Stepbrother

EMILIA ROSE

Trigger Warning

This book includes mention of sexual assault, sexual exploitation, slapping, name calling, degradation, death, and other potentially triggering topics. If you don't feel comfortable with the topics listed above, place the book down now.

Chapter One

JACE

"Oh, yes, baby ..." Nicole said, leaning her head against one of the glossy red lockers in the Redwood Academy football team's locker room. Dressed in a cheerleader uniform that was a size too small for her, she thrust a hand into my teammate's thick blond hair and tugged his face closer to her pussy. "Just like that."

I balled my hands into fists and wondered why the fuck I was watching my girlfriend cheat on me with the quarterback of the best high school football team in New England. She was supposed to be mine. I was the only guy who should've been pushing her up against the lockers like that.

Anger. Rage. Hurt. Betrayal. It all rushed through me.

I wanted to kick his ass more than anything, but I was paralyzed to the damn spot, knowing that I couldn't touch him or else I'd be kicked off this damn team right before finishing the season. And I loved football more than I'd ever cared for Nicole.

Reacting like Dad had when Mom cheated on him would make me just like that fucking loser. So, I took a couple deep breaths, promised that I'd get revenge on Carter in practice, and told myself that I should've known better than to date a cheerleader in this shitty town.

Nicole curled her toes. "God, you're so much better at this than Jace."

Fuck holding back. I punched my fist right through the wall, feeling the blood already start to drip from my knuckles.

"What the fuck are you fucking doing?" I said through clenched teeth.

They both pulled away from each other, eyes wide in fear. Nicole pulled down her skirt and jumped up.

"Jace!" she said, cheeks flushed. She fiddled with the ends of her sleeves. "I-I … it's not what it looks like. I promise!"

I grabbed Carter by the throat and thrust him against the lockers, digging my fingers as deep as they would go. He might've been the quarterback, but he was weaker than me. I could've killed him with my bare hands, but I resisted, even as much as it hurt me.

"Jace, stop!" Nicole screamed.

Carter stared at me with that damn smirk on his face, knowing that he had the upper hand. "What're you going to do to me, Harbor? The principal is riding your ass, looking for a reason to make Coach sit you for the rest of this season."

I growled and slammed him into the lockers, released my grip, and charged out of the locker room. *Fuck him and fuck Nicole.* Neither one of them was worth it. I should've never fucking dated a girl like her. Girls like her were trash.

I stormed out of the building and toward my car, letting the crisp fall air hit me. Rain started to drizzle overhead. We were so close to finishing this season, and I wanted to end my high school football career on a high note to spite my father.

We only had a couple more months for the season.

"Jace, I didn't mean for it to happen," Nicole said, hurrying after me in all that tight cheerleading uniform.

I took longer strides toward my car to get the fuck out of here.

If I didn't leave now, I was going to punch Carter in the throat and ruin all his chances at playing college football.

I yanked open the door to my black Maserati, but Nicole stepped in front of me. "Please, Jace. It only happened a couple times. It didn't mean anything. I promise, baby. We were both drunk that first night, and you had to go pick up your stepsister. It just ... happened."

"Just fucking happened? Things like that don't just happen." I balled my hands into fists, aching to hit something so fucking hard to displace all this betrayal.

I should've never gotten into a relationship with a lying piece of shit. Everyone I opened up to broke my fucking heart.

I was done with this shit.

"Jace—"

"Get the fuck out of my face, Nicole," I growled.

She crossed her arms over her chest, sneering at me with those ugly red lips and acting like it was my fault she had slept with one of my teammates. Fuck her. I wasn't about to let some rich, bratty-ass cheerleader talk me down.

"Move," I said again.

"Make me."

"You're not fucking cute," I said, talking myself down from pulling her out of the way because she'd yak off to her daddy, who was the chief of police, and get me thrown in juvie again for not doing shit.

Girls like her weren't worth throwing my dreams away. Not many were.

"I'm going to say it one more time," I said through clenched teeth, jaw twitching. "Get. Out. Of. My. Fucking. Way."

The rain poured harder down around us, matting her hair and uniform to her petite body. All that makeup she wore started dripping down her face; it was almost laughable. She wouldn't last another minute out here, or she'd start melting like the wicked bitch she was.

Nicole flared her nostrils at me, then stormed away. "Fuck you, Harbor."

Before she could get far, I stepped in front of her. "You tell that fucking asshole that the next time I see him, he's going to be fucking sorry," I said through clenched teeth.

I slid into my car before she could rant at me for what *she* had done. I had no sympathy for a liar and definitely no sympathy for a damn cheater. She was just like Mom.

After locking the car, I punched the steering wheel hard with my bloody fist. *Fuck.*

I fucking hated this shit. I couldn't wait to get out of this town.

Nicole sprinted through the rain to her car on the other side of the parking lot. I'd never wanted to be with that bitch anyway. Dad had forced me to, holding my mom's death and his money over my head, telling me that if I didn't get my *head on straight* and stop *acting out*, he'd take my future away.

I shouldn't have believed him, but I had because he had taken someone's future away before. And he'd do it again, especially to his problematic, football-loving, business-hating son.

Chapter Two

ALLIE

There were many people I hated in this world, and Jace Harbor was literally all of them.

Sopping wet clothes, drenched in rainwater, brown hair stuck to my face, I pulled open the front door.

"Why the hell didn't you pick me up?" I screamed as soon as I stepped into the damn mansion I lived in now.

Water dripped from my soaked jeans and onto the ground, creating a puddle underneath me. That man had absolutely no idea how aggravating he was.

All I'd asked was for a ride since my car had broken down. One simple ride. That was all.

The house was quiet, and I stormed up the stairs, tracking mud and water on the hardwood floor to his bedroom. I hated Jace, absolutely hated him. If I had known Mom was dating his dad before they got engaged, I would've screamed at her not to say *I do* ever.

It was the worst decision of *my* life.

Even after a year of living with them, navigating this damn house was harder than a freaking maze. Mom barely visited Dad's grave with me anymore. Harlan tried acting like my father. But what really ticked me off was that I had to see Harlan's son's ugly face every freaking day—at school, at home, at Redwood's football games.

After sophomore year, I'd promised never to associate myself with him again.

But now, senior year, he was my damn stepbrother.

When I made it to Jace's room, I ripped open his closed door, not caring what kind of shit I was interrupting. "I'm going to kill you," I said through clenched teeth as I stared into a bedroom made for a king.

Jace was lying back on his gray sheets with Jenny, the Science Club president, between his legs, his cock all the way down her throat. When she heard me, she jumped up, covering her half-naked body with the sheets, and adjusted her glasses.

To say I was surprised would be a total exaggeration.

I tapped one wet sneaker on the floor. "Leave," I said to her.

"She's staying," Jace said, not even moving from that position to hide any of his junk. It *definitely* wasn't impressive—that was what I told myself at least.

I tore my eyes away from him and watched Jenny throw on her clothes and shoes. Jace growled and stood up, pulling on a pair of gray basketball shorts that still hid absolutely nothing. Jenny shuffled out of the room.

When she pushed past me, I stepped in the doorframe to block Jace from following her out and crossed my arms over my chest, staring up into those brown eyes.

"Why didn't you pick me up?" I asked.

"I'm not in the fucking mood, Allie. Move."

"No," I said, trying to look intimidating even though I was five-two, sopping wet, and had glasses that were fogged up and covered in rain droplets. "I walked five miles in the pouring rain because my damn phone died and nobody could pick me up."

He took a threatening step closer to me. "That's not my problem."

"Yes, it is!" I screamed, throwing my hands into his chest to push him away. "Harlan told me you'd pick me up."

He snatched my wrists in one of his large hands and pulled me closer to him. "I told you that I'm not in the fucking mood. Now, move out of my way before I have to move you myself ... unless *you* want to finish sucking me off."

I blew a breath out of my nose and pushed him away again. "You're disgusting."

But I knew that he wasn't kidding. Jace Harbor had a thing for nerdy girls. I'd learned that the hard way two years ago, and it was *never* happening again. He freaking repulsed me. Every time I looked into those brown eyes, watched him ruthlessly slam into another player during one of his football games, saw him lifting in our in-home gym, his biceps flexed and covered in a layer of sweat, I wanted to vomit.

"My backpack, my laptop, my books are all ruined because of you."

After pausing for a moment, he cracked that infamous smirk of his that had haunted my dreams for the past two years. "I thought you liked being wet," he said, voice terrifyingly low and husky, insinuating more.

His words were slurred slightly, and I almost didn't catch on that he had been drinking.

"I like the rain, idiot, not getting drenched in a downpour!"

"You sure liked being wet sophomore—"

I slammed my hands into his chest again, not even letting him finish. "Can you not?"

He stepped closer to me, snaking his hand around my throat and pinning me to the wall, like he used to. All those memories came flooding back, and I had to resist the urge to shiver at the thought of everything we used to do together—in the back of his car, late nights after his games, him touching me under the desk in Geometry.

It was the lowest point in my life.

He leaned down slightly, his hot breath in my ear. "Listen to me, Allie." He strummed his fingers against the side of my neck, and a rush of heat warmed all those sinful parts of me. "The next time you interrupt me when I have a girl over, it's going to be your ass sitting in the bed with me when she leaves, finishing off what she started."

After I gathered all my strength, I pushed him away. "Gross," I said in a breathy whisper, afraid that if I spoke any louder, my voice would betray me. I crossed my arms over my chest, wanting to put as much space between us as possible.

I hated living with him. It was shit like this every day.

"Why do you even have a girl over anyway?" I asked. "What happened to Nicole? Did she decide you were a shitty boyfriend and dump your annoying ass?"

That smirk disappeared from his face and was replaced with anger and hatred and a tinge of what looked like hurt.

"Fuck you," he said under his breath. He pushed me out into the hall and slammed the door shut.

I slapped my palm against it, still seething. "This is not over, Jace."

And it wasn't over. *We* weren't over either.

Chapter Three

JACE

She was a brat.

And, no, I wasn't talking about Nicole, who was practicing her cheers on the track with the rest of her peppy team. Nicole was a *bitch*. She irked me, but not as much as Allie did every time she had the chance.

I stared at Allie, sitting with her friend Imani on the bleachers during football practice. Face stuffed inside a Biology textbook, she pushed those thick-as-hell black-framed glasses up her nose and tapped the top of her black ballpoint pen against her chin.

My fingers dug into the leather football, and I clenched my jaw.

After I hadn't picked her up from school last night, she'd told my fucking dad, who chewed my ass out and punished me by sticking me with Allie for the next two weeks while he and his trophy wife went to celebrate their one-year anniversary on a boat somewhere.

As soon as they left the house tomorrow night, I was going to put Allie's bratty ass in her place, let her know not to fuck with me again or else there'd be consequences. I didn't care how long it'd take for her to break, but it was going to happen.

"Harbor, move your ass," Coach Carol called from the sidelines. "We don't have all day."

I growled through my helmet, tossed the ball back to fucking Carter, and jogged to the line, getting in my stance. All I wanted to do was hit him hard right in the fucking chest, show *him* that he might've been the quarterback, but I wasn't to be fucked with again.

Carter stared at me from the other side of the line of scrimmage, standing behind his center and readying for the hike, and fucking smirked. As soon as the damn ball was hiked, I tore through the players defending him and hit him as hard as I could in the side before he could throw the ball.

He grunted as I drove him into the mud, making it hurt. His mouth guard came flying out and landed next to us. I dug my elbow into his exposed stomach and pushed myself up before Coach Carol could catch me.

"What the fuck?" Carter asked, struggling to stand. "You still mad about Nicole?"

"You can have that bitch," I said through clenched teeth, gripping his jersey and pushing him away because Coach was watching us with those hawk eyes of his. I walked back toward the line with Jamal. "She's fucking garbage."

"Like your stepsister?" Carter asked.

I turned right the fuck around to slam my fist into his jaw, but Jamal jumped in front of me, grabbed my jersey, and pushed me back.

"He's not worth it, Jace."

"I wonder how she'd be in bed," Carter said, walking backward toward the line.

I pushed against Jamal harder, slipping out of his grip, ready to end this fucking boy's ass for talking shit.

Jamal and another guy from the team each grabbed one of my

arms, holding me back. "Don't be stupid. He's trying to rile you up, so you get kicked off the team. He wants all eyes on him."

"It's not like you don't wonder the same thing." Carter smirked at me. "She's got a fat ass."

"Harbor!" Coach Carol shouted as they struggled to hold me back.

Coach waved me over, and I cursed myself for not ending Carter right then and there. I should've, so he couldn't touch anyone else.

"I'm going to kill that fucking kid," I said, storming to the sidelines.

"Practice is over," Coach said, waving everyone off.

I grabbed my shit from the sidelines and tore off my helmet, shaking the sweat off my hair.

Coach pulled me aside. "What's going on with you today, Jace?" he asked, stuffing his clipboard under his arm and pushing his phone into his pocket.

"Nothing, sir," I said, glaring at Carter, who disappeared into the locker room, and wiping the sweat from my forehead.

Sure, Coach might've been worried about me, but I was fine. Completely fucking fine.

"I saw you staring over at the girls," he said, nodding to the cheerleaders.

I lifted my gaze and met Allie's eyes. One of her brows was arched as she stared at me, her book resting in her lap. I tightened my jaw, remembering how my hand had felt around her throat last night. Her pulse had been so fast, racing underneath my palm, as she stared up at me through those glasses of hers. God, I wanted to see her staring up at me like that through them, my cock stuff—

"Don't let those cheerleaders distract you, son," Coach continued.

I shook my head and tore my gaze away from her. What the

fuck was I even thinking? She was my bratty, annoying-ass stepsister. Nothing more than that—and she'd never be more than that.

"Keep up your training, and you're going to make it to big places," Coach said, giving me a strong smile. "I see you in the NFL, playing this game for the rest of your life."

I stared at him, pressed my lips together, and nodded, trying not to show him how much it meant to me that someone believed I could make it, that this wasn't all a big waste of my time, like Dad thought.

When he let me go shower, I sauntered into the locker room, knowing that Coach had never thought this about anyone else on our team and maybe not even during his twenty-five years of coaching football at Redwood. We had a good team, some guys had made it into big colleges, but nobody had made it to the NFL.

I tore off my jersey and tossed it into my locker, sweat dripping down my abdomen. "Party at my place tonight, boys," I said because I needed something to forget about Nicole and to get my mind off Miss Know-It-All, who I'd have to deal with for the next two weeks. "Don't be late."

Chapter Four

ALLIE

It was Thursday night. I had a Biology test tomorrow that I needed to ace, and all I could hear was loud music blaring through the house from all the way in the living room. The stench of pot drifted through the hallways, under my door, into *my* room, driving me insane.

Imani lay on her stomach, tapping through PowerPoint slides on her computer. Since mine had broken because of the rain, I was stuck with a print-out copy of them and this three-hundred-pound textbook.

"Jesus Christ, I'm going to kill him," I said under my breath.

"Why don't we stop for tonight? We've been at this for six hours now," Imani said.

I glanced over at her and nearly smiled. She was stunning, and I knew people said that about their best friends all the time, but it was true. Piercing brown eyes against her flawless dark-brown skin. Ugh, I was so jealous of her genes. All I had was terrible vision, thighs decorated with stretch marks, and twenty-four-seven frizzy hair.

I frowned and slumped back in my seat, knowing that stopping was probably a good idea.

"Or, if you want, you can come to my place to study," she said.

"No, it's fine." I threw my papers onto my desk. "I'll just fail."

Imani rolled her brown eyes and shook her head, her curls bouncing all over the place. "Girl, stop. We all know that you're going to get over a hundred, especially with all the extra credit that Barnes gives." She pushed her laptop into her backpack. "And if you don't, you can always ask Barnes for *more* extra credit. You're hot enough to seduce him."

I nearly choked. "Ew, gross. He's, like, seventy."

Imani giggled. "All I'm saying is that you don't even have to *work* for that A-plus, just shake a little ass," she said, shaking her hips for emphasis.

After she gathered all her things, we walked down the hall to the living room. The music got louder the closer we got, smoke sitting heavily in the air.

"I can't wait to get out of this shitty town," I said under my breath, staring at all of Jace's friends, who were drunk and littered around in our living room.

The entire cheer squad—except Nicole—was in the living room with their tits nearly hanging out of their tops and dancing on guys that they were way too good for. I was all for being a bratty slut, but, damn, some of these athletes didn't even shower.

I shook my head and entered the room, grasping Imani's hand. People in this town were either filthy rich, like Jace and his father, or dirt poor, like I used to be. There was no in between. And while the rich might've thought that they were better than the rest of us, they hadn't been to the poor side of town. The side where Poison hung out. They ruled the poor, did favors for the rich, ruined people's lives, all to make a quick buck and to get the hell out of this town one day too.

"You can come back to my place for the night," Imani offered again, tugging on the straps of her backpack.

I pushed people out of the way to get us to the front door and made eye contact with Jace's best friend, Jamal. My gaze lingered for a moment longer than it should've, but I quickly pulled it away, my cheeks flushing.

"Well, I guess that's a no." Imani laughed. "Just be careful with him. You know how guys like him act. He's like your stepbrother, and he will break your heart too, if you let him."

"Jace didn't break my heart," I said through clenched teeth.

Memories of sophomore year flooded my mind, and I shivered. I opened the front door, and a few more people stumbled into the house. It wasn't just any people, but the three notorious Poison boys.

One of them, Landon, looked Imani up and down as he passed, and Imani's cheeks flushed even more than mine had. She tucked some hair behind her ear and looked down at the ground.

"And you're telling *me* to be careful," I said, narrowing my eyes at her. "The Poison boys are no good. You should know that."

Imani tried to play it off by rolling her eyes. "I know. Don't worry about me."

After waving her off, I made eye contact with Jamal again and walked toward the kitchen to grab some water before I went back upstairs to try to study more. Jamal appeared a few moments later with a can of beer.

"You want a drink?" Jamal said, handing me an unopened can of beer.

I pushed it back. "No, thanks. I have a test tomorrow morning."

Jamal smiled at me and stepped closer, one foot between mine, his fingers brushing against my forearm. "Come on, Allie," he said, his voice deep. He leaned down closer to me. "One won't hurt."

I stared up into those dark brown eyes. "One leads to two, and two leads to me having a hangover tomorrow morning and not being able to focus."

He chuckled. "You're no fun," he murmured against my ear.

Was I flirting with another football player after what happened sophomore year with Jace? Maybe. Would I choose to fool around with Jace's best friend because I wanted to spite Jace? Absolutely.

Jace stumbled into the kitchen, pushing a cheerleader off him. "Later, babe." When he saw us, he stopped and clenched his jaw. "Party is out here, Jamal," he said through clenched teeth. He grasped my upper arm and pulled me away from him. "Allie wasn't invited. She should be upstairs, studying, shouldn't she?" He glared at me with those evil, sinful eyes, filled with so much hatred.

"I'm finished studying," I lied in a matter-of-fact tone. I snatched the beer from Jamal. "But I don't mind going back upstairs." I glanced at Jamal. "Care to join?"

Jamal took one long look at Jace, who was giving him the hardest death stare, and stepped to the side. "Maybe some other time, Allie," he said and then disappeared into the living room.

I tightened my jaw and glared at a smirking Jace. "You think you're so fucking cool, don't you? Why don't you just leave me alone? What is your problem?" I asked. "You're always in my love life."

He leaned around me to grab a beer from the counter, his body too close to mine. "I can't be in something that doesn't exist," he said.

I huffed and opened my beer, taking a huge gulp of it and wanting to relax. "Says the guy who can't keep a girlfriend," I said, blowing out a breath.

He growled and grasped my jaw harder than he had last night, pushing me against the counter. "Says the girl who hasn't had a boyfriend her entire life. You must be really lonely, spending every night alone. Haven't been touched by a man in, what? One, two years?" He chuckled menacingly at me. "You know, if I remember correctly, I was the last person to touch that pussy of yours, wasn't I?"

I thrust my beer at him, making it spill all over us both. "You drive everyone I like away because you're an annoying asshole."

"That didn't answer my question." He tightened his grip and stepped closer to me, his cock pressed against the side of my hip, his lips against my ear. "I am, aren't I? There's no harm in admitting that you try to get on my nerves every day to get it again."

"You're drunk," I whispered, knowing that everything he was saying might or might not have been true. But I would never admit it.

He was my stepbrother, which made everything so much more complicated.

"And you're a brat," he said into my ear.

Heat rushed to my core as he made me feel things that I really shouldn't.

"You know what I like to do to brats."

Someone walked into the kitchen, half-drunk off his ass, and I pushed Jace away.

"I'm going to go study," I said. "Take your damn beer." I shoved the can into his hand and hurried through the kitchen and back toward my bedroom.

Study.

As if I wasn't going to lock myself in my bedroom and touch myself for the next damn hour, thinking about *Jamal*. Definitely not Jace. Not his hands running up my sides or his fingers dipping into my pussy or his raspy breath in my ear.

Chapter Five

ALLIE

"You're fucking kidding me," I said, hurrying after Mom through the spacious hallways.

It was Friday night, and she'd broken the worst possible news to me.

My day had been going great. I had definitely aced that test, Jamal had texted me about going out with him this weekend despite Jace breaking us up last night, and I'd found out that Nicole cheated on Jace.

I thought cheating was the shittiest thing someone could do, but Jace was also the most annoying prick I had met and had been tormenting me for the past two freaking years. He deserved to hurt just as bad as he'd hurt me.

"You're really going to leave me with *him* for the next two weeks while you and Harlan are gone? Why didn't you tell me this sooner, so I could've made plans with Imani?"

"Because, dear, Harlan and I want you and Jace to get along." Mom stopped in the hallway with her suitcases and everything.

"Oh dear, I almost forgot my sunglasses." She hurried back toward her bedroom, completely ignoring me.

I followed after her with my arms crossed over my chest. "Mom, please. He's going to party the whole time and have girls over and ... ugh ..." I wrinkled my nose and shivered at the thought.

"It'll be fine, sweetheart," Mom said, grabbing her sunglasses and pushing past me to hurry down the hallway again. "Your step-father told him to behave. There will be no partying, no alcohol, and certainly no girls."

I rolled my eyes. Sure, that was what he would say. But I'd bet he'd be sleeping with another one of his whores as soon as they left the house.

Harlan and Jace were standing in the living room, waiting for Mom, when we made it downstairs. Jace glanced at me when I walked in, those cruel eyes lingering on me. His arms were crossed over his chest, making his biceps bulge. His hair—usually slicked back with grease, like all frat boys' hair—was soft today, a strand of it falling against his forehead. And his lips—which I definitely hadn't thought about while *studying* last night—were curled into a smirk.

"Honey, we should get going," Mom said to Harlan.

I pressed my lips together and pulled out my phone, typing to my best friend, Imani, that I would be staying at her house every single night for the next two weeks because I would *not* be staying here.

Harlan grabbed Mom's suitcase, carrying it to the door.

I stood in the middle of the living room, fuming. How could they do this to me? How could they leave me with such an idiot? Did they not see how terrible Jace was to me?

Without even acknowledging all my problems with this, Mom and Harlan hopped into their car and sped down the street, leaving me alone with Jace. I was used to being alone with him for a few hours, but not two entire weeks.

"Looks like it's just me and you," Jace said, lips curled into a smirk.

His dark brown eyes were on me, giving me that look he had given me so many damn times before. I sucked in a breath, crossed my arms over my chest, and turned away from him. I couldn't spend two weeks here. I'd lose more than my mind.

"Stay out of my hair, and I'll stay out of yours," I said to him.

Then, I turned on my heel and started back toward my room to gather my clothes for the next two weeks. If Imani didn't have room for me, I'd sleep in a hotel.

Jace snatched my arm and yanked me back. "You're not going anywhere."

I tried to pull myself away from him, but he held me tighter. "Let me go."

"I have plans for us."

"I'm not doing anything with you."

He smirked even wider. "Oh, Allie, did I say you had a choice?" He wrapped a hand around my throat and pulled me to him until my chest was pressed against his. "You've fucked me over one too many times. Have been waiting for me to lose it, haven't you?"

I clenched my jaw. "No." *Maybe.*

Something about him was screaming at me to run back to my bedroom and lock the door because being this close to him was surely not going to turn out good. He had that same look on his face he'd had two years ago when he asked me to *hang out* and I stupidly said yes.

"No?" he asked, harshly brushing his thumb against my jaw and forcing me to look up into his dark eyes. "Sounds like you need to learn some fucking respect."

I yanked myself out of his grip and stormed to my room. "Fuck you, Harbor."

He followed after me, his strides longer and quicker than

mine. I went to slam my bedroom door in his face when he placed a firm hand on it and pushed it back open.

"Get out of my room!" I yelled, jaw clenched. I hurled my phone onto the bed and slammed my hands into his taut chest. "Get out."

After closing my door, he grabbed my hands and stepped closer to me. "Maybe I should teach you some respect, some manners."

My cheeks flushed ever so slightly because part of me wanted to know *how* he would teach me. Would he push me into my bedroom, bend me over the bed, and take me finally? Two years. Two fucking years, and this hadn't changed between us.

"You're gross," I said, watching his jaw twitch.

He growled under his breath, pushed me onto my bed, and stalked toward me. My eyes widened, heart pounding against my chest. His muscles flexed under his shirt, and his cock pressed hard against his gray sweatpants.

I hate him. I hate him. I hate him.

"Jace," I said, voice shaking.

I hated him, but I made no move to stop him. I didn't push him away. I didn't scream at him to stop looking at me with those sinful brown eyes. I didn't want him to stop. Maybe I was fucked up, but I wanted my stepbrother to finally give in after two years of torture.

Chapter Six

How the hell could I want him to fuck me when all he had done was torture me these past two years?

I scurried back to the headboard and pulled my knees to my chest. It was wrong—so damn wrong—that I felt so pulled to him that I would allow myself to be with him like this again.

He was an asshole, a player, and, worst of all, my damn stepbrother.

Seizing my waist, he slipped his fingers under my sweater, gazed between my legs, and smirked at my black silk panties that I definitely hadn't worn because I knew I'd be alone with Jace tonight.

"My stepsister is wet for me," Jace said, voice low and husky.

I clenched as a wave of heat warmed my core. "Get off," I whispered, lightly kicking my foot toward his chest in my weakest attempt to convince myself that I didn't want this, that I hadn't been thinking about this moment for the past two freaking years.

Before my foot collided with his chest, he snatched it and

yanked me to the edge of the bed by my ankle. Wetness pooled between my thighs at the way he was rough. He had never been like this before, but it seemed, tonight, there was something feral lurking deep within him, something that even he couldn't stop himself.

And I didn't want him to stop.

"Jace ..." My heart was pounding. "I'm not going to say it again."

What the hell was wrong with me? Why was I wet for my damn stepbrother?

He snaked his hand around my throat and pulled me to my feet, so we were chest to chest. "You prance around in this short schoolgirl skirt"—he grabbed the bottom of my skirt and looked down at my body—"fucking knee-high stockings, and your nerdy little glasses, and you expect me not to want to bend you over the fucking bed and take you, Allie?"

I furrowed my brows and stared up at him through my lenses, nipples hardening underneath my sweater. "Yes, I do," I said, but my words came out choppy and weak.

"You know how much I fucking love it, don't you?" he asked, dark eyes fixed on me. He trailed a finger up the front of my thigh and looped it inside my panties. "Do you wear all this shit for me too?"

"No." *Yes.*

"I bet you've been dreaming about the day I'd finally snap and take you."

I pressed my lips together, my cheeks flushing. "No."

He curled his lips up slightly and chuckled, gaze flickering down to my tits under my sweater. "You expect me to stay in fucking control when you refuse to wear a damn bra when we're alone." He tugged on my nipple through my sweater. "And your nipples are always this fucking hard."

Pleasure shot through me as he drew on it harshly. I took a

shaky breath, loving every single moment of this but knowing that it was wrong ... so wrong.

"Please, Jace," I said, my voice barely above a whisper. "This is wrong. I'll do whatever you want, just stop. You're my stepbrother now."

He paused, slowly releasing my nipple and watching my breast bounce in my sweater. "You'll do anything?" he asked, brow arched.

I actually believed he was serious, so I nodded.

Before I could stop him, he snatched a fistful of my hair and pushed me to my knees. My eyes widened slightly, a rush of heat going to my core as I stared up at him. The ache between my legs wasn't going away ... it was intensifying with every second that passed.

"Good." He grasped my chin in his callous hand and swept his thumb across my bottom lip. "Because you're going to wrap your lips around my cock, like you used to. Finally suck me off after interrupting me the other night."

"Are you crazy? I'm not going to suck your cock."

He stared down at me and undid his pants, watching as *I* watched him pull out his long, pulsing cock. So many fucking nights, I had dreamed of this happening again. So many mornings, I woke up, thinking about him inside of me. So many wishes, hoping that it would happen just once ... once—that was all I asked for.

His dick was hard and thick, and I knew it'd feel so good inside of me.

"Jace ..." I trailed off, my voice quiet.

"Lost for words, Allie?" he asked, tugging on my hair and making me gaze up into his eyes through my glasses.

I clenched and tried hard not to think about him plunging it inside of me, about him filling me all the way up and stuffing me full.

Stop it, Allie. He is your stepbrother.

I shoved my hands against his thighs, wanting to push him away before I slipped. "Fuck you."

He wrapped one hand around his cock and the other around the back of my neck, slapping the head against my lips. For a moment, I almost instinctively parted my lips, then pressed them back together as quickly as I could.

But it was too late.

"You want it, Allie." Jace could already see how much I needed it. "Don't deny yourself the simple pleasure of having my cock down your throat."

My wet lips pressed against his head, and I took a deep breath through my nose, my eyes closing softly. This was wrong. So fucking wrong. Yet I didn't stop. Instead, I opened my mouth and let him push himself into me, inch by inch until his cock was sliding down the back of my throat.

When he was all the way inside of me, he stilled and wrapped his hand around my neck, feeling the bulge inside of it and slowly jerking himself off. "God, Allie, you don't know how fucking long I've been waiting to feel your throat close around my cock like this again."

I stared up at him, my cheeks flushing, my pussy clenching, my tits pressed hard against his thighs. He shoved himself deeper into me, slid his hand to the back of my head, and pulled me to him until my lips were pressed against his hips.

"I want to see your eyes," he demanded.

I glanced up at him, my pussy aching, and gagged on his cock. He slapped my tits and watched them bounce in my sweater.

"You're a fucking whore, Allie. *My* fucking whore."

Spit dripped from my lips, rolled down my chin, and fell onto my sweater. I placed my hands on his thighs and pushed on them, needing to breathe. But he knew I could take more, so he began to pump himself faster into me.

Wet with my spit, his cock hit the back of my throat with every thrust. I pushed against his thighs harder, needing so desperately to breathe. And when he knew I couldn't take it any longer, he grabbed me by the throat, pulled me to my feet, and pushed me toward the bed.

I gasped for breath, wiping the spit from my chin, and stumbled onto the mattress on my hands and knees.

He crawled onto the bed from behind me, pushed my panties down to my knees, and snaked a hand around the front of my neck, forcing me to arch my back and stare right into my bedroom mirror that was attached to my dresser.

"You're going to watch me fuck your tight pussy," he said, gazing at me through the mirror.

My pussy clenched harder. *Oh my God. This isn't really happening. My stepbrother isn't really going to fuck me, is he?*

He pressed down on my lower back so my ass was in the air and ready for him, and he rubbed his cock against my tight entrance. I took a deep breath, feeling him press against it.

"Please, Jace ..." I whispered, unsure if I was asking him to stop or asking him to do it already. I gazed down at the bedsheets. I had dreamed of this moment for so long.

Snatching my chin, he forced me to look into the mirror again. "I said to watch," he said through clenched teeth.

I stared at those sinful, dark eyes and bit the inside of my lip. This was not what I'd expected. I never thought we'd be together like this ever fucking again.

Jace's eyes softened a bit as he rubbed his bare cock against my entrance. I furrowed my brows at his reflection and tilted my head down slightly, as if to give him permission. He swallowed hard. A hundred emotions crossed his face, and stupid me thought he was going to be gentle for our first time together, like he always promised.

He pushed himself inside of me slowly, his cock bigger than any toy I had ever used. My pussy wrapped tightly around his cock, and he pushed himself deeper and groaned in my ear.

"Please ..." I whispered.

His cock was so big that he barely fit it inside. He was stretching me out, and all I could do was whimper.

"Jace …"

"My slutty little stepsister can't take my cock?" he asked into my ear as he pulled my sweater over my head and let my tits bounce out of it.

He slapped one of my breasts over and over and over until it turned a light pink. My pussy tightened on his cock.

"You like that?"

I pressed my lips together. "No." *Yes.*

He tugged harder on my nipple. "Your pussy is getting wetter and tighter for me."

"This is wrong," I whispered. "So wrong."

He released my chin, grabbed my hips, and continued to pump into me. "I have been dreaming about taking you for so long, Allie, about feeling your pussy tighten on me, about filling you with my cum."

Just the thought of my stepbrother filling me made me clench.

I'd be lying if I said that I hadn't been dreaming of that too.

"I'm going to come inside of you, and you're going to take it like the slutty little whore you are," he said against my ear, strumming his fingers up the column of my neck. With his other hand, he dipped his fingers between my legs and rubbed my clit.

"Jace, please."

He pumped faster into me, and I moaned, the pressure rising in my core and driving me higher and higher. He slapped his palm hard against my clit, still driving into me. Wave after wave of pleasure pumped through me. My body trembled in his hands. I grasped the bedsheets and cried out, unable to hold back my moans and my orgasm any longer.

Jace slowed down slightly. "Did my sister just come on my cock?" he asked, lips curling into a smirk against my neck. "You must really want it."

"Jace …" I breathed. "Please."

He thrust harder, his cock swelling inside of me.

"Jace ... Jace ... please. I'll take it down my throat or between my tits or on my face."

"I'm going to fill my stepsister's pussy," he said, making sure I knew that was where all his cum would go, that there was no other place he was willing to put it.

He wanted to claim me.

"Tell me you want my cum inside of you."

My pussy tightened even more around him, pulsing over and over again. He continued to tease my clit, and I grasped the bedsheets in my fists even harder, the pressure starting to rise once more. He bucked his hips hard against me, and I moaned softly.

"Please." My voice was barely a whisper.

He groaned against my ear and stilled inside of me. My entire body was filled with ecstasy, shaking and trembling and pulsing. And when I finally came down from that high, from all my secret little hopes, my eyes widened.

Oh my God.

After years of cursing him out and hating him, I'd let Jace Harbor fuck me.

And I'd liked it.

I squirmed in his hands, trying to break out of his strong hold, but he wrapped his arms around me tighter to hold me in place as he pushed his cock deeper inside of me, making sure all his cum stayed in there.

I should've hated it.

But I didn't. I wanted more of it, needed more of *him*. Now.

My tits bounced against his arms as I struggled against him. I could feel his heart beating rapidly against my bare back, and his arms ... they felt so good around me, holding me to him like he always used to do.

I shook my head. *What the hell am I thinking?*

I don't like this. I don't like this. I don't like this. I repeated the words to myself, as if saying them over and over would get me to actually believe them.

Only when he finished did he pull out of me and let me collapse onto the bed. I rolled onto my back and spread my legs, staring down at my creamed pussy under my skirt.

"Jace," I whispered, brows furrowed together. "I can't believe that we just ... that you ..."

"Came inside of you?" he asked, watching my pussy push out some of his cum.

He glanced from my pussy to my face, the smirk never disappearing but his eyes softening a bit. He paused, and I looked down at his lips, his soft lips.

I wanted him to crawl up into my bed with me and tell me that he was sorry for everything that had happened between us, that he hadn't meant any of it, that it was all some sort of mistake ...

But instead of doing any of that, he took one last look at me, crawled off the bed, and grabbed his jeans. "I don't know about you, Allie, but I think we're going to have a long two weeks ahead of us."

Chapter Seven

JACE

"**Y**ou're just going to leave?" Allie asked from her bed, still naked, except for a blanket and her skirt covering everything but those thick thighs of hers that I wanted to tease until she was squirming in my arms again. I had touched her thighs, grabbed them, groped them so many fucking times before; all I wanted was to do it again.

I opened her bedroom door and glanced back at her. "Do you want me to stay?"

A hundred emotions crossed over her face, but after a few moments, she settled on fury. "No," she spat at me, covering her thighs and pushing her glasses up her nose. "I didn't expect you to anyway. Don't you have a football game or something? It's Friday night."

My gaze traveled over her, and I clenched my jaw to hold myself back. I didn't have anywhere to be tonight. I could stay here with her, touch her again, kiss her neck, feel her legs squirm around me ... but nothing good would come from staying in here with her.

Things would get sticky between us. *Hell*, they already were. And I needed them to be fucking clear as day. I didn't care about Allie, not one fucking bit. All I cared about was getting her and her mother out of this damn house and going off to play football in college.

"It got canceled," I said.

And with that, I walked out of the room and shut the door behind me, resting my head back against the doorframe and blowing out a long breath. Something deep down inside of me didn't feel right.

We shouldn't have had sex. We shouldn't have kissed. We shouldn't have even touched each other. She was my stepsister, a girl I'd once wanted to spend my entire life with, a girl I used to sit with on the rocks at the Overlook, watching the snow drift down from the dark gray sky and melt as soon as it touched the ocean waves.

My hands balled into fists, and I shook my head.

This was never how Allie and I were supposed to turn out.

She shuffled around inside her room, and I walked back to mine, slammed the door shut, and threw a fist into the wall, easily breaking through the drywall yet again. This spot had become my own personal punching bag since Mom had died.

Fuck, why the hell was I getting fucking upset? I didn't give a fuck about Allie. *I can't.*

She and her mother had needed to get out of our lives months ago. She didn't belong in this house, under the same roof as me, sealed with the same fate as me. She fucking didn't.

I'd tried to get rid of them as soon as I found out about Dad and her mom dating. But neither of them would budge, no matter how much hell I raised. I had just been sent to juvie and a boarding school in the summer to *straighten myself out*, as if that was going to make me change.

I hopped onto the bed, grabbed the football from the side table, and threw it into the air. I would do it again and again and again if that meant Allie didn't live here with me. I wanted her out. I had tried to make *her* life a living hell despite everything inside of me telling me that it was wrong, that I shouldn't hurt her.

My phone buzzed from the side table.

Dad: Behave this week. I don't want to hear that you were terrorizing Allie again.

I stared down at the phone, picked it up, and clenched it in my fist until my knuckles turned white. I hated him. He should've never fucking married Allie's mom. It was the worst fucking decision *she* could've made.

Dad: There will be harsher consequences next time.

Instead of responding to him—I'd be chewed out for that when he got home—I turned off my phone, changed into my gym clothes, and decided on a run for tonight. Since the game had been canceled, Coach would want us to be twice as ready for our game next Friday night. We were playing our rivals, the Leeside Phantoms. Between them and Carter, I still had a shitload of steam I needed to blow off.

Opening my bedside drawer, I snatched my Apple Watch from inside and snapped it around my wrist for training. Inside were the usual—condoms, lotion, pills I refused to take that Dad had made some therapist give me, weed from Poison, and a picture.

My eye caught on the photo that I had folded in fourths. I sat down on my bed, resting my forearms on my knees, and pulled out the picture. Gaze flickering to the door to make sure it was closed, I slowly unfolded it and let myself smile.

It was of Allie and me sophomore year after one of my football games—homecoming, to be exact. Snow fell around us, blowing her brown hair into her face, nearly hiding her grin. With her arms around my waist, she stared up at me through those thick glasses, and she was happy—so fucking happy.

I shook my head and stared down at it for a long time, until my watch buzzed.

Nicole: Can we talk?
Nicole: I'm sorry for what happened.
Nicole: Please, speak to me, Jace.
Nicole: Jace, baby ...

Four messages, all within one fucking minute. I silenced my watch and glanced back down at the picture, noticing the Cartier diamond bracelet that I'd bought Allie but she hardly ever wore because she *didn't care about all the fancy stuff*. Back then, she'd only wanted me.

She had worn the bracelet that night though because I had asked her to. I just didn't think the next morning, she'd be throwing it at me with tears racing down her face as she sobbed and asked me why.

"Why, Jace? Why?"

That was the last night I had seen her that happy. And truth was, that was the last night I had been happy too.

Chapter Eight

ALLIE

It was Saturday night, and Jace was nowhere to be found when I left the house for my date. He was probably at Jenny's house or with another girl from my Biology class, making them suck him off because he was king of Redwood and kings got everything they ever wanted.

I gnawed on the inside of my lip and stared off into space.

Last night ... I'd never thought it would happen. I never thought I'd actually ever sleep with Jace. It had been sophomore Allie's dream to spend the night with him, to have him whisper sweet nothings to her that he never told anyone else, to have him touch her in places that nobody ever had before.

But all I'd gotten was a filthy mouth that made me wet and his cum deep inside of me. As if he deserved to come inside of me after leaving me in tears, after I begged him to answer me, wondering why I wasn't enough for him anymore two years ago.

"Allie?" Jamal said, waving a hand in front of my face.

We were parked at the Overlook. The rocks overlooked the Atlantic Ocean, which was how it had gotten its name. This place was busy in the spring and summer, but in the fall and winter, it was almost completely empty.

I glanced over at Jamal. "Sorry. I'm just tired," I said, shifting my body so it was turned toward him. My knees brushed against his, and I wanted to feel my heart race like it had with—I shook my head—but it didn't.

"I can take you home if you want," Jamal offered.

My lips curled into a smile, and I wrapped a knit blanket around my body and leaned into him to snuggle closer. "No, I'm good."

I felt so bad about this. Part of me really, really wanted to give Jamal a chance, because he was actually one of the nicer athletes on the football team and had always been so sweet to me. The other half wanted to kiss Jamal, make out with Jamal, have Jamal's hands run all down my body, just to hurt Jace.

Jamal stared off into the endless Atlantic Ocean and smiled. "I've been wanting to take you out forever," he said, gently brushing his knuckles against mine.

Chills ran down my spine from the wind.

"But I wanted to do something a bit more ... I don't know, active?"

"More active?" I asked, brow arched. "That's a funny way of saying you want to get in my pants. Not many guys are as forward as you are, Jamal Simmons."

He let out a deep chuckle. "Nah, I mean, go out to dinner or to the movies or break into the boarded-up arcade down by the beach and let you kick my ass at Pac-Man or some shit."

I couldn't help the grin on my face. Only kids from the shitty side of town knew about the bankrupt, boarded-up arcade three blocks away from the overcrowded tourist seaside. The rich kids wouldn't be found dead anywhere even close to there. They had the Cherry Hill beaches, which were only for the higher class, supposedly.

Jamal was from the shitty side of town, had grown up a few

houses down from where I used to live before Dad died. He had helped out around the house, mowing our lawn and keeping things the way Dad had had them before Mom met Harlan.

"But I'm down for this too." Jamal grinned at me with those gleaming white teeth, almost as bright as the full moon tonight.

My lips curled into a soft smile, and I suddenly found myself clutching the necklace Dad had bought me the night before a drunk driver killed him.

Spent almost twenty years in the military and got killed for someone's senseless decisions. The world was cruel, so freaking cruel and rude and uncaring, especially to a girl just trying to make it out of this town and live a happy life.

"How's your mom?" Jamal asked when everything got quiet.

I shrugged. "Same, but now, she gets to go out to fancy dinners and travel to exotic places and can buy anything she wants. She's spending two weeks in some other country to celebrate her anniversary instead of going to Dad's grave with me to commemorate his death this year."

I pressed my lips together. That made it two years in a row now.

Part of me felt like she didn't care even though she had spent twenty years with my father.

Jamal frowned and looked back at the ocean. "Life's a bitch sometimes. You just gotta deal with it."

My lips curled into a small smile. "That makes me feel so much better, Jamal. Thanks."

Jamal winked at me. "Anytime." Then, he shook his head, as if to say life *really* did suck sometimes for some people and that it wasn't fair to even the best of us. "How are *you* doing?"

"As good as I can be," I said, thinking back to last night. All those emotions and feelings I had tried to suppress were suddenly back and nagging at all my insides. Raw pain and agonizing hurt from wanting something I knew never really was or would ever be mine.

Jace ...

Jace fucking Harbor.

My phone buzzed, and Imani's name popped up on the screen along with the time—12:04 a.m.

"I should get back home," I said, standing up and brushing off the dirt from my backside.

Jamal stood up and twirled the keys of his nearly broken-down 2005 Dodge Neon around his finger. I slid into the passenger side and looked over at him, knowing that I shouldn't have asked him to take me here out of all places. If Jace found out that Jamal and I had hung out in *our* spot, he'd kill the man.

"I had a good time tonight," I said with a smile. "A really good time."

Chapter Nine

JACE

"Where were you last night?" I asked Jamal during our last three-minute break at practice. I grabbed a towel from the track and wiped the sweat off my face. For it being thirty degrees in October, I was fucking sweating today, like at every practice.

My gaze locked on to Carter on the other side of the field as he talked to Nicole, who was sitting on the bleachers. I rolled my eyes and glanced around. Allie was usually here during the week, but since it was Sunday, all I got to see was Nicole and some of her slutty friends.

Jamal shrugged. "At the Overlook," he said as if it were nothing.

"The Overlook?" I asked, looking back at him.

He never went to the Overlook. He must've had a date, as he would never spend the gas, driving from his house all the way across town, for nothing.

"You bring a girl?"

Jamal stared back out onto the field, refusing to make eye contact with me. "You know how it is. Saturday night shit."

Coach blew the whistle, and Jamal jogged back onto the field before I could get a chance to grill him about whoever she was because if she was any one of the cheerleaders or even any of the rich and snobby girls, he'd be bragging about it.

I tossed the towel and jogged back to the line, taking my spot toward the end and keeping my eye on Carter, who was calling out a play. He stood behind his center, his hands between the center's legs and his gaze fastened on to mine.

Was I still pissed that he was fucking Nicole behind my back? Not really. What was ticking me off today were those snide comments he'd kept throwing at me about my stepsister. It was like he was never satisfied, always wanting to be the center of attention. As if being the fucking quarterback wasn't good enough for him.

Guessed he wasn't *that* talented to be the talk of the town, even as the QB.

"Hut, hut."

I watched his movements and sprinted down the field toward the receiver he was passing the ball to, jumping out in front of him and intercepting the ball before it got into the receiver's hands.

"Keep it up, Harbor," Coach called from the sidelines. "That's the kind of play I want to see every game for the rest of this season."

Carter shook his head in his helmet, and I tossed him the ball, purposely making sure it didn't reach him but fell a few yards in front of him. Our defensive coach called a second play, and I lined up again, keeping my eyes on the quarterback and readying for a blitz.

When the ball was hiked, I sprinted ahead and hit Carter right in the side, knocking him to the ground and making him lose the ball before he got a chance to toss it or hand it off. He hopped back up and dusted himself off, grabbing the football and throwing it back to the center.

"No wonder Allie hates you," he said to me, looking down the field. "Did you treat Allie the same way you treat your teammates? Is that why you two broke up sophomore year? You hit her, talk her down, huh?"

He's trying to get under your skin, Jace. Don't fucking listen.

"I guess that's why she'd rather hang out with Jamal all night than spend any time with her stepbrother," he said.

I froze, and he chuckled.

"Didn't know?" Carter continued before looking over at Jamal. "Well, if I had known you and Allie were a secret, I wouldn't have said *anything*."

I cut my eyes to Jamal. He'd brought Allie—*Allie*—to the fucking Overlook last night? Out of all the fucking people he could've brought and all the places they could've gone, he had taken my stepsister to what used to be *our* spot.

"We just went out," Jamal said, brushing it off. "Nothing happened."

Coach blew the whistle, probably sensing things tensing up between us. "Bring it in, boys!" he called.

My nostrils flared, and I tore off my helmet. "Nothing had better have fucking happened between you and her," I said through clenched teeth, knocking my shoulder into his as I walked by.

Allie was mine to fuck with.

Hands on my hips, sweat dripping down my neck, I waited for the rest of the team to bring it in, so Coach could talk, and then I could get the hell out of here as soon as possible to clear my head.

"We have a big game this Friday," Coach said, stuffing a pen behind his ear. "Leeside High isn't going to go easy on you. They're six and one for the season and looking to defeat *us* to keep their record almost perfect. They want blood. They want us to break. I expect you to give it your all this week during practice." He paused and looked at me. "And I expect absolutely no fighting during practice this week either."

I clenched my jaw. I wouldn't make any promises over that one.

Chapter Ten

ALLIE

It was Monday morning at the *best* school in the region, Redwood. Note the sarcasm because I hated this place more than I hated Jace Harbor, and I *loathed* Jace Harbor with my entire heart.

I stood by my locker, depositing my books from my first class and trying to retrieve my books for the next two classes because I didn't want to sprint back here from across the campus in my five-minute break. There was far too much trouble I could run into, like the Poison boys dealing weed, cigarettes, drugs, and weapons to the rich kids.

One time, I'd caught Jace with them and nearly gotten beaten the fuck up for it. Nobody saw Poison make their deals—they made sure of it. If someone did, there were consequences, which was why I steered the fuck clear of them.

I might've been from the same side of town as them, but I didn't want to associate myself with them at all. Now, I was considered one of those *rich kids* that they preyed on. No, thank you.

Someone poked me on the shoulder, and I looked back and locked eyes with Jamal, who was leaning against his locker with a football in his hand, talking to his teammate but looking at me. My cheeks flushed slightly from the sudden attention.

Imani popped up next to me. "God, I tap you on the shoulder, and suddenly, you're in love with Jamal, the football flirt." She inched closer to me and lowered her voice. "Just like your step-brother, if I *have* to remind you."

I playfully rolled my eyes at her. "Nothing happened between us, I."

She arched her brow, held her books to her chest, and leaned against the locker next to mine, smirking. "Mmhmm, sure. That's what we're calling it nowadays ... *nothing*." She narrowed her eyes at me. "Come on. You went on a date with Jamal to the *Overlook* —that's where everyone goes to hook up."

Scrunching my nose, I frowned. "Maybe people hook up there in the summer, but not now in the fall," I said, remembering all those nights when *he* had had his arm around me and we watched snow fall from the sky and into the sea.

Someone slapped a hand against my locker door, slamming it shut. My eyes widened. I'd totally expected to see Jace, but I came eye to eye with two members of Poison—João and Landon. João was a third of Poison, tall and stalky with big brown eyes, half Brazilian and one entire jerk.

"Where's your brother?" he asked me, crossing his huge tattooed arms across his chest.

From the corner of my eye, I saw Landon start talking —*flirting*—with Imani, and I cursed her for all her help on how to get out of this one.

I shrugged and opened my locker back up, refusing to show him that he fucking terrified me. "I don't know. He's not my problem."

"If you see him, make sure he knows we're looking for him."

And then, with that, he nodded to Landon, and they retreated down the hall toward the gymnasium. I doubted they actually had gym class. They were probably going there to jerk around in the locker room and smoke a blunt.

"What was that about?" Imani asked.

I arched a brow at my best friend and decided to give her a hard time. "You would know if you weren't gawking at Landon," I said, my lips curling into a smile.

She rolled her eyes and then tensed as her gaze fell behind me.

Imani nudged me and gestured down the hall. Jace was stalking through the crowd of people, who moved for him, and toward me. My heart leaped in my chest, and I turned away from him, pretending like I didn't care about him. Last night, I had slept over at Imani's, so I wouldn't have to see his stupid fucking face.

Something must've happened between Friday night and this morning.

"I guess I'll be going," she said, leaning in. "Meet you in Bio."

I glared at her. "You are not leaving me." I seethed, hurrying to organize my locker to find all my books for class. "I am not spending a second alone with him." My cheeks flushed. I hadn't told her yet what had happened on Friday between Jace and me.

"Imani," Jace said, stepping closer to me. "I need to talk to Allie alone."

Imani gave me a pitiful smile and hurried down the hall. She surely wasn't going to be late to any class, and neither was I.

The first bell for second period rang through the busy halls.

I gathered the five damn textbooks Mr. Barnes made me drag to each class and pushed my locker closed with my shoulder. "I have to get to class, Jace. Move."

Jace stepped in front of me and placed his hands on the locker above me, trapping me in. "You're not going anywhere. I said that we need to talk."

"And I said to move," I said, glaring up into his brown eyes. I wanted to slap him right in that gorgeous face of his for fucking me and straight-up leaving the other night, for not talking to me all weekend, for making me wonder when the hell *that* was going to happen again.

Instead of moving away, Jace stepped closer, making me pull my books to my chest, my glasses fogging up slightly from all this body heat. As soon as everyone—except for one of the Poison boys, who was lingering by the restrooms with a lit cigarette in his mouth, and a rich kid nearly up his ass about weed—was out of the halls, Jace wrapped a hand around my throat and pinned me to the lockers.

"What the fuck is going on between you and Jamal?" he asked.

I sucked in a breath, my heart pounding in my chest. "Nothing."

"You're fucking lying to me," he said through clenched teeth.

"I'm not."

Just like you didn't lie to me years ago, telling me that you wanted me more than anything, just to get into my pants, I thought.

Jace stared down at me with those raging brown eyes, a strand of his dark hair falling into his sculpted face. He slid his tongue across his lower lip and roughly grabbed my chin in his hand, burying his face into the crook of my neck. "Was I not enough for you Friday night?" he asked, drawing his nose up the side of my neck and growling deep in my ear.

I shuddered against him and glanced down the hallway to make sure nobody was watching. I wouldn't be caught dead with him this close to me, especially now that he was my stepbrother.

"Did you have to go be a slut with one of my teammates?" he asked, his words coming out rough and raw.

I didn't know whether he was fucking with me or if he was hurt.

He pushed his thumb hard against my jawbone, stroking it. "I'm the only one you get to slut around with," he said, slipping a hand into my leggings and drawing a finger down my folds. "I'm the only one who gets to touch your pussy, fill you with my cum ..." He slapped his palm against my cheek, and I clenched. "Slap this pretty little face of yours."

Wetness pooled between my legs, and I could feel the heat crawling up my neck. My nipples hardened under my bra. All I wanted was for him to slip his fingers into me and make me beg for him to slap me again, spank me even. It was so fucking wrong to feel this way after everything that had happened between us ...

But he knew exactly what he was doing.

He pressed his lips against my ear. "Remember that your step-brother still owns this pussy."

Still. Not now. Not two years ago. *Still*.

He and I both knew that I hadn't been with another guy since him. I refused to get my heart hurt again ... or maybe I didn't want to give my heart away because he still had it. Maybe that was why I was filled with so much hurt and agony around him, watching him be with so many other girls when all I wanted was for him to be mine.

I swallowed my pride and stared up into his eyes, refusing to give him any satisfaction that I was enjoying this. "*If* I was seeing Jamal, I don't think that's any of your business, Jace," I said through clenched teeth, returning his intense glare. I pushed myself into his chest to get him to move. "Now, let me go to Biology in peace. I'm already late."

Jace stared at me with a twitching jaw and anger in his eyes ... maybe there was even hurt in them too. I couldn't tell. He was always good at hiding his feelings, at acting like he didn't give a fuck at all, kicking me to the curb like I was nothing.

"Go." He surprisingly stepped out of my way. "Don't want to ruin that perfect reputation of yours because of me."

I stared at him for a few moments, completely taken aback. Why was he so frustrating to understand?

I don't care, I reminded myself.

I shook my head and pushed past him, leaving for Biology and leaving him behind. But I didn't want to. I wanted to stay and try to understand him.

Maybe tonight, I would.

Chapter Eleven

ALLIE

"I can't believe he's giving us another quiz." Imani pulled out her laptop at lunch and opened the slides from Bio class. "We literally just had an exam last Friday. What is his problem? Give us at least three days before the next one."

I tugged out my textbook, promising myself that I'd ask Mom about fixing my computer when she got back from her trip. Harlan would get me a brand-spanking-new one if I asked him because he wanted me to like him, but I didn't want his money. He had produced the infamous Jace Harbor, and I didn't take any money from the Harbors.

"He's a grumpy old man," I muttered, flipping through the five-hundred-page textbook.

Of course Barnes would give us a freaking quiz. He probably didn't have anything better to do than sit in his house, chuckle menacingly as he wrote the hardest damn questions ever, and wrote Fs on a bunch of papers.

I sipped on my chocolate milk and sighed, unable to focus, as my thoughts had been all over the place during the lecture. I couldn't even pay attention. I'd never be able to absorb all this information by tomorrow. All I could think about was that stupid fucking man.

My gaze flickered to Jace, standing by the entrance of the cafeteria and talking to all three of the Poison boys. My stomach clenched, and I had the urge to go over there and scream at him for ever getting involved with them. They were no damn good ... but neither was he.

If he wanted to ruin his life and all his chances of getting into the NFL, I didn't care.

Nope. Not one bit.

He could go back to juvie for all I cared.

"Hey," Jamal said, sitting next to me at the empty table.

My eyes widened slightly at the sight of *him* sitting at the "Outcast Table," as designated by the great Jace Harbor after he broke up with me. He usually sat with Jace and the rest of the football team at the table by the windows, the one with all the cheerleaders and popular girls. No athlete would be caught dead sitting here with us.

Except him, apparently.

I unclenched my fists and gently rubbed the nail marks on my palms. "What are you doing here?" I asked, brows raised.

Imani clicked away on her computer and smirked behind her screen, pretending as if she were still studying, but I knew she was listening to every word of our conversation. "Hey, Jamal," she said, giving him just an ounce of acknowledgment.

"Thought you girls could use some company," Jamal said, shrugging his shoulders.

I glanced at Jace, who was watching us with a tense jaw as he walked away from the Poison boys to his usual table. After swallowing hard, I turned back to Jamal and nodded, not knowing what to say to him.

"Yeah, sure." I took another gulp of my milk.

Jamal stuffed half a meatball sub into his mouth and bumped

his shoulder into mine. "What're you up to?" he asked, still chewing.

My lips curled into a small smile, and I pushed his jaw up. "Chew with your mouth closed." I turned back to my books. "Mr. Barnes is giving us a quiz tomorrow."

He finished chewing and leaned closer to the table to look at the textbook, putting his arm around the back of my chair. Imani raised her brows at me and narrowed her dark brown eyes at the gesture. And I ... I sucked in a breath because Jamal had *never* gotten this close to me in front of Jace.

"Didn't you have an exam on Friday?" Jamal asked.

"That loser decided to give us another one," Imani said, tapping on her keyboard.

I looked over at the popular table and tensed when I saw him.

Jace had sat down at his usual table with Jenny—Jenny, not a cheerleader, not a popular chick, the Science Club president— sitting next to him. She curled her arm around his, drawing her fingers up and down against his forearm. Nicole sat at the opposite end of his table, looking pissed the fuck off.

I glanced back at him, my heart racing when I saw that he was looking at me. What was his damn problem? First, he'd hated me. Then, he'd told me that I was his. Now, he was letting another girl touch him. My hands balled into fists again. Fuck, I didn't care. I hated—*loathed*—the dickhead.

Turning back to Jamal, I clenched my jaw. What was wrong with me? Why couldn't I get over Jace, even after two years of him torturing me every fucking day? I just wanted to be happy, and Jace would never bring me happiness again. I knew he wouldn't. He had made it clear as day when he broke my heart sophomore year.

"So ..." I took a deep breath, slammed my book closed because I knew I wouldn't be able to study with him next to me, and smiled over at him. "Are you ready for the game on Friday? It's against our rivals, isn't it?"

Jamal grinned at me, a small gap between his two front teeth. When he used to come over, he always told me how much he wished his parents had the money for braces so he could fix it. But I kinda, sorta liked it.

"Coach is worried about it, but we'll kill 'em as long as Jace keeps his head on straight." Jamal glanced over at Jace, who was now whispering something in Jenny's ear and making her blush. Jamal shook his head. "He's been off lately, more than he usually is."

Off.

Hadn't we both been a little off lately? We had both made the biggest mistake of our lives Friday night and gotten back together. It had been a moment of weakness. A moment of weakness that would *never* happen again.

If only that were true ...

$$Chapter\ Twelve$$

ALLIE

"You have Calc?" Jamal asked, stopping by my locker after lunch.

I deposited my lunch box inside and pulled out my textbook for Math with Mrs. Dawson, the middle-aged teacher who flirted with almost all the athletes at our school. It was kind of gross, but nobody said anything to her about it, especially if it got them passing grades.

The first bell rang, and Jamal swore under his breath. "Shit, I'd walk you there, but if I'm late to English one more time, Mr. V is going to write me up, and Coach will make me sit out the game on Friday."

"Guess you'll have to walk me to class tomorrow," I said, closing my locker and smiling at him. "I'm going to hold you to it too."

Jamal walked backward down the hall and smirked at me. "I'll be there."

When he disappeared, I picked up my pace and rushed down the corridor to get to Math. It was all the way on the opposite side of campus, past the gym and the science wing. I hated being late more than anything, hated all the judgmental stares from everyone when I walked into the room, hated the disappointed head shakes teachers would give me, hated this freaking town.

People hurried down the hall, trying to get to class before the second bell. I passed the gym. Fuck this school. Who thought it was a good idea to have two buildings on one campus and give students a measly five minutes to get from one building to the other in the damn sleet?

Someone stupid—that was who.

Someone slapped a hand over my mouth and pulled me right from my sprint-walk into a hallway. I screamed into their palm, my heart already pounding hard against my chest.

"Shut up, Allie," Jace said into my ear, pushing me into the empty boys' locker room.

I wriggled out of his grip, turned around, and smacked him in the chest. "What the fuck was that?" I seethed through clenched teeth. "Are you trying to give me a fucking heart attack? I'm late for class."

I stepped to the side, but he moved in front of me, his jaw clenched hard.

"Did you do it to make me angry?"

My eyes widened. "Did I do what?"

He stepped closer to me, towering over me. "Go to the Overlook with Jamal."

"What? Are you stalking me now?" I asked, crossing my arms over my chest.

How had he found out about that? Was he keeping tabs on me or something? I didn't understand the damn man, didn't think I ever would.

"And you have no room to talk, sitting with Jenny at lunch." The words came out laced with so much damn jealousy that I regretted opening my mouth.

Jace raised a single brow for a moment, as if he was surprised.

Then, all the surprise was gone from his face and replaced with a look of fury. He pushed me against his locker in the locker room.

Don't ask me how I know which one is his.

"You go with him to the Overlook, then sit with him at fucking lunch after I told you …" He placed a hand on the lockers next to me, his fingers curling against the metal. "After I fucking told you that this"—he grasped my pussy through my leggings—"is mine."

"It's not yours," I said through gritted teeth as he started to move his fingers in tortuous little circles around my clit. "I'm not"—I took a deep breath, trying to ignore the heat between my legs—"yours."

He chuckled deeply in my ear. "Is that why you're wet for me? I just started touching you, and I can already feel you through your leggings, Allie." He brushed his nose against my ear. "I bet you taste good."

I closed my eyes, my nipples hardening in my bra. We shouldn't be doing this.

"Sit down on the bench," he said, gesturing to the bench right in front of the locker he had me pressed against.

God, this was wrong—so fucking wrong.

Yet I sat.

The corner of his lips curled up, and he kneeled between my legs, hooking his fingers under my waistband and pulling my leggings down to my ankles. His breath warmed my core.

"We can't do this here," I said, back already arching to give him better access to eat me out. I glanced at the locker room entrance that we were basically sitting in front of and shook my head. "What if someone comes in?"

He sucked on my thigh, definitely leaving a blotchy red bruise. "I'm the only one who's going to *come* inside you," he murmured against me.

I tensed when two of his fingers brushed against my entrance. "What if your coach comes into the locker room or one of the gym teachers, one of your teammates, Jace? We can't ..." I parted my lips, feeling the tips of his fingers slip inside of me. "We can't ..." I said breathlessly.

"You'd better be quiet then," he said, pumping them in and out of me. He dipped his head and flicked his tongue against my already-swollen clit. "No screaming my name this time."

This time.

Because last time when he had touched me like this, we had been at the house, and I could scream as loud as I wanted. This time ... this time, if we weren't careful, we'd get caught. And I would never get caught with Jace Harbor between my legs.

Yet ... I didn't want him to stop.

He flicked his tongue against my clit, over and over and over, sucking it between his lips, making me whine and whimper for him to give me more. I closed my eyes and shuffled around on the bench, feeling way too good.

"Look the fuck at me," Jace said, his face buried between my legs.

I glanced down at him through my glasses, feeling so exposed in such a public place. Anyone could walk right in and find out that I was being touched by my stepbrother, the man I was supposed to hate.

"My stepsister thinks she's not a slut, but her cunt is dripping fucking wet, tightening around my fingers." He pulled his fingers out of me and watched the juices stick to them. He stuffed them into my mouth. "Clean them for me, like I know you want to."

My core was pulsing wildly as I sucked them into my mouth, wrapping my lips around his fingers and taking them as deep as he wanted to push them. He smirked down at me with those dangerous, dark eyes.

"How do you taste?"

I furrowed my brows at him, still sucking. The tension was building higher in my core.

He pulled his fingers out of my mouth, wrapped his hand

around my throat, and pulled me closer. "How. Do. You. Taste?" he asked, his voice husky yet rough in my ear. He pressed the front of his jeans against my bare pussy, getting my juices all over the material and making me feel how hard he was already for me.

"Good," I whispered. "So good."

He gazed from my eyes down to my lips, letting his stare linger for a few moments. I furrowed my brows and grasped his jeans, needing them off now.

"Call me a slut again," I said in a breathy whisper.

"You're not just a slut, Allie. You're *my* slut. Nobody else's." He undid his zipper and pulled out his hard cock. "Your little pussy is just aching for me to put my cock back inside you, isn't it? I bet you haven't stopped thinking about me between your thighs, fucking you from behind, making you watch as I ruined you."

It was so close ... so close to slipping inside of me.

"Be rough with me. Slap my face. Fuck me, Jace. Please, fuck me."

I was a desperate little slut for him.

He groaned and slipped himself inside of me, pushing himself as deep as he could go. His eyes fluttered closed. "Fuck, fuck, fuck," he said, the words drawn out. "You feel so fucking good. So good, baby."

After a few moments, he started to pump in and out of me. He wrapped a hand around my throat, pinning me to the lockers. He tore my shirt open with his other hand and slapped my breasts through my bra, watching them bounce with every thrust.

He roughly slid his thumb across my chin, pushing my head to the side. He slapped my exposed cheek hard, then rubbed it with his fingers softly. I tightened around him and waited ... just waited for more. Again, he slapped me hard against the face, and I moaned out loud.

This felt so much better than I remembered.

Another slap against my cheek, and he gently released the grip on my neck. He tugged me to a standing position, turned me around, and thrust me against the lockers. He placed a hand on the locker next to me, his fingertips white against the red metal, the veins in his hands swollen. Then, he slipped inside of me again, pumping into me from behind, his strokes quick and steady, pushing me against the lockers.

After pulling a fistful of my hair, he twisted my head so I looked back at him. Then he slapped me across the cheek, then tugged me into a kiss.

Slapped me across the cheek again, then kissed me hard.

Smacked me across the cheek and stuck his tongue into my mouth and claimed it.

Every time he kissed me, I inched closer and closer to the edge of an orgasm. I intertwined my fingers with his on the locker.

"Jace, I'm so close," I whispered, my toes curling. "I'm going to come for you."

"Come for me, baby," he murmured against me. "Just like you used to."

My fingers curled harsher around his, and I slapped a hand over my mouth, feeling nothing but pure bliss filling every inch of my body. Tingles shot up and down my arms and legs, and I doubled over, clutching on to the locker for dear life.

One of these days, Jace Harbor was really going to ruin me.

And my horny ass was going to fucking let him.

Chapter Thirteen

JACE

Allie sat on one of the benches in the locker room, leaning against a red locker with her cheeks flushed and a look of satisfaction written all over her face. I imagined her with my jersey on again, sporting the number 46 on her back. I imagined having her in here after one of my games, pressing her up against the lockers again and letting her know that I wanted her on those bleachers at every game. I imagined her ditching Jamal and finally fucking being with me again.

It wasn't fucking fair that Dad had had to ruin everything I fucking had with her.

After what he had done, I would never forgive that fucking asshole. I would always want Allie and her mother to leave the house, would always fuck with their lives until they couldn't take it anymore and were gone for good.

Allie quickly came to her senses, hurrying to put on her clothes. She rushed out of the locker room with a quick, "I have to go. I'm late for class," refusing to look me in the eye.

I watched her walk out those doors and frowned at her departing figure.

Since this morning, I hadn't been able to get her off my mind. Hell, since *yesterday*, when I'd found out my best friend had taken her to *our* spot, I hadn't been able to get her off my mind. I wanted to show her that he was not even half the man that I could be to her, but we'd already crossed that bridge once, and I'd already broken her heart.

I tugged on my jeans and wet my hair, trying to make it look like I hadn't just had the time of my fucking life in the locker room. I didn't care what people thought of me, but I didn't want people asking questions about me and my stepsister.

The doors to the locker room opened. For a moment, I thought it was Allie coming back for seconds, but when I felt those fake nails drag against my back, I tensed.

"What the fuck do you want, Nicole?" I asked, turning around and stepping away from her.

"Jace, baby," she purred. "I just want to talk. Please."

I suppressed the urge to roll my eyes and pushed past her. "I don't want to talk to you."

She stepped in front of me, blocking my passage to the exit. "You don't want me to tell my dad about you hanging out with Poison again, do you?" she asked with a smirk. "You know what could happen."

I clenched my jaw, refusing to flip out on her because that bitch *would* go straight to her daddy, who would go straight to the principal. She'd get me kicked off the damn team and thrown in juvie again, just for talking to Poison.

"What do you want?" I asked.

"I want you to take me to homecoming. I want to fix this ... fix us ..." She dragged her fingers down my chest. "Please, baby. You're the best thing that has ever happened to me."

"My father's money was the best thing to happen to you," I said through clenched teeth. It was never me ... nobody ever liked *me* for *me*, except maybe Allie at some point. Nicole didn't give a fuck about who I was, just wanted me to give her everything her father couldn't. "Not me."

She rolled her eyes, her inch-long eyelashes batting against her cheeks. "Jace, you know that's not true. I love you for you. Carter was a mistake, a silly little mistake that I will try hard to make up for every single day."

"Why?" I asked, shaking my head from side to side. "Why do you want to get back together with me?"

"Because I love you."

"Name one fucking thing you love about me," I said, staring at her and feeling so hollow and empty on the inside.

This was why I didn't fucking date in this town anymore. Nobody really gave a fuck about you unless you were someone or had something they wanted.

She shook her head, pausing for a few moments. "I love that you love football."

"Forget the athlete. Forget the money. Tell me what you love about *me*." I waited, and I waited, and I waited. "That's what I thought," I said, throwing my backpack over my shoulder.

I stormed out of the locker room, away from a seething Nicole and right into Jenny. After sighing through my nose and rolling my eyes because I couldn't seem to get away from the two most annoying people on the planet—except Allie, of course—I stopped.

"What do you want, Jenny?"

Jenny smiled at me and stared up at me through her glasses. "Come over tonight," she said boldly. She tugged on the ends of her hair and nervously sucked on the inside of her cheek. "My parents have a business meeting tonight. They won't be home until late."

"No," I said, stepping past her and starting toward my class.

She grabbed my wrist and pulled me back. "Come on, Jace,

please. We can finally …" Her cheeks flushed red, and she looked down at her feet, licking her dry lips. "You know …"

"We could what?" I asked, brow arched as I watched her squirm uncomfortably. "Fuck?" I let out a low chuckle and continued down the hallway, thinking that this entire situation was actually laughable. "No, I don't want to fuck you."

"What about what you said at lunch?" she asked, shaking her head.

My chest tightened as a wave of shame washed over me. All those lies to make Allie jealous. I fucking hated myself for it … but I had to push her away as hard as I could. Yet I still couldn't stay away from her.

I turned around. "If I wanted to fuck you, you'd know it. Don't beg for it. It doesn't look good on you."

"You know, I heard a rumor," she said, crossing her arms over her chest and staring at me through her glasses. She tapped her Converse on the tiled floor. "You can't keep up your *I fuck the entire Redwood female population* bad-boy image forever, Jace. Girls talk, you know. You don't fuck half of the girls everyone claims you do."

I let out a breath through my nose in an attempt to laugh. Did she really think she had one up on me? Was she as stupid as the rest of Redwood, who believed all those rumors too?

I turned on my heel again and walked down the hall. "I haven't fucked *any* of the girls people claim I do," I shouted over my shoulder. "And I'm not about to start with you."

Chapter Fourteen

JACE

Dad: Football is a waste of time. You should be studying with Allie instead of going to those nonsense games of yours.

I thrust my phone into my football locker, clenched my jaw, and grabbed my helmet for tonight's game. I fucking hated him. All he cared about was me taking over the family business, becoming one of those asshole CEOs that he always hung around, forgetting my dreams of making it to the NFL.

"Bring it in, boys," Coach said, standing by the doors. "Leeside High is going to bring their all tonight. I expect you to play better than you have in practice. Carter, I want you throwing the ball. They have a good defense, so stay sharp. Harbor"—he turned to me—"make sure those sacks are perfect. No slip-ups."

We ran out onto the field, rain already starting to drizzle overhead. The bleachers were filled with students from Redwood and from Leeside, all here to cheer on their teams. I stared off into the bleachers, spotting Nicole on the sidelines and Jenny mixed in the senior section, and frowned.

"Offense, you're up," Coach called.

I crossed my arms, pacing up and down the sidelines as our offense ran out onto the field. Carter called out a few plays and threw twenty yards for a touchdown—annoying prick. When we were up, I sprinted out onto the field, trying to clear my head. I was here to play football, not care about who showed up in the bleachers.

Yet, all throughout the night, I couldn't stop looking up at them. After Mom had died, Allie was the only person close to me who came to my games. Dad refused to go, as he hated football—or any sport for that matter. I didn't even think he'd been to one of my games in my entire life.

Right before halftime, I spotted her in the stands, her body bobbing up and down, probably trying to stay warm. I pushed my shoulders back and tossed the ball to the referee.

"Harbor!" Coach shouted. "What are you doing out there? Pick it up!"

I crouched at the line, gaze fixed on the quarterback, all sense of cockiness and confidence back. I was here to play fucking football. When he hiked the ball, I followed a receiver back toward the end zone.

The Leeside quarterback dropped back and scanned the field for an opening. He threw the ball toward one of his receivers, who stood at the four-yard line. I sprinted toward him, jumped in front of him right before the ball could slip into his hands, and snatched the ball out of the air, intercepting it.

As soon as my feet hit the ground, I ran toward the other end of the field, dodging linemen and receivers who all tried to get in my way. One grabbed on to my arm, slipping on the mud and nearly taking me with him. But I shook him off and continued to sprint toward the end zone, running into it and giving our team a six-point lead.

The crowd went wild, but all I could see was Allie standing in the bleachers. I wanted her to be happy, to be excited. But instead of being excited like everyone else, she crossed her arms over her chest and looked away from me and toward Jamal, who had his arms up in victory on the other end of the field.

I threw the ball to the ref, growling under my breath, and walked to my team's side of the field. Coach slapped me on the back. The guys shouted at me. I pushed through them and slouched on the bench, grasping my water bottle until my fingertips turned white.

At halftime—when we were supposed to be going into the fucking locker room—Jamal stayed behind and ran over to the bleachers, calling out Allie's name. I balled my hands into fists, watching her jog down the bleachers and hanging over the side to smile down at him through the rain.

That should've been *me*—fucking *me*. Not him. Not my best friend.

"Jamal," I shouted.

I tore off my helmet, about two seconds from sprinting over there and ripping him away from her so everyone in this school knew she was still off-limits. Jamal didn't get a special fucking privilege because he was my friend.

"Jace," Coach called.

But I ignored him.

I started toward Jamal, teeth clenched together, fingers curled around my face mask.

Coach grabbed me by the jersey. "Harbor, get in the fucking locker room. Don't start shit now. The principal is here, watching your every move, waiting for you to screw up."

Rage exploded through me, the vein in my neck pumping wildly. I wanted to kill, wanted to drive him into the ground, shout at him for even thinking about *my girl* ...

But she wasn't my girl, and she could never be my girl again.

Everything was too fucked up now. *Dad* had fucked everything up.

I ripped myself away from Coach and started toward the

locker room, trying to calm my anger before I ran into the bitch Carter, boasting about throwing three touchdowns in the first half and acting as if he owned the damn school and everyone in it, including Allie.

"Some of the guys are throwing a party at Bubba's house tonight," Jamal said, jogging up to me as I stormed to the locker room. He grabbed my shoulder and stopped me, wiping the sweat off his forehead with his forearm. "You going?"

I stared at the mud on my shoes, felt the rain beating down on me, and frowned. My heart fucking hurt. Jamal was my best friend. I shouldn't be angry with him for going after the girl I kept pushing away. As much as I fucking hated it, Jamal would be good for Allie. He could make her smile. All I did was make her cry.

My lips twitched. No, fuck that. He wouldn't be good for her. I would.

"No." I shook my head even though I wanted to rip *his* off and clenched my jaw. "I have somewhere else to be." I tore myself away from him and continued to the locker room, knowing if I waited any longer, I'd slam my fist right into his pearly-white teeth.

Chapter Fifteen

Sometime during the football game, the drizzle had turned to full-on sleet. Almost everyone but those in the student section left before the end of the game. I stayed and sat in the bleachers with my hood on, watching Jace make hit after hit.

When he and I had dated, I'd always loved coming to his games. Now, I went because I wanted to, not for him. It was something to do in this town that didn't involve drugs or alcohol, just sweaty, muscular boys who had to get their aggression out on someone.

After we won, I decided not to wait for Jace to get out of the shower. He would probably be off to another party to celebrate his win against Redwood's rivals. And he wouldn't want to drive me to the cemetery anyway.

Today was the anniversary of Dad's death. The last four years without him had been some of the hardest years of my entire life. I hated not seeing his crooked grin when he came home from deployment or not smelling the blueberry pancakes he made for me as often as he could.

I walked to three stores within half a mile of the cemetery to try to find some marigolds—Dad's favorite flowers—to bring to his grave. When nobody in walking distance had any marigolds, I settled on a bunch of pink roses for him. I bought an umbrella too, not that it would do much in the diagonal-falling sleet.

After waiting in CVS for five minutes, hoping the weather would clear, I hurried out into the storm and started my short walk toward the cemetery. It was freezing outside, and my waterproof rain jacket definitely *wasn't* waterproof, as I could feel the water sticking to my arms.

When I made it to the cemetery, my heart ached. I didn't come here as much as I should have. I tried to avoid it because I hated the feeling of helplessness, knowing that I didn't have anyone to hold me as I broke down in tears in front of his grave. Mom didn't come with me anymore, only on their anniversary. I didn't want Imani here. And Jamal ... that'd just be weird.

I sat on the wet grass and rested my head against Dad's gravestone, my fingers brushing against the dog tags that I always kept in my backpack, in my purse, almost everywhere I went. Mom didn't want them anymore. She'd told me that she didn't want Harlan to get angry or jealous over them.

"I'm sorry that I'm here alone," I said to him, wanting a response back but knowing that I'd never get to hear him say, "It's okay, kiddo," again.

I let the sleet pound against my thin jacket and drench me. Tears welled up in my eyes, some spilling down my cheeks.

"I'm sorry that Mom's not here. I asked her to come, but she's out with Harlan."

I sat there for an hour, maybe two, twisting and turning his dog tags between my fingers. My phone had died during the game, so I couldn't tell exactly how long the rain and sleet had been pouring down on me.

"I wish you were still here," I whispered. "I miss you so much. I try to make you proud every day, but lately ... lately, I don't know what I'm doing down here without you." I swallowed hard, closed my eyes, and let a couple more tears fall down my cheeks. "I hope I'm making you proud."

When I heard the purr of an engine, I opened my eyes to see someone parking on the side of the road near Dad's grave. The headlights pierced through the dark fog sitting overhead. Crying in a cemetery in the middle of the night probably wasn't my best choice.

I gazed over at the car, my heart racing when it turned off and the darkness consumed the cemetery again. And in the midst of the rain and the sleet, I saw Jace Harbor get out and walk over to me with a bunch of marigolds in his hands.

Chapter Sixteen

ALLIE

"What are you doing here?" I asked, my voice barely above a whisper as Jace Harbor approached me.

Rain beat down around us, plastering his hair to his forehead. His pretty dark brown eyes were fixed on me. He should have been at a house party, lighting up a blunt with Poison and letting Jenny suck him off. Not here, not with me.

He shrugged his shoulders and thrust the flowers into my hands. "It's the anniversary of your dad's death. I wasn't going to let you come here alone."

My chest tightened. Not once this entire week had I told him that I was coming here to see Dad after the game. He must've remembered when we used to go a few years ago … unless his dad had told him to come with me.

I glanced down at the flowers in my hands.

But the marigolds? Harlan wouldn't have known about the marigolds.

My chin quivered, and I couldn't stop the tears from spilling down my cheeks. I wrapped my arms around his torso and pulled him into a hug, letting myself be vulnerable with him again for just a moment. Times like this ... I didn't know what Jace Harbor thought about me.

If he hated me, like he claimed to, he wouldn't be here.

But if he loved me, like he used to, he wouldn't be a dick to me all the time.

Jace tensed, then hesitantly wrapped his arms around my shoulders to pull me closer to him. Rain and sleet were pounding down around us, my toes were numb, and I was crying like a maniac in front of my father's gravestone, but for that single moment ... everything felt a little bit better.

Then, I remembered that Jace Harbor had broken my heart, and I stepped away from him. I placed the marigolds on the ground in front of Dad's grave and watched Jace nod to the car.

"Why don't we get back home? You look cold."

After giving him a curt nod, I said good-bye to Dad and slid into Jace's Maserati in all my wet and soaked-through clothes. Jace slid in next to me and started the car, glancing over a few times as he drove us home.

"Are you okay?" he asked.

"Yeah, I'm fine." I gnawed on the inside of my lip, not liking how nice he was being to me. It made me feel weird and awkward and cared about by Redwood's cruelest man. "Are you?" I asked, staring at the sleet hitting the windshield. "You got hit pretty hard in the third quarter. Thought you blacked out."

Jace cut his eyes to me and shut off the car as we pulled up to the house. "Always got to say something, don't you?"

I trudged out of the car and kicked off my wet shoes and soggy socks at the door to the garage. Beads of water dropped off my raincoat and onto the ground beside me. Jace scrunched up his nose when he saw it.

"Why do you still wear all these cheap fucking clothes?" he asked, tugging on the corner of my jacket from Target.

I looked his expensive ass up and down as he took off his raincoat, his clothes dry, unlike mine, and basically dripping with money—*definitely* unlike mine. I pulled off my raincoat and stripped off my nasty-ass jeans, not caring that he was staring at me with those intense brown eyes of his.

My jacket might've been cheap for him, but I had spent a good thirty dollars on something that barely kept me warm during his football games and didn't even try to keep the rain away. I rolled my eyes and walked toward the second-floor bathroom near our rooms.

"Unlike *you*, I don't have money to spend on expensive clothes."

"My dad loves you," he said, following after me.

"I know he does," I said.

"He'd buy you anything you could ever want."

And I knew that he would, but that didn't mean that I wanted or needed any of that shit. Mom might've taken it and all the other expensive things he'd gotten her without question, but Dad had raised me better than that. I didn't take things; I earned them.

"I don't want them," I said, shrugging my shoulders and walking into the bathroom.

I went to close the door, but he smacked his hand on it and held it open. Crossing his big arms over his chest, he leaned against the doorframe. I turned on the hot water and narrowed my eyes at him.

"What?" I asked, hoping he'd leave me to shower in peace because that ache in my core hadn't disappeared since Monday afternoon in the locker room.

It was getting worse. My need for him kept growing, and I couldn't fucking get a grip. He was my stepbrother, my damn stepbrother. I shouldn't feel this way toward him. I should *never* have felt this way toward him.

"If all your clothes are ripped, you'll have to get new ones," Jace said.

I cut my eyes to him and gritted my teeth. "Don't you fucking dare think about destroying my closet. Why do you even care about what I dress in anyway?"

He paused for a slight moment, then tilted his head to the side in the way he always did when he wanted to say something to his dad but didn't want to offend him or start a fight. But with me, he didn't care what he said. "If you're going to be representing the Harbor name, you can't be wearing shitty clothes."

"I'm not *representing* the Harbor name in any way." I balled my hands into fists. "I'd never take the same last name as someone like *you*," I said, tearing off my shirt and glaring at him right in the eyes.

He stepped closer to me. "You'd rather freeze your ass off in this winter than accept some warm clothes?"

I gnawed on the inside of my cheek, knowing that this winter was about to be the absolute worst. Another reason that I couldn't wait to move out of this town. But if I took clothes from this man, I'd end up owing him.

"No," I said, shaking my head and placing my hands on my hips. "I don't need you to buy me clothes."

Another moment, and I wanted him to leave. When I realized that Jace wasn't going anywhere, I stepped closer to him, wanting nothing more than to hop into the shower and be done with the night. "What I need is for you to stop sending me all these weird, fucked up signals."

Steam poured over the glass shower door, yet I couldn't get myself to take off the rest of my clothes and step into it. Jace was staring at me with those devilish brown eyes. He stepped closer to me, and I stepped back. No, I couldn't let this man get close. Not again. I was finished with whatever we had going on.

It was sex and then hate and then sex and then hate.

"First, you hate me. Then, you fuck me. You go back to hating me again, and then you show up at my father's grave because you didn't want me to go alone." I shook my head and sucked in a breath as he came even closer to me. "I can't keep fucking around with you like this."

Inches away, Jace Harbor grasped my chin and pushed me against the shower door. "I could make love to you, if you'd prefer," he whispered into my ear. "Caress you ..."

He moved his fingertips down my forearm, the touch so light. I sucked in a breath and tensed.

"Tease your cute little cunt until you're crying and begging for me to be inside of you."

I furrowed my brows, heat gathering between my legs. I didn't like this. I definitely didn't like this.

"Jace," I whispered.

He brushed his thumb against my cheek and pressed his lips to mine. And because I was a dumb, stupid girl, I let him.

Chapter Seventeen

After opening the shower door, Jace pushed me into it, not caring that he was still fully clothed. The water beat down on him and plastered his white V-neck to his taut abdomen. He pushed me against the side of the shower, his body against mine and his tongue in my mouth. I wrapped my arms around his neck and kissed him back, tugging on the ends of his hair, gnawing on his lip, trying to get him closer and closer to me.

"Take this off," I said to him, toying with the ends of his shirt and slipping my hand into his pants to feel his hardness inside them. I stroked him up and down, imagining him inside of me.

Now. I wanted him now.

He pulled his shirt over his head and pushed down his pants, letting his cock spring free. I kneeled in the shower, stared up at him, and took him inside my mouth before he could even ask. My pussy was pulsing. My core was aching. My nipples were hard. I wanted this. I really did.

When I pushed him down my throat, he groaned and laced a hand in my hair. "Fuck," he said, dragging the word out. "Fuck, baby, just like that." He slowly started to thrust his hips, sliding his cock deeper and deeper down my throat.

I bobbed my head back and forth and stared up at him. The water hit his chest, traveling down to his abdomen, making him look so godly above me. But that was who Jace Harbor had always been. Redwood's football god.

Wrapping one hand around my throat, I squeezed to make him feel good and lightly gripped his balls with the other, gently massaging them. Jace parted his lips and moaned—fucking moaned for me.

Jace fucking Harbor moaning like that was the sexiest thing I had ever heard.

"If you keep doing that, Allie, you're going to fucking make me come."

"Come for me then, Jace."

He pulled out of me. "No," he said, blowing out an unsteady breath through his nose. "Not yet. Now, turn around and look back at me," he demanded. After I turned around, he pushed me against the glass door, pressing my tits against it. "Spread your legs."

I curled my fingers against the glass, tried to breathe evenly, and stared back at him, watching his gaze travel down my body—from my shoulders to my ass and then back up to my face. I spread my legs, and he stepped closer to me, taking his cock in his hand and jerking it against my entrance.

"You're such a good little slut for me," he murmured against my lips, pushing himself into me as far and as deep as he could go.

I wrapped myself around him, tightening until he stilled.

He slapped my ass and gripped it harder. "One day, Allie ... one day, I'm going to fuck this nice ass of yours and make you watch as my dick slides so deep inside of it. Buy you a toy, so you can play with your little pussy and stuff yourself full with it as I fuck you."

My pussy tightened around him as I thought about watching

him in my bedroom mirror as he fucked me again. He'd love making me watch him do whatever he wanted with what was *his*.

"Jace," I whispered, pushing my hips back against his. "More."

"I bet *my* innocent little Allie would love that, wouldn't she?" he asked, rubbing his finger against my backside.

I tightened even more on him and turned my head slightly, letting him kiss me hard on the lips.

"Yes," I mumbled against him. "I would love it."

He continued to thrust into me, picking up his pace. After intertwining his fingers with mine and pinning both my hands to the shower wall, he kissed down my back and stilled. "Oh fuck, baby. Keep moving your hips like that. You're going to make me come."

I continued to move my hips back and forth on him, feeling his cock slide in and out of me. Steam filled the shower and rolled over the door, making it hot inside the bathroom. When he groaned against me and his teeth lightly dug into my shoulder, I moved faster, needing his cum.

Letting go of my fingers, he placed his large hands on my waist and suddenly held me still, fingers digging deep into my stomach. He pushed his cock as deep as it could go. "Fuck, fuck, fuuuck. I'm coming inside of that tight little pussy, Allie."

As soon as the words left his mouth, I came on him, too, my legs shaking, my heart racing, my pussy pulsing over and over and over on his dick. I rested my forehead against the shower door and tried to even out my breathing as waves of pleasure rushed through me.

Jace turned off the water and twirled me around. He grasped my face in his hands and crashed his lips down onto mine, moving them needily. Surprised at first, I tensed. Since Jace and I had started to hook up again, we never did this afterward. One of us left before we could even think about what we had done.

Yet he opened the bathroom door and didn't even bother wrapping a towel around either of us to dry us off. Instead, he picked me up and walked with me toward his bedroom, resting me on his soft mattress and crawling up next to me, his lips moving up the column of my throat.

"I could be sweet with you again, but that slutty little cunt wouldn't like that. At least, not as much as she likes this ..." He stuck two fingers into my pussy, filled with his cum, and moved them around, letting me hear just how full I was for him.

Don't do this again, Allie. Don't let him touch you like this again.

"More," I whispered, sinking into his sheets. "Give me more."

Chapter Eighteen

JACE

Sunlight flooded in from the window, hitting my closed eyes and forcing me awake. I grumbled and stuffed my face into Allie's hair, dragging her body closer to mine and trying so hard not to wake her.

My heart raced in my chest as I remembered all those mornings we used to wake up like this, when I'd watch her mumble in her sleep, the way her nose would scrunch up as she opened her eyes, how the sunlight would flicker off them and make me smile.

She had fallen asleep in her glasses last night, so I gently pulled them off her face and placed them on my side table. She turned toward me and buried her face into my chest, resting her ear right over my rib cage, no doubt hearing my racing heart.

I trailed my fingers over her cheek and smiled to myself.

Fuck pretending that I woke up next to a different girl every morning. I wanted this.

On the nightstand, Allie's phone buzzed. It was six in the fucking morning on a Saturday. Who was messaging her now?

Imani was probably still half-asleep. From what I'd gathered when she stayed over, they both got up early but not *this* early.

I moved slightly in the bed, closing my eyes and telling myself to enjoy the moment I had with her because I didn't get moments like this often—moments I could actually smile down at her and not see her angry face glaring back up at me, moments I wasn't filled with dread because of what Mom and Dad had done to our family, moments I could just feel good and at peace because the girl I loved was sleeping in my arms.

The phone buzzed again, and Allie stirred in my arms.

"Shh, shh, shh," I whispered, brushing my fingers over her cheek like she always used to love.

She mumbled something but didn't open her eyes.

I glanced over at the phone, hearing another message pop up. Jamal's name flashed on the screen, and I tensed, feeling both anger and jealousy raging through me.

Why is he messaging her so early?

Allie turned back over and groaned. "Why is my alarm on? It's Satur—" She paused halfway to reach for her phone and tensed. She glanced over her shoulder at me with wide eyes, looking like she had gotten caught doing something she shouldn't have. "Fuck."

My heart hurt as I watched her face contort into one of anger. I wanted to have her, to be with her, to love her. That was all I needed, all I fucking needed to be happy with my life.

"What are you looking at?" she asked, pulling the blankets up her body to cover her chest. She shook her head and turned away from me. "You should've brought me back to my bedroom last night. Why would you sleep next to me?" she asked, her voice filled with such pain and anger.

Tossing some strands of hair over her shoulder, she put on her glasses and grabbed her phone. When she turned it on, she realized that it wasn't her alarm, but Jamal texting her this early, wishing her a good morning, asking her if she wanted to have breakfast with him at the Overlook.

I pressed my lips together, feeling like I was being stabbed in the heart over and over and over again. She shuffled to her feet and twisted the sheets around her torso to hide her naked body from me, typing out a text to him.

"You're leaving?" I asked, wishing she'd stay. Just another minute, just a little longer.

She glanced at me and swallowed, turning toward the door. "I'm going out to breakfast with a friend," she said.

She didn't know that I knew it was him—my best friend, my *only* real friend.

Before she could leave my room, I stood up in front of her. "Wait."

She paused and shook her head, her voice quiet. "What, Jace?"

I licked my lips, trying to form words—any fucking words to get her to stay. She was mine, mine ... yet I couldn't tell her how I felt. I couldn't tell her that I still wanted her. I couldn't explain my actions from sophomore year. She'd be fucking terrified if she found out what had really happened and why I had really broken up with her.

"If you're not going to say anything, move," Allie said, stepping to the side and trying to sneak by me. She grasped the door handle and opened it up, hurrying out into the hall.

"Do you love him?" I asked before I could stop myself, my heart clenching.

She stopped in the middle of the hallway, her entire body tense. "What?" she asked, but she had heard me the first time.

"Do you love Jamal?" I asked, turning around and staring down into those big, wavering eyes. They were suddenly glossy and filling with tears, the same way they had the day I broke her heart.

"Jace," she said, voice almost inaudible. She wrapped her arms around herself, as if she was protecting herself from me yet again. "Don't do this."

My jaw twitched. "Tell me it's not true," I said—*begged*. "Tell me you don't love him, Allie."

I didn't want it to be true. I didn't want any of this to be true. It had started as innocent little moments and turned into breakfast dates. Soon, it'd be more, and the thought of us would be lost for-fucking-ever.

She couldn't like my best friend. She was mine.

After a few moments of silence, she shook her head. "How can I love him?" she whispered, pressing her lips together and looking down at her feet. There was hurt in her voice—so much fucking hurt that I had caused. "How could I ever love him?" The question was almost rhetorical, and yet she answered it herself. "I couldn't, I can't, and I don't."

I wanted to reach out to her, to pull her into a hug, to take another stupid high school picture with her that I could keep in my drawer and smile at whenever I felt sad. But all I had the confidence to do was nod my head.

She paused and stared at me, as if she was waiting for something more than a head nod. And when she realized that was all I could ever give her, a look of sadness washed over her face, and she turned away from me. "I don't love him *yet*."

Chapter Nineteen

ALLIE

Jamal grabbed a box of doughnuts from Yummy Nutty Doughnuts and walked over to the rocks at the Overlook. I sat on a rock next to him, bundled up in my winter jacket because it was freezing, and stared out at the raging sea.

Something about being here with Jamal felt … pretty fucking terrible.

I couldn't stop thinking about what Jace had said to me earlier —that one little question that made me rethink how shitty I had been to him lately. *"Do you love him?"*

His words had been so soft, so fragile, so freaking vulnerable. They brought back so many raw memories of being together with him, of laughing by the sea, of the first time I could be somewhat happy after my father's death.

When I told him that I didn't love Jamal yet … his face dropped. But I wanted him to tell me that he fucking loved me still, that he wanted to be with me more than just screw around with me. I wanted him to tell me not to go with Jamal, to rip me away from the front door and press his lips to mine.

You're mine, Allie. Mine to love.

That was all I had wanted to hear. If he had said those six little words, I would've stayed with him. I wouldn't be here with Jamal at the Overlook, having cream-filled doughnuts and pretending like I could ever be truly happy without Jace.

"How was your night?" Jamal asked, opening the box and pulling out a powdered doughnut. He glanced over at me. "And your father?" he asked, words coming out almost too quiet.

I tore apart a Boston cream doughnut, watching the cream ooze out. "It was as good as it could've been," I said. "It was pouring. The ground was muddy. I nearly got hypothermia. But ... I'd do it again to see him."

And who could forget that Jace had come with marigolds?

Jamal scratched the back of his head, as if he didn't know what to say. But what could you say to someone who was still grieving over her father's death?

He looked down at my doughnut. "Are you going to eat that, or are you gonna let it cream all over you like that?" he asked, catching some of the cream filling on his finger right before it dropped on my black jeans. Lips curled up into a smile, he pushed his finger toward me, wanting me to suck it off.

I pushed his hand away and let out a giggle. "No!" I said, shaking my head and trying to move away before he could stuff his finger into my mouth.

Yet he wrapped an arm around my waist and was holding me closer.

"Come on, Allie," Jamal said.

After rolling my eyes, I grasped his finger, acting as if I were going to suck off the cream. He gazed from my eyes to my lips and watched me pull his finger closer. And right before I sucked it off, I thrust his hand right back into his face, getting the cream all over his cheek and nose.

I shot up and hopped from rock to rock, playfully running away from him.

"Allie!" Jamal shouted.

I glanced over my shoulder to see him tossing the doughnuts down on the rock and following after me.

"Get back here!" he said, voice entangled with laughter.

But I didn't stop. I continued leaping from rock to rock, trying to be careful not to slip on the slush. It was fun, a breath of fresh air—something I hadn't thought would happen since Jace and I had broken up.

Yet here I was, with Jamal, his best friend, finally smiling again.

He wrapped his arms around my waist and tugged me to him, pulling me into the air and throwing me over his shoulder. "You're not going anywhere, Allie," Jamal said, walking back to the rocks and our doughnuts.

I let out another small laugh, trying to wiggle out of his grip.

When he placed me down on the rocks, I sat and grabbed the box of doughnuts. "No more Boston cream. They're too messy."

Jamal widened his dark brown eyes and wiped the cream off his cheek with his finger. "Are they? Or do *you* just make a mess with them?"

We stared at each other for a few moments, my smile fading slightly. Guilt washed over me, and I didn't know what I felt guiltier for—sleeping with Jace last night or being here with Jamal now.

I was so lost in my own thoughts that I didn't catch Jamal leaning in to kiss me. Not on the lips. Not on the cheek. Right on my jaw.

I tensed up for a moment but let him do it because it felt good to be wanted like this again. Years ago, Jace used to talk to me at the Overlook, tell me his deepest and darkest secrets, and make me pinkie promise that everything we said was between us and us only.

If I said that I didn't crave that kind of love again, I'd be lying.

But then one day, out of the total blue, Jace had stopped talking to me altogether, told me that everything between us was fake, that we couldn't ever be together, that he'd rather be with someone like Nicole, who wasn't using him for his money or his looks or his talent in football. Someone who loved him for him.

Maybe I hadn't shown him how much I loved every part of him back then.

Maybe he hadn't noticed all those times I stared at him lovingly in class, all those times that I had made him smile so wide when he was broken down in tears, every time I would curl my fingers into his chest when he was sleeping, all those lovable little moments.

I fucking loved the real Jace Harbor with my entire heart.

"Sorry." Jamal pulled away, his eyes wide. "I didn't mean to make it weird."

I grasped his hand, still lost in my past, and hoped tears wouldn't form in my eyes. "No," I whispered to him. "It's okay. I don't mind it. I was just thinking about"—I brushed my fingers against his forearm and looked out into the sea—"us."

Chapter Twenty

JACE

Fuck.

I stared at the front door, paced around in the foyer, and growled to myself. Allie had left almost an hour ago, and I couldn't stop thinking about her being with Jamal at our spot, him telling her all those things I used to, running on the rocks with her, staring off into the sea.

The doorbell rang, and I cut my eyes to the window, seeing the three Poison boys standing outside the house. *What the fuck is Poison doing here?*

"You know not to show up at my fucking house," I said through gritted teeth, opening the door and letting João, Landon, and Kai saunter into the foyer.

João patted me on the shoulder. "Oh, don't worry about it, Harbor. We love coming to pay you a visit in your daddy's mansion. It's always a pleasure." He walked around the foyer and glanced down the halls. "Is Allie home?"

I clenched my jaw. "Don't push it."

"Is lover boy jealous?" Landon asked, cracking a smirk.

"Heard she's been going out with Jamal. Your best friend and your stepsister." He shook his head. "Must be hard, especially since you still love her, huh?"

Kai swung his backpack over his shoulder, tugged out a manila folder labeled *Harbor*, and handed it to me. I swallowed hard and opened the folder, blowing out a breath through my nose. There were papers about my father, about his money, about *me* inside of it, but nothing useful.

"You know that I can't fucking use this." I slammed it back into Kai's chest. "I asked you to find me something useful, not shit that won't hold up in any fucking court."

Landon leaned against the wall, posting a foot on it and crossing his tattooed arms over his chest. "If you want more than this, you have to pay more, Harbor."

"You're asking us to break into the police chief's house in a guarded neighborhood, steal a stack of papers from a locked safe, and not get caught by Nicole's father or Nicole," João said, leaning back on the leather couch and hanging an unlit cigarette out of his mouth.

"Can you fucking do it or not?" I asked through gritted teeth.

"Of course we can do it." Kai walked around the living room, staring at all the expensive shit that he was probably thinking about stealing. "But it's going to cost you."

"How much?" I asked, knowing that this was going to cost a fucking fortune.

But I'd spend hundreds of thousands to punish that man like he had punished me by throwing me in juvie and nearly having everyone in Redwood breathing down my fucking neck. With Dad, I had to be fucking perfect, couldn't spill the family secrets.

Not anymore.

João lit his cigarette and puffed on it. "Two mil."

My eyes widened slightly. "Are you fucking kidding me?"

"How much is it worth to you, Harbor?" João said, standing up and sauntering over to me. He slung an arm around my shoulders and nodded out the window to Allie, who was being dropped off by Jamal in front of the house. "How much is *she* worth to you? You *are* doing this to keep her safe, aren't you?"

Two million was nothing, but Dad had been a fucking prick with my inheritance lately, had been tracking my every fucking expense to make sure I was staying in line, never straying or trying anything against him again.

I balled my hands into fists. "Two mil," I agreed.

"We also need entrance into Nicole's neighborhood," Kai said. "They watch the gates and the perimeter like fucking hawks. And we don't fuck with anyone in the police chief's neighborhood after what happened last time."

I cursed under my breath, fucking hating myself for ever even needing to do this.

"Don't worry about Nicole and getting onto their property," I said, knowing that I could easily distract her by *wanting to talk* or asking to come over. She'd think I was there to have a good time with her. "I'll get you into the neighborhood. You need to fucking deliver shit that's better than what's in that folder."

"Money in cash by next Friday. You'll hand it over after the game, back of the parking lot by the dumpsters. Make it look like we're giving you weed. Don't be suspicious about it, Harbor. The chief of police and the principal watch your every move."

Chapter Twenty-One

ALLIE

A surprisingly sleek black car sat in the driveway when Jamal dropped me back home. It wasn't as fancy as a Maserati or any of the cars Harlan drove, but it was sure a lot better than any car someone from the bad side of town could afford.

I stared at the car for a few moments, knowing that it looked familiar, but not knowing who it belonged to.

Jamal leaned over the center console. "Do you want me to come in with you?" he asked, though he looked hesitant, probably because Jace was here.

"No, it's fine," I assured him because I *didn't* want him to come in with me.

Though I hated Jace, the look on his face when he had asked me if I loved Jamal broke my heart. I didn't want to rub it in Jace's face, show him how much better Jamal could try to make me feel, show Jace what he was missing because those small, intimate moments with us were ... everything to me and it felt like shit to be hurt.

When I opened the front door, the three Poison boys stood in the foyer with Jace. João slid a baggie into Jace's hand, and Jace stuffed it in his pocket, staring at me with a blank and cold expression.

Kai nodded in my direction, as if to say, *What's up?*

Kai had grown up with Jamal and me on Pierce Road and had been friends with us in elementary school. He still lived there but was gone so much with the other boys that I rarely saw him when I visited my old neighborhood.

"Catch you later," Jace said to the guys.

I crossed my arms over my chest. The boys walked out the door, and Landon smiled at me.

"Tell Imani I said hi," he said and shut the door behind him.

I arched a brow, knowing that was the last thing on my mind, and turned on my heel toward Jace, who had left the room.

"Jace!" I shouted, following him up the stairs to his room. After opening his closed door, I found him shutting his bedside drawer. No doubt where he had stuffed the weed from Poison. "Do you want to ruin your life?"

"Why don't you go back out with Jamal?" Jace sneered at me, standing up from his bed.

Something between now and this morning had changed with him, and I couldn't tell what. He seemed angrier than usual.

I clenched my fists by my sides. "If you ever want to get out of this deadbeat town, you can't fucking smoke Poison's shit," I said through clenched teeth, anger boiling inside of me.

"What I do is none of your business," Jace said. "Now, leave."

"Not until you get rid of it," I said. "I don't care how much you paid for that shit. Dump it."

Jace moved toward me. "Get out of my room."

Deep breaths, Allie. Deep freaking breaths.

"If you won't do it, I will." I stormed past him and grasped the handle to his drawer.

"Get the fuck out of my stuff, Allie," Jace said through

clenched teeth, wrapping one arm around my waist and pulling me away from the side table before I could even open it.

I scrambled out of his hold and crossed my arms over my chest. "What are you doing with Poison?" I asked, unable to fathom why he would ever even attempt to risk his chances at getting out of this town and making something of himself. "They lace their shit with harder drugs, Jace, to get you hooked and coming back for more. If you're fucking caught with that shit"—I pointed to the side table, really trying to hit home my point—"all your college football offers will be freaking revoked. You won't be able to make it to the NFL."

Jace seemed harsher, angrier than when I had left with Jamal this morning. "You think I'm that fucking stupid?" he asked, seething down at me with hatred in his eyes. "Poison has the cleanest shit. They don't mess with the hard stuff."

"They're called Poison for a reason."

"Stay out of my business," Jace said. "Don't mess with my shit. I've suffered the fucking consequences before, and I'll do it again."

My eyes widened. "Are you serious? Do you think your money will be able to clean your *second* juvie record when the principal has been out to get you for literally anything?"

Jace paused for a long moment, jaw twitching. He tore his gaze away from me. "You don't know what money can buy, Allie. Who it could pay off. The damage it could do." He turned back toward me. "Especially to *you* ... Redwood's good girl, who is all up in her stepbrother's business."

It hurt. It hurt a fucking lot to hear Jace threaten me ... but this wasn't really him. When we had been together, Jace hadn't smoked, hadn't hung out with Poison, hadn't gotten into any trouble. This was Jace Harbor speaking from a place of hurt and heartbreak. I couldn't believe that this man was the same one I used to love.

"You're going to ruin all your chances of playing in the NFL," I said, quieter this time.

He stared at me with cold and dead eyes, yet I saw them tremble. It was so slight that I almost missed it, but I didn't, and it made my heart clench.

"Leave me the fuck alone, Allie." He turned away from me and walked back to his drawer, pulling out the weed. Staring me straight in the eye, he rolled a fucking joint.

Jace Harbor loved football more than he loved anything. He wouldn't give it up to smoke some weed with the Poison boys. He was smarter than most people gave him credit for.

He grabbed a lighter from the side table, and I stormed out of the room before I got the chance to see him light the joint and ruin his life. I didn't want to see years of hard work go right down the drain for nothing.

As much as I hated to admit it, Jace deserved to get out of this shithole. Maybe it was my past that had blinded me or the way he had begged me to stay with his eyes this morning, but I wanted Jace Harbor to succeed in his life. Even if he wasn't in mine.

Chapter Twenty-Two

JACE

Allie was right. It was so fucking risky to work with Poison. They did shit nobody would ever consider doing, shit that I wanted no part in, shit that could ruin *any* rich kid's life, no matter how much money their family was swimming in.

I had worked my ass off, both on and off the field, for years to be so good that college football teams vied over me. Football was my entire life, one of the only things I could do where I completely forgot all my problems, could run, tackle, intercept. I made myself important. It wasn't Dad's money.

The NFL had been my goal for over a decade now. But there were far worse things in life than boarding school, juvie, and not achieving those goals. If it was Allie or football, I'd choose Allie every single time.

"You think about letting me hit your stepsister yet, Harbor?" Carter asked, getting up from a sack during our Tuesday afternoon practice.

I turned away from him and stormed to the line. One day ...

one day, I was going to slam my fist so hard into his face that he wouldn't be able to play in the next few games. And it was going to be fucking glorious.

The ball was snapped again, and I traced the ball downfield moments too late. Offense caught the ball and ran it in for a touchdown. I sighed through my helmet and walked back to the line, trying to clear my head.

"Harbor, get your head out of your ass. This is practice," Coach yelled.

But all I could think about was how I was going to have to go behind Allie's back and pretend to be interested in Nicole *again*, just to keep Allie safe. My gaze flickered to Nicole on the sidelines, practicing her cheers with Redwood's sluttiest girls. The bleachers were empty today. Allie must've gone to Imani's house.

If Allie found out about what I was doing or even *why* I was doing it, she'd be in danger.

"Those cute schoolgirl skirts keep getting shorter and shorter," Carter said before he called for the ball to be snapped. The guys on the line laughed. "Makes it hard to concentrate in Math."

"You've been failing Math since freshman year, Carter," Jamal spat at him from beside me, earning some *ohh*s from the line. "Allie ain't the reason you can't get a passing grade in Math, even when you flirt with Mrs. Dawson."

"Sticking up for your girl?" Carter asked Jamal. "You stick it in her ass yet?"

The center snapped the ball, and Carter scanned the field for an open receiver. I sprinted around the guys who were protecting him, pushing them out of the way, and knocked him over so hard that he doubled over to catch his breath.

"Oh, come on," Carter said, standing up after a few moments. He held his arms out, gesturing to the rest of the team, who was gathering by the line again. "I'm not the only one wondering how tight it is."

Coach blew the whistle. "Practice is over, boys. Get your asses to the showers."

I tore off my helmet and walked toward the locker room, not even waiting for Jamal. Every time Carter mentioned Jamal and Allie together, it made me hate him for it. He was supposed to be my best fucking friend, not the guy who moved in on my stepsister.

Coach grasped my shoulder before I could get far.

"What's going on with you, son?" Coach asked, crossing his arms over his chest. He was giving me that fatherly look that I had always wished Dad would give me, growing up, but from Dad, I only got looks of disappointment and dirty grimaces whenever I mentioned football.

"Nothing," I said, wiping the sweat off my face with the bottom of my shirt. "Just problems with my dad."

"Anything you want to talk about?" Coach asked.

My gaze flickered from him to the kicked-up dirt below my feet. If I told him, he wouldn't believe me. Nobody fucking believed me. Not the principal. Not the police chief. I was a nuisance to them, and it put me on their radar.

"No."

Coach gave me a long look, then nodded. "If you need to talk, Harbor, you know where I am." He gestured to the locker room. "Get out of here. Clear your head. Focus on your goals."

When I finished with my shower, everyone was already gone. I gathered my things and walked to my car parked in the student lot. As if it was perfect timing, Nicole had just finished cheer practice and was strolling to hers too.

"Nicole," I shouted as she walked to her car.

She turned around. "Is that Jace Harbor calling for *me*?" she asked, smirking at me.

I grabbed her scrunchie that she had left at my house weeks ago. I had known that it would come in useful at some point if I needed to get out of trouble. Or in this case, get *into* it. I tossed it to her. "You left this."

She caught it and glanced back up at me. "My game-day scrunchie." Her lips curled into a smile, eyes twinkling because she had so much damn sparkly eye shadow on. "Where'd you find this?"

In my fucking garbage with the rest of your shit.

"I kept it," I said, looking at the ground and back up. "It smells like you."

Like your nasty fucking perfume.

Nicole's smile turned into a full-blown smirk. "Miss me, Jacey?"

I twirled my keys around my finger, trying not to be suspicious about this. I needed to get into her house to let Poison in, and I couldn't do that if she thought I wanted something from her other than a good night.

"Don't get your hopes up." I opened the door to my Maserati, looked back at her, and threw her my signature smirk. "Not yet, Nikki baby."

Chapter Twenty-Three

ALLIE

Jamal sat at the nerd table with me and Imani again at lunch. I welcomed him today, giving him a warm smile and wondering if I could finally be happy with him someday. We ate in silence as Imani typed on her keyboard, only looking up when Poison walked into the lunchroom.

I narrowed my eyes at her. "What's going on between you guys?" I asked.

She looked back at me with wide brown eyes. "Who?"

I playfully rolled mine and gestured to the table Poison had claimed for themselves.

Imani tugged on one of her curls and blushed. "Nothing," she said a bit too quickly, turning back to her screen and trying to look busy.

"Way to *not* seem sus," Jamal said to her.

"Sus?" she asked, furrowing her brows.

"Suspicious," I clarified, placing down my chocolate milk. "Landon keeps asking for you."

She closed her laptop, giving me that narrowed gaze again. "When do you talk to him?"

My lips curled into a smirk. "Is someone jealous?"

Jamal rested his forearms on the table and leaned forward. "Landon's bad news. If you're going to go for any of them, try Kai. He's chill. Allie and I grew up with him on Pierce Road."

Imani gave me a small smile and looked down at her lunch. "*Or* I can try all three." She threw me a wink, which made Jamal scrunch his nose and look away, as if he hadn't heard the football team talk about doing worse with the cheerleaders.

"If you're going to hang out with us, this is what you get, Jamal," Imani said, laughing. "Sarcasm, sexual innuendos, and anxiety about Bio. We aren't those innocent, geeky girls everyone thinks we are."

Jamal chuckled and gave me a look. "I know that."

Imani kicked me under the table and gave me those *what the hell happened between you two this weekend* eyes. I shrugged my shoulders and stuffed a ham sandwich into my mouth.

My gaze flickered to the head of the cafeteria, where João was talking with Jace. Jace shook his head and continued into the room, leaving João behind and sitting at his table, next to a couple guys from the football team. Nicole sat across from him, giving him those *fuck me* eyes that I loathed.

I clenched my hands into fists and continued eating my lunch in peace. But today, I had a mission to stop Jace from ruining his life. So, against my better judgment, after lunch, I skipped fourth period and searched for Poison in all the hallways, slipping into restrooms and empty classrooms when I saw a teacher walk down the hall toward me.

Who knew skipping would be so fucking hard? Maybe I just wasn't used to it.

I wandered down the corridors, finding no sign of Poison anywhere. The windows at the end of the second-floor hallway were fogged up, so I swiped my hand across the glass and saw one of the boys on the front steps.

Hurrying down the stairs, I bumped into Principal Vaughn.

"Miss Allie Hall, what are you doing out of class?" he asked, a hairy gray brow arched hard. He clasped his hands behind his back and stared down at me from nearly six foot five in the air.

"I'm just, um ..." I crossed my legs. "Going to use the restroom."

"You haven't shown up to class. Your teacher is worried."

My cheeks flushed. "I'm sorry," I got out, heart pounding. "Girl problems have been bad this week, sir."

He hummed to himself and gave me a curt nod. "Well, make sure you get to class. You have a perfect record. Wouldn't want to ruin it." He continued up the stairs and walked onto the next floor.

I cut my eyes to his departing figure and continued down the stairs to the front door.

Kai sat on the steps, smoking a damn cigarette, right out in the open, like he didn't care about anyone asking him to put it away or to get back to class. I stared out the door window at him, my heart racing in my chest.

Am I really doing this? Yes. I had to for Jace. I wasn't going to let him ruin his life.

I pushed the door open and stepped out into the cold, tugging my jacket around my body to stop the frigid air from giving me hypothermia.

Kai waved his cigarette in the air. "I'm not going back to class, Vaughn. Don't even try."

After I stood there for a few moments, not knowing what to say, Kai looked over his shoulder at me.

"What're you doing, skipping class?" he asked, holding out a cigarette for me to puff on.

I ignored his offer and sat next to him. "I need to talk to you about Jace."

"We don't talk about jobs or clients." Kai tossed the cigarette on the step in front of him and stomped it out. "You know that, Allie. I can't give up shit about him, or he doesn't pay."

Snow drifted down around us, my breath coming out as a white fog, looking like I *was* smoking with one of Poison's finest. "I don't need information on him. I just need you to cut off communication with him, stop giving him drugs. It's going to ruin his chances of getting to the NFL, if he gets addicted."

Kai paused for a moment. "I thought you hated him after what he did to you. Why do you care about what happens to him from his own senseless decisions?"

I pressed my lips together and glanced down at the slush by my feet, watching it melt as I stomped on it. I shrugged. "I don't know," I whispered. "Just, please, don't give him any more shit."

The front door opened, and João walked out of the building, zippering up his coat. I swallowed hard and stood up before João could ask any questions. I didn't particularly like the man, but I could tolerate Kai.

"What's going on here?" João asked.

"Nothing," I said quickly.

Kai stood up next to me and stuffed his hands into his pockets. "If he pays up, he gets what he wants, Allie. We can't do anything for you."

After staring between him and João, I excused myself to go back into the building, wishing that I could've convinced him otherwise but I couldn't get through to Kai with João there. João was the boss, made the decisions, and told them what to do and when to do it. He was intimidating, to say the absolute least.

I hurried into the building and up the stairs, needing to get back to class so I wouldn't seem suspicious.

But as I was passing the restrooms, Jace walked out of the men's room and grabbed my upper arm. "We need to talk."

Chapter Twenty-Four

ALLIE

After tugging me into Mr. Barnes's empty Bio class—he must've been on break during this period—Jace shut the door and slammed me against it with his hand around my throat.

"Why are you talking to Poison?" he asked through clenched teeth. "I told you to stay out of my business."

My breathing hitched, and I had the urge to slam my hands into his chest to push him away, but we were alone yet again in school, and all I could think about was the last time we had been together in Redwood—when he snuck me into the locker room and fucked me senseless.

"I was just talking to Kai," I explained.

"Just talking to Kai?" Jace asked, narrowing those dark eyes at me and strumming his fingers against my throat. He raised his brows at me and hummed, as if waiting for me to admit the truth to him. "João texted me that you were asking about me, telling them not to deal with me and my shit."

Slamming my hands into his chest, I pushed him back. "You're ruining your life."

He snatched both my wrists in one hand and pushed me harsher against the cold wooden door. "I do what I want, Allie," he said, his lips against my ear. He pushed himself against me, pressing his hardness against my stomach. It felt so big, huge, thick against me. "You should know that better than anyone else."

I let out a shaky breath. "Jace, I have to get to class." It was almost the end of the period by now.

"You're not going anywhere," he said, drawing one finger up the column of my neck to my chin and lifting it slightly. "I'm going to make sure you know not to ask around about me *ever* again."

Swallowing hard, I shook my head. "I won't, I promise. We can't do it here, please."

He let go of my wrists, grabbed one of my hands, and placed it right on his erection, stroking himself with it. "Feel that, baby?" he asked.

I pushed my thighs together, feeling the warmth gather in my core.

"You're going to put that all the way down your pretty, tight little throat and suck me off until I'm coming down into it."

Breathe, Allie, breathe.

"When I let go of your hand, you're going to continue stroking me until I tell you to kneel," he said, letting go of my hand.

I cursed myself for ever being so submissive to him and continued to stroke his hard cock, wishing that he were inside of me.

After smirking at me, he dropped his gaze from mine to my skirt. "Let's see how wet you are under this skirt of yours."

He fingered the bottom of my skirt, slipped a hand under it, and drew a single finger up my thigh. When he reached my panties, he grew even harder and chuckled menacingly at me.

"Oh, baby, these panties are soaked through."

He rubbed my clit through my underwear, sending a wave of pleasure through my entire body. I stroked him harder and faster, my fingers almost trembling with how good he felt.

Slipping his fingers under my panties, he stuck two inside of me and forced me to listen to the wet and sloppy sounds my cunt made for him. When he pulled his wet fingers out, he stuck them into his mouth and blew an unsteady breath out of his nose.

"Knees," he ordered.

I furrowed my brows and kneeled in front of him, unbuckling his belt and pulling down his pants enough to pull his cock out of them. My lips wrapped around the head of it, and I sucked it into my mouth willingly.

Bobbing my head back and forth on his cock, I stared up at him through my glasses.

He grasped the side of my face, stroking his thumb across my cheek. "Fuck, baby, you look so beautiful on your knees."

I continued, wanting nothing more than to accept this *punishment* for ever trying to get into his business. If Jace Harbor wanted to punish me for trying to stop him from ruining his life like this ... I would take it any way he gave it.

"I'm going to empty my cum into your mouth, and you're going to hold it there until I tell you that you can swallow it," he said, standing over me with his cock all the way down my throat.

He grasped the sides of my head and started to really throat-fuck me, moving his hips hard and fast until I was a gagging, drooling mess.

One last thrust, and he groaned and slowly pulled himself—inch by inch—out of my mouth, leaving his warm cum inside of my mouth for me to hold for him.

He smirked down at me and tapped my chin with two fingers. "Let me see that cum, baby."

I opened my mouth slightly, showing it to him. It was wrong, but I couldn't stop. I really fucking couldn't. I loved this raw, real

Jace Harbor and all his dominant ways—sneaking into public places, touching me in ways that he shouldn't, doing things that should've been forbidden, *even* for normal couples.

"Good girl." He picked me up and set me on Mr. Barnes's desk, tugging me to the edge. Gripping the backs of my thighs, he spread my legs, held them up into the air, and rested one on his muscular shoulder.

Without even taking my panties off yet, he pressed his lips against my core. All I could feel was his hot mouth moving across my lace panties, leaving sloppy and wet kisses, tugging on them with his teeth, sucking and nibbling. My legs trembled slightly, and I gripped the edge of the desk.

This was wrong. We should've left and gone home to do this.

Jace pulled my panties off of me and stuffed them into his jeans pocket. He trailed his nose up my inner thigh, letting his breath warm against my core. "All my cum is still in that bratty little mouth of yours, isn't it, Allie?"

When I nodded, he spread my folds with his fingers and pressed his lips against my clit, his tongue flicking out to lick it. He stared up at me with those dangerous, dark eyes, eating me like how a fucking animal ravished its prey. I pressed my lips together, holding his cum inside of me and clenching my pussy over and over, waiting for him to slip a finger into my tight little hole and destroy it.

He reached up and tugged on one of my nipples through my shirt. "Good ..." He sucked my clit between his full lips. "Because if you swallow before I tell you that you can, you *will* be punished for it."

After sucking my clit into his mouth one last time, he pulled away. "Spit some up on these nice tits of yours."

He ripped the buttons of my shirt open and pulled down my bra to let my tits bounce out. I let some of his cum drip from my lips onto my breasts as I stared into those unruly brown eyes.

He smirked and rubbed the cum against each of my nipples,

flicking them with his fingers when he was finished. He gazed back up at me from between my legs. "Swallow the rest, Allie. Tell me how I taste."

Swallowing the rest of his salty cum and licking my lips like the hungry little slut I had always been for him, I whispered, "Good."

After he stood and gripped my waist, he picked me up, sat on the desk where I had been, and placed me on top of him. "I want you to ride me."

I stared at him with wide eyes. "Jace, we can't ..." I shook my head and glanced over my shoulder to the closed door. The clock on the wall read twelve thirty, which meant we had fifteen minutes before next period and probably less than ten before Mr. Barnes came back.

He rubbed his cock against my pussy and slid it into me before I could tell him to stop. A wave of pleasure rushed through me, tingles shooting up and down my arms and legs.

I curled my fingers into his chest. "*Fuck.*"

"Hands behind your back." He grasped my wrists behind my back and held them there, forcing me to sit up taller. "I want to see your glistening, cum-covered tits bounce as your slutty little pussy gets fucked raw."

With my arms trapped behind my back, I pulled myself up just a couple inches to hover above him. He rammed himself up into me, over and over and over, watching my tits bounce. I tightened around him, squeezing him as tightly as I could.

"Oh, Jace," I moaned.

My glasses started sliding down my nose, strands of hair falling into my face. He let my arms go.

When I pushed my glasses up and stared down at him, he groaned and grasped my hips. "Ride me, baby."

I placed my hands on his hard chest, curling my fingers into his shirt, and bucked my hips back and forth, feeling every inch of his cock slide into me. He gazed at my tits, staring at them with dilated eyes as they swung near his face. He captured one of my nipples between his fingers and tugged on it.

Tension rose in my core, my toes curling.

Five minutes … we had five damn minutes before Mr. Barnes came back in to prepare for class.

"My pathetic little slut is going to come from riding my cock, isn't she?" he mumbled.

I nodded and squeezed my eyes shut, heat raging in my core.

"Scream for me, baby. I want you to scream for me as loud as you can when you come."

Jace squeezed hard on my nipple, and I screamed. I screamed so fucking loud that the students in the classrooms beside us could definitely hear.

"Jace," I cried out, on the verge of damn tears from how good it felt. I collapsed in his arms and buried my face into the crook of his neck. "Oh, Jace."

He wrapped his arms around my body and pulled me tight into him. After a few moments, he groaned into my ear and pulled out of me, his cock leaving a trail of cum as it slid from my pussy lips and down my thighs.

I lay in his arms for a few moments, wishing I could stay here a bit longer, but we were at school, in Mr. Barnes's classroom. So, I pulled away from him and readjusted my bra. Jace hopped off the desk and pulled his briefs up.

Suddenly, the door opened, and Mr. Barnes walked into the room with wide eyes.

"What the hell is going on in here?" he asked, voice pinched and groggy, like the old professor he was.

I pulled down my shirt, heart racing in my chest, and felt my face flush the deepest color red. *Fuck. Fuck. Fuck. Fuck. Fuck.* This was not happening. We hadn't really just gotten caught by the most annoying professor in all of Redwood.

Jace pushed his shoulders back and buttoned up his pants

with his cock still hard inside of them. "You didn't see anything," he said to Mr. Barnes with so much damn confidence.

"Mr. Harbor," Mr. Barnes said, shaking his head, "I have to report it to the principal. I can't let you off with doing something like this, especially in my classroom out of all places. I—"

"My father pays your bills, *Mr. Barnes.* Keep quiet if you want to keep that Porsche of yours," Jace continued, pulling out a wad of hundred-dollar bills from his wallet. "And while you're keeping that mouth of yours shut, here's some spare change to buy yourself a new desk."

I glanced over at the desk, which had a huge, nasty spot on it from Jace's cum and my pussy juices.

Jace thrust the money against Mr. Barnes's chest and smirked. "Looks like you're gonna need it."

Chapter Twenty-Five

JACE

At the end of our game Friday night, the scoreboard read 29–28, Redwood win. I tore off my helmet, my chest rising and falling quickly. This had to have been the worst fucking game I had ever played. I had missed three sacks, fumbled an interception, and let the other team score twelve points they shouldn't have made.

"It's a win," Coach said in the locker room, glancing over at me. He was giving me that *we need to talk* look, which meant I had to avoid him for as long as I could. "Not our best performance, but you boys did good tonight. No practice tomorrow morning. Rest up."

I didn't want to talk to Coach. I knew my mind hadn't been in the game tonight. It was on the two million I had stuffed in bags in my car, how I had to flirt with Nicole later, and Allie, who had been in the bleachers, wearing Jamal's fucking number on her back, even after what had happened the other day in her Bio classroom.

"Party tonight, boys," Carter shouted through the locker room once Coach was gone.

I usually didn't go to his stupid fucking parties, but I knew that Nicole would be there, and I had skipped last week. I had to keep up the reputation of being one of the rich, spoiled kids just a bit longer.

After showering, I told Jamal I'd meet him in the parking lot in twenty minutes because I had to bring Allie home. It was probably my worst lie yet since Allie was getting a ride home from Imani, but I had to think of something believable.

I snuck out the back door, slid into my car, and drove to the back of the parking lot by the dumpsters. Two fucking mil was too much in my opinion for this kind of thing, but Poison set the price, and I was desperate as fuck.

Kai was waiting for me, leaning against his motorcycle with a laptop in his hands. I parked out of sight from the cameras and got out of the car.

"Cameras are off for the next fifteen minutes," Kai said, closing the computer and stuffing it into his backpack. "Don't worry about it."

"Where are they?" I asked, crossing my arms over my chest and leaning against the car with anxiety rushing through my body.

If we were caught, everything I'd worked so hard for would be over. Allie. Football. My inheritance.

João's sleek black car pulled into the parking lot, right next to mine. He and Landon both exited the car and walked over to us.

"You got it?" João asked.

Landon arched a brow. "Anxious tonight, Harbor? You almost lost the damn game for us."

"You want the money or not?" I asked through clenched teeth, opening the trunk.

João, Landon, and Kai walked around to the back.

João nodded, a smirk crossing his lips. "Didn't think you'd be able to get this much in time," he said to me. He nodded to Landon and then to the trunk. "Take it."

Landon gathered the bags and put them in João's trunk.

"Text the details to Kai," João said, shutting the trunk. "We'll count the money tonight. We can do it tomorrow at the earliest."

Then, he and Landon climbed into the car and sped out of the parking lot.

Kai got on his bike, grasping his helmet. "Do me a favor," he said before putting it on. "Whatever you do, don't hurt Allie. She's a nice girl. She's the only one who grew up on the shit side of town who has the chance of going anywhere in life."

He pulled the helmet on and drove off into the night. I swallowed hard and drove back to the student parking lot, finding Nicole and some of the football players and cheerleaders still there, hanging out by their cars.

I got out of the car and walked to the group, hands stuffed in my pockets. I didn't know why the fuck we were still here if Carter was having a party … but I would rather get this over with now than later, when I was going to be shit-faced drunk.

Nicole glanced at me from across the group, and I offered her a smirk, tilting my head to the sidewalk and away from the group. She walked over to it, and I followed after her, hating that I was doing this shit.

"Good game," she said, biting her lower lip. "But you looked a bit stressed the entire time. Why don't you come over tonight? I can help with that," Nicole said, drawing her finger up and down my chest.

All I wanted to do was push her away and tell her to screw off, but I needed her to trust me. I needed Poison to get me my fucking information.

"Party tonight," I said, brushing off her advances like I used to. I slung an arm around her waist, tugging her closer to me so her chest was pressed against mine. "But what about tomorrow?" I whispered into her ear.

"Mmm, Jacey." She sprawled her hand across my abdomen. "Why don't we sneak into my car and get it over with? I bet you've been aching to fuck me hard, get all that anger out, *hurt* me."

I snatched her jaw in my hand, telling myself not to hurt her like I wanted to because *nothing* about it would be pleasurable to her. I wanted to rip her face off and make her so ugly that even plastic surgery would never be able to fix her.

"I said tomorrow," I said.

"I love when you get all dominant like that." She giggled and stepped away. "If you want to wait for tomorrow for this"—she gestured down her body—"then I'll see you at my house at seven." Gaze flickering behind me, she smirked even wider. "Don't be late, lover boy."

She climbed into her car, and I turned around to get into mine. But Allie stood behind me with wide eyes that told me she had heard every single word of that worthless conversation. Her eyes were filled with tears, and I could feel her pain. It felt like sophomore year all over again.

Chapter Twenty-Six

ALLIE

Nicole sped out of the parking lot while I stood there in complete and utter shock. *No, no, no, no, no.* I couldn't have fallen for Jace's stupid little games again. I couldn't. I …

My chest tightened until I felt like I couldn't breathe, until I had to open my mouth to gasp for breath.

It couldn't be true.

But it was because Jace stared at me with those wide brown eyes, like he had been caught doing the same thing he had done to me sophomore year. He had that same guilty look on his face, that same pain, that same hurt.

"Wh-what was that?" I whispered to him, wanting it to not be true.

Jace stepped toward me. "Allie, please, it's—"

Some of Jace's friends and teammates looked over at us from their cars. I moved back and wrapped my arms around my body, so I wouldn't tremble, but tears were already welled up in my eyes, threatening to spill down my cheeks.

"Don't tell me that it wasn't what it looked like." My voice cracked. "What was that?" I repeated, voice shakier.

Jace looked down at his feet and shrugged. Not even giving me the damn respect by looking at me.

I barreled forward at him, anger taking hold of me. When I shoved my hands into his chest, he stumbled back. I did it again and again and again until all his damn friends were looking over at us, wondering what was happening. But I didn't give a fuck about them.

"Look at me when you answer," I demanded, tears rolling down my cheeks. "What was that?" My voice was filled with such heartbreak and hurt. "What was it? Tell me. Are you fucking sleeping with her again? Huh? Just say it."

Jace grabbed my wrists and stopped me from shoving my hands against him again. "Stop shoving me, Allie, and drop it. I told you to stay out of my business. Stay out of my fucking business."

"No." I shook my head, not believing that Jace couldn't fucking own up to it. He'd had no problem owning up to it sophomore year. "I'm not going to drop it. This is *my* business, Jace. So, tell me. Fucking tell me!" The tears were coming so much quicker, and I couldn't stop them.

Jace threw my hands back to me and shook his head. "What do you want me to say?" he shouted back. "That I'm sleeping with her? Is that what you want to hear, Allie? Do you want to hear all the fucking things I'm doing with her that I used to do with you?" Jace glared at me. "Why are you making such a big deal out of this?"

"Because I love you, Jace!" I shouted so loudly that everyone heard.

Everyone fucking heard me confess my never-ending love for my stepbrother.

I dropped my hands, chest tightening at the mere sound of

saying it out loud. It was out there in the world, and I had finally given myself permission to feel everything I had sophomore year. All the pain, all the hurt, all the anguish I'd had to endure the days, weeks, months after Jace Harbor—the man I'd thought I was going to marry—broke my heart into tiny pieces and stomped on them to make sure I could never truly love again.

Stepping away from him, I stared at the ground. "I love you, and you can't love me back," I whispered. I shook my head, unable to keep the tears from spilling down my cheeks. "You can't."

The cruel and angry expression on Jace's face shifted to one of hurt. He furrowed his brows together for the slightest moment, his pupils dilating. He blinked a few times as the silence captured us.

"You love me?" he whispered so quietly that I didn't think I'd heard him. But then he said it again, this time a bit louder. "You really still love me?"

My glasses fogged up from all my heated anger and all the damn tears falling down my cheeks. I ripped them off, so I wouldn't look stupid, standing in front of him, and wiped the glasses with my thumb. When I pushed them back on my face, I swallowed hard and turned away from him.

Imani stood by her car, arms crossed over her chest and a frown on her face. She hurried over to me, ready to capture me in her arms and drag me back to the car, where I could cry in peace without the entire football and cheer teams watching.

Jace snatched my wrist. "Allie, wait."

I ripped myself away from him for the last time. "No, I'm not waiting for you anymore. I waited for you for two years." I pushed some tears off my cheeks with the back of my hand. "Go be with her, Jace. You've always wanted to be with her."

Go be with the girl you left me for sophomore year, the girl who cheated on you, the girl who will never love you with her entire heart the way I do.

Imani enveloped me in her arms, opened her car door for me, and pushed me into the car. When she shut the door, she turned around to say something to Jace that I couldn't quite hear while I curled into a ball, my knees to my chest, and screamed through the tears, through the pain, through all those memories that I couldn't stop from running through my mind.

Chapter Twenty-Seven

JACE

I snatched an entire bottle of whiskey from the kitchen, collapsed on Carter's couch, and put the bottle to my lips. I fucking hated myself, loathed myself, wanted to kill myself for what I had done to Allie. It was worse than sophomore year—so much fucking worse—to break her heart now.

Worst of all, I had fucking driven her further into Jamal's arms.

Some cheerleaders from the team tried sitting next to me, but I told them to fuck off. Nicole knew to stay away. I spotted her a couple times in the other room before I drank so much that I couldn't see straight.

My phone buzzed in my pocket, and I ripped it out, hoping that it was Allie.

Dad: We're extending our vacation for a few more days. How's Allie?

After typing out the words *fuck you*, I erased them and shut the phone off without ever responding. He'd fucking beat the fuck out of me for ignoring him these past two weeks, but I didn't fucking care. I took another swig. This was his fucking fault.

Grabbing a second bottle, I took another gulp of it and lay back on the couch, closing my eyes. My entire body fucking ached, and it wasn't because of the shit game tonight. It was the same kind of pain I had experienced sophomore year after I purposely lied to Allie and made her feel like trash.

That pain never fucking left. It was a constant reminder that I'd learned to deal with.

I hated seeing her in Redwood's halls with tears in her eyes and a pain that I could feel deep in my bones. I wanted her back, I wanted her with me, I wanted to love her freely again. But that would never happen.

Someone walked into the empty room and turned on the light, making it shine brightly.

"What the fuck?" I mumbled. "Leave me the fuck alone."

Jamal sighed. "Get up, Jace."

It was that fucking asshole.

"Do me a favor and stay away from my fucking stepsister," I said to him, my words slurred.

Fuck him being my best friend. A best friend wouldn't go after the one girl that I fucking loved with my entire fucking heart.

Jamal grabbed the bottle from me. "I'm bringing you home."

I shoved him away from me and stood, almost toppling over. "Give me that fucking back." I reached for the bottle and stumbled when Jamal pulled it out of reach from me. I curled my hands around his collar. "Give it to me, you fucking asshole."

"You're drunk," Jamal said.

"Why do you fucking care?" I asked, shaking my head and finding a beer bottle that someone had left on the coffee table. "You don't give a fuck about me. You're fucking around with my sister."

Jamal pressed his lips together, flaring his nostrils. "Let's go."

Snatching his collar, I pulled him closer to me and glared right into his eyes. "You're screwing the only woman I have ever loved. This entire time, you knew that I loved her. Yet you still fucking did it."

"Because you treat her like shit." Jamal shoved me away. "You have for two years now."

I wanted him to hit me. I wanted him to fucking hit me so hard, knock me out so I could forget for a couple hours, so I didn't have to live with all the stupid fucking things that had led me here, to this very moment, feeling like this.

"And you think you could fucking please her the way I could?" I asked, curling my lip.

I shoved him back and made him stumble into the wall. Some people looked over at us.

"You think you're fucking man enough to make her happy?"

"Get your hands off me," Jamal said through clenched teeth.

By the way the vein in his neck twitched, I could tell that he was getting angrier by the second, but Jamal always kept his cool. It was hard as fuck to get him so angry that he hit something or someone.

I grabbed on to his collar and thrust him against the wall again. "Or what are you going to do, Jamal? Hit me? Fucking do it then. Fucking hit me," I shouted at him. I wanted him to do it so fucking bad.

"I'm not going to hit you," Jamal said so damn calmly that it made me angrier.

When I knew he really wouldn't, I shoved him away from me and stumbled out of the room, shaking my head and trying not to topple over on my ass. "Fuck you, dude. Fuck you. Leave me the fuck alone."

Pushing through a group of people, I walked out of the house and toward my car. My keys weren't in my pocket—Jamal must've fucking taken them—but I didn't give a fuck anyway. I wasn't driving. I just wanted to be alone.

After slamming the door shut, I hurled my fist against the

steering wheel over and over and over until it was numb. I slumped back into the seat and cursed myself out. I hated my life. I really fucking did.

Ten minutes later, Jamal knocked on my glass window. "Get out, Jace." He pulled the door open and dragged me out of the fucking car. "I'm bringing you home, dude. Don't try to stop me."

I stumbled to his car and sat in the passenger seat. Staring out the foggy window, I shook my head. Allie would never be mine again. Never.

Chapter Twenty-Eight

ALLIE

Wrapping my arms around myself, I bounced up and down on my toes and stared out at the ocean at the Overlook as I waited for Jace. The Cartier bracelet that he had begged me to wear last night for his game glided back and forth around my finger. I had taken it off because I didn't like wearing something that expensive—especially in my neighborhood—but I made sure to keep it on me all the time.

I sat on a rock and glanced down the road to look for his car. Jace had asked me to meet him here a half hour ago and hadn't offered to pick me up like usual, so I had to walk here in the raw January cold. I'd tried calling him two times, but he hadn't picked up.

My teeth chattered, a puff of white air forming in front of my face. Where is he?

When I heard a car drive toward the Overlook, I turned around and hopped into the air with a big smile on my face. Finally, he was here. My stomach tightened with little fluttering butterflies.

Jace parked beside me, taking a couple of minutes in his car. I *peeked into his window and waved at him. He turned the car off and got out, staying a good five feet away from me when he did. I furrowed my brows at him, wondering what was wrong.*

Dark circles lay under his eyes. Those tan cheeks were flushed. He couldn't look at my face.

"We need to talk," Jace said, his voice cold and distant.

I clasped my hands together and rubbed them to keep my fingers from freezing off. "About what?" I asked.

Is it about his mother again? He has been—

"Us," Jace said.

My eyes widened, and I stepped toward him. "What about us?" I asked, thinking the absolute worst of the worst. What could he possibly want to talk about us? We hadn't fought about anything recently, and last night ... last night, we had been great.

"We're over."

My heart dropped, tightened in my chest. "What do you mean, we're over?"

"We're over, Allie," Jace said, glaring at me. "Done. Finished. Over."

Tears welled up in my eyes, and I shook my head. "Why?" I whispered.

Jace paused for a long moment. "Because I don't want a girlfriend who's going to use me for my fucking money and popularity, just to fucking feel better about her shitty life," he said harshly, yet he couldn't look me in the eye.

"Wh-what?" I whispered, shaking my head. A tear slid down my cheek. "I'm not, Jace. I'm not. I would never do that to you. You know that. You know that ..." My voice sounded so hurt, so defeated, so betrayed.

The corner of Jace's lips twitched, and he looked me right in the eye. There was hurt in his yet more pain than I had ever seen in them before. Even more than when he had found out his mother died.

"Did you think you could keep this act up forever? Did you think

I wouldn't find out?" he asked me. He gave me a lifeless kind of laugh and shook his head, glaring at the ocean. "It's good that we were never fucking serious, huh?"

I stepped toward him and grasped his arm. "Jace, what are you talking about?"

"Did you think I wanted to build an entire life with you, Allie?" He blew out a breath through his nose in an attempt to laugh again.

All I could feel was my heart breaking. Jace doesn't want to build a life with me? Has everything he told me been a complete lie? All those late nights and early mornings? All that fucking love? All of it's an act?

"Stop, Jace," I pleaded.

Why is he acting like this suddenly?

A car pulled up to the curb, and Nicole got out.

"Jacey!" she squealed, wiggling her fingers at us.

Jace looked in her direction. "You should leave, Allie."

I stared between them, tears spilling down my face. "What are you doing?"

I shook my head, not able to believe this was happening. He couldn't be … he couldn't be with Nicole. He couldn't.

"Are you cheating on me?" I whispered, hugging my arms around myself. When Jace didn't answer me, I dropped my arms, the bracelet dangling from my fingers. "You are," I whispered. "You are, aren't you?"

"We were never exclusive," Jace said, jaw clenched.

"In our spot, Jace?" I asked, voice barely over a whisper. "This is our spot."

He blew an annoyed breath out of his nose and glanced back at Nicole. "You think that this was our spot? You think I didn't bring any other girl I fucked here this past year? Huh? Are you still that naive little Allie?"

I threw the bracelet at him and shoved my hands into his chest, feeling nothing but an unbearable amount of pain. "I hate you! I hate you! I fucking hate you, Jace! Why would you do this to me? Why would you fucking do this to me?"

The Overlook meant nothing to him. All the dates he had taken me on meant nothing to him. I meant nothing to him.

"Allie, wake up!" Imani shouted above me.

She straddled my waist and had my hands pinned to the pillow. My body was trembling underneath hers, and real tears were sliding down my cheeks.

It had felt so real, so fucking real.

I sobbed loudly and curled myself into a ball underneath her, clutching my knees to my chest. The pain physically hurt every part of my body, especially my heart. Tears streamed down my face, hiccups exiting my mouth, and my body shook so badly that I couldn't control it.

"I'm so dumb. I'm so fucking dumb and stupid." I threw my head in my hands. "I tried everything to get him to love me again, fucking everything. Sleeping with him, making him jealous in hopes that ... he'd show me he fucking cared."

Imani wrapped her arms around me and rested her head on my shoulder, holding me tight to her. "Stop it, Allie. He's not worth your tears."

"Nothing worked. He'll never love me like I love him. I'm not good enough for him. He kept me around to fuck. That's all I was to him, a stupid fucking fuck buddy that he could use to get off. He never cared about me."

The truth ... it hurt.

Imani stroked my hair and pushed some tears from my face. "He's a rich, spoiled brat. You deserve so much more. You don't want someone like him, who doesn't care about your feelings."

I hiccuped again and sobbed. It hurt so bad, so fucking bad. "But I love him so much that it hurts. I will never stop loving him.

I've tried so many times, Imani. He's fucking sewn himself into my heart, and he keeps stabbing me with the needle."

And while Jace Harbor had broken my heart yet again, my stupid hurting heart still wanted him.

But I couldn't ... I wasn't supposed to even like him again. It was wrong.

Chapter Twenty-Nine

JACE

Pulling up to Nicole's gated neighborhood, I blew out a deep breath. Last night, I'd nearly drunk myself to death before sitting by the toilet and puking while Jamal watched from the bathroom door. And yet, I was still here to spend the night with Nicole because I needed this information.

"Jace Harbor," the guard at Nicole's neighborhood gates said, flashing his light into the car to look into the backseat of Dad's Escalade. My trunk wasn't big enough for Poison to fit. "Who are you here to see?"

I wrapped my hand around the steering wheel and swallowed. "Who I come to see here every time, Jack. Nicole," I said with distaste. I fucking hated the way her name sounded on my tongue, and I loathed why I was here to see her, all to get some evidence.

The guard stared at me for a few moments, scanning my license. He opened the gates for me, and I rolled up my window as soon as I could. Fuck talking to anyone in this fucking neighborhood.

After I drove far enough onto the property, my phone lit up with a text from Kai.

Kai: Cameras are down.

I pulled over to the curb near some large shrubs and popped the trunk. Poison hopped out and slid into the car through the side doors, João sitting next to me in the passenger seat. He lit a cigarette and took two puffs on it.

"Last chance to turn back, Harbor."

There wasn't any turning back now. I'd fucking hurt Allie for this. She thought I was a fucking cheater, a fucking liar, a fucking prick. If I'd ruined my chances with her, the least I could do was protect her.

"Huh?" João said after I pulled into Nicole's driveway.

"We're going through with it." I yanked the key out of the ignition. "Get me what I need."

Once I calmed myself down enough to put on my best act, I stepped out of the car, leaving it unlocked, and walked to Nicole's front door. I knocked twice and waited patiently for her. She opened it in nothing but a set of lacy black lingerie.

Make it up, Jace. Make it all fucking up.

"Hey, Jacey," Nicole said, pulling the door open wider. "I was just freshening up."

I stepped into the house. "You look good."

Good? That isn't going to be the fucking way to distract her.

After closing the door, she wrapped her arms around my torso from behind and pressed her breasts against my back. "Just good?" she asked, hand slipping down my abdomen and to the front of my pants.

I tensed and stepped away from her. "I brought wine," I said, walking toward her kitchen to keep my distance. "Go sit in the living room and wait for me. I'll bring you some out."

I didn't want to sleep with her. I would do anything not to sleep with her. I hated her more than Allie probably hated me at the moment.

Quickly finding the corkscrew in her kitchen drawer, I popped the wine open and poured myself a huge fucking glass. It was the strongest shit I could find from Dad's wine cellar because I needed it.

After drinking an entire glass, I poured two more, glanced into the living room—where Nicole was mindlessly scrolling through her phone, distracted—and disabled the security system the way that Kai had told me to so they could get into the house. I hurried back, brought out the two glasses of wine, and handed one to her, then sat on the opposite side of the couch.

"So," I started, wiping my sweaty palm on my jeans, "what do you want to do?"

Nicole giggled. "Oh, come on, Jace. We both know why you're here."

She crawled on top of me, straddling my waist, and wrapped her arms around my shoulders. I rested my hands on her waist, hating every fucking second of this, and let her stick her tongue into my mouth.

I need to distract her. I need to distract her. I need to distract her.

Grinding herself against me, she moaned slightly. I squeezed my eyes shut, thinking of Allie, about protecting her, about doing this all for her. I had to be the fucking shittiest person to ever live on this fucking earth, but it was the only way. The only fucking way.

"You feel so good, baby," Nicole murmured against my lips. She reached behind her and undid her bra, letting it fall between us, then reached for the front of my pants again. "Let's take care of this," she said, grasping my cock. "It's so hard."

I hate myself. I hate myself. I fucking hate myself.

"Nicole," I said, voice above a whisper. "Not now, please."

Nicole grasped my hands, put them on her chest, and ground herself up and down against my hardness through my jeans. She pouted her big, fake pink lips at me. "Jacey, let me have it, please."

I pulled my hands away and stared her right in the eyes. "I ... I ... not now."

I couldn't explain myself to her. I couldn't get it out that I could never fucking do this with her. I couldn't admit to her how much I loved Allie. Allie was my entire life.

"You want to take it slow?" Nicole asked, running her hands through my hair. "Is Jace Harbor *afraid* that I'm going to break his cold little heart again? Because I won't, Jacey." She crawled off me and dropped to her knees, hands running up the inside of my thighs. "All I want to do is please you."

My breathing hitched, and I stared right through her. She undid my pants and ran her fingers across my cock pressed against my briefs, slowly moving her manicured fingers. Placing her mouth on my underwear, she sucked on it lightly, all the way up until she reached the head of my cock.

I squeezed my eyes closed and thought of something, anything, so I could keep Nicole distracted because I couldn't do this. I couldn't fucking go through with this. *What the fuck was I ever even thinking?*

Nicole paused. "Why is your dick getting soft?"

My eyes snapped open, and I zippered up my pants, gathering myself together. "I need to use the bathroom," I said, hoping she'd be stupid enough to believe that excuse. I stood up and hurried over to the bathroom connected to the living room.

When I closed the door, I placed my hands on the sink and took a deep breath. I stared at myself in Nicole's bathroom mirror, wanting to punch it to pieces.

My chin trembled as I stared at the man in the mirror—tears in his eyes and that *sorry for a fucking man* expression on his damn face. I balled my hands into fists and stared at myself—really fucking stared at the man who was supposed to love Allie. Now, I was at Nicole's house, letting her touch me, letting her grind her body against mine and kiss me in places only Allie should.

A tear—a fucking tear—fell from my eye.

Fuck me. Fuck this.

I wanted Allie to hold me, to stroke my hair, to tell me that everything was going to be okay, like she had after Mom died. Yet Allie was the only person that I was doing this for. I didn't give a fuck what happened to me or to my father. I just wanted to keep Allie safe.

If I had to give up any hope of ever having her in my arms again as anything more than a measly hookup, then I would do it to keep her safe. She couldn't know what this was all for; she couldn't know how dangerous my father was. She'd tell her mother, and her mother would try to leave him. Nobody could leave him.

Chapter Thirty

Jace Harbor had ruined my life. I wanted to ruin his.

I walked down Pierce Road and knocked on Jamal's front door. After I had convinced Imani that I was fine—because I fucking was—I had decided that Jamal was my only hope for making Jace hurt and for actually being with someone who could love me for me.

I might've been a bad person for coming here, but Jace had made me into one.

Jamal's mom answered the door in an extra-large Redwood Academy nightshirt and her signature purple silk hair wrap. "Baby, it's been so long since I saw you!" She opened the door wider for me to come into the house and enveloped me into a hug.

After promising myself that I wouldn't cry—because being hugged by someone motherly felt so good—I hugged her close. Jamal's mom had baked so much food for Mom and me after Dad died. We'd had dinner with her almost every night.

"Jamal!" she shouted up the stairs. "Get your ass down here." She turned back to me. "How you doing?"

I gave her my best smile, lips quivering. "Good."

Jamal's ten-year-old brother, Marquis, ran down the stairs and leaned against the wall, smirking at me in his Spider-Man pajamas. "Hey, Allie. Here for me?"

Jamal's mom smacked him on the back of the head. "Get your ass back to bed. She ain't here for you. Tell your brother to come down."

Marquis rubbed the back of his head and stomped back up the stairs. "Jamal! Mom wants you. She's gonna beat your ass if you don't get down there."

Jamal's mom shook her head and followed him up the stairs. "Marquis!" she shouted, disappearing into the upstairs hallway.

A door slammed shut, and Jamal appeared at the top of the steps, smirking down the hall toward Marquis's room.

He jogged down the steps in a pair of gray sweats that did him wonders. I swallowed hard and smiled at him, curling my arms around his waist and pulling him close to me. When he rested his arms around my shoulders, I relaxed almost fully in his arms, not because I was a girl falling in love with another football athlete, but because he felt like my childhood—when I hadn't had problems like this.

"Let's go out," Jamal said, glancing up the steps and listening to Marquis screaming and crying like all out-of-control ten-year-old kids did after they knew they had done something wrong but done it anyway.

After grabbing a coat, Jamal drove us to the better side of town, where we could walk around and not be afraid of getting jumped by the Poison boys or any other goons who acted like them. He parked on the side of the road and walked with me to a fast-food joint, ordering large fries to split.

I slid onto a chair and grabbed one, trying hard not to think about Jace being out with Nicole tonight, about him touching her the same way he'd touched me, about him whispering to her all those sweet nothings that I'd believed.

"You wanna talk?" Jamal asked.

I thrust my head into my hands and blew out a shaky breath. "I don't know. I—"

"Allie Hall!" Someone clapped their hands onto my shoulders and squeezed hard. Carter—Redwood's most annoying quarterback—leaned down close to me. "Out of all the athletes you could come out with, you chose Jamal?"

Jamal tensed and stood up. "Get your fucking hands off her, Carter."

Carter pulled his hands away and lifted them into the air. "Didn't mean to insult you, J." He threw Jamal a wink and walked toward the other side of me, grabbing a fry from the center of the table. "Think Allie deserves a bit more than you and a shitty large fry for dinner."

I flared my nostrils and clenched my jaw, nails digging into my palms.

"How about you, me, and a steak dinner at Charlons?" Carter said to me.

"No," I said, keeping my gaze on Jamal. "I'm quite fine with fries and ketchup."

Carter smirked at me, grabbed a hundred-dollar bill from his wallet, and tossed it toward Jamal. "Treat her to something nice, J." He leaned in close to Jamal and stared at me. "Then, tomorrow at practice, tell me how long you lasted in bed with her tonight."

Jamal shoved the money and his hands right into Carter's chest. I stood up and maneuvered my way between them before Jamal lost his shit and made Carter eat his fist. Snatching the fries and Jamal's hands, I pulled him out into the cold.

"Forget about him," I said, glaring back into the restaurant at Carter, who wiggled his fingers in my direction to say good-bye.

We walked in silence for a few moments until Jamal calmed down.

"We need to talk," I said after some time, thinking about Carter's comment. "Jamal, I can't sleep with you," I blurted out.

"And I really can't give you all of me," I whispered, glancing down at my fingers. "I'm sorry for leading you on and making you think that there was more between us than just friendship, but I loved Jace for so long ... it's so difficult to get him off my mind, and this —between us—is so wrong."

"It's wrong from both ends, Allie. You're my best friend's ex-girlfriend *and* stepsister," Jamal said, brushing a piece of hair from my face. "I shouldn't have kissed you or taken you out, but I was tired of seeing him treat you like shit. He dumped you like you never meant anything to him and constantly makes your life hell. I've told him to cut that shit out, but he won't." He paused. "I know I don't have much, not even a bit of what Jace has, but I want to treat you how the always-smiling Allie I grew up with deserves."

"Jamal," I sighed, letting his name run over my tongue with such sorrow. I shook my head, knowing that though Jace had broken my fucking heart, I didn't think I could ever truly love Jamal as more than a friend.

I wanted to love him—I really did. But I couldn't—and I wouldn't be able to. Not now. Not until I healed.

"I can't," I whispered. "I don't want to hurt you just because he hurt me."

"At least stay over then," Jamal said. "One night. Give me one night."

"One night," I whispered. "Just one."

Chapter Thirty-One

ALLIE

"Take the bed." Jamal slouched down on a kitchen table chair he had brought up from downstairs. He tugged on a Redwood sweatshirt and closed his eyes, resting his head against the wall.

I arched a brow at him and threw a pillow at him, knowing how hard those wooden chairs were—I had sat on them too many times, crying my eyes out after Dad died. "You're not sleeping on the chair, Jamal. You wanted me to stay over, so get in the bed."

Jamal didn't even open his eyes. "It's fine, Allie."

After sitting up, I rested my back against the headboard and crossed my arms. "You have football practice tomorrow. Just lie down. I don't mind."

Jamal opened one eye. "You're not going to let me sleep, are you?"

I pulled the blankets open and pointed to the empty side of the bed. "No."

He groaned inwardly and walked over to the bed. "I didn't want you to come over so I could sleep with you," Jamal said, sliding under the sheets with me. "I hope you know that. I mean, you're hot as fuck, but ..."

Turning on my side, I faced him. "Then, why'd you invite me over?"

There was awkward silence between us for a few moments, and then Jamal sighed again. "Because I knew you wouldn't want to go back home and Imani is out with her family tonight."

"How'd you know about that?"

He widened his eyes, the moonlight bouncing off them. "She wouldn't shut up about it at lunch this entire week," Jamal said.

My lips curled into a smile. "Oh yeah. I forgot that you sit with us."

Jamal let out a quiet laugh. "Am I not that memorable?"

I playfully pushed his shoulder. "Stop it."

After staring at him for a few moments, I gazed back up at the ceiling. I shouldn't be here, but he was right. I didn't want to go home to that big-ass mansion, knowing that Jace was out, banging Nicole at her house. But even now, how would I confront him in the morning? What would I freaking say to him?

"I want to be with you, Allie," Jamal said.

Neither one of us could sleep, apparently. Maybe it was from the police sirens going off every five minutes or our racing thoughts.

"But I know that we can never really be together."

I stayed quiet, not knowing what to say.

"Jace loves you," Jamal said, his voice sounding so hurt. "He really does."

My lips turned into a sour frown. "He doesn't. He never did."

Jamal turned toward me, the moonlight making his dark face glow. "I know that it might not seem like it. I know he's treated you like shit these past two years. I know he does some shit that doesn't make sense. But last night, he got so drunk that he couldn't walk straight. I took him home and stayed with him the entire night as he puked and cried about how much he fucking loves you but can't have you."

Pausing, I turned my face toward him. "What do you mean?" I whispered.

Jace Harbor never cried, not even when his mother had died.

"Listen, Allie, I don't know what's holding him back, but I know that you know there's more to him than who he tries to be in front of everyone. You've been hurt by him more than once. I get you're pissed at him. I just wanted you to know that he still loves you."

"Why are you trying to defend him?" I asked, brows furrowed together.

I wanted to hate the man in peace for everything he had done to me.

"Because he's my best friend. I want to love you. I want you to smile again. But I see the way you are with him, even when we're sitting at lunch. You want him, even after everything you've been through, and he wants you."

"I don't want him," I clarified, balling the sheets up in my fist. "I don't fucking want him."

Jamal blew a breath out his nose in disbelief. "Look at me and tell me that, since sophomore year, you haven't thought about being with him again. Tell me that you don't wish things were different between you two."

I glanced over at Jamal, fully prepared to tell him that I had been over Jace Harbor the second he broke up with me two years ago. But when I opened my mouth, all that came out was a sob. I slapped a hand over my mouth to quiet myself, so Marquis and his sisters wouldn't wake up in the other room.

Jamal tugged me to his chest and shushed me. "I know how you feel about him. You don't have to hide it from me."

"You don't ... don't deserve th-this," I cried into his chest. "I shouldn't be here ..."

Jamal continued to stroke my hair, his breathing uneven and chest tight. I clutched on to him, my arms around his shoulders.

"You're a really good friend, Jamal," I whispered into his chest, relaxing once I finally calmed myself down enough. "You deserve someone wonderful."

Chapter Thirty-Two

JACE

"Jacey, why don't you stay the night?" Nicole asked, clutching on to my arm.

I had been here for four hours and had somehow managed to preoccupy her with things other than having sex. Don't ask me how I'd fucking done it, but I had. I had done everything I had to do to keep her busy, including letting her dress me in makeup because she kept complaining that all her friends wouldn't let her.

Of course, they had refused. They all knew how shitty she was at it. She couldn't stop her hand from trembling the entire time. Part of me felt bad about it because tremors ran in her family. But the other part of me didn't give a fuck because she couldn't keep her hands off me, even after I told her no.

I curled my finger around a lock of her hair and tugged. "You know I don't stay over."

She frowned. "We didn't even do anything fun."

"You caked me in makeup, Nicole." I felt myself getting annoyed with her, which I couldn't if Poison hadn't gotten what I needed yet, so I took a deep breath and smiled at her. "Isn't that what you wanted? You never get to do that."

Lips curling into a small smile, she nodded. "Fine. I'll see you on Monday."

When she shut the front door, I sighed and slumped my shoulders forward. God, that had taken longer than I'd expected it to take. Keeping up a front with Nicole after spending so much time with Allie had really taken a toll on me.

"Damn, what was she doing with you in there the entire time?" Landon asked when I slid into the car with a makeup wipe in one hand and my dignity in the other. "Prettying you up, Harbor?"

I backed out of the driveway and parked by a bunch of shrubs, opening the mirror and wiping off all the damn makeup Nicole had put on my face. When I got it all off, I threw the sheet into the garbage on the side of the door.

"Did you get my shit or not?" I asked through clenched teeth.

João handed me a folder. "This is what we found. There's a ton of shit in there that could put a lot of people in this town away. That prick is probably blackmailing the rich to get money from them; that must be how he got enough cash to move into a guarded neighborhood."

I opened the file and blew out a breath through my nose. There was a lot of shit that I hadn't even known happened in this town, but I flipped through the paperwork until I found my father's name.

There were a couple documents, but I saw the one that I had been looking for over the past two years. Copies of messages to a Rick Santos and a copy of a check written to the police chief himself for over a hundred million.

"Is this enough?" I asked.

"How would we know?"

"You guys have been to fucking jail," I said.

"So have you," Landon said.

João went to grab the folder back from me, but I pulled it away.

"This is worth more than two million dollars," I said to them. "I take what I need about my father, and I'll give you the rest, but then you promise to do whatever the fuck I need you to do for me. Understand?"

João looked at the guys in the backseat. After a few moments, he nodded. "Deal. Anything you need, you got it."

I grabbed what I needed from the folder, stuffed it into the glove compartment, and handed him the rest of the documents. I drove Kai and Landon to Landon's house on the shitty side of town and parked the car for them to leave.

"I told you that there would be consequences if you hurt Allie," Kai said, looking into the car through the passenger window. "The job you asked for is done. Watch your fucking back."

João nodded to Kai before I rolled up the damn window and sped off, thinking nothing of his threat. *This* was for Allie, and he knew it. I had other shit to worry about. I would worry about Kai later.

"Plan it strategically," João said as I pulled up to his place on Pierce Road. "Whatever information you're planning on taking out of that folder, make sure it won't get you sent to jail. You're eighteen now. You won't be sent to juvie this time, if you can't convict him."

I rubbed a hand over my face. I had to be strategic about this, but I also couldn't wait. Dad would find out that the two million was missing and *talk* with me about it. If he sent me back to finish senior year at boarding school, I couldn't protect Allie.

After he got out, I drove to Coach's house and parked on the curb. Coach lived on Crestwood Drive—the street bordering the bad side of town and a few streets down from Jamal. My car would be gone by the morning—people worked quick when they saw something this expensive sitting on their road—but I didn't give a fuck. It was Dad's anyway.

All the lights were off in his house, yet I got out, grabbed the papers from the compartment, and knocked on the door anyway. I'd had to hold myself together the entire night, and I couldn't anymore. I needed to talk to someone about this because it was eating me a-fucking-live on the inside.

After the third knock, Coach finally answered, his eyes wide when he saw me. "Jace, what are you doing here this late?"

I opened my mouth to say something—to say what I had wanted to say all night—but nothing would come out, except, "Can I stay here tonight? I don't want to go home."

His wife appeared behind him in a cheap, plush robe and a warm smile. With graying brown hair pulled into a braid down her back, she reminded me of Mom. "You're always welcome here, Jace."

<h1 style="text-align:center">Chapter Thirty-Three</h1>

ALLIE

I woke up to Marquis screaming downstairs. Turning over, I pulled a pillow over my face to block the sound and the sunlight blaring into the room from the window.

"Jamal," I whispered. "Are you awake?"

When he didn't answer, I tugged the pillow off me to see the bed empty. The clock read eight forty-five a.m. I sat up and wiped my hand over my face, my eyes puffy from the lack of sleep and all the thinking I had done about Jace last night.

My phone lit up with new messages from Jamal.

The first message was at seven-fifty a.m.

Jamal: Practice at 8 a.m. today. Mom will feed you breakfast if you want it.

The second message came seconds ago.

Jamal: Shit.

Jamal: When I was at your house the other night, my license must've dropped out of my wallet. Can you look for it in Jace's room? He won't pick up and isn't here.

Jamal: I put it on his nightstand.

I furrowed my brows at his rampant text messages and arched a brow. Why hadn't he asked Jace to get it for him later? He knew how much I didn't want to face Jace today or anytime soon. Gnawing on the inside of my lip, I frowned.

Me: Do you need it today? Can't you wait until Jace gets it back to you? Didn't you have it yesterday when we went out?

Three little bubbles appeared on the screen, then disappeared.

Jamal: Can you look when you get a chance? It'll take two seconds.

Scrunching my nose, I sent back **Sure** because he had taken me in last night. I tugged on one of Jamal's sweatshirts since it was freezing and walked downstairs, wanting to sneak past Marquis if I could. That boy had had a crush on me since he was four years old, and it had only gotten worse.

When I walked downstairs, Marquis sat on the couch fiddling with his mother's phone while she folded laundry in the kitchen.

"Morning, baby," she said, placing the last shirt into the bin. "You doing good?"

I mustered my best smile to hide the hurt. "I'm good." No, I wasn't. "Thanks for letting me stay the night. I appreciate it. Jamal is a sweetheart."

"Anytime, honey," she said. "You're always welcome here." She glanced into the other room when Marquis started to get antsy on the phone. "You'd better head off before he realizes that you stayed over last night. You know he won't shut the hell up about it."

I tugged her into a hug and walked to the door. "Thank you," I said again because I really appreciated her with all my heart.

She had done so much for me, and I had wanted to repay her for so long. Maybe one day, I'd be successful enough to do it myself—without using the Harbors' money.

After the thirty-minute walk home, I stepped onto our driveway to see Jace's Maserati sitting in the driveway. Harlan's SUV was gone, so I was hoping that Jace had taken it. I didn't want to be here alone with him.

I clenched my hands into fists, praying to whoever the fuck was watching me that Jace Harbor wasn't home, and snuck into the house, hearing nothing but silence.

Hurrying right up to the bedrooms, I clutched Jace's doorknob in my hand. What was I doing this for again? Jamal because he had let me stay over last night so I wouldn't have to come home to face Jace.

Slowly—very fucking slowly—I opened Jace's door to find an empty room. I sighed in relief and hurried to Jace's bed, looking around the nightstand and under the bed for Jamal's license. I swore to God that he'd had it yesterday when he brought me out because I couldn't find it anywhere here.

I didn't want to tear apart Jace's bed because I didn't fucking know who had slept in it last night, and I didn't want to contract any diseases that Nicole might've had.

After looking nearly everywhere, I sighed through my nose and tore open his nightstand drawer to look for it in there. Jace had scolded me last time for attempting to go through his things, so I wanted to make this quick. If it wasn't in there, I'd be the hell out of this bedroom for good.

I stared down into the drawer at two bags of weed from Poison that hadn't been touched. They both were filled completely, and I had sworn that the other day, they'd only handed him one baggie. Was he not smoking it, like I'd suggested?

After pressing my lips together, I rolled my eyes. I didn't care. I didn't fucking care.

I pushed them out of the way, scrambling through the bottle of lube and … the bracelet that he had given me two years ago. I stopped and picked it up, letting it tremble in my hands. *He still has it? He hasn't given it to Nicole or Jenny or any of his other sluts?*

My chest tightened. *He's really kept it all these years?*

No. He'd kept it because it was expensive. That was it. He hadn't kept it for me. He couldn't have. I was just making up all these fake scenarios again, hoping that we could be something that we would never be—together again. Jamal had gotten into my head.

Once I threw it back into the drawer, I continued my search. In the back of the drawer, something white caught my eye. I sighed through my nose, so thankful that I had finally found Jamal's license so I could get out of here. I picked it up and turned it over, frowning when I realized it wasn't a license, but something folded up.

For moments, I contemplated if I wanted to unfold it. It would make me hurt even worse if it was a picture of him and Nicole or even him and Jenny. I didn't want to hurt anymore. So, I sat on his bed and let my fingers trail against its edges. I couldn't open it.

I thrust the picture back into the drawer and snapped it shut.

Walk out of the room, Allie. Walk out and don't look back.

After hurrying to the door, I slammed it behind me and pressed my back to it. I didn't care if he had pictures of Nicole. There was nothing between us anymore. If he wanted to date the annoying bitch, then I would let him.

When I thought I had enough self-control, I stepped away from the door, but then I found myself tugging it open again and yanking the drawer open. I pulled out the picture and unfolded it, my chest tight.

It wasn't of him and Nicole.

It was of us.

Chapter Thirty-Four

JACE

The clock on Coach's nightstand read 10:58 a.m. I shot up in the bed, scrambling to pull on my shirt and get to the two minutes of practice that I had left because I had fucking slept through it. I hadn't missed a single day of practice since Mom had died, and I didn't want to start today even if it meant showing up and doing laps around the field as all the guys showered.

Someone knocked on the door, and Coach's wife peeked her head into the room.

"You're finally awake," she said, opening the door wider. With a plate of French toast, eggs, and bacon, she walked into the room and set the tray on the dresser. "Don't worry about going to practice. Steve told me to make sure you rested up. He's on his way home."

I frowned at her and nodded, sitting back down on the bed. "You didn't have to—"

She waved her hand at me. "Nonsense. It's nice to cook for someone again. All my kids are off to college." She looked toward the plate. "Oh dear, I almost forgot. Do you like orange juice? Or I also have some apple juice or milk downstairs."

The corner of my lips curled up slightly. "Orange juice is great. Thank you, Mrs. Carol."

She gave me a curt nod and smiled. "Good, good. Well, would you like to come eat in the kitchen or eat in here?"

By the way she teetered toward the door, I could tell she wanted to talk to someone. Or maybe it was me who wanted to talk.

I grabbed the tray and walked with her down to the kitchen, sliding onto one of the chairs and grabbing a piece of bacon.

She sat across from me, sipping on a cup of coffee. "Steve told me that you've been contacted by many colleges for football. Have you chosen which one you'll be attending?"

"Michigan," I said.

"Michigan?" she asked, eyes lighting up. She reached across the table and gently grasped my wrist. "That's amazing, sweetie. Michigan is a huge football school—well, I'm sure you already know that." Her cheeks flushed, and she looked down at her coffee.

The front door opened. When Coach walked into the house, his wife stood.

"Honey, you're home." She handed him some coffee. "I'll leave you two alone. I have some washing to do."

She disappeared into the hallway and then into one of the back rooms.

Coach sat across from me and took a sip of his coffee.

I rubbed the back of my head and frowned at him. "Sorry that I slept in. It won't happen again. I was—"

"You're fine, Jace. You show up to every practice early and stay late when you can. You need some time off," he said. After a few moments, he cleared his throat. "I, uh, heard about what happened with Allie after the game on Friday," Coach said, running his tongue over his bottom teeth, as if he didn't know what else to say or how to approach the subject. "Word gets around fast in Redwood."

Sunlight flooded in through the windows, and I closed my eyes, feeling nothing but hurt. I balled my hands into fists. Tears welled up in my eyes. "I love her, Coach. I fucking love her so much."

"Why don't you tell her, son?" he asked me. "You're gazing up into those bleachers during every practice and every game, just looking for her, then pick on her every chance you get. That's not how to win someone over."

My lips curled into a frown. "That's how to protect her."

"Protect her from what?" he asked, graying brows drawn together.

I couldn't tell him the entire truth because I hated the mere thought of it, but I could tell him some of the pain that I had endured for years—even before Mom's death.

"My dad abuses me," I said aloud for the first time ever.

Everything rushed to the surface, all the emotions that I had been trying to suppress since I was a kid, and I sobbed, throwing my head into my hands.

"The principal, the police chief, the fucking counselor he made me fucking go to after Mom died ... nobody believes me when I tell them that he's dangerous. Everyone turns a blind eye, thinks I'm lying for attention, that my dad couldn't be a monster because he has fucking money. I have been trying so hard—so fucking hard—for someone to believe me."

It'd been too hard, too much some days. I was getting tired of the facade that I had to keep up at home, on the field, at school, and especially with Allie. I had wanted to tell someone the real, deep truth for years now.

"Son."

Coach pulled me into a hug, wrapping his arms around me and holding me close as I shook uncontrollably. I wrapped my arms around him and shook my head, the tears actually falling.

"Why didn't you tell me before? I would've helped you out sooner."

"No one can help me," I whispered more to myself. "Everyone in this town can be paid off." I rubbed a hand over my face. "I'm so fucking terrified that he's going to hurt Allie. I don't let her ever be alone with him. I get him pissed off before she can, so he hits me and not her."

"Allie's mother?" Coach asked after a few moments of silence. "Does he abuse her too?"

I shrugged. "I don't know."

Allie's mother seemed happy, but I tried hard enough to seem happy too. I could hide the pain, the hurt, the fucking fear. I had done it for the past two years without a problem, so Dad wouldn't put me in boarding school or throw me in jail just because he felt like it again.

"There's more, isn't there, son?"

I stared down at the floor and lied because part of me didn't think he'd believe me either. He might've believed the abuse, but he wouldn't believe that Dad could ...

I swallowed hard and pressed my lips together. "No, there isn't any more."

Chapter Thirty-Five

ALLIE

Still sitting in Jace's bedroom, I clutched the picture in my hand and swallowed hard. It had been an hour at the least, and I couldn't get myself to put it down and walk out of the room again. I loved Jace Harbor so much. This picture had to mean something to him too, right?

Maybe Jamal wasn't lying about something holding Jace back.

The crease in the picture looked like it had been folded and unfolded hundreds of times. He had been looking at it since we had taken the picture together the night before he broke my heart.

Downstairs, the front door opened and closed. I should've put the picture back and left the room, but I couldn't move. Jace cursed as he walked up the stairs to the bedroom, getting closer every second.

I gnawed on my lip, everything in me hurting.

"Fuck. I screwed the fuck up. I screwed the fuck—" The door opened, and he stood in the doorway with wide eyes. He gazed down at the picture in my hand and sucked in a deep breath. "Allie, I ..."

I stared up at him through teary eyes, the picture trembling in my hand. "What's this?" I whispered. "Why do you still have this picture of us in your drawer?"

Jace stepped into the room and glanced down at the picture again. He opened his mouth and snapped it shut, no words coming out. He looked at me for a long time, tears forming in his eyes.

It was the first time I saw Jace Harbor cry.

His lip twitched, and suddenly, he charged toward me, threw his arms around me, and picked me up. He spun me into the air, holding me tightly to his chest, and buried his face into the crook of my neck.

"I love you, Allie," Jace mumbled into my neck, his fingers digging into my sides. He sat on his bed with me in his lap. After a few moments, he pulled away slightly and stared into my eyes with his teary ones. "I love you so much, and I don't ever want to lose you. You're the only thing I look forward to every day."

Taken by surprise, I hesitantly rested my hands on his strong shoulders, still clutching the picture. "Jace," I whispered. Everything in me warmed at the sound of Jace admitting that he loved me again after years of him putting me down time and time again.

It would be stupid of me to believe him after everything that he had done to me. I had made that mistake one too many times and couldn't afford to be hurt again.

"You have to believe me," Jace said, a tear falling down his cheek.

"Then, tell me why," I whispered. "Why do you hurt me? Why have you made my life hell for the past two years? Why do you choose Nicole over me time and time again?"

"I don't want Nicole. I never have." He paused. "I'm trying to protect you."

I shook my head, fury washing over me. For the past two years, I had felt like I came in second place to Nicole and every other girl he had been out with. Now, he was telling me that he never wanted any of them. If I had a clear mind, maybe it would add up, but to me, right now, it didn't.

"Protect me from what, Jace? You?" I asked harshly.

Jace looked down between us and shook his head. "I can't tell you. I can't."

My lips curled into an angry frown. "Why?" I asked. "Why not? Why are you doing this to me? If you can't tell me why you continue to hurt me, then I can't do this." I shook my head, trying to think clearly as the tears flowed down my cheeks. "I can't, Jace."

When I went to crawl off of him, he grasped my wrist. "I'm protecting you from my dad."

"Harlan?" I whispered.

What had he done? Though he was a bit annoying, he seemed nice at the very least, and he made Mom happy as far as I knew.

There was so much pain in Jace's eyes. He grasped my face and rested his forehead against mine. "You won't believe me if I tell you. You'll think I'm looking for attention too. That I'm crazy."

I placed my hands on his and trailed my fingers down his long ones. "Tell me," I whispered. "Please. I'll believe you. You don't have to hide things from me, Jace. You should've always known that."

We stayed like that in silence for a few minutes until Jace finally opened his mouth. "My dad killed my mom."

Chapter Thirty-Six

JACE

Allie pulled away and stared at me with wide, confused eyes. I sat there—completely vulnerable—and held her in my arms, hoping that she believed me because I needed someone on my side. But the more time that passed, the stupider I felt about letting it slip out of my mouth.

Why would she believe the one person who had lied to her for two years? Why would she believe the man who had dumped her for Nicole not once, but twice? Why would she believe me after all the shit I had put her through? She probably thought that this was another one of my lies to get her to feel bad for me.

"Jace," she said, voice above a whisper.

I tore my gaze away from her, picked her up, and placed her beside me on the bed. After throwing my head into my hands, I shook my head and cursed to myself. What the fuck was wrong with me? I couldn't do anything right.

"Forget I said anything," I snapped, standing up and hurrying to the door. I didn't know where the hell I was going to go, but I needed to get away from this hellhole. Maybe getting out of this town and going to Michigan for football would do me some fucking good.

Just as I was about to rip the door open, Allie wrapped her arms around me from behind and pulled me tight to her. She inched her way around my body until she stood directly in front of me. Head buried into my chest, she tensed in my hold. "Please, don't go," she whispered, staring up at me through glasses stained with tears. "I believe you, Jace."

One moment passed. Then two.

So much weight felt like it had suddenly fallen off my shoulders, and I could breathe again.

"You believe me?" I asked, doubting everything.

She nodded as more tears raced down her cheeks. "I believe you."

I wrapped my arms around her shoulders and pulled her tight to me, clutching on to her harder than I ever had before—even after Mom's death. I'd tried to stay strong. I'd fucking tried hard not to cry in front of her.

But nobody had ever believed me.

I had thought too much about Mom's death these past few days, and ... and after the two longest, hardest years of my life, I could finally be myself with Allie again.

My body trembled back and forth, and I doubled over into her. Allie wrapped her arms around me, holding me up, and pushed me to the bed. She crawled onto it, resting her body against the headboard, and pulled me up toward her.

I lay between her legs with my head on her stomach and wrapped my arms around her body. She stroked my hair gently, like she always used to, and lay there with me as I sobbed into her shirt.

"I'm sorry for everything I've done to you," I said, shaking my head. "I'm so fucking sorry. I hate myself more and more for it every fucking day. I don't deserve you. You deserve someone who cherishes you, who gives you the world."

She wiped tears from her cheeks with her thumb. "You are my world, Jace. You have nothing to be sorry for," she whispered. "But why? Why did you hide this from me? Why didn't you think you could tell me this?"

I stared up at her and pushed a couple more tears away, hurting so fucking bad because of what I had done to us. It wasn't Dad's fault. It was my fault. I had been shitty to her as my way to protect her. At least, I'd thought I was protecting her.

"Because when I learned that he had killed her, I found out that he was dating your mother. I told the principal and the police chief, even the fucking therapist," I said. "Nobody believed me. If they did, my dad paid off everyone to turn a blind eye. I've been so alone. I wanted your mother to fucking hate me, so she would break it off with him before they got married. I didn't want you to worry about anything. I wanted to protect you."

She stayed quiet for a long time.

"Do you really believe me?" I whispered, almost unable to believe her myself. I had been alone for so long, so fucking long.

She nodded and tugged on the ends of my hair. "Yes, I believe you. I'm just in shock. Your dad said she died of cancer."

"My dad is a fucking liar."

"Why would he kill her?" she asked me, confusion written all over her face.

"Because she cheated on him with one of my coaches from pee wee football. They had an affair for years before my father found out that she was pregnant with someone else's child. And when he did, he flipped and murdered her in cold blood. I found the pictures of it on his laptop. A bullet straight through her head, her eyes so empty."

My entire body hurt, thinking about it. I had suppressed the thought of those cold eyes for so long. I missed her. I really fucking missed her, and I didn't want Allie to feel the same pain that I did, especially after her father had died.

"Is my mom in danger?" she asked, lips quivering. "Will he try to kill her too?" Tears fell from her eyes. "I don't want my mom to die. She's the only family that I have left."

I scurried up in the bed and wrapped her up in my arms. "She won't die. I promise that I won't let him kill her. Poison found me some information that the courts can't fucking deny. I need time and a plan to come out with it, so he doesn't throw me in jail again before I can prove it to everyone."

Allie clung on to me for dear life, pulling me tight. She buried her face into my side and stared up at me. "I promise to stand by your side through all of this," she whispered. "As long as you don't keep anything from me anymore."

I tucked some hair behind her ear. "No more secrets. No more lies. No more hurt. I'm going to love you this time, Allie. I promise you that I will protect you with my life."

Chapter Thirty-Seven

ALLIE

Jace kissed my cheek, then my jaw, then just below my ear on my neck. I shivered under his touch. Tears still welled in my eyes at the mere thought of everything that he had told me. Everything for the past two years had been because of this, because Jace wanted to protect me in his own messed up way.

"I promise to love you," Jace said against my neck, trailing kisses down my collarbone.

I breathed out slowly and curled my fingers into his hair, tugging on it slightly.

"I promise to care for you," he said, moving lower down my chest and to my stomach.

Arching my back, I whimpered softly and curled my toes. I stared down into his big, tear-filled brown eyes. His kisses were so soft that I could barely feel them, but as he peeled away the layers of my clothes, I could feel every sensation on my skin. Every touch, every kiss, every word etching into me.

"I promise to protect you with everything I have," Jace said, fingers looping around the waistband of my leggings. He pulled them down slowly and continued to kiss down my stomach to my pussy. "I fucking love you, Allie, with my entire heart."

He pulled my pants off me and tore off his shirt, placing his hot mouth on my cunt and sucking my clit between his lips. I squirmed in his hold, but he sprawled a hand across my stomach to hold me still.

He continued to eat my pussy, dipping a finger into me and hitting my G-spot with ease. Pressure rose in my core, warmth exploding inside of me. I moaned out and tugged him back up to kiss him on the lips.

After positioning himself right at my entrance, he brushed some hair out of my face. "Tell me you love me back, Allie. Tell me that for these two years, you loved me too," he whispered, almost sounding desperate.

"I've loved you for so long, Jace," I admitted.

He thrust himself inside of me, rested his forehead against mine, kissed my lips softly and passionately. Hand wrapped around the front of my neck, he gently brushed his thumb across my jaw and pumped into me again.

My pussy tightened around him, and I lifted my lips a few inches again to meet his lips and kissed him harder this time. I wrapped my arms around his shoulders and pulled him closer to me, needing, wanting, and desiring to love him again.

At first, he thrust into me slowly, so I could feel every inch of him. I wrapped my legs around his torso and pulled him down closer to me. He leaned his forearms on the pillows and pressed his muscular abdomen against mine.

"Faster, Jace," I breathed, fluttering my eyes closed. "Please, harder."

"Oh fuck, baby," Jace groaned into my ear, thrusting harder.

I curled my toes, my legs shaking slightly, and dug my fingers into his back. He wrapped his arms around my torso, pulled us into a seated position, and kissed down my chest again, sucking one of my nipples into his mouth. Continuing to pump into me, he sucked on my breast and stared up into my eyes.

Tightening on him harder, I scratched my nails down his bare back, leaving dark red marks on it. With harder and faster and rougher thrusts, the pressure rose in my core until my legs were shaking around him.

"Come for me, baby," he mumbled against my breast, tugging on my nipple.

I moaned out, threw my head back, and came all over his cock. My body relaxed in his arms, wave after wave of pleasure rushing through me. He groaned against me, burying his head against my chest. His cock pulsed inside of me as I tightened willingly around him.

"I missed you, Jace," I admitted, brushing some hair out of his face. "I missed you so fucking much."

Chapter Thirty-Eight

ALLIE

Snow drifted down outside the window, the chilly air fogging up the corners of it. I shifted in Jace's bed to cuddle closer to him and to steal all his warmth because my feet were frozen.

"Get your cold-ass feet off me, Allie," Jace mumbled into my ear with that groggy morning voice I had missed oh-so-much. He gently nibbled on my ear, grasped some of my belly fat in his hand, then buried his nose into my hair. I went to push his hand away, but he moved it back almost instantly. "Go back to sleep. It's not even nine yet."

I sank into the mattress next to him, then snapped my eyes open. "Did you say nine?" I asked, shooting up in the bed. "It's Monday, Jace. We're late for school." I hurried out of the room to my bedroom, ripping apart my closet to find something to wear. "Oh God. Mr. Barnes is going to kill me."

A few moments later, Jace leaned against my doorframe in a pair of tight gray briefs, giving me that sinful little smirk and those dangerous brown eyes. He looked me up and down, eyes lingering on my ass.

I cut my eyes to him and clenched my jaw. "Get dressed. If you miss school, you can't go to practice tonight. And I need you to drive me there. I've already missed first period. If I miss Barnes's class, he'll slaughter my grade, especially after catching us fucking on his desk."

Instead of getting dressed, like I'd politely asked him to, he sauntered into my room, opened my drawer, and pulled out one of my plaid skirts. "Why don't you wear this and a pair of black stockings?" he asked.

"I'm not going to wear it just to satisfy your schoolgirl fantasies," I said, glaring at him, but feeling my lips about to curl up into a smile. I pointed to my glasses for emphasis. "These glasses aren't an accessory. I need them to see, not to be your little—"

"Slutty schoolgirl?" he asked, finishing my sentence. He stepped closer to me, fingers brushing up my bare thigh and curling around the hem of my underwear. "It doesn't make you all hot and bothered, knowing that it'll make me hard the entire day? I'll have to walk around Redwood, trying to hide my boner because I can't get you off my mind."

My nipples hardened under Jace's T-shirt, heart racing. I snatched the skirt from him and grumbled to myself that I would never wear this again for him even though I would wear whatever he asked as long as we were on good terms like this.

Jace Harbor always made me hot and bothered. It was my turn to do the same to him.

After pulling on a sweater, that damn plaid skirt, and a pair of thick black stockings—because it was nearly ten degrees Fahrenheit outside—I slid into Jace's Maserati and rested my backpack on my knees, scrolling through my phone at the tens of messages from Imani, threatening to kill me if I left her alone for the entire day.

Halfway into our drive, Jace placed his hand on my knee. I sucked in a sharp breath, staring at how his fingers curled around my thigh like they had so many times before. It was such a weird feeling to let him touch me so freely after two years of hating him.

Jace noticed my tenseness and pulled his hand away. "Sorry," he said, sneaking a glance over at me. Snow drifted down from the white sky around us as hot air blew through the vents toward me. "I just missed this."

I'd missed this too ... but I didn't know if I was ready to be full-on boyfriend and girlfriend yet. My heart still ached, and the thought of facing the entire student body after last Friday was making me anxious.

Jace pulled into the parking lot. Instead of waiting for Jace, I jumped out of the car and hurried toward the building. If I waited for him, he might try to hold my hand or something. And while I had wanted Jace Harbor to be mine again for so long, I had stupidly admitted to all of Redwood that I loved him. Everyone had witnessed him flirt with Nicole and reject me like it was nothing. I didn't want *any* attention on me today.

Maybe in a couple weeks, when I was more comfortable with us.

But now ... now, I just wanted to get through Mr. Barnes's class.

I slipped into the building and hurried down the corridor toward my locker. People glanced over at me as I rushed past them, whispering about Friday night. Heat crawled up my neck, and I stared down at the shiny floor and tried hard to make myself small and invisible.

"Aren't they, like ... brother and sister?"

"Why would Jace Harbor ever date someone like her? She's not even pretty."

"Does she really think that outfit looks good?"

"I heard he was at Nicole's Saturday night anyway. It's probably just rumors."

After telling myself that they didn't know shit about me, I found myself standing in front of my locker, trying to undo the lock with shaky hands. My stomach twisted and turned at their comments about me. I ... I wasn't the prettiest girl that Jace had been with, but I didn't think I was ugly.

Heat erupted through my entire body, and I pushed back the tears. It seemed like everything had been so raw these past few days, yet I refused to cry my eyes out in front of all of Redwood Academy.

When I finally got my locker open, more books than I owned tumbled out of it and onto the ground around me. Everyone really looked over at me now. I scrambled to pick the books up, not knowing where they had all come from. But some of them weren't books at all, but *Playboy* and *Mayfair* magazines and porn DVDs, with the word *Incest* in all of them.

My fingers shook as I picked them up and tried to stuff them into my locker before anyone could see. But people were crude as fuck and had already whipped out their phones to start recording the entire mess.

Once I got everything into my locker, I glanced up at the damn thick-as-hell ten-inch dildo suction-cupped to the inside of it. I pulled it off with a *pop*, hitting my hand against the other inside wall of my locker and letting a single tear fall from my eye.

Why were people so cruel? Who would fucking do this to me?

The first bell rang, and I tried to find my books for Barnes's class in the mess of magazines, DVDs, and now, a dildo. I shouldn't have even come to fucking school today. I should've stayed in bed with Jace and enjoyed the entire day with him, drinking hot chocolate and watching the snow fall outside his window.

Just as the second bell rang and I found my books, someone slammed my locker closed. I expected Jace to be standing behind it. But it was none other than Carter, the quarterback. And he was staring down at me with a smirk that told me he wanted to do more than just talk.

Chapter Thirty-Nine

ALLIE

"Your date with Jamal go good?" Carter asked, leaning against the locker and crossing his muscular arms over his chest. He sent me that smirk that all the other girls probably went nuts for. "You finally let him hit it after those soggy Saturday night fries?"

"Fuck you, Carter," I said through clenched teeth, opening my locker *again* to get the damn books that I had finally found out of it. I was going to be late for Mr. Barnes's class and get another period closer to Imani killing me for leaving her alone.

Carter glanced into the locker and pulled out the dildo. "You buy this because Jamal isn't big enough for you, baby?" He stepped closer to me and rested his hand on my shoulder, leaning in. "You wouldn't have to worry about that with me. I'd fill your tight little ass up until you screamed."

Turning around, I punched him square in the jaw. He stumbled back a bit, gently rubbing his face, and smirked.

"Feisty," he said, stepping back toward me again. "Just how I like them. You'd fucking learn to be a good little"—he placed a single finger on my thigh, beneath my skirt—"whor—"

Suddenly, he tensed, and Kai appeared behind him, sticking something against the back of his neck. "You fucking move your finger a fucking millimeter up her thigh, and you'll get a bullet in your skull."

Carter chuckled—like the fucking psychopath he was—and put his hands into the air. "You got me." He walked past us and down the hall, turning around to face me. "You want to get your world rocked, Allie? You know where to find me after school."

Kai stuffed his gun back into his waistband and scowled at his departing figure. "You're welcome," he said to me, like I owed him an apology.

All the Poison boys acted like they owned the world and that everyone owed them everything. I couldn't see how Imani could like them.

"Thanks," I said, finally retrieving the books out of my locker. "What do you want?"

"To talk," Kai said, looking back at me and leaning against the locker. "About Jace."

I arched a brow. "What about him?"

"He's hurt you for the past two years," Kai started. "Don't you think it's time for a little payback?"

"I don't have money to pay you to get Jace back for me," I said, not really wanting him to know that Jace and I were ... kinda, sorta a couple or thing again. I didn't really know what to call us, especially after this morning, when he'd placed his hand on my thigh and told me that he missed us.

"Free of charge, Allie," Kai said, sprawling a hand across his chest. "I'm doing this out of the goodness of my heart."

I snorted. "You and the rest of Poison don't have any goodness in your hearts."

"True, but I owed your dad a favor before he died. We'd be even after this."

"Why'd you owe my dad a favor?" I asked, crossing my arms.

"That's none of your business," Kai said, stuffing a hand into his pants pocket. "You want my help or not? I have some ways to torture Jace that you'd be interested in—rumors, embarrassing pictures, money you can donate to whatever kind of charity that you want, and some other stuff that can't be discussed on school grounds."

I slapped my hand against his chest. "How about you take all the porno magazines, DVDs, and the dildo out of my locker, and we'll call it even?" I asked, not wanting him to fuck with Jace anymore. He had been through hell and back already.

Kai arched his brow, a smirk crossing his face, as if I had given him permission to do something terrible to Jace. "Deal."

Walking into the cafeteria, I tried to ignore the stares from the entire student body. Everyone had seen the pictures of me with the dildo and those porno magazines at my locker. And everyone— even the damn teachers—were talking about me confessing my undying love for my stepbrother on Friday night.

I kept my gaze low and made a beeline for the nerd table. Poison sat in their usual corner, staring over at me as I walked in. Kai arched a brow at me and slightly nodded toward the football table, where Jace had to be sitting. After peeking a glance at it, I saw Jace sitting next to one of his teammates on one side and an empty seat on the other.

When he made eye contact with me, I turned away and sat across from Imani, who leaned forward.

"Do you want to eat in the library?" she asked me. "People are pissing me the fuck off with those pictures of you. I don't want you to feel like we have to sit here."

Before I could say two words, Jamal sat next to Imani and gave me a half-smile. "Don't listen to them, Allie. They're immature fucking brats. I'll find out who stuffed all that shit in there."

Imani gave him a side-eye at how close he was to her and scooted an inch to her left. "Yeah, don't listen to them. They mean nothing anyway. They're not going anywhere in life, and they will stay in Redwood for the rest of their lives, especially Nicole."

"Fuck that bitch," Jamal and Imani said at the same time.

Imani gave Jamal another stink eye, then continued to eat her sandwich. I sank in my seat, shoulders slumping forward as I tried to make myself small again. Everyone was staring. Every-fucking-one. Even Nicole and Jenny and some of the nerdy kids on the debate team.

I peeked a glance at the football table to find Jace suddenly gone. Someone sat down beside me, placing their lunch on the table and their hand on my knee.

"I saved a seat for you," Jace said.

Almost instinctively, I pushed his hand away and stared at Imani. She had her eyes narrowed at me in a death glare. Even Jamal looked surprised that Jace had come to the Outcast Table and was eating with us as the entire school looked on.

After the whispers finally died down, Imani cleared her throat. "So, Allie, where were you this morning? And what happened between you and Mr. Barnes? He couldn't make eye contact with you all class."

I shifted uncomfortably in my seat and glanced at Jace. "We, um, woke up late."

Imani grabbed my wrist. "Okay, we need to talk," she said, dragging me away from the table and the boys. When we were far enough away, she slapped my chest. "What the hell?" she whisper-yelled. "I thought you weren't getting back together with Jace. What happened to 'I hate him with all my heart. He's a dickhead. He deserves to die'?"

Glancing back over at the table, I noticed Jace smiling at me. I didn't know how I wanted us to be in school. I wanted him, and I didn't want to hide it anymore ... but those rumors and those pranks and all that shit this morning had almost been too much.

"He had a reason," I admitted, "for doing everything that he did to me."

Imani scrunched her nose. "Come on. Are you seriously going to believe him? He's a player, and everyone knows it."

I grabbed Imani's hand and squeezed it hard. "I can't tell you what it is, but I can promise you that I'm not being stupid ..." At least, I hoped I wasn't. "Jace has been through so much. I ... I still love him. I always will."

"Just know that if he fucking hurts you again, I will get Poison on his ass to kill him," Imani threatened, glancing over at Poison.

Landon smirked at her and blew her a fucking kiss.

"You know that they would too. They hate rich, bratty kids like him."

I held out my pinkie and let her curl hers around mine. "Deal. If Jace breaks my heart again, you can get Poison on his ass," I said, letting out a chuckle. "Make them do anything that they want to do to him. Kai has some ideas."

Chapter Forty

JACE

As I opened my locker after football practice, porno magazines and a huge purple dildo fell out of it and onto the locker room ground in front of all my teammates. The room erupted into a fit of laughter, dickhead comments being thrown my way.

"You having fun with that cock, Harbor?"

"Who's been using that on you?"

"Do you like Allie pegging your ass?"

I rolled my eyes, picked up the dildo between two fingers, and suctioned it to Carter's locker. Screw that fucking guy. He was probably the one who had put it in Allie's locker this morning. Whoever had, I was about to beat their ass in. Pictures had been circulating around all of Redwood's social media with Allie in tears as she picked up all the stuff from the floor before putting it back in her locker.

After I threw magazines into the trash and walked back to my locker, Jamal nudged me. "We need to talk." He leaned close and glanced at Carter, who walked into the room and saw the dildo stuck to his locker. "It's about Carter."

I snickered as he pulled it off with a pop and gave me the finger.

"You suggesting something, Harbor?" he asked me, grabbing his cock through his football tights. "You want it?"

The other guys laughed and shook their heads. I rolled my eyes and turned back to my locker.

Jamal nudged me again. "Come on, dude. It's important. You should—"

"Why the fuck should I listen to you?" I asked him, slamming my locker closed. "You tried to fucking take Allie from me over and over, knowing how I felt about her. I heard that you fucking took her home Saturday night."

The blood drained from his face, but he quickly shook his head. "We didn't do anything," he said. "I promise that we didn't. We went out to get fries, and Carter showed up and—"

"She stayed over at your fucking house," I repeated, having heard a rumor about it after lunch.

It fucked me up that they had been together, but I couldn't get angry with Allie about it since I had been out with Nicole. Jamal though ... my best fucking friend?

I pushed him. "Did she sleep in your bed too? Huh? You don't have an extra one for her to sleep in."

Jamal grabbed me by the collar. "Will you fucking settle down?" he asked me, pushing me against the locker. "Fucking listen to me. Carter was being a dick to Allie when we saw him out. He wanted to take her home, and a rumor is going around that Carter was hitting on Allie this morning, had his fingers up her skirt."

I shoved Jamal off me. "You're fucking lying."

"Ask him," Jamal said.

I turned to Carter, who was stripping off his sweat-soaked shirt. "You touched Allie?" I asked.

He turned his head and curled his lip up slightly. "What's it to you?"

Rage rushed through my entire body as I sprang forward at him. Jamal tried to hold me back, but I slipped out of his hold and slammed my fist right across that pretty fucking face of Carter, hearing a crack.

"You won't be able to keep her all to yourself," Carter said, pushing me back. "She actually wants to be pleased. You think Nicole left you because you could fuck her right? She let me eat her tight cunt because you couldn't make her come, just like Allie will soon—"

I slammed my fist into him again, knocking him down. After straddling his waist, I continued to rain punches down onto his face, relishing in the blood that spurted out of his nose, the way his eyes already turned black and swelled, all of the pain written across his features. Jamal and another teammate grabbed my shoulders to pull me back, but I wasn't going anywhere.

I would kill Carter, just like he fucking deserved. I wanted him dead and away from Allie. He deserved to rot in the worst shithole there was.

Coach blew his whistle. Everyone backed away from us, creating a path for him to walk through. Carter shielded his face with his arms as Coach and one of his defensive coaches grabbed my arms, tugging me off the piece of shit.

"Settle down," Coach said, getting in my face. "What the fuck are you doing?"

"Fucking piece of shit," I said, spitting down at Carter as some guys helped him stand.

Coach placed a hand on my chest to push me against the lockers. Overcome with so much pain and hurt and pure rage, I glared at Carter. I'd find a fucking way to destroy his life one of these fucking days.

"Look at me, Jace," Coach shouted.

The entire room went silent and stared at us, even Carter.

"Cut the shit and leave your fucking differences off the field and out of my locker room. I don't give a fuck what Carter said to you. You should control yourself." A look of hurt crossed Coach's face. "You sit out the next game, Harbor."

"He fucking—"

"You want to make it two games?" Coach asked me.

I pressed my lips together. "No, sir."

He pointed to the door. "Get out of here and cool down."

I snatched up the rest of my things and hurried out of the room, forgoing any good-bye to Jamal or the rest of the team. Carter smirked at me on the way out, holding an ice pack to his eye. He fucking deserved it.

Chapter Forty-One

ALLIE

"So, how do you like them?" the associate at All Your Eye Needs asked me after school.

I stared at myself in one of their mirrors and scrunched my nose at my new glasses. I had vowed to try to switch things up and take care of myself for once, so I switched from semi-rimless square frames to circle ones.

My eyesight had been getting worse this past year, and I had been saving up money to buy new glasses for the past six months because I refused to use Harlan's money, especially after Jace had told me that Harlan had a dark past. I just hoped to God that he didn't hurt Mom.

"Can I have a minute alone?" I asked, wanting to hold in my disappointment until he left.

The man nodded and walked toward his desk. I gnawed on the inside of my lip and inched closer to the mirror. I'd had those square frames for almost four years now. Something this dramatic wasn't what I was going for. Hell, when I had picked them out a couple days ago, I'd thought they looked fine, but now, I was regretting everything.

My phone buzzed in my pocket, and I pulled it out. "Hello?"

"Where are you?" Jace asked. "You weren't at the field. We need to talk."

"I'm at the mall, getting new glasses."

Jace paused. "Did you walk? I would've brought you if you—"

"No, I didn't walk. Imani brought me, but she had to leave."

"I'll be there—"

"You look beautiful in them!" the associate said, walking back to me and staring me down in the mirror.

This man must've *wanted* me out of the store as soon as possible or something. He probably knew that a young girl with a damn hole in her sweater wouldn't be spending any more of her money here and didn't want the brand of the store to depreciate with me standing next to the hundreds of dollars' worth of merchandise.

"Who is that?" Jace asked, an edginess to his voice. He almost sounded ... jealous.

It made me warm and giddy on the inside.

"Nobody," I said with a smile. "Better get here before any guy tries to pick me up."

Before he could respond, I hung the phone up and stuffed it into my pocket. "These are good," I said to the associate, taking the glasses off, setting them back in their case, and putting on my old ones. "Thanks. I don't need them readjusted. I'll be leaving now."

So, you don't have to worry about all the billionaires in Redwood not coming into your store because a homeless-looking kid raised on the other side of town wanted to see better.

Walking back through the mall to the exit, I rubbed my sweaty palms together. As soon as Jace pulled up, I would be out of here because I didn't want him coming in and walking around with me. I'd barely survived lunch today when he sat next to me. I really wouldn't be able to survive the constant stares as Jace and I shopped together.

"Waiting for me?" Jace asked, wrapping his arms around me from behind and stuffing his face into my neck.

I tensed up and stepped away from him, heart racing inside my chest. He stood there, brows furrowed together and looking sad that I had pulled away from him.

"Where did you come from?" I asked.

"Entrance on the other side of the mall," he said, hiking his thumb back toward the shops. He furrowed his brows harder. "Where are your glasses? I thought you were getting new ones?"

I gnawed on the inside of my lip and glanced down at the case in my hand. "I did."

"And ... you're not wearing them?"

My cheeks flushed. I didn't want him to feel bad for me. I had spent all the money I'd saved to buy new glasses, only to be disappointed in the way they looked on me. I couldn't return them, and I didn't have any more cash to buy new ones.

"I, um ... I think they look kinda weird on me."

Jace reached for them. "Let me see them on you."

Some people from school walked by us and waved at Jace. I pressed my lips together and looked down at my toes, stepping farther away from him so it wouldn't seem like we were a couple. I wanted to be with him again more than anything, but I wanted to be cautious and didn't want to run into this blindly.

"No, Jace. Not now."

"Come on, Allie. Who cares what they look like? You need them to see."

I glanced up into his big brown eyes and opened the case. "Okay," I whispered.

I pulled out the glasses, my stomach tightening with nerves, and took off my old ones. After promising myself that I wouldn't cry because of how bad I thought they looked, I pushed them onto my face and peered up at Jace.

With a big, goofy grin, Jace grabbed my chin in his hand to pull me closer and pinched my cheeks until my mouth formed a lopsided *O*. He pressed his lips to mine. "You look so"—wet kiss on my jaw—"fucking"—wet kiss on my neck—"cute.."

Cheeks flushing red, I gazed up at him. "You really think so?" I asked, my stomach filling with butterflies and tingles. "I just ... I don't think I'm used to them yet."

Jace grabbed my old glasses and put them into the case, stuffing them into his back pocket. "Well, get used to them because they're adorable, Allie." He smiled down at me, his eyes big and wide and filled with ... love, like they used to be. He scooped my hand in his and pulled me toward all the shops. "Come on. Let's buy you some winter clothes and a raincoat. All yours are too thin."

Lost in thought and all these little gooey feelings, I forgot all about me wanting to keep my distance from him until I noticed people from Redwood looking over at us as we walked by them. I pulled my hand out of Jace's hand and stuffed them into my pockets, ignoring the heartbreaking glance he gave me.

I walked toward Forever 21, something simple and cheap because I knew Jace would want to pay and I didn't want him to waste his money on me. But he shook his head and continued walking past it toward higher-end boutiques that cost a fortune for damn socks.

"Jace," I said, grabbing his bicep.

He tensed under my touch, sucking in a breath, and then looked down at me quizzically.

"These stores are expensive, and I don't have any money left. Let's go to—"

"No."

"But, Jace—"

"No. *I'm* taking you shopping, and *I'm* paying."

"Jace ..."

Jace tilted his head and stared down at me. "Allie ..."

I slapped him on the chest for mocking me and glanced into one of the many shops, where the salespeople were dressed in their finest attire and were waiting to pounce on the first customer that walked into the store.

Jace went to wrap his arm around my shoulders, then stopped and stuffed his hands into his pockets. "How about I take you shopping and then we go out to eat?"

After trying to suppress a smile and pretty much failing, I glanced up at him. "Like a date?"

Jace gulped and cracked a smile. "A date."

Chapter Forty-Two

JACE

After I convinced Allie to let me buy her winter clothes, I took her out to her favorite restaurant from sophomore year—Mustang Ranch. License plates on the walls, '90s music on the stereo, and burgers the size of my fist, Mustang Ranch hadn't changed one bit.

"I haven't been here in so long!" Allie said, sliding into the red booth. "It's too far away from Redwood to walk, and Imani hates burgers this big. I think the last time I came here was ... with you." Allie opened the menu and glanced up at me. "When was the last time you were here?"

I grasped the menu in my hands and told myself not to fuck this up.

"Sophomore year," I admitted, nervously looking back up at her.

What was wrong with me today? Allie had never made me this nervous before, but ... that had been when I wanted her to loathe me. Now, I wanted her to love me again. I had waited two entire years for this moment—to be able to bring Allie out on dates again. If I said or did the wrong thing, I could lose her for good.

Through those cute-as-fuck, new circular-framed glasses, she stared at me with wide eyes. "You haven't been back here since we stopped dating?" she asked in disbelief. "You didn't bring Jenny or Nicole or anyone else here?"

A wave of disappointment washed through me, and I slumped my shoulders forward. I had screwed Allie up so much by bringing Nicole to the Overlook that Allie didn't trust me not to spoil any of our other places. It had shown in the way she didn't want me to touch her at the mall, the way she'd kept pulling away and walking a few steps ahead.

Those little rejections fucking hurt me bad. But not as bad as I must've hurt her.

"This is your favorite restaurant," I said to Allie, placing the menu down and leaning forward.

I glanced at her hand, wanting to wrap it up in mine but then thought against it. When she noticed me looking, she didn't pull her hand away but instead inched it closer a few millimeters, as if she wanted me to take it but didn't have the courage to ask.

I placed my hand inches from hers and smiled. "I was a dick, but I didn't ruin every one of our places. I promise."

Her chin trembled slightly as tears filled her eyes. "I love you," she whispered, so low that I almost didn't hear it. "I want to pretend like nothing happened and go back to the way things were before, but ... I can't forget, no matter how hard I try. I'm so nervous that you're going to hurt me again and leave me." More tears raced down her cheeks. "I want to be with you so bad that it hurts."

I gulped down the lump in my throat and brushed her tears away. "Take your time, Allie," I whispered, tucking some hair behind her ear. "I can wait until you feel comfortable. I know it's going to take time."

To my surprise, Allie placed her hand on mine and interlocked her fingers with mine. She pulled it away from her face and kissed my thumb, smiling against it. She stayed quiet for a few moments, then sat up taller and leaned forward, trying to let go of the pain with a forced smile and a different conversation.

"So, um … I heard from Kai that *you* were hiding a dildo in your football locker," she teased.

Of course it was fucking Kai who had embarrassed me in front of the entire damn football team. But if that was his payback, I'd be fine because Poison did some pretty fucked up shit. This was an easy punishment.

My lips curled into a smile, and I decided to go along with it. "Was it big enough for you?" I asked, sending her a wink. "Thought we could test it out. Let you put it in your tight little pussy, like I'd promised, and make you watch me take you from behind."

Allie scrunched her nose. "Gross. I don't know where that thing has been. For all I know, Carter could've put it in his ass, then stuffed it in my locker along with all the other shit I found in there." She shivered. "I wouldn't put it past him."

I tensed at the sound of his name and pushed my shoulders back. "You need to stay away from him and *tell* me the next time he tries to talk to you. He's not fucking sane, Allie, and I don't want to hear from *Jamal* that Carter was flirting with you."

All the blood drained from her face, yet she shook her head. "He's just being a dick, like the rest of the guys on the football team. I can handle him, Jace. He's not your problem."

"Everything you do is my problem. I have to protect you."

It was what I had been doing for years now. Just because I had football and Dad to worry about didn't mean I could stop trying to protect her from other stupid-ass people, like Carter, who wouldn't stop talking about her at practice.

Allie rolled her eyes. "Come on, Jace. If anything happens, I can talk to Kai about it. You need to focus on your dad and football. Don't let Carter get you kicked off the team during your senior year."

I glanced down at the menu in front of me and drew circles on the table with my finger.

Allie tensed. "Oh my God. Please don't tell me that you already got kicked off."

I clenched my jaw and tightened my hand into a fist. If Coach had let me fucking finish him, I would've been happily kicked off the team. Nobody touched Allie without her permission, and nobody flirted with my girl, especially not a dick like him.

Allie smacked my chest from across the table and shook her head. "Jace!"

"I didn't get kicked off the team," I said.

She sighed in relief. Despite all the rage and anger I felt for Carter right now, I actually smiled. Allie cared so much about me playing football. Even when we hadn't been speaking, even when it was negative two degrees Fahrenheit outside, she showed up for my games and cheered on Redwood.

Dad refused to even think about me playing football, and Mom ... well, she had only come to my games to fuck around with the peewee coach in the restroom. But Allie had always been there for me. *Always.*

"Earth to Jace," Allie said, waving a hand in front of my face. "What the hell happened, and why do you have that goofy grin on your face again?"

I shook my head and wiped the grin off my face because *this* was nothing to be happy about. Carter—Redwood's *finest* quarterback—had gotten me kicked off the field for the next game.

"Coach told me I'm sitting out Friday's game," I said.

"Because of Carter?" Allie asked with wide eyes. "What'd you do to him?"

"Nothing."

"Jace!" She playfully kicked me under the table. "What'd you do?"

"I just talked to him, Allie."

I should've done a lot fucking more than give him a few good hits. But the entire school, the principal, and the police chief would be watching my every move these next few weeks. I couldn't risk getting thrown out of Redwood now that I had everything I needed to bring Dad down.

I'd have to get Poison to do my dirty work, and they'd deliver the finest results.

Chapter Forty-Three

ALLIE

"On your next exam, you will be asked about the differences between mitosis and meiosis, so I suggest that all of you go home and study this weekend. This will be one of the hardest exams of the semester," Mr. Barnes said and stared down all the students in his class like a fucking hawk.

The entire class stayed quiet, giving him slight nods. To say that everyone in Redwood was terrified of his exams was an understatement. People tried hard to avoid Mr. Barnes's class if they could because that man had it out for the entire student population.

"Did you see Carter's face?" Jenny whispered behind me to her friend.

"Someone fucked him up bad," another student whispered.

Imani leaned closer to me. "Have *you* seen him yet? I heard he looks like shit."

I swallowed hard and shook my head. Jace had told me he *talked* to Carter, but I highly doubted it. For Coach to sit him out, there must have been some kind of fight. Coach knew that they probably wouldn't win without Jace in the game. It had to be bad.

"No," I said. "I'm too nervous."

Mr. Barnes cleared his throat and narrowed his eyes at me. "Do you have a question?"

Jenny and the other student smacked their lips closed and looked at me, as if I were the only one who had been talking during the lecture.

I shook my head and took one for the entire Biology class. "No, sir."

After Mr. Barnes grimaced and looked away, I slumped down in my seat, thankful that he hadn't called me out. I couldn't deal with more drama this week. Between Jace and Carter and Kai yesterday, I wanted one peaceful day in this hellhole town.

"Class is dismissed. Allie, stay behind. We need to chat."

All the blood drained from my face. This was the first time since Mr. Barnes had caught Jace and me in his classroom that he had spoken my name or even looked in my direction. If he was going to start something about it, I didn't know what the hell I was going to do.

Everyone started packing up their materials.

Imani glanced over at me. "What's that all about?" she asked, taking off her reading glasses and placing them into her case.

I envied her that she only had to wear them for reading and wasn't as blind as I was when it came to seeing things mere feet in front of me.

"I don't know," I said, gathering my belongings and walking up to Mr. Barnes's desk. "I'll meet you in the hall."

Mr. Barnes waited until all the other students were out of class and the door was closed. I hugged my books to my chest and shifted uncomfortably back and forth on my feet. He sat at his *new* desk and handed me an envelope.

"What's this?" I asked, voice barely above a whisper.

"The letter of recommendation that you requested for your

scholarship, not that you actually need one, seeing who your mother married, but—"

"You actually wrote one for me?" I asked with wide eyes.

"Of course I did. You're the most hardworking, driven, and intelligent Biology student I have seen in my twenty-two years of working here. And before you ask, there is nothing in that letter about what I"—he cleared his throat—"walked in on the other week."

My lips curled into a smile, and I clutched the letter to my chest. After thanking him, I walked out of the class to find Imani gawking at someone across the hall. With piercing blue eyes, a sharp jaw, and a shirt that looked a size too big for his scrawny body, a guy was trying to push the key into a classroom diagonal from us.

"Who is that?" I asked, brows furrowed.

"A new professor," she said, squinting at the door. "Computer Science, it looks like."

"Doesn't Mrs. Goldman teach Computer Science?"

Imani looped her arm around mine and began walking down Redwood's halls. "Mrs. Goldman got caught hacking into some of her students' parents' computers and accounts," Imani said, shaking her head. "She had been taking money from them. I think she stole almost a half-billion dollars."

My eyes widened. "What?! When did this happen?"

"Last week. You've been too preoccupied with your stepbrother's cock to listen to the gossip, it seems."

I cut my eyes to her, and she laughed.

"What? It's true, isn't it? You guys have been sleeping together for weeks now." She playfully narrowed her eyes at me. "I don't approve of the man after what he did to you, but you can't keep something *that good* from me. I picked up on it."

Since our lockers were right across the hall from each other's, I stopped at hers and leaned against it. "So ... you talk to the Poison boys lately?" I asked, arching a brow at her. "If you want the gossip about me and Jace, you gotta give me some juicy details about your life."

Imani bit her lip and glanced down the hall toward Landon, who was leaning against his locker and talking to Kai. I glanced their way, feeling giddy for Imani. Those boys were nothing but bad news, yet ... I knew Imani wouldn't be able to stay away.

The good girl always ran to the bad boy—or *boys*, in Imani's case—who would break her heart.

It was damn close to the oldest cliché, but it was one hundred percent true.

"So, they're kinda, um, blackmailing me," she whispered, rubbing the front of her neck.

"What?!" I said.

A couple people looked over, including Landon and Kai.

Imani placed her hand over my mouth. "Don't yell about it!" When she thought I wouldn't say anything else, she removed her hand and tucked some curly black hair behind her ear. "Long story short, they found out about ... my freaky side and—"

I snorted. "Your freaky side?"

Imani grinned at me. "Okay, don't judge me, Ms. I Love Having Public Sex with My Stepbrother after He Fucked Me Over." She gestured up and down her body. "A girl has needs, and ya girl is a freak."

"Who's a freak?" Jamal said, walking up to us.

Imani rolled her eyes and closed her locker. "Allie, but you'll never find that out."

Jamal held a hand to his chest. "Ooh, that hurt. That was mean. Goddamn."

Imani smirked but then dropped the smile when she gazed behind us. "Oh God. I think I know why everyone has been gossiping about Carter today. He looks like he got run over by a fucking train."

I swallowed my fear and turned around to see Carter standing at his locker with two eyes almost swollen shut and large bruises down the side of his face and his neck.

My eyes widened as he made eye contact with me and mouthed the words, *This is your fault, bitch.*

And part of me actually feared for my life because Carter hadn't had a problem with touching me before. He really wouldn't have a problem with really trying to hurt me now that Jace had beaten him to a pulp.

Chapter Forty-Four

JACE

"I can't even practice?" I asked Coach.

Sure, he could sit me out during the game on Friday, but I still wanted to get out onto the field, help my team, and work on my skills. If I was going to Michigan for football, I needed to be ready. I didn't want to sit around and do nothing.

Coach placed a hand on my shoulder and ushered me to the sidelines. "You need to relax and take some time off. I understand what you're going through, and I heard the other side of the story from Jamal after you stormed off yesterday. But the principal and everyone in Redwood are watching you. If you screw up out here in the open, I can't hide it for you. And I can't lie to the principal if Carter get his parents involved for you hitting him. You understand me?"

I clenched my jaw and growled to myself. I understood, but that didn't mean I liked it.

Coach nodded to Allie, who sat on the bleachers in the freezing cold. "Why don't you go spend time with her?" He cracked a smile. "Word around town is that you took my advice, stopped being an ass, and are back together with her. Is that right?"

My lips curled into a soft smile. "Yeah, it is."

"I'm proud of you," he said, making me smile even harder. "Take some time off. We'll be here on Friday night. Don't be late for the game. I need you to help me coach."

After grabbing my bag, I jogged past Carter toward the bleachers and tried hard not to lose my cool. Instead of making a huge deal out of what had happened, like I'd thought he would, he had been awfully quiet at school today about the fight.

"Allie," I shouted from the sidelines. "Come on. We're going home."

Stuffed in her new winter coat that seemed to swallow her body, she bounced up on her toes and hurried down the metal steps. "Already? You didn't even practice."

"It doesn't matter. Now, come on."

When she stepped off the bleachers, I wanted to reach for her hand more than anything. But she kept her hands stuffed into her pockets and was staring down at the ground all the way to my Maserati. I opened the door for her and watched her slide into the car.

"Did Carter talk to you today?" I asked on the ride home.

"No," she said, rubbing her hands together. "But ... he makes me nervous."

"What'd he do?" I asked her, grasping the steering wheel.

"Nothing yet, but you were right. He's unstable."

After clutching the steering wheel even harder, I growled and pulled into our driveway. A sleek black car with tinted windows was parked in front of the house. Just the people I needed to see, though I didn't quite know why they were here.

"What's Poison doing here?" Allie asked.

"I don't know," I said, stepping out of the car.

Poison got out of their car and nodded to the front door,

wanting me to let them in. I blew a breath out of my nose, snatched Allie's hand, and ushered her inside.

"What do you want?"

Allie rocked back on her heels, standing behind me and staring between the three of them. She crossed her arms and glanced at Kai. "Before you leave, I need to talk to you," she said to him, then disappeared into the living room.

"You have a problem," João said.

"*Me?*" I asked.

"Nicole's father found out about the missing evidence," Landon said, crossing his arms over his chest. "He doesn't know who did it, but he knows that it was sometime between Friday night and Tuesday morning."

I tensed and glanced into the living room. If he found out that it was me and Poison, he'd throw us in jail or do something much, much worse to hurt me, like fuck with Allie and all the opportunities that she had worked so hard for.

"Since it wasn't only your mother's case that was stolen, he can't pinpoint who it was. It could literally be anyone. Nicole has so many people over at her house all the time. The cheerleaders, football players, even some nobodies that she likes sleeping with. But he knows that it's gone."

"If you don't want Allie hurt, you'd better have a plan to come out with it all," Kai said to me, following my gaze into the living room. "Soon."

I ran a hand over my face and groaned internally. "I need more time. I'm not ready. I don't have everything I need or the people I need to get this information out. Once I release it, all of Redwood is going to rally behind my father's back, and you fucking know it."

João smirked and pulled a pack of cigarettes out of his back pocket, lighting one up. "Not if all of Redwood's richest burn with him," he said. "We have the information to blackmail and destroy some of the most prestigious families. They can't defend anyone else when their reputations are on the line."

"You want to blackmail all of Redwood?" I asked.

It was a brilliant idea if it worked, but a stupid one if it failed.

João blew out a puff of smoke. "Redwood billionaires have treated the poor like we're trash for the past hundred years. I know you would never understand that, as your daddy has given you everything, but it's fucking time we push back. Fuck the billionaires. I want to watch them desperately grasp on to their hope as we crush them under our fucking boots."

I rubbed my forehead and cursed. This had been coming for years now. I just hadn't thought I'd ever take part in it. The Redwood rich had always been too corrupt for their own good.

"Are you in?" João asked.

I ran my tongue against the front of my teeth. This was beyond risky, but if it helped me put that man behind bars or in the ground, where he deserved to be, then I would do it. I would do anything to destroy the man who had ruined my entire life.

"Once you take care of Carter for me, I'm in."

Chapter Forty-Five

ALLIE

After I hammered into Kai, because I was way more comfortable with him than the others, about blackmailing Imani—to which he snarkily replied that he didn't know what I was talking about—I left Jace and Poison in the living room and strolled into the kitchen, grabbing some strawberries from the fridge.

Once Jace showed Poison out, he eyed me through the kitchen door from the living room.

I hummed and popped a strawberry in my mouth. "Mom and your dad are coming home today."

Jace placed his phone down on the coffee table and appeared at the kitchen door, giving me those dangerously sultry eyes. Sauntering over to me, he trapped me between the kitchen island and him and chuckled down at me. "If you think that's going to stop me from coming inside you today, you're wrong," he said, drawing his fingers against the front of my skirt.

He cupped the mound of my pussy in his hand and rested his fingers right over my wetness. I tensed at his possessive, dominant touch and bit my lip, glancing up at him through my glasses. Jace had been so careful these past couple days not to touch me in any way that I didn't want.

But now, I wanted it. More than anything.

"You don't want them to find out that my stepbrother has been touching me, do you?" I innocently asked him, batting my lashes. It would drive him crazy, absolutely insane, just how I loved him.

He grabbed a fistful of my hair, making me squeal, and pulled my head back. "I do what I want with you, Allie," he murmured against my neck. "You should know this by now. They won't find out about us, and you won't tell them."

"And if I do?"

"Then, you'd be the slut I always thought you were. Telling everyone that your own stepbrother fucks you to sleep every night. That you enjoy watching his cum spill out of this tight"—he rubbed his fingers over my clit—"little"—harder—"pussy."

I seized his hand to yank him off.

"Let go," he said.

Almost immediately, I dropped my hand as my nipples hardened under my shirt.

"Take off your shirt. Let me see your tits."

"No," I said, giving him my most defiant look. "I don't want—"

After he captured both my nipples between his fingers and squeezed harshly, I yelped out and grasped his wrists. Yet he tugged on them even harder and pulled them toward the ground. I stumbled onto the hardwood floor and landed on my hands and knees.

"That's what I like to see," Jace said, still squeezing my nipples.

"Please, let go," I pleaded.

"Are you going to take off your shirt?"

After a few moments, I nodded. When he released me, I rubbed them gently and then pulled my shirt over my head, my tits bouncing out of it. Jace unbuttoned his pants, pulled out his cock, and smacked it right across my cheek.

"Open your mouth," he demanded.

I sat back on my knees as my skirt rode up my legs.

He slapped his cock against my cheek again, making me flinch. "Open your fucking mouth."

When I refused to open my mouth, he smacked me across the cheek. I snatched my jaw, let out a moan, and pressed my legs together. Warmth spread throughout my core. I parted my lips slightly, and Jace shoved himself into my mouth.

He thrust his dick all the way down my tight throat until his balls were pressed against my lips. I gagged on him, my eyes teary. And then he forced more of himself into me, resting his balls against my tongue. I placed my hands on his thighs to push him away, but he held me tighter to him. Spit and drool dripped down my chin and onto my tits, making them glisten.

My gags turned into raspy gargles, and he pinched my nose closed, so I couldn't breathe. I pushed a hand between my legs to touch my pussy, getting it wet and ready for his cock to slide into me because this felt too good—too fucking good.

"Jerk off your stepbrother, Allie," he said down at me, outlining his cock in my throat with his finger.

When I refused, knowing that it would piss him off, he slapped me harder across the face. I whimpered and reluctantly wrapped my hand around my throat to jerk him off while bobbing my head back and forth on his cock.

The doorknob jingled in the foyer, and Jace pushed me behind the kitchen island, where no one could see me. Instead of pulling out of my mouth like a normal human being would, Jace thrust in and out of me wildly until I couldn't breathe. When he finally pulled out, I doubled over onto my hands and knees, coughing up spit. I gasped for breath, my breasts swaying.

Jace rested his hands on the counter and leaned over it, acting as if nothing was happening. "Put my cock back into your mouth."

"Jace, we ca—"

He snatched my nipples between his fingers again before our parents could come into the room, and I squealed. I sat up and took his cock back into my mouth, staring up at him with nervous, wide eyes. He wrapped a hand into my hair and held me down.

Our parents walked into the kitchen, dragging their luggage behind them.

"Jace," Mom said. "Glad to see you again. Where's Allie?"

He thrust his hips against me, and I tried to suppress my soft gagging. "Out with friends," Jace said, his cock so fucking deep inside me that it hurt.

All I wanted was for him to be buried this deep inside my pussy, fucking me until I could barely stand.

"Well, sweetie, we need to shower, but we'll be back out to tell you all about our trip!" Mom clapped her hands together and hurried up the stairs.

Harlan gave a grunt and seemed to follow her.

When they were gone, Jace pulled out of me, picked me up, and set me on the kitchen island. He yanked up the bottom of my skirt and rubbed his fingers against my wet panties.

"Jace, we can't do this here!" I said, scrambling to back away. I pushed my knees together, my face flushed.

Yet Jace showed no signs of stopping.

Instead, he kneeled in front of me, pulled down my panties, and pressed his lips to my clit. I gripped the edge of the island, digging my nails into the granite. His tongue moved in circles around my clit, and he pushed my legs apart even farther, devouring what was his.

He pushed a finger inside of me, then another, and I clenched around him. My pussy felt so good, being filled by him, and I couldn't wait to let him fill my pussy with cum.

After spitting on my clit and letting it drip down my mound to my entrance, Jace stood up and rubbed the head of his cock against my tight hole. "Make sure you keep your legs spread for me," he said, wrapping his hand around the front of my throat and staring down at my tits as he pushed the head of his cock into my wetness.

As my pussy clenched even harder around his head, he rubbed his thumb over my clit. I dug my nails into his chest and furrowed my brows.

"Jace, please," I whispered. "Please."

"Please what?" he mumbled against my ear, holding back a groan.

"Please, put your cock inside of me," I said.

He rubbed my clit faster, and I moaned.

"Please."

Jace dug his teeth into my shoulder, biting lightly to keep from groaning out loud. And then he thrust himself deep inside of me. I threw my head back and slapped a hand over my mouth, moaning into it.

"Harder," I breathed, lips parted in delight.

He pushed his fingers into my mouth and slammed into me harder, burying his dick as deep as it would go. "I have so much control over you, Allie," he murmured, thrusting harder into me. "I can make you scream so fucking loud with our parents upstairs."

He smacked me on the cheek, and I let a moan slip out of my mouth. Then, he smacked me again and again and again until I was about to explode around him. Teetering on the brink of an orgasm, I whimpered in an attempt to stop myself from screaming.

"Beg me not to come inside of you," he said.

"Jace," I said softly, my pussy clenching around him. "Please, don't come inside of me. I-I didn't take my pill this morning."

He pumped in and out of me harder, wrapping both his hands

around my throat. I shook my head, fear racing through my body at the thought of forgetting to take the pill. I had been so preoccupied lately.

"No, Jace, I-I'm being serious. I—"

I threw my head back, wave after wave of pleasure rushing through me.

Jace stilled in my pussy, his cock so deep inside of me that he was nearly pressing against my cervix, letting all his cum shoot up into me. When he pulled out, his cum dripped out and coated my pussy lips, showing me that I was his to play with whenever and wherever he wanted.

"Put your clothes back on before they come back down," Jace said, buckling his belt.

I hopped off the counter as his cum ran down my thighs, put on my clothes, and wrapped my hand around his. Jace glanced down at our hands and smiled, lightly grasping my face with his free hand and rubbing my red cheek, where he had slapped me.

"Can you take me to the pharmacy?" I asked.

Instead of nodding his head, Jace looked down at my stomach and then back at me. He clenched his jaw, as if he wanted to say something, wanted to *refuse* to take me, but then he squeezed my hand tighter and said, "Sure. I'll take you *this time.*"

Chapter Forty-Six

JACE

Did I want to see Allie pregnant with my child? Fuck yes. Maybe three or four or even five of them one day? Nothing turned me on more.

All I had been thinking about for the past three years was having a family with her. And for the past two, it'd seemed like it would never come to fruition. But we were back together, and I couldn't fuck it up now because all those chances of starting a big, loving family with her would go straight out the fucking window if I wasn't careful.

"Be back for dinner!" Allie's mom called from upstairs. "We're going out."

After peering up the stairs and frowning, Allie turned to me. "Do you think my mom is going to be okay here alone?" she asked me, clasping her hands together, that dazed look on her face quickly fading. "I don't want anything to happen to her."

"She spent almost three weeks alone with my dad," I said.

It wasn't a good answer, but I didn't have one for Allie. I didn't know Allie's mom that well. I didn't know if anything she did ticked my dad off to the point where he would hit her like he had with Mom countless nights for *going out with the girls* and spending time away from him.

Staying quiet, Allie nodded and walked to the car. I glanced up the stairs and swallowed hard, my stomach tightening. I fucking hoped that he hadn't hurt her because once he landed that first slap, punch, or kick, that man went off the rails and lost complete control.

Allie rested her arm on the center console as I drove us to the nearest pharmacy to pick up Plan B.

After pushing her glasses up her nose with her finger and gnawing on the inside of her lip, Allie finally turned to me. "What did you mean by *this time*?"

I tensed and gripped the steering wheel harder. "What?"

"After we had sex, you said that *this time*, you'd take me to the pharmacy. Why?"

Don't fuck this up, Jace. You're trying damn hard to get her to be comfortable with you.

Instead of telling her that I had fantasized about her being pregnant like a fucking creep, I clenched my jaw, turned into the parking lot of CVS, and parked in the back, where no loser from Redwood could spot my car and decide to come stalk us as we bought Plan B.

"Because if we're going to have sex all the time, you can't go a day without taking your pill," I said, deciding on handling this situation in a dickish manner because it was what I did best. "You should get an IUD or one of those shots in your arm or—"

"Or maybe you should wear a condom," Allie snapped from the passenger seat.

When I looked over, there was anger written all over her face, but at least it wasn't disgust. She crossed her arms over her chest and stared out the windshield at the beige siding of the building.

After a few silent moments, she looked back at me. "Is that really why?"

I stared at her for a few moments. It wasn't Allie's job to worry about contraception if *I* was the one who couldn't keep it in my fucking pants around her. I sucked on my bottom lip nervously as she continued to search my face for any trace of a lie.

"No, that's not why." I got out of the car, stuffing my hands in my pockets and walking toward the entrance of CVS. The last thing I wanted right now was to lie to Allie or to have Allie think I was the biggest creep in all of Redwood.

Allie shuffled out of the car behind me and hurried to keep up. "My legs are short. Stop walking so fast." She grabbed my hand to stop me, and it worked because Allie hadn't wanted to hold hands in public *yet*. "I can hardly keep up with you."

Instead of pulling away like she usually did, Allie glanced down at our hands with her lips twitching up in a small smile and took a deep breath.

I smiled down at her, my heart racing inside my chest. "You want to hold hands?"

"Don't push it, Harbor." She walked into the pharmacy, tugging me behind her, and headed straight to the feminine products and condom aisle. She stopped in front of the knock-off brands of Plan B and dropped my hand. "Which one should we get?"

"Not the off-brand."

I picked out the most expensive one they had because while I wanted Allie to have my babies one day, that day wouldn't be so soon. We had to finish high school, get away from this shitty town, and cut ties with my murderer father.

"How about these too?" I asked, taking some condoms from the rack.

Allie turned on her heel, smiled up at me, and plucked them from my hand. "Just one for tonight. I'll get an IUD soon." She stood on her toes until she was inches from my face, grabbed my collar, and whispered in my ear, "Because I love the way you feel inside of me."

I grasped her jaw and pulled her closer. "Do you like the way I feel inside of you or the way I plug your tight little cunt up with my cum?" I asked her, a smirk making its way onto my face.

Allie smirked cheekily at me and then kissed me—fucking kissed me—in the middle of the aisle. Her lips felt soft and warm as they moved against mine, like they used to. It was like Allie was slowly starting to feel comfortable with me again and wasn't a pit of stress every time she saw me.

"Maybe a bit of both," she said quietly.

She grabbed my hand again and headed straight for the candy aisle, grabbing some chocolate bars and a bottle of root beer. "Movie night after dinner with me?" she asked, batting her dark lashes at me.

"Are we actually going to watch something?" I asked her, brow arched.

"Maybe ..." she said, giggling. "Maybe not."

Chapter Forty-Seven

ALLIE

"It was so beautiful there, darling!" Mom cheered over a glass of red wine.

I nodded along happily as I scanned her arms and neck for any sort of bruise. For the past hour, she had been going on and on about all the things she and Harlan had done on their tropical getaway to a place that I couldn't even pronounce. And for the past hour, I had been suppressing a scowl every time I looked at Harlan.

From the moment I had met that man, I had known something wasn't right. Despite the amount of money he had, he *always* tried too hard to be the father figure in my life and would always somehow get Mom out of going to the cemetery with me. Last time, it had been with a trip to an island.

"So, Allie," Harlan said.

I gulped, forced myself to look over at him, and gave him my best smile. "Yes?"

He sipped the rest of his drink and set it down on the table.

"Did Jace bother you while your mother and I were gone? Any parties that I should know about or any disruptions? Anything?"

It was like he was fishing for a reason to punish Jace. He had gone almost three weeks without it. I bet that man was waiting for a moment to smack Jace upside the head for making fun of me.

My chest tightened. And I had been the cause of Jace getting hurt so many times. I'd told Mom about Jace being rude to me, and Mom had blabbed to Harlan, and Harlan had kicked Jace's ass for it. I just ... if I had known, I wouldn't have done that. I would've kept it to myself.

"Sweetie?" Mom said.

I shook my head to get rid of those horrid thoughts, promised that I'd make it up to Jace one day, and smiled at Harlan. "No," I said. "No parties. No girls. No disturbing me while I studied. It was peaceful these past few weeks." I glanced over at Jace and smiled. "Really peaceful."

Harlan sat back in his chair and called for the waiter. "I see."

"Dad," Jace said, watching the waiter pour his fourth scotch of the night.

"What, Jace?" Harlan asked, staring tensely at him.

I had never noticed it before now, but it almost looked like a damn warning in his hazy green eyes, like he was daring Jace to make a big deal out of him drinking *four* entire glasses of scotch.

Jace tensed beside me and sat up taller, looking down at his steak. "I'm glad you had a good time," Jace said instead of scolding him like he usually did to get him angry.

Jace seemed to think things through a bit more now before he spoke with his father.

At least, I hoped.

Whether he was loving me or hating me, Jace had always been there for me these past few years. I didn't want anything to happen to him because I didn't know what I would do without him. He was the only person, besides Imani, who had been there through all the shitty things in my life.

After we finished dinner tensely, Harlan asked for dessert, and Mom stood up to use the restroom or probably to really make sure nothing was in her teeth because everything had to be perfect for Harlan.

"I need to use the restroom too." I stood up and followed Mom to the restroom, knowing that it would be one of the only times I would get to talk to her alone.

Harlan was always around, almost too much. And ... I needed to make sure she was okay.

When I made it to the restroom, I shut the main door behind us.

Mom looked at herself in the mirror and smiled at me as she fixed her lipstick. "How was your week, darling?"

I swallowed hard, not knowing what to say to her. She had changed so much. I barely knew her anymore. We never had girl chats like we used to when Dad was alive. I missed that old life and would take being poor again over not talking to Mom and being rich any day of the week.

"Good," I said, shifting from foot to foot in front of the mirror. "I got new glasses."

Mom looked over at me and smiled widely. "Oh, you did. They look good."

I glanced down at the sink and watched the beads of water run down the white bowl and into the drain. I had to do it. I had to ask her if Harlan had hurt her in any way, but I couldn't let her know that Jace knew about what had happened with his mother. She'd tell Harlan.

She placed her lipstick back into her purse and puckered her lips.

"I want to get an IUD," I blurted out to keep her in the restroom.

She looked over at me with wide eyes. "An IUD? Are you having sex?"

Fuck. I didn't mean to say that.

"Yes," I said. "A lot of it, and I need an IUD."

"With who?" she asked me, narrowing her eyes. "You don't have a boyfriend."

"Um ..." I teetered back and forth and turned toward her, pushing my glasses up my nose. "Just someone from school. I don't want anything to happen, especially while I'm still in high school."

"Well, sure, but ..." She looked at me oddly and furrowed her brows together. "Is everything okay with you, darling? You look pale. Nobody is forcing themselves on you, are they? I can get Harlan to deal with them if they are."

More blood drained from my face.

I shook my head. "Everything is fine. Is everything okay with *you*?" I asked, gnawing on my cheek.

Why the hell was I so awkward about this entire thing? Why couldn't I just ask her outright?

Mom smiled brightly at me. "Everything is wonderful!"

"And Harlan? How ... how is he?"

Mom's smile didn't falter, but it hadn't faltered when Dad died either. "He's wonderful too."

"Oh, okay," I whispered.

She looped her arm around mine and tugged me to the door. "Come on. The boys are waiting. We still have so much to tell you and Jace about our trip!" she said, as if nothing was wrong.

And I followed her out because I didn't know what else to say.

If Harlan had really hurt her, I couldn't force her to admit it.

Chapter Forty-Eight

ALLIE

When we got home from dinner, Jace pushed me into my bedroom, pressed me against the door, and ground his cock into me from behind. "You don't know how long I've wanted to do this," he said into my ear. He wrapped his hand around the front of my neck, pulled it up gently, and sucked hard on my soft spot, definitely leaving a big red hickey.

Snaking his other arm around my waist, he pulled me closer to him. I turned around in his hold, pulled his face to mine, and kissed him hard. Fuck that movie we were going to watch. I pulled his shirt over his head and let my hands wander down his thick, muscular abdomen. He tugged off my bra, leaving my shirt on, letting my tits bounce out of it and press against the thin material. And when they did, he dipped his head and took one of my nipples into his mouth. My head rolled back, and I moaned as he bit down on my nipple.

"More," I said in a hushed breath since our parents were down the long hallway.

He kissed up my body and roughly grabbed my throat with his callous hand, pulling me to him. "My little slut wants more already?" he asked. Within a moment, he picked me up, grinding his hardness against my underwear from under my skirt, and walked with me to the bed. "She's desperate for it, isn't she?"

He groped my ass and pulled it apart, his fingers disappearing underneath my skirt and underwear and touching me in places he hadn't before.

I threw my head back, my nipples rubbing against his chest, and nodded. "So desperate for it."

After pushing a finger inside of me, he massaged my tight hole. I whimpered into his chest, pressure rising in my core. All I needed was him. Him right fucking now.

"You like that? You want your stepbrother to fuck this tight little ass one day?"

I nodded in a daze and ground my hips harsher against his hard cock, trying to displace the ache between my legs. He pulled his finger out of me and tossed me onto the bed, pulling off my skirt and underwear.

He kneeled on the side of the bed, threw my legs over his shoulders, and pulled me to the edge of the bed. His mouth met my wet pussy, and he sucked my folds between his lips. I gripped on to the mattress, lifting my hips slightly and pushing them forward to give him better access.

My brows furrowed together, the pressure in my core sending me higher and higher. Heat rushed through my body, and when he flicked softly at my clit, I let out a throaty moan.

He gripped my waist tighter, pulling me closer to him.

My legs began shaking. "Yes ..."

He smirked against me and continued making circles around my clit with his tongue. He trailed his fingers up my body and squeezed my nipples hard. He twisted them, and I moaned, my legs shaking furiously.

A wave of pleasure rushed through me, and my entire body

tingled. I slapped a hand over my mouth and came hard, rubbing my pussy over his mouth. When I finally came down from the high, he stood, pulled me to my feet, and spun me around, pushing me over the side of the bed.

"Fuck, Allie," he said, rubbing his cock against my ass. "I've been waiting for this all day." He slapped my ass with his hand, watching it bounce, then slapped between my cheeks with his cock. "Your ass is perfect."

My core tightened when his cock slipped lower and brushed against my entrance. He grabbed my wrists and pulled them behind my back in one hand. With his other, he pushed down on my lower back and made me arch it for him.

He slapped my ass again and rubbed his cock against my hole. I pushed my ass back, wanting him to enter me, and he slid the tip in. But I needed more than that. Then, he entered me so fucking slowly until his hips met mine.

"More. I need it," I said. His thrusts started slow, and I clenched around him. "Make it hurt."

He quickened his pace and deepened his thrusts, his free hand wrapping around my throat and forcing me to arch harder. He placed his lips against my ear. "Is this what you fucking want?"

"I want you to fuck me harder than this," I said.

He tightened his hand around my throat, and pleasure rushed through my body. He pounded his big cock into me and forcefully pulled my head back as his lips met mine. Our tongues tangled together, and he released my hands. He roughly slapped the side of my face, making me clench on him.

I tried to pull away from him to breathe as he rammed himself into me, but he forced me to kiss him and slapped me harder on the cheek. When he finally released me, he pushed my face all the way down against the mattress and held me there.

I shifted under him and stared back, watching my ass bounce as he fucked me. He took a handful of it and groped it as he thrust inside of me. He slapped it hard before pulling out and sitting on the bed next to me. He wrapped his arms around my waist, picked me up, placed me on his lap, and spread my legs. I posted my legs up on his knees, and he thrust hard into me again.

His hands wrapped under my legs, holding them up in the air as his thrusts became harder and deeper.

"Harder," I moaned out.

His fingers trailed up the inside of my thigh before harshly rubbing my clit.

Heat rushed to my core. His touch became rougher, and I threw my head back, clenching around him. My legs began shaking as I came for the second time tonight. When I finished, he pulled out of me.

"No, please, don't stop. You feel so good inside me," I begged.

I wanted more. I needed another release.

"I'm not done with you yet." He smirked against my neck and pushed me away from him. "Get on your knees and suck off your juices. Tell me how you taste."

I kneeled on the bed, crawled between his legs, and sucked his cock into my mouth. My nipples rubbed against his thighs every time I bobbed my head up and down on him. Heat rushed to my core.

He twisted my nipples with his fingers, and I tightened around him as he forced himself deeper inside of my throat. He picked up his pace, thrusting faster inside of me, and placed a hand around my throat. Pleasure rushed through my body as I felt him squeeze my neck harder. I gripped his thighs and stared up at him through teary eyes.

"You fucking love this, don't you?" he asked, hitting the back of my throat. When I didn't answer him, he smacked me hard on the face again. "Answer me." Another slap.

I clenched and nodded, trying to get out a solid verbal answer, but only able to make a sloppy, wet, gagging sound.

He pulled out of me fully. "What was that?"

"Yes," I breathed out, trying to catch my breath. "Choke me harder, please."

He wrapped his hand around the front of my neck again as I felt the pressure begin to build up in my core. He forced himself back down my throat and slapped my face when I gagged on him. I threw my head back and moaned loudly, waves of pressure washing through me.

"Allie! Jace!" Mom shouted from somewhere in this large house.

"Fuck, baby," he said, pumping faster into my mouth, making me taste all my juices on him.

My eyes were teary, throat sore from taking his huge cock. But I sucked him off because my pussy was pulsing and I wanted him to put it back inside of me. I'd do anything for it again.

"You're such a fucking slut, and I love it."

My tits bounced around wildly as he thrust into me. He slapped one and groped it hard in his hand.

"Come inside of me, please, Jace. I need it. All of it."

He growled under his breath, slid on a condom, and pulled me back onto the bed, thrusting into me from behind almost immediately. Someone knocked on my door, and Jace slapped a hand over my mouth, yanking the blankets up over our bodies and grabbing my TV remote from the side table, turning it on.

When the door opened, he let go of my mouth.

Mom stared at us with wide eyes. "What's going on in here?" she asked us, staring at our position under the blankets.

Jace, being the asshole he was, continued to thrust into me, so slowly that it was barely noticeable. "We're watching a horror movie." He nodded to the movie on the screen. "Your daughter got … scared and wanted me to come watch it with her."

Mom glanced at the TV, a look of relief crossing her face, and she held a hand to her chest. Jace stilled inside of me, groaning against my ear. I could feel his cock pulsing inside of me. My pussy throbbed on his cock, wanting to make sure he gave me all of it.

"Oh. Well, it looks like you two got along quite well when we were gone," she said, smiling.

All I wanted was for her to leave, so I could scream out into Jace's palm and fucking ride his cock until I came again.

"I'm so happy you're finally working things out," she said. Jace's dad called her from the kitchen, and she looked over. "I'll be back later on."

She said something that I couldn't quite hear and walked away, leaving the door open.

"Sweet little Allie is such a whore," Jace said into my ear, rubbing my clit.

He slapped a hand over my mouth, and I came for the third time tonight. A whore, only for him.

Chapter Forty-Nine

ALLIE

The next morning, Jace drove us to school and parked near the rear of the lot.

"Do you want to get out before me?" Jace asked me, glancing over at me from the driver's seat. "Like you did Monday?"

I parted my lips, glanced at the school, and shook my head. "No. It's fine."

"Are you sure?"

My entire body warmed at the thought of holding Jace's hand yesterday. It was so stupid and such a small gesture, but it was a huge step for me to do that out in public. Nobody had seen us, but it was something. And walking into school together—without holding hands—would be something too.

Small steps for Allie.

When Jace turned off the car, I stepped out and glanced around at the students in cars around us, giving us weird stares. I brushed off their looks, pulled on my backpack, and watched

Poison pull up next to us. Landon, Kai, and João got out of the car.

Kai nodded to Jace. "Carter is taken care of."

I arched a brow and eyed Jace. "What'd you do?"

"Nothing," Jace said, nodding back to Kai in some sort of agreement.

Kai inched closer to me. "I have to talk to you later about that shit in your locker."

Landon smacked João. "Look who it is ..." he said, staring into the parking lot.

With snow getting caught in her curly black hair, Imani sprinted toward us and grabbed my hands. "You should go home," she said to me, glancing back at the school and all the passersby who looked over at the two nerdiest girls at Redwood hanging out with Poison. "Don't step foot in the hallways, Allie. I mean it."

I furrowed my brows together. "What're you talking about?"

The first bell rang, and I stepped beside Imani to walk toward school. I had already skipped one of my classes the other week because I needed to talk to Kai. I couldn't afford to miss another class or day. My attendance had been close to perfect during all of high school.

Imani moved in front of me again. "Allie, please, just leave."

"What's wrong?" I asked, continuing to the building. "I can't miss class."

Jace and Poison walked behind us, talking about something I doubted I wanted to know about or take any part in. As long as Jace wasn't getting himself into more trouble with his father and could get back on the football field next week, I was content.

"I'll skip with you," Imani said.

I stopped dead in my tracks and stared at her with wide eyes. Imani *never* skipped school, never a day in her entire life. She had had perfect attendance since preschool, never got sick, and was proud to be almost at the top of our class. If she volunteered to skip with me, that meant that this was serious.

"What is it?" I asked, heart pounding. "What don't you want me to see in there?"

Imani frowned, tears piling up in her eyes, and glanced over my shoulder at Jace. She parted her lips to say something, then pressed them back together three times in a row. When she finally got something out, she shook her head. "There are pictures ..."

My heart dropped. Before I could stop myself and despite my best friend telling me to walk away, I found myself storming up the stairs to Redwood's entrance and shoving the door open to see this for myself.

Pictures? What kind of fucking pictures are up in the halls?

Colored flyers of Jace and me at the pharmacy yesterday—holding hands, kissing, and picking up Plan B—were posted on almost every damn locker, where everyone could see them, accompanied by the words *whore, slut, incest,* and things I couldn't even read through the tears.

I plucked the flyers off the lockers as quickly as I could, my cheeks flushed as people stared and whispered in my direction until I reached my locker and found people crowded around it and staring at something. I pushed my way through the crowd and collapsed when I saw the pictures of Jace and me in the locker room two weeks ago.

They weren't just any pictures either. They were of Jace eating me out, of him fucking me, of his fingers in my mouth and my brows furrowed together in a lustful stare.

"Oh my God," I whispered, body heaving on Redwood's dirty hallway floor.

My chest tightened to the point where I had to physically force myself to breathe the same way that nurse had taught me to breathe when I found out Dad had died. Yet even with that stupid fucking way, I felt like my chest was being crushed by a hundred thousand pounds.

Naked.

Naked and fucking Jace.

Everyone at Redwood had seen me naked and having sex with my stepbrother.

Imani shoved her way through the crowd and ripped the flyers off my locker. "I'm sorry, Allie. I didn't see these ones. I would've taken them down. I'm so sorry." She continued to rip them all off until there weren't any more naked pictures of me in Redwood's locker room.

"You think this is fucking funny?" Jace shouted through the halls.

For the first time ever, all the chatter stopped, and Redwood's halls were completely silent. Students shuffled to the sides of the hallways and stared wide-eyed at Jace, who looked like he was on the verge of losing control.

Imani wrapped her arms around my body and pulled me into her lap, stroking my hair. "I'm going to take you home," she whispered to me and wiped tears from my cheeks. "Don't cry. People are mean, Allie. People are so mean. I'm so sorry."

"Who the fuck did this?" Jace shouted.

When nobody answered, Jace stormed through the halls toward us. "Allie is my stepsister. We're not related by blood, and all of you fucking know that already." Jace grabbed my hand and tugged me to my feet. "You can continue to talk shit about us, but I love Allie, and nothing you do is going to change my mind about it. Grow the fuck up and stop being childish about a relationship you know nothing about."

Everyone stayed quiet and glanced between us, then started whispering again.

"If you want to call Allie a fucking whore or slut or mention anything about incest, say it to my fucking face," Jace said, glaring from person to person. "Because you have to deal with *me* now. Nobody insults Allie ever fucking again."

The second bell rang through the halls, yet nobody moved.

"Do you understand me?"

Nobody spoke a word.

"Do you. Fucking. Understand me?"

A flurry of yeses echoed through the hallway, and then everyone scurried to their classes.

Jace wrapped an arm around my waist and pushed the tears off my cheeks. "Allie, I'm so sorry. If I had known that someone was fucking watching us, I would've never done that. Fuck school. Let's go home."

"I can't miss another day," I whispered.

Imani scoffed. "If I can miss a day, you can too." She grabbed my hand. "Come on."

"Jace Harbor." Principal Vaughn stepped out of his office with his arms crossed over his chest and hairy gray brows furrowed together in a furious stare at us. "My office. Now."

Chapter Fifty

JACE

Always had to deal with some shit from Principal Vaughn.

I had been staying under his radar for nearly two years now. And now, because *someone else* had posted flyers around campus with Allie and me naked, *I* was the one in trouble. It was fucked up.

"Take Allie home," I said to Imani.

"Jace," Allie whispered, shaking her head. "Don't go."

She knew that Principal Vaughn would expel me for fucking her in the football locker room because he was the biggest dick in all of fucking Redwood, who had just been waiting to throw me out. *So many people* fucked on campus. I had seen it with my own two eyes with Carter and Nicole. We weren't the only ones.

"My office now, Harbor," Vaughn said.

Allie pulled herself out of Imani's hold and walked to my side. "I'm coming too."

"You have class," Principal Vaughn said, staring at her for a moment longer than he should've.

"Allie, go," I said to her.

She crossed her arms over her chest. "No. If you expel him, you're going to have to expel me, too, for what I did with him." Allie looped her arm around mine. "You can't put the entire blame on him. He doesn't deserve it."

I removed my arm from hers. "Go home, Allie. This isn't your fight."

Though he looked surprised at first, Principal Vaughn cleared his throat. "If that's what you want, then I'd like to see both of you in my office." He held the door open and pointed into the room, glaring between us.

"She doesn't want that, sir," I said through clenched teeth. "She's going home. Now."

"No, I'm not. You're not going down alone."

"My office now."

"If you expel them, you're going to have to expel me too." Imani stepped forward. "I fucked Poison in your office after school yesterday."

Principal Vaughn, Allie, and I looked over at Imani with wide eyes. She swallowed hard, her cheeks flushing red, and uncomfortably crossed her arms over her chest. She gave Allie a small smile and nudged her.

"That's enough. I don't want to hear about anyone else's sexcapades. All three of you, inside my office before I call security." Principal Vaughn walked into his office and sat at his desk.

Imani wrapped her arm around Allie's and walked with her into the room. I followed after him and collapsed into the chair beside Allie. Well, we were all fucked now. Allie and Imani could lose their acceptances to college, and football for me was long gone.

Poison followed us into the room and locked the door behind them.

"You're not expelling anyone," João said to the principal, sliding his ass onto the desk and lighting a cigarette right in

Vaughn's face. "If you do, we'll release your file to the community."

Vaughn went to snatch the cigarette from João's hand, but he pulled it away.

"Don't you want to know *which* file? There are tons of them out there on you. And all the damn money in the world won't save your ass this time."

Principal Vaughn flared his nostrils. "I don't know what you're talking about."

"The cameras that you installed *yourself* in the girls' locker room two years ago."

All the blood drained from Vaughn's face. Allie tensed and looked at me with wide eyes. This must've been something that was in that damn file from Nicole's father's house. There had been loads of shit in there.

"H-how do you know about that? It's erased."

Landon walked around the desk and clasped his hands on Vaughn's shoulders, clamping down tightly. "Once it's out in the world, you can't erase anything. You can hide it behind money, but money won't buy our silence about it."

Kai grabbed the papers from Imani's hand and uncrumpled them, showing him the pictures of Allie and me from the locker room. "Do those look like they were taken by a phone or a video recorder, Jace?"

My eyes widened as it all started to come together. "You have cameras in the football locker room?" I asked through clenched teeth, standing up. "What the fuck do you do? Jerk off to naked and underage high school kids?"

"You have no proof," Vaughn said.

"Kai, can you pull up the security camera recordings from last night?" João asked.

Kai pulled out his computer, hacked into the security footage with ease, and played a recording of none other than Vaughn hanging up those pictures of us late last night.

Overcome with rage, I swung my fist at him and hit him across the face.

Vaughn's head swung back, blood spurting out of his nose. "I'm going to get you arrested for that. You're going to be—"

João held up a finger and waggled it. "No, you're not. You're going to remove those cameras and not say a word to anyone for the rest of the year. You won't expel Jace or Allie or especially Imani. You're going to be *our bitch*."

"Why?" Allie asked suddenly with tears in her eyes. "Why would you do that to me, to us? Why would you put those DVDs and dildo in my locker and post pictures around campus of us?"

Vaughn wiped the blood from his nose with his sleeve and looked away from Allie and me. Landon slapped him hard across the cheek, and I ached to hit him harder than that. He fucking deserved it.

"She asked you a question," Landon said.

"Because ..." Vaughn answered.

"Say it," João said.

"Because I fucking love watching innocent schoolgirls like you squirm."

I hit him right across the face again, giving him a black eye. "You fucking disgust me," I said, spitting in his face. I snatched Allie's hand and led her to the door. I wasn't going to let her deal with another second of this. "Imani, come on. I'm taking you home. Poison will deal with this."

Chapter Fifty-One

ALLIE

"I don't think you want to do that, Harbor," Principal Vaughn said.

Just as he was about to walk out the door with Imani and me, Jace stopped. "And why's that, Vaughn?" he asked through clenched teeth.

He turned his entire rigid body around, and I scooted closer to Imani, wrapping my arms around hers.

Vaughn glanced at me, his gaze flickering down my body. I felt so exposed, too exposed around him. He had seen me naked. If he had the audacity to post all those pictures around the school, then he had probably jerked off to the damn videos over and over and over again.

It was disgusting. I felt violated.

Principal Vaughn yanked himself out of Poison's grasp and straightened out his suit. "How was your father's vacation?" he asked Jace, rocking back on his heels and clasping his hands behind his back. "He was gone for longer than expected, wasn't he?"

Jace tensed and clenched his jaw. "What do you care?"

Vaughn grinned like a maniac with his crooked yellow teeth. "He called me this morning and asked what happened when he was gone. I mentioned that there were some interesting things that I found while he was out."

I tensed up at the thought of Vaughn showing Harlan everything we had done in the locker room and telling him about Jace hitting Carter. Harlan had probably paid for the information and paid for Vaughn *to make things up* about Jace. If he found out and kicked Jace out, I'd be left in the house with Mom and Harlan. Alone.

"He's bluffing," I said, swallowing my nerves and stepping forward. "He hasn't told Harlan anything yet because Harlan hasn't paid him. Has he?"

Vaughn cleared his throat and scowled at me. "That doesn't mean that I won't tell him."

Vaughn took a threatening step toward Jace. Poison looked at Vaughn, then looked back at Jace to see how he'd react.

Vaughn crossed his arms. "If you leave school today, I will tell your father everything that has been going on with you, so I can watch Redwood's notorious Jace Harbor fall into oblivion and lose out on all his chances of making it big, and then I get to get off to the videos of his girlfriend."

Overcome with rage, I lunged forward to hit him myself. How dare he even threaten that! He should've been six feet under already for even suggesting such a thing and for *everything* he had done to the girls and boys here.

Before I could make impact, Kai caught my wrist to hold me back, and Jace had Vaughn shoved hard against the wall.

"You won't fucking do a thing," Jace said through clenched teeth, brown eyes wide in fury. "I will fucking kill you for even thinking about touching her."

Though I wanted to see Vaughn dead, Jace couldn't do it here or now. Harlan would find out that Jace had killed our principal on school grounds and send him away for good.

I wrapped my arms around Jace and tugged him off. "Jace, please, stop."

When I finally pulled Jace off Principal Vaughn, Vaughn straightened out his clothes again and smiled.

"Your father is looking into you right now, Harbor," Vaughn said. "I won't tell him anything I know if you all keep your mouth shut, or I can tell him that you've been fucking your sister on school grounds and getting into fights in the locker room."

"You don't have proof," Kai said. "You can't show him proof without him knowing how fucking perverted you are."

"That's where you're wrong," Vaughn said. "Mr. Harbor doesn't need any evidence. He has money, and he has me as a witness. All he needs to do is slide some money into some people's hands, and everything will be taken care of."

Jace tensed and pressed his lips together. It was true. Harlan had done the same thing with Jace's mother, had gotten rid of her like it was nothing, pushed everything under the rug and bribed people with millions of dollars.

It was fucking sick.

"So, Jace, what's it going to be?" Vaughn said, arching a brow. "Are you going to keep this quiet? Or do you want me to tell your father everything, so he can toss you in jail and I can keep your sister for myself?"

It was an impossible decision that Jace would never be able to make.

Jace growled at him, grabbed my hand, and tugged me toward the door. "Don't say anything to my father," he said and walked out into the hallway toward my second period class, giving me his full attention now. "We're staying here for now. It's the only place that's safe. As soon as school ends, meet me by my car. We'll go home once I know my dad is gone. Don't leave with anyone."

I furrowed my brows. "We're just going to let him continue to video innocent people?"

Jace pressed his lips together, flared his nostrils, and looked down. "My dad is far more of a threat than Vaughn. Let me take care of him, and then we can take Vaughn down along with the rest of Redwood's most corrupt." He brushed some hair out of my face. "Okay?"

It was pitiful to think and even more pitiful to say out loud. But I wanted Vaughn to hurt more than this. It wasn't fair that he could record us at our most intimate, post the pictures around campus so I'd get bullied, and not be punished for it. I hated it so fucking much because I knew there would be more of it.

He would continue recording. He'd ruin someone else's life. He would get away with it.

A vicious cycle that was so difficult to put a stop to.

"Jace," I whispered, "we can't let him get off. He's ruined my life."

Jace took my face in his hands and stroked his thumbs against my cheeks. "He won't. I promise that I'll take care of him. Redwood is about to be blown to pieces and crumble. We just have to give it a little more time."

My lips trembled, yet I held out my pinkie. "Pinkie promise me."

Jace curled his pinkie around mine. "I promise you that I'll make everything right again."

Chapter Fifty-Two

ALLIE

"We're grabbing the files on my dad, and then we're out of here," Jace said, tugging me through the eerily quiet and empty house.

My stomach tightened at the thought of Harlan being back in town and the house being this ominous. Something didn't feel right to me.

Harlan wasn't home, but we still had to be quick. He could be back at any fucking moment and could trap us here. Between Vaughn and the police chief, God only knew what Harlan had found out since he had gotten back from his trip.

Jace jogged up to his room and shut the door, tearing out a floorboard and plucking a file from it. He opened the manila envelope, flipped through the stack of papers inside, and blew out a relieved breath. "They're all here."

I sat on his bed and rubbed my sweaty palms against my jeans. Today had turned out to be complete shit for both of us. I was glad that we had a win and that Harlan hadn't found and stolen this back. If he did, we'd both be screwed over to no end. Harlan might even try to kill Jace too.

My heart raced at the thought of finding Jace with a bullet straight through his head, all his blood seeping out of the hole, his eyes a dull and lifeless brown. I shivered at the thought and pushed away the tears. I couldn't cry now. We had to get out of here.

Just as Jace grabbed my hand, someone rattled the doorknob.

"Jace. Open the fucking door," Harlan said, his words slurring toward the end. It wasn't even five at night yet, and Harlan was ... drunk.

Jace cursed under his breath, pushed the file into my hands, and shoved me into his closet. "Don't come out and don't watch, Allie. You don't want to see him like this," Jace said, grasping my face. He stroked my cheeks, pushing the tears off them. "Promise me that you won't."

"If you don't open this door now, Jace, I fucking swear I'll kill you."

I gulped and looked back at the door, which was nearly coming off the hinges. "Go open the door, please," I whispered, more tears racing down my cheeks. My chest tightened, and I pressed my lips together to not make a sound.

Jace couldn't die.

I fucking loved him.

He couldn't fucking die.

"I love you," he whispered, then slid the closet door closed.

But I could still see out of the small crack in the door. As soon as Jace opened the door, Harlan barreled into the room. I had never seen Harlan wasted until tonight. He must've thought that I wasn't home or wasn't coming home, that I was out with Mom or something because Mom would never stand for this shit.

At least, I thought she wouldn't.

Standing behind the door, I curled my hands into fists and jumped when a bottle shattered against the closet door.

"You're a fucking brat." Harlan seethed, words slurred, as if he had had one too many and didn't give a fuck. "You're the fucking reason your mother left us. Don't you dare blame it on me. I gave her the fucking world, and you destroyed it."

"It's not my fault she cheated on you," Jace said.

There was silence, and then a smack … but it sounded harder than a palm on the cheek. It sounded like a fist right to the face, like a jaw cracking, like Jace had just gotten hit hard.

"Don't talk back to me. I told you to quit football. I told you to fucking quit it, and you fucking didn't. And you still won't after what she did with your coach. You fucking look up to your coach like he's your father."

I bit my lip, so I wouldn't let out a cry. There I was again, stupid Allie crying for stupid reasons … but … but I felt it. I heard the hurt in Harlan's voice, but I saw the pain in Jace's eyes every time I looked into them.

"He's a better father than you ever were," I heard Jace mutter under his breath.

Something banged against the wall, and I heard Jace suppress a groan. But why wasn't he fighting back? He was strong enough to do it. Why stay here? Why endure this pain? Why not report his father to someone?

He once told me that I didn't know what money could do, who it could pay off. And I thought I finally understood him. But I wouldn't truly understand those words for a long time. I wouldn't understand that a billion dollars could do more than buy fancy things.

Jace continued to groan, and I couldn't take it any longer. I burst right through the door to his bedroom, grabbed Harlan's wrist, and tried to pull him off of Jace, who was getting the shit kicked out of him by a man half his size. Harlan's hand flew back, knocking me off him and onto the ground. My head hit against Jace's dresser, and I saw tiny black stars in my vision.

As I cradled my head, blood seeped into my hair and made it stick together. I sucked in a raspy, ragged breath and tried hard to catch the breath that had suddenly left my lungs at the sheer force of Harlan.

"Allie," Jace said, scrambling to his feet and rushing over to me. He grabbed my hand and pulled me to my feet, ushering me out of the room and away from a shocked Harlan. "Are you fucking crazy?" Jace asked, gripping my upper arm, pulling me down the stairs and to his car, and pushing me inside of it. He slid into the driver's side, started the car, and sped down the road, going about a hundred miles an hour.

I sat back in my seat, my bloody fingers shaking, my heart racing, my thoughts everywhere. Did Harlan get abusive with Mom too? She would never take it after living with my dad all those years. He'd taught us to be strong, but ... maybe when she was in that position, she'd be twice as nervous as I had been.

Deciding to hide the blood from Jace, I wiped my palm across my jeans. "Jace," I whispered, staring out the windshield as we zoomed past trees.

Jace didn't say anything for the longest time. He clenched and unclenched his hand on the steering wheel and shook his head. "I fucking told your mom not to marry that fucking asshole, and she still fucking did. Do you see why I wanted you gone?"

"Jace, it's worse than you let on," I whispered, glancing over at Jace for the first time tonight. His lip was busted open, his eye black, blood dripping down his neck. "Jace, you can't let him continue to abuse you like this. He-he can't."

It broke my heart to see Jace like this.

"You don't think I've tried calling the fucking police on him? Hitting him back? It either ends with him threatening to shoot me fucking dead, the cops not fucking believing shit because he's paid them off, or me in juvie. And I can't have any of those things happening now that we're better."

Silence fell upon us again, and I didn't know what to say to him. He'd tried to get out of this before, time and time again, yet nobody believed him. And if they did ... Harlan paid them off.

Apparently, people in this town liked money more than they liked putting murderers and abusers behind bars. Another reason to get out of here as soon as I could.

We pulled up to a run-down house in the bad part of town. The siding was chipping, and some of the windows were cracked. The entire place reeked of pot and bad decisions. Definitely not a place I wanted to be after what had happened.

"Get out," he said to me.

I fumbled with my seat belt and followed after him as he walked to the back door and banged on it three times with the side of his fist.

Landon answered, a cigarette hanging out the corner of his mouth. "What?"

Jace pulled out a wad of cash and slapped about five hundred-dollar bills in his hand. "Watch Allie."

Landon glanced over at me, lit the cigarette, and took a puff on it. "Looks like you need a smoke," he said, handing it to Jace.

Jace started toward his car. "Don't let anyone fucking touch her. I'll be back."

My eyes widened, and I followed Jace back to his Maserati. "You're leaving me with them?" I asked, grasping his wrist and tugging him back.

Jace snatched his hand out of my grip and turned toward me. Under the moonlight, I could see just how bad his bruises were, and my heart ached for him.

"Please," I whispered. "Don't go back."

"Get in the fucking house," he said.

I gently grasped his hand. "Please, let me at least clean you up."

When my fingers touched his, he tensed, but his eyes softened so much that I thought he was going to let me. But then his phone buzzed in his pocket, and he pulled away from me.

"Later. I'll be back for you." He slid into his car, threw it in reverse, and sped back in the direction we had come.

I stared at his car until his taillights disappeared from my view.

Landon flicked his cigarette onto the ground and stomped it out with the heel of his boot. "You coming?"

I walked into the house, my palms clammy at the mere thought of Jace going back to that tonight. Part of me was terrified that I'd get back to the house and find him in a pool of his own blood with a bullet straight through his head.

Chapter Fifty-Three

ALLIE

Landon walked down some creaky-ass steps into a basement and shut the door behind us. A shirtless João was sitting on a beaten-up and stained couch with Kai, each with a video game controller in their hands. They looked over at me when I walked in, Kai raising his brows at Landon.

"Jace," Landon said, and that was it.

João and Landon went back to their video game.

Kai nodded to another couch across from the boys for me to sit on and handed me a cold beer. I sat on the couch awkwardly, crossing my arms over my chest, and glanced around the room, seeing their backpacks thrown in the corner of the room as if they didn't give a fuck about school, weed on the coffee table, beer bottles gathered in the corner of the room.

"Fuck you, dude," João said, tossing his controller onto the coffee table with the weed. He looked over at me, then at the unopened can. "Loosen up, buttercup. Take a swig." He took the can from me, opened it up, and handed it back.

The stench hit my nose and almost made me gag, but I took a

sip of it anyway, needing something after what I had witnessed. I never thought I'd ever see something like that in my life, never thought that *Jace* would be the one getting abused. In football, he was always so ... so ... rough and violent and had that *don't fuck with me* attitude.

"Feel better?" João asked, his mouth curled into his signature smirk. His dark hair was a tousled mess on his head, and a metal feather earring hung off one of his ears. His body was covered with tattoos.

I blew a breath out my mouth and decided not to lie. There was no point in it. I was going to be a mess all night with them, worrying about Jace. "No," I said, grabbing some napkins from the table and placing them on the back of my head to stop the blood. "I'm not."

Landon sat on the couch next to me and tossed the cash Jace had given him onto the table. "Don't worry about Jace. He'll be all right. He always is."

"You don't know what he's going through."

"Oh, come on." Landon laughed. "His daddy hits him. Everyone here knows it. He brought you here because he doesn't want you getting hurt. Daddy is probably off drinking or some shit." He waved his hand dismissively. "It's not a secret to us. He's handled worse shit than that."

Worse shit. I didn't believe it.

"Am I right, or am I right?" Landon said.

I stayed quiet and took a huge fucking gulp of the drink, wanting to erase everything about tonight from my mind. First, Vaughn. Then, Harlan. We should've never gone home tonight. Imani would've let us stay in one of her spare rooms if I'd begged. Jamal might've even let us stay with him too.

The two boys went back to playing video games, and I watched them aimlessly, not being able to forget about it. This damn beer wasn't helping, so I pulled out my phone to check to see if Jace had texted me. But I had no notifications. Part of me wanted to call Jace to make sure everything was okay, but I didn't want to make it worse.

"So, how's Imani?" João asked me, lighting up another cigarette and blowing the smoke out of his nose.

I arched a brow at him and narrowed my eyes. "Why are you guys blackmailing her?"

Landon looked over and chuckled. "Wouldn't you love to know? What we do with Imani is none of your business."

"Yes, it is. She's my best friend, and I don't want you guys ruining her life like you ruined Jace's. I'm sick of you butting into everyone's business." I put all my insecurities aside and told them off for the first time ever, and it felt *damn* good. "Stop bothering good people and bringing them down."

While Landon and João looked over at me, Kai flicked his cigarette into the ashtray and slumped down on the couch next to me.

"She's had a hard night," he said, waving off the guys to let them play more games. "Let it slide."

When the guys turned back to the TV, I glared at Kai and crossed my arms over my chest. "I want to go home. I need to make sure that Jace is okay. He can't stay with Harlan tonight. You know what he'll do to him."

"You're staying here tonight. I can't let you go back over there. Jace would try to kill me." Kai placed a hand on my shoulder and turned toward me. "And, plus, it's the only way you're safe."

"Why does he trust you?" I asked, crossing my arms over my chest.

"Jace?" Kai asked, brows furrowed together. "Because we do good work for him."

"And why did my dad trust you?"

All the emotion on Kai's face evaporated. He sat back up very uncomfortably and shifted in his seat. "What makes you think your dad trusted me?" he asked. Not trusted Poison, but him—

Kai. Something had gone on between my father and Kai, and I needed to figure out what it was.

"You said he did a favor for you. What was it?"

Kai tore his gaze away from me and grabbed my beer. "You keep asking me questions that you know I can't answer about our business." He was suddenly cold and even distant. "Ask me something I can answer."

"No." I crossed my arms and lay back on the couch, knowing that I wouldn't get anything out of him. "I want you to answer this for me. He was my father. I want to know what kind of business he was in before he was killed."

"Keep dreamin'," João said from the floor, tossing his controller on the ground and looking back at us. "If you want to know what happens when we do business with someone, why don't you offer up a job, and we'll show you how it works?"

I narrowed my eyes at him and then tore my gaze away. I didn't know how the hell Imani dealt with their shit. They were the three most annoying assholes on the planet, almost even worse than Jace during the past two shitty years.

Not caring that the blood was seeping into their stained couch, I closed my eyes and prayed that Jace would still be alive tomorrow morning and that he'd come back to get me. All I wanted was to spend my life with him.

Chapter Fifty-Four

JACE

I hated that fucker more than ever.

After dropping Allie off at Poison's, where she'd be safe for the night, I pulled into the driveway and cursed myself for ever coming back. I should've stayed at Poison's with Allie to make sure she was all right after what had happened. She had hit her head, yet I had been too blindsided by rage to ask her if she was okay.

But I needed to set things straight with that fucking asshole. He could slap me around all he wanted, but he would never touch Allie ever again. There wasn't a reason for it. She had done nothing but be nice to the man.

Harlan and Allie's mom were both in the dining room, eating a late dinner when I arrived.

As if nothing had ever fucking happened, Allie's mom smiled at me with her perfectly corrected and straight teeth and patted the seat next to her. "Come sit."

Dad cleared his throat and looked at Allie's mom. "Sweetheart, I need to talk to Jace alone," he said to her. He opened his wallet and handed her his credit card. "Why don't you go out and get yourself something nice?"

Allie's mother hesitantly grabbed the card, looked between us, and then pushed the card back toward him. "I think I'll stay. I have some things to clean up around the house. So much work to do. Jace, do you want to—"

"Leave." Dad didn't stutter and didn't even look in her direction.

She scrambled to her feet, pressed her lips together, and grabbed his card. "I'll be back in an hour," she said, hurrying to the door before she could witness my father lose complete control and slap me across the face.

"Don't come home until morning," Dad said.

Allie's mother stopped at the door and gulped. She didn't look back, yet she nodded. "I love you, Harlan," she said. To me, it sounded like she was trying to calm him down, so he wouldn't hurt me so badly that I ended up in the hospital.

"I love you too, sweetheart."

Allie's mom hurried through the hallways to the front door. I stood in the doorway with my heart racing in my chest. I hated being alone with him, would try to find any reason not to be here while he was here. But I couldn't put this off any longer.

"Don't ever lay a hand on Allie again," I said to him through clenched teeth when the front door closed. My voice trembled slightly, and my chest tightened at the memory of terror on Allie's face after my father had knocked her off her feet.

I should've stayed with her. I should've fucking made sure she was okay.

Harlan stood to his full height and looked me in the eye, grasping a glass in his hand. "You stole my money, Jace."

He hurled the glass in my direction, and I didn't duck in time. It shattered across my cheekbone, the glass centimeters from my eye.

"You fucking stole two million dollars from me."

I stepped back from him, pulling glass from my face. "On alcohol," I said, as it was the only thing that came to my mind. I couldn't let him know that it had gone straight to Poison in exchange for information. "I'm becoming a raging alcoholic, just like my father."

Lunging forward, Harlan grabbed my collar and slammed me into the wall. I pushed him back, tired of being beaten up over this shit over and over. Why couldn't I have a normal fucking family for once? Why couldn't we go back to the way things used to be?

Yet Dad had seen it coming and slammed his fist into me so hard that my head bounced off the wall. I could feel the indent of his wedding ring against my jaw. He hit me again before I could regain my balance.

"Where'd the money go, Jace? Where'd my two million dollars go? Because it surely didn't go to alcohol. You can't spend that much in the three weeks I was gone."

"I spent it on alcohol," I said as I spit up blood. "And Allie. That's fucking all."

He didn't take that as an answer. "Are you trying to put me in fucking jail? Did you use that money to try to get some kind of evidence?" he asked me. "Try all you fucking want, but you'll never find anything. What happened to your mother is the past."

I went to hit him back, but he slammed his fist into my mouth. I stumbled back again, unable to move. Maybe this was how Mom had felt. She was tired of constantly putting up with his bullshit too. I used to hate her for cheating on Dad, but if she lived like this all the time ... I didn't blame her for trying to find love elsewhere.

"You're shit, Jace."

Punch.

"You keep this up, and I'll put you back in jail."

Punch.

"Or ..."

Punch.

"Fucking ..."

Punch.

"Worse."

He landed one more punch that knocked me off my feet. I stumbled back into the wall and slid down it, my eyes closing despite my trying so desperately to keep them open. He wasn't going to kill me like he had killed Mom. I couldn't let him be alone with Allie and her mother.

I went to grab his leg, somewhere, anywhere. But he snatched me by the back of the neck.

"We're not finished," were the last words I heard from him before I passed out.

Chapter Fifty-Five

ALLIE

I ended up staying at Poison's place last night, not wanting to come home and witness any more of drunk Harlan. He wasn't a pretty sight, and neither was him hitting Jace right in his pretty face. *I* wanted to hit Jace in the face sometimes, too, but I didn't act on it, and I wasn't some murderous sicko father.

Only Jace's car was in the driveway when Kai pulled up on his motorcycle. I had basically begged him all morning to take me back home because Jace hadn't returned any of my calls.

When Kai parked, he lit a cigarette and nodded to the house. "You want me to stay?"

"No." I glared at him and hopped off the bike, needing to get away from that disgusting stench of cigarette. "I'm fine," I said.

He sped off, the motorcycle louder than a damn thunderstorm.

I turned back to the front door and tried hard not to hyperventilate.

Breathe, Allie, just breathe. Harlan isn't home.

After persuading myself to get this over with, I walked into the house.

"Jace!" I shouted, racing to his room. "Jace!"

No response.

"Are you home?" I asked, keeping my voice steady even though it was about to falter.

I pushed his bedroom door open. Unlike last night, there was no blood, no hole in the wall, no shattered beer bottles either. It was almost like nothing had ever happened. My stomach tightened in knots, and I frowned as I gently grasped his bedsheets.

Where the hell is he? Why isn't he here? Is he okay?

I walked to my room and stood still when I saw a Fendi shopping bag sitting on my bed. My brows furrowed slightly as I peered inside of it, seeing a card that had *Love, Harlan* on the blank side.

Inside, there was an emerald-green crocodile-leather Fendi bag that must've cost at least thirty thousand dollars or more. The only reason I knew that was because Nicole—Jace's stupid fling— wouldn't stop gossiping about it when he had bought her a similar one for Christmas last year.

I felt dirty, holding the bag, knowing that he had only given me this to make up for last night.

After thrusting it back into the shopping bag, I threw it to the side of the room and pretended like it didn't exist. I didn't want it to exist. I didn't want *any* of this to exist. I just wanted things to be good, safe, and normal again. Now, I was going to have to watch over my shoulder, see if Mom was being abused too, try to find a way for us both to get out of this shitty life that she seemed to love.

Instead of spending another minute despising the damn thing, I tore open my closet door to find my entire closet turned upside down with thousands of dollars' worth of clothes, twenty new pairs of shoes, and purses that I would never ever use.

I clenched my jaw to stop myself from crying. All the clothes Dad had bought me, all those little gifts from him were gone. Not in boxes. Not in the trash. Not in the back of my closet. Gone for fucking good.

"No," I whispered, shaking my head.

I grasped his dog tags around my neck and held on to the wall, so I didn't double over in painful heartbreak. Besides the chain around my neck, those were the only damn things that I had left of him. After a drunk driver had ripped Dad from my life, I had those gifts to remember him by.

Now ... now, I fucking didn't.

My heart pounded against my chest, and I forced myself to take deep breaths for the second time in the past two days. If I didn't, I would have a panic attack, alone, here in the house. After I took ten deep breaths, air was getting back in my lungs.

"I can't believe this," I whispered, tears racing down my cheeks.

Anger built up inside of me, and I found myself tearing the clothes off the hangers so forcefully that the hangers snapped in half and littered the ground of my room.

Fuck Mom for ever agreeing to marry Harlan.

I hated that man more than I hated anyone, and I hated her for ruining my life.

After destroying my closet, I grabbed the backpack in the back of it. I needed a getaway bag, if anything ever happened. Hell, I needed a bag for tonight because ... I couldn't stay here. I needed to get my shit and leave, drive Jace's car around Redwood like a maniac to try to find him.

He couldn't have gotten far.

Unless Harlan had done something to him.

My stomach dropped.

No. No. No. No. No. No.

Harlan couldn't have done anything to him. He couldn't. Maybe he had gone for a walk down the road to think through his next few steps, or maybe he and Harlan had gone on a drive to talk about what had happened with his mother. But the more I thought about it, the less likely I knew something like that had happened.

Somehow and for some reason, Jace had left to go somewhere without taking his car.

From my bedroom, I listened to shuffling in the hallway.

"Jace?" I shouted, packing up the rest of my essentials with my back turned toward the door. I needed to get us out of here as soon as fucking possible.

Suddenly, the door closed behind me. I turned around and sucked in a deep breath to find none other than Harlan Harbor standing inside my room with a small smile on his face and fiendish blue eyes.

"Allie," he said, stepping closer to me. He looked at the bed, then at the purse on the floor, and then gestured for me to sit. "Sit down. We have much to talk about."

Chapter Fifty-Six

ALLIE

I stepped back until my legs hit the blue suede blankets covering my bed. My heart pounded against my chest. Running wasn't an option, climbing out the window in the middle of winter wasn't an option, and fighting with Harlan definitely wasn't an option.

Harlan was capable of murder.

Cold-blooded murder.

If he had done something to Jace or even Mom, I would avenge them. I had to. It wasn't only what I wanted to do, but it was also what Dad would have wanted me to do. He had always served to protect his family and our country. If I couldn't protect them at this moment, I had to do something.

After locking the door behind him, he smiled at me as if nothing was wrong, a complete one-eighty from last night. But behind that big, fake smile, I saw the real drunk and delusional Harlan Harbor, the man who beat his own son because he felt small and wanted to feel powerful.

"Where's Jace?" I asked, straightening my back and trying to seem as if I wasn't terrified.

"Jace is going to be gone for a bit," Harlan said, walking over to my trashed closet.

"Where is he?" I asked through clenched teeth.

"He'll be back next week. Don't worry."

"I am worrying," I said, biting my lip.

Because you could've killed him.

"Why?" Harlan stopped in front of my closet and picked up some of the clothes I had mercilessly thrown all over the floor. Harlan stared at me and waited impatiently for my response, one hairy graying-black brow raised. "Jace is taking some time off, resting and relaxing before he goes back to *football*. There is no reason for you to worry."

After placing the piece of clothing on my bed, Harlan grasped my shoulder harshly. "Or maybe you're worried about something else ..." he said, dangerously close to my ear that I could feel the hairs on his cheek brush against my neck. "Did Jace tell you anything? You and he do seem to be closer than you two were before I left."

My entire body tensed. This wasn't what I was prepared to answer. I had just wanted to come home, get some clothes and Jace, and sprint out of here before anyone had the chance to talk to me. If I had known Harlan was here, I would not have even come in, never mind let Kai leave me stranded.

"And this?" Harlan pulled a file from his suit jacket and waved it in the air.

All the blood drained from my face. I had dropped it last night. I'd fucking dropped it. Jace had told me to stay in that damn closet and let him take a merciless beating, but ... God, why was I so stupid?

"He hasn't said anything to me," I said, voice above a whisper.

Harlan walked behind me, tucked the file underneath his armpit, and placed both hands on my shoulders, leaning in close. I sucked in a deep breath and didn't let it out. I was too fucking scared that Harlan could see right through my lies.

Where the hell is Jace? And Mom?

"What has he said to you about me?" Harlan asked.

"I-I don't know what you're talking about."

"You hate Jace, yet you're calling for him?"

"I love Jace," I whispered, balling my hands into fists. "I've loved him for all these years. I have wanted him more than anything. When you left ..." I had to think of something quick, had to tell him some truth and something believable to get him off my back. "When you left, Jace and I got back together, and I care about him. That's why I called for him. I don't want to see him hurt."

After seeing what you did to him.

And like that, the nice Harlan was gone.

I saw his true colors. He thought that his son was unworthy of love.

Harlan stepped back and clenched his jaw. "I bought you an entire closet of clothes and a purse to help you forget about last night, but I can see that you aren't grateful for it, as all the hangers are torn to pieces and the clothes are scattered on your filthy floor."

"I never asked for your clothes," I snapped, overcome with so much anger. "I want my old clothes back, the ones my father bought me." I stepped forward and crossed my arms over my chest. "Where are they?"

Harlan clenched his jaw. "Those clothes were old and ragged. You deserve more than what that man could have ever bought you. You're a Harbor now. You have a name to represent. You don't ever have to suffer like you did on the bad side of Redwood ever again."

"You think that I suffered there?" I asked, shaking my head.

I wanted to scream at him that I had never suffered more than being in this house with him and his son. These past two years had been hell for me, not only because Jace had hurt me, but also because Harlan had taken Mom away from me. As soon as we had moved in, everything had turned sour between me and her. She didn't care like she used to, not about me and especially not about Dad.

Instead of blowing up at him—because I could see it in his eyes that he was seconds away from breaking again—I turned away and looked toward the closet. "Where is my dad's stuff?"

"At the dump. Shredded. Covered with more trash. With a family that actually deserves ripped clothes like that." Harlan stared at me with rage in those green eyes of his. "They're long gone, Allie. Forget about them and forget about him. You have a new father."

The words coming out of his mouth disgusted me more than anything. A new father? Did he think that I would *ever* call him my father? He didn't even deserve the word *stepfather*. He was more like a piece of shit.

"You're not my father," I said, grasping Dad's dog tags between my thumb and forefinger. If I didn't have any more clothes from him, then at least I had these and all those memories of better days. "You'll never be half the man he was."

Storming toward me, Harlan grabbed the chain and ripped it off my neck. I reached, screamed, scrambled to get them back, but Harlan stuffed them into his pocket, gripped my hand harshly, and stopped me.

"You'll get them back later," he said to me. "But I never want to see them again. *Never.*"

"Give them back to me now!"

Harlan grabbed my upper arm and pulled me out of the room. "We're going to spend some much-needed time together. Just me and you, Allie … me and you. And then, if you're good and you do as I say, you'll get your father's filthy chain back."

<h1 style="text-align:center">Chapter Fifty-Seven</h1>

JACE

Darkness.

I clutched my stomach and rolled onto my hands and knees, struggling to hold myself up. My left eye was swollen shut, and I could only see a sliver of darkness out of my right one. Every part of my body ached worse than it had after Dad beat me.

For the first time last night, I'd actually tried fighting back. For years, I'd wanted him to kill me to stop the fucking agony I had felt since Mom had died, but now that Allie was back in my life, I didn't want to die. I needed to protect her with everything I had. I had to get back to her before he could touch her.

The chalky gray concrete underneath my hands was covered in my blood. I grunted, sucked in a breath, and willed myself to my feet. Clutching the wall, I followed it blindly until I reached a door. Some light flickered out from underneath it.

After opening it up, I heaved myself up the long, cold staircase and squinted when I made it into a brightly lit room.

God, where the fuck am I? In the eighteen years that I'd been alive, I had never once been here.

"You're up?" someone said from my left.

Turning my head toward the voice, I nearly stumbled over my two feet toward a table with a man I didn't recognize. I grasped a wooden chair for support and collapsed into it, staring at the Russian with a thick black mustache.

"Who the fuck are you?" I asked, eyeing his gun on the table.

I didn't have any doubts that he would pull it out if I tried to run.

The man shone his pearly-white teeth at me. "Call me Rick. Rick Santos."

"No." I shook my head in disbelief. "No, you can't fucking be."

"I've heard much about you."

I pushed myself to a standing position and stumbled back until I hit the wall. I scanned the room as my heart raced faster. There was one exit, one fucking exit behind the man who had taken part in burning my mother's body. We'd had to have a fucking closed casket because of that fucker.

But if he was here with me, had Dad told him to get rid of me too?

When Rick smirked, I wanted to charge at him. I wanted to hurt him as much as I wanted to hurt Dad, but I had no energy. My muscles felt extremely weak, and he had a fucking gun. I couldn't make any rash decisions until I at least figured out a plan to get out of here without dying.

"What kind of fucking name is Rick Santos for a fucking Russian?" I spat at him.

He knocked his knuckles against the wooden table. "Sit down, Jace. Let's talk."

"Where is Allie?"

"Allie?" Rick polished the barrel of his gun with a cloth. "As in your pretty stepsister?"

I clenched my right fist and held myself up with my left hand on the wall. "Where the fuck is she?" I asked through clenched teeth.

If she was alone with my father, I swore to fucking God, I would lose it.

She had probably gone back home, seen my Maserati in the driveway, and thought it was safe to go back into the house alone. That fucking asshole was probably all over her, trying to make things right, buying her gifts upon gifts to keep her mouth shut. But Allie could never be bought out. She had hated when I bought her clothes just because, and she had a better head on her shoulders than I ever had.

"She's with your father," Rick said.

As soon as the words left his mouth, I slammed my fist into the wall and relished in the pain that shot through my body. It wasn't enjoyable, but it reminded me that I was alive still and that I had someone to protect. I hated that it had to be this way. I hated being this far from Allie, where I couldn't protect her and where she had to protect herself.

I had *never* left her alone with my father. *Never.*

I didn't fucking trust him. By the way Allie's mother had acted terrified of my father yesterday, I could tell that he had either been threatening or hitting her too. She had herself and her daughter to protect. She'd walked out of the house, and I fucking couldn't have been more thankful. I didn't want her to see what my father was truly capable of and didn't want Allie to lose another parent.

"Your old man really fucked you up, didn't he?" Rick taunted. "You think he'd do the same to her too?"

Without thinking, I spat at Rick because it was the only thing I could physically do at the moment. Rick stood up and swung at my face for the disrespect. Before it could collide, I ducked and hit him in the ribs, making contact and hearing something crack, expending the last of my energy. But it was all I could do before he kneed me in the bruised gut and made me double over in pain.

He slammed his fist into the side of my face, banging my head off the concrete and making everything go dark.

Chapter Fifty-Eight

ALLIE

Despite my silent protests, Harlan brought me out to breakfast, to the mall, out to dinner, then asked me to watch a movie with him in the home theater. I wanted to decline every offer, but that cruel look on his face warned me not to retaliate. And I didn't want to end up like Jace's mother *or* put my mother in danger.

And, plus, Harlan still hadn't told me where she or Jace were.

I sat at the end of the couch, inching closer and closer to the armrest until I couldn't get any farther. Harlan sat on the other end with his legs kicked up on a footrest and crossed over one another.

He looked too fucking comfortable for a man who had just beaten his son senseless.

Suddenly, the screen went dark, and the end credits started rolling. I shot up from my seat, completely checked out for the entire fucking day, and stepped closer to the door.

"Are we done now?" I asked, holding out my hand. "I did everything you asked. Please, give me my necklace back."

Harlan stood and turned the light back on, cocking a finger in my direction. "Come, Allie ..." He held the door open for me to exit the theater. "There's one more thing I'd like us to do together."

Something told me to fucking run.

I walked into the hallway and made sure to stay a solid four feet from him at all times.

Instead of heading into the kitchen for some ice cream—I thought he'd want to do something *fatherly*—he walked to his office and gestured for me to enter. I sat on the very edge of his suede maroon guest chair, itching to leave already.

"We're going to end these rumors once and for all," Harlan said. He opened his drawer, set his file on the center of his desk, and placed a lighter over it. He nodded to the file that had everything about him and his wife's murder. "Burn it."

My eyes widened, and I stood. "No."

He slammed his palm against the desk. "Burn. It. Now."

"No."

When I refused a second time, Harlan grabbed the lighter and paper himself. As he turned on the lighter and started to burn the bottom of the page, I sprinted at him to try to salvage it. But Harlan backhanded me harder than he had last night and sent me flying down.

Jace had worked so fucking hard to get this information. It was my fault—my fucking fault—that Harlan had it and was going to destroy it. A slap was nothing compared to the pain Jace must've felt after learning how terrible this man was.

So, I jumped back to my feet and lunged at him again.

I kicked him. I screamed at him. I bit him even, trying so desperately to get the papers away from that fire and to stop them from burning. And when the last of the paper burned, I didn't stop hitting him. He deserved it all.

Harlan tossed the lighter down and grabbed a fistful of my hair in one hand and my jaw in the other. "You need to learn fucking respect, Allie. Don't make me lose my patience again with you." He threw me down and walked to the door. "It won't end well."

"You're not the man you want everyone to think you are," I said to him, staring him right in the eye.

I wanted to hold myself back, but I couldn't anymore. This man disgusted me so much more every day—even before had Jace told me about Harlan murdering his mother.

I glared at him. "You are weak and a disgusting excuse for a man. You can buy me the entire world, and I'll never treat you as my father. My father was strong and fought for truth and justice."

Darkness flashed in Harlan's eyes—the same darkness that I had seen in them as he beat Jace last night. Instead of hitting me again, Harlan clenched his fists and stormed out of the room, slamming the door behind him like a bratty and immature teenager would.

I dug my nails into my palms, waited until I saw Harlan speed out of the driveway from the second-floor window, and hurried through the house to Jace's room. I gathered enough clothes for him for a couple days, the football he always threw around, and a pair of keys from the kitchen counter.

There were about eight cars parked in the garage. I hit the unlock button on the keys, hoping that it was a car I could drive, and heard the white Porsche beep twice. I needed to find my Jace.

The car was small, so fucking small. I slid into the driver's seat and hit my head on the car top. Pain shot through me, and I winced, but I ignored it. I went to slam the key into the ignition, but there wasn't a slot. I hit a button on the top of the car, hoping that a light would turn on, but the garage door started opening, the loud gear sound scaring me.

"Fuck," I whispered.

Fingers dancing across all sorts of buttons, the fog lights turned on, then the headlights turned on, then the high-beams turned on. *What the fuck? Why is this so damn hard?* I needed something quick and easy to get out of here before he came back.

After finally figuring out how to turn the car on, it revved to life, and I sighed deeply through my nose. God, I really needed to get my shitty car back. The fender might've been dented, the engine going, the back windshield cracked, but at least I could drive the damn thing.

After figuring how to put the car in reverse, I backed out of the driveway, not caring if I totaled the car because Harlan could buy a hundred of these and still be a fucking billionaire. I sped out of the driveway and toward Jamal's house.

I wanted to sink into Imani's arms, but I couldn't put her in danger. Too many of the people I cared about were already at risk with a crazy murderer living in the same house as me. Jamal kinda knew about what was happening.

Kinda.

At least, I trusted him more than I trusted Poison with this.

<h1 style="text-align:center">Chapter Fifty-Nine</h1>

ALLIE

After speeding past five cops and getting away with it because I was driving Harlan's car, I parked out in front of Jamal's house. I hurried to the front door and banged on it twice, my fingers shaking as I continued to glance over my shoulder to see if Harlan had followed me.

Jamal's mom opened the door with a big smile on her face, but then it dropped. "Allie, baby, what's wrong?" She held the door open, snatched Marquis's hand, and pulled him aside. "Come in, honey. It's freezing outside tonight. Coldest night of the winter so far."

I rubbed my frozen hands together and stepped into the house. "I need to talk to Jamal. It's important," I said, heading for the stairs.

"Allie, he—"

"J has a girl over," Marquis said, wiggling his eyebrows at me.

Jamal's mom smacked Marquis on the back of the head. "Go shower."

He rubbed the back of his head and ran to the staircase. "You know, my room is always open if you want to watch *Paw Patrol* with me. My sisters will be sleepin' later, if—"

"Marquis! Don't make me smack you again!"

Marquis widened his eyes and sprinted up the stairs. I glanced up the stairs at Jamal's room and gulped. If Jamal had a girl over, I didn't want to ruin his chances with her. This was important, but …

"It's fine," I said before his mom could call his name.

"Jamal!" Jamal's mom shouted anyway. "I seen that girl whoring around with another guy this weekend anyway. I taught my baby better than that. Jamal! Get your ass down here now," she continued. When he still didn't open the door, his mom said, "Allie is here!"

The door flew open, and Jamal stepped out with wide eyes. "Allie, what's going on?"

"Get your ass down here before Marquis hits on her again."

Jamal rolled his eyes, said something into the bedroom, and held the door open for Jenny—the same girl I'd found with Jace a few weeks ago. Jenny scurried down the stairs and past Jamal's mom, who was giving her major stink eye.

After she left, Jamal jogged down the stairs. "Is everything okay? You didn't show up for school. Imani couldn't get in contact with you either today. We were worried about you," he said, gripping my shoulder.

"Have you seen Jace?" I asked.

He furrowed his brows. "I thought he was with you."

"You're bleedin'." Jamal's mom spotted blood that must've been dripping down my neck, then grabbed my arm and brought me to their downstairs bathroom, turning on the sink and running a torn rag underneath it. "Why is the back of your head bleeding?"

My eyes widened, and I touched the spot where I'd hit it last night. I'd thought it had closed up, but my fingers felt wet. I swallowed hard as the tears filled my eyes and glanced over at Jamal. As much as I wanted to tell them about the true reason, I couldn't.

It would be a betrayal to Jace, and it would put them into danger.

The less people who knew about this, the better.

"I just ... hit my head last night."

Jamal's mom placed the rag on my head and pulled my hair aside. "Honey, this is deeper than it should be from a fall. What happened? And don't even think about lying to me. I can spot when someone's lying." She wagged a finger at me. "Especially you."

"Nothing," I whispered. She narrowed her eyes at me, but before she could say anything, I shook my head. "Please, do you have anything to seal the wound for now so that it doesn't open back up? I really need to find Jace."

After grimacing at me, she guided me to the kitchen, sat me in a chair, and disappeared into the bathroom to find some stuff. Jamal's mom was a nurse, so I hoped to God that she had something lying around that could help me for now.

Jamal glanced down the hallway to make sure nobody was listening in, then turned to me. "Allie, that wound is so deep. What the hell happened, and where was Jace when it did? He'll fucking kill whoever touched you. It wasn't Carter, was it?"

I pressed my lips together. "Harlan," I whispered, and that was it.

Jamal tensed and pressed his lips together when his mother walked into the room. She shook her head, parted my hair to the side to give herself better access, and started to clean the wound.

Jamal's mom looked between us as she continued, "You ain't gonna say anything?"

I pressed my trembling lips together, still able to feel Harlan slapping me earlier.

How does Jace do this day in and day out? Has he used football to hide his injuries? Does he play through the pain? Where the fuck is he?

I needed him, and I needed him now.

Once Jamal's mom was done, she stepped back. "Harlan?" she asked without either of us saying a word. "Is that who done this to you?"

"H-how did you know?"

"I can spot an abusive man when I see one. And with all the money in the world, Jace still comes and stays here whenever he has the chance," she said, shaking her head. "If you ever need anything, baby, you know where to come. You and Jace are always welcome here."

"I need to find him," I whispered, glancing from her to Jamal.

It made my heart swell that I still had someone to talk to, that I didn't have to hide this from everyone, but ... this couldn't be her problem. She was a single mom, trying to raise a houseful of kids.

"I thought Jace would've come here. He's been missing all day. His car is at the house."

Jamal tensed even more and grabbed his keys from the counter. "Let's go find him ... or find someone who might know where he is." Jamal took my hand and led me to the door. "Poison."

Chapter Sixty

JACE

When I opened my eyes and came back to consciousness, it was dark again. I didn't know what day it was or how much time had passed, but I must have been out for a long fucking time because Rick stood on the other side of the room with a fresh set of clothes on.

Has it been one day? Two days? Three?

I made sure not to make any sudden movements and listened to his conversation on the phone. He walked to the only window in this dingy place and glanced out at the snow as it fell from the dark sky. He grunted and nodded.

"How long will you be? I can't spend another fucking night here. I'm not a babysitter."

My entire body tensed, and I opened my eyes as wide as I could. His gun wasn't on his hip, but on the table, like it had been earlier. The cloth he polished it with lay next to it. But there it was … out in the open and ready to be fucking used.

When Rick turned in my direction, I closed my eyes and lay like a dead man.

"If you want me to kill the kid, say the fucking word," he said through the phone.

When his voice faded and seemed a bit farther away, I opened my left eye and winced at the pain coursing through my body.

If he had plans to kill me, I needed to kill him first.

"You sure?" he said, looking out the window.

Fuck, I needed to act quick.

After a slight pause, he nodded. "All right, see you in thirty."

Gathering all the strength I had left, I pushed myself to my feet and sprinted to the table. Rick turned around as I started for the gun and rushed after me. I grabbed the grip at the same time he did. We fumbled back and forth with it for a few moments, the muzzle pointing toward the ceiling.

It went off once, a bullet going straight through the drywall.

Then, another bullet fired off, the kickback nearly making my hands slip off the grip.

Rick slammed his shoulder into my cracked ribs, probably in hopes that I'd let go but I couldn't. This was my only fucking chance to kill the person who had disposed of Mom's body and to escape death. I didn't want to see Dad again, and I surely didn't want Allie to see me like this.

So, using all the strength that I had gained from years of football, I turned the gun in his direction, pointed it straight at his head as he continued to struggle against me, and shot the gun three times until his body fell limp.

Blood splattered everywhere—on the walls and on me. I'd thought I'd feel better, but I couldn't feel shit. My hands shook as I dropped the gun. I had never killed a man before, never fucking used a gun. I ... I didn't want to be like my father, had vowed to never kill anyone like he did.

"Fuck," I said, backing up until my back hit a wall. I needed to clean this up.

But first, I needed to find Allie.

I pushed the fears running through my head aside and grabbed his cell phone from the floor, picking it up and dialing Allie's number. I held the phone to my ear, searched the room for a pair of car keys, and waited impatiently as the phone rang and rang and rang.

"Allie, baby ..." I said through the phone.

When she didn't answer, I hopped into an SUV parked out front, stuck the key into the ignition, and sped away from the abandoned cabin in the woods, where Dad would come to see me.

"I'm coming for you."

<h1 style="text-align:center">Chapter Sixty-One</h1>

ALLIE

As soon as Jamal pulled up to the curb near Landon's house, I jumped out of the car and banged the side of my fist against the door. A chilling winter wind seared my cheeks. I jumped up and down on my toes, my anxiety eating me alive.

"Poison!" I shouted toward their window. "Open the door, for fuck's sake."

The door opened, and the three boys stood in front of it. Someone pushed their way between them, and Imani appeared before me with wide eyes.

"Oh my gosh, what happened to you?" she asked, pushing open the screen door and tugging me into a hug.

Despite telling myself that I wouldn't shed any more tears, I sobbed in her arms. "I—Jace ... he-he's gone. I haven't heard from him in over twenty-four hours. When Kai dropped me off this morning, he was gone. I'm so afraid that he's dead."

Imani looked back at the guys. "Have you heard from him?"

Before any of them could answer, a black SUV with tinted

windows skirted around the bend and screeched up to the side of the road. Kai grabbed Imani's waist and pulled her to the ground, as if someone was about to pull up and start shooting.

The driver's door swung open, and Jace shot out of the car toward me. My heart dropped as he scooped me up into his arms and buried his face into the crook of my neck.

"Thank fucking God that you're okay."

I ran my hands against his cheeks and shook my head in disbelief as blood coated my fingers. Jace *looked* like he had gone to hell and come back. There were so many bruises over every exposed place of his body. But ... but he was back here with me.

"The fuck happened to you?" João asked, opening the screen door and nodding inside.

Jamal wrapped one arm around Jace's torso to hold him up, and Jace flinched.

"Sorry, dude," Jamal said, helping him inside.

Imani pulled me into her arms and ushered me inside the house and to the basement, where I had slept last night. There were beer bottles scattered around the room, an empty box of condoms on the coffee table, and bongs near the couch.

After Jamal rested Jace on the couch, I sat next to him and gently grasped his knee.

"What happened to you?" I asked, searching the room for something clean that I could wipe the blood up with.

João grabbed a cheap bottle of vodka from the dirty white refrigerator and held it out for Jace. Jace went to grab it, but I tore the bottle out of his hand and glared at João.

"What's your damn problem? This is not a time to get drunk. He needs to be healed. Now."

"We could go see my mom, but she's, uh"—Jamal glanced down at his watch and frowned—"probably at work right about now. Her night shift starts in, like, five minutes. She leaves at ten-thirty p.m."

"My mom should be home," Imani said, eyeing the Poison

boys. She gnawed on the inside of her lip and shook her head, as if saying *screw it*. "If we leave now, she'll probably still be awake, too, but she has a surgery scheduled for early tomorrow morning, so we need to hurry."

Imani's mom was the most respected neurosurgeon in the entire northeast. I didn't know if she'd be able to heal Jace or at least close up his wounds, but she was our only hope. Nobody could know about Jace's father, not yet, especially not when we didn't have any evidence anymore.

"Imani, are you sure?" I asked, eyeing the boys.

Imani's mother definitely wouldn't approve of the three boys that Imani had been hanging around for the past however many weeks she had gone behind my back to sleep with them.

She nodded. "Let's go."

Before Jace could follow after Imani to her car, I grabbed his hand. "Jace, I need to tell you something first about ... about your father," I whispered.

I couldn't believe how stupid I had been. If I had stayed in the damn closet while Jace got his ass kicked, none of this would've happened.

But I knew that I'd do it again. I couldn't sit back as my boyfriend was abused.

Jace froze and tightened his grip on my hand. "Don't tell me that fucker touched you."

I shook my head and lied to Jace. Harlan had hit me more than once, but Jace was too banged up to go back home and fight him. I didn't want Harlan to *kill* him this time. I needed a couple days to gather my thoughts.

"He-he burned those papers and all the evidence in that file you told me to protect." Tears streamed down my face. I hated myself for this. It was all my fucking fault. Everything was going to shit because of me. "I'm so sorry! I-I tried to stop him. I really did."

Jace slumped his shoulders forward and blew out a deep

breath. "Don't fucking scare me like that. I thought he'd hit you," Jace said, wrapping his arms around my shoulders and pulling me closer to him. He gently stroked my hair. "Don't worry about it, Allie. Everything in that file was a copy. The real ones are somewhere where nobody will ever find them."

"You have them?" I asked, looking up at him. "You really do?"

He gave me the smallest of smiles. "I do, but don't say anything to my dad. We're going to let him think that he hasn't been caught and won't be caught. Then ... we'll watch him burn."

Chapter Sixty-Two

ALLIE

"Listen ..." Imani crossed her arms and glared at the Poison boys as João pulled up to her house.

Jamal had left to watch his brother and sisters while his mom was at work, so it was her, them, Jace, and me.

She eyed each one of them. "Don't say anything to my parents. They don't like you guys, so don't be fucking jerks."

Landon wrapped his arm around her shoulders. "We wouldn't do that, babe."

She elbowed him hard in the ribs. "I mean it this time."

After she hopped out of the car, I followed her. "You introduced them to your parents?"

Imani glanced back at the boys and Jace. "No, but that doesn't mean that they didn't show up while I was out at dinner with my parents and try to hit on me." She scrunched her nose. "My mom hasn't stopped talking about it all week. She won't let me live this down."

"Why don't you ever invite us over?" Landon said as Imani pushed her key into the front door lock.

"Because you steal shit and my parents don't like you." She cut her eyes over to him as her upper lip curled up. "I'm not in the mood. Don't push it, Landon." She looked back at the other two, daring them to say something to her. But they both kept their mouths shut. She pushed the front door open. "*Mom!*"

"In the office," her mother shouted back. "What do you need?"

"I need you. Now."

"Not the first time we've heard that," Landon said.

I rolled my eyes and intertwined my fingers with Jace, not wanting to spend any more time away from him. Being away from him for an entire day, wondering if he was dead or alive, had eaten me alive.

Mrs. Abara appeared in the foyer and sucked in a deep breath, hurrying over to Jace. "Oh my goodness, what happened to you?" she asked, taking him to the other room and sitting him on her white couch. It was bound to get stained, but Imani's family was rich enough to have ten identical couches like this here within the damn hour.

Everyone looked at everyone, not knowing what to say.

Jace grimaced at me and shook his head. "I got into a fight with someone on the football team," Jace lied straight through his teeth. "And got my ass kicked."

Mrs. Abara blew a breath out her nose. "Looks like it." She glanced up and noticed the Poison boys for the first time tonight. She gave them a hard and long look, then pressed her lips together and nodded to the other room. "I'm going to grab some supplies. Allie, please help me."

I followed her into the other room, glancing back at Jace in the living room.

"Sweetie, make sure they don't steal anything," Mrs. Abara said, leaning in close. "Those boys are bad news. I told her not to see them. Why is she bringing them into the house? Can you try to talk some sense into her?"

I glanced back at Imani, who sat on the other side of the living room, trying to distance herself from the Poison boys as much as she could. She widened her eyes at me, giving me that *what is my mom saying this time* look.

"They're just, um ... *friends*," I said, not sure of how to get out of this one.

Imani was way more than friends with those boys. And I had warned her endlessly not to get with any of them, but *someone* didn't listen. They had caught her doing something that she shouldn't have been, and now, she was paying for it. But I couldn't tell her mom that.

She gathered some supplies from her bathroom closet and handed them to me. "I'm telling you, those boys had better not distract her. She is set to be top ten in your graduating class, and you know how hard it is to get to the top at Redwood with everyone having the best tutors around."

When we walked back into the living room, Mrs. Abara started to clean Jace up.

"Allie!" Mr. Abara shouted as he walked into the room. Despite his wife's hesitation with four of Redwood's *finest* boys in his living room, he didn't seem to mind. He squeezed my shoulder. "You think about that internship yet?"

Mr. Abara was a biochemical engineer who had been suggesting I apply for an internship at his work for months now. With everything going on, applying to colleges, and dealing with Jace drama during the summer, I had brushed it off. But I had wanted to go for it for so long now.

"Internship?" Jace asked.

"Don't move, honey," Mrs. Abara said to him, stitching up his head.

"We're working on finding someone for a bioengineering internship. I know you're going to school for biology next year. Why don't you give this a try? A new position just opened." Mr. Abara smiled at me. "So? What do you say? You going to apply?"

"Um …" I glanced over at Jace, not sure if this was the right time. I wanted to do it so bad, but with Harlan and with Poison about to expose the whole town's secrets … I wasn't sure if I could right now.

"Do it," Jace said.

"Didn't I just tell this boy not to move?" Mrs. Abara said, eyeing the Poison boys.

I nodded. "Sure. I'll do it."

Mr. Abara clapped his hands. "Great! I'll set up an interview with the hiring manager."

Though I appreciated the offer, an internship was the last thing on my mind.

When Mrs. Abara was finished, she pulled out an orange bottle of medication and handed it to Jace. "I'm not supposed to do this, Jace, but you're going to need this." She leaned closer to us and grimaced. "Don't speak a word about this to *anyone*. I'm doing this because you're Allie's stepbrother, and that's all."

After Jace nodded and thanked her, I grabbed his hand. "Jace," I whispered. "I need to make sure that my mom is okay. I haven't seen her in twenty-four hours, so … I need to go back to the house. I'll meet you at Poison's place in an hour."

When I went to stand, Jace grabbed my hand. "I'm coming with you. You're not going there alone."

"But, Jace …" I shook my head and lowered my voice even more so only we could hear. "He's going to kill you."

"Don't worry about that," Jace said with so much certainty that it frightened me.

João placed a hand on each of our shoulders and stepped between us. "Wherever you're going, make sure you show up to the football game tomorrow. You're going to want to be there. Shit is going to go down."

Chapter Sixty-Three

ALLIE

When we pulled up to the house and saw Harlan's car in the driveway, my mouth dried up. I rubbed my sweaty palms together and scolded myself for reacting this way. The way that Harlan treated me was nothing compared to how he treated Jace. He had nearly killed him. I needed to be strong for Jace.

But I was scared.

Scared for Jace. Scared for Mom. Scared for myself.

Jace placed a hand on my knee and squeezed. "It'll be okay."

"Don't lie to me," I said to him.

Lights glared through the front windows and onto the snow in the front yard. This was not and would never be okay. We needed to both be strong for Mom because God only knew why that woman was still with him. If he had no problem with hitting me, I doubted he had a problem with hitting her.

"I'll protect us." Jace opened the glove box of the stolen SUV. "Don't worry."

"A gun?" I whispered, eyes wide in fear.

There was a gun covered in blood, sitting in the glove box.

I glanced between him and the gun and swallowed hard, placing a hand on his shoulder. "What did you do when you were gone?"

Jace tore his gaze away from me, clutched onto the steering wheel with one hand and the gun in his other. "I killed the man who had burned my mother's body. He trapped me in one of my dad's cabins. I thought he was going to kill me." Tears welled up in Jace's eyes, but he pushed them away, as if he didn't want me to see him so weak.

But we were in this together.

I brushed my fingers across his cheek and frowned. "You did what you had to do."

"I killed someone, Allie," Jace whispered. "I don't want to be like my father."

"You're not like your father. You killed him because you thought he would kill you. Not out of jealousy. Not out of rage. Not to feel better about yourself. To survive. You will never be like your father despite how afraid of becoming like him you are."

After a few moments of tense and saddening silence, Jace cleared his throat and straightened his back. "Whatever you say to your mother," Jace started, shifting uncomfortably in his seat. He glanced at the front door and cursed to himself. "Don't tell her to leave him. My mom wanted to leave him since I was eight, way earlier than when she cheated on him." Jace swallowed hard. "I listened to him threaten to kill her if she did." Jace bit his lip, as if he was biting back emotions along with it. "I just didn't think he would actually go through with it."

I swallowed hard and shook my head. This was going to be so much harder to get out of without a scratch. We were in deeper damn shit than I had originally thought. Jace had tried so hard to get us to leave years ago, so we wouldn't be stuck like this forever.

As we walked to the door, my stomach tightened. I hated this place so much, even more now. We walked into the room, Jace guiding me with his hand on my lower back to the living room, where Mom and Harlan spoke in hushed tones.

When we entered, everyone went silent. Mom gazed at Jace with wide eyes, yet she didn't say two words to him to ask if he was okay even though he looked like pure and utter shit. Instead, she grasped Harlan's hand and squeezed tightly. "You kids are home. Jace, what—"

"I got into a fight," Jace said, not even sparing a glance at his father, who sat deathly calm in his grand living room chair.

He was so still that it fucking frightened me to no end.

"Mom …" I bravely walked into the room and toward them. I grabbed her hand and tugged her away from Harlan. "I need to talk to you about Imani. I need your advice. She's stressing me out."

Harlan easily let me pull her aside, yet he kept his gaze on her like a damn hawk. Jace stood by the door, lips fixed in a scowl. I pulled my gaze away from both of them and looked at my mother, who I really hadn't spoken to in years.

"Mom," I whispered, gazing into her dull eyes. The brightness had faded when she lost Dad. "Mom, are you okay? Where were you last night and all of today? You didn't answer any of my calls."

She gave me a tense *fake* smile. "Oh, sweetheart, I was just out with the girls."

"You couldn't return my calls, couldn't send me a text?"

She peeled my hand away from hers and leaned an inch closer. "This is not a good time, Allie. Please, drop this now. We can talk sometime later," she said with a smile.

She pushed some hair from my face, yet I saw the way her eyes wavered.

Nothing was okay.

"Now, tell Imani to come over anytime she wants," Mom said louder. "Whenever her parents are fighting, she's always welcome here." She looked over her shoulder at Harlan. "Isn't that right, Harlan?"

Harlan gave a curt and tense nod, and Mom walked away from me and back to him. Before I could pull her away, Harlan wrapped his arm around her waist and pulled her into him, daring me to try to tug her away again.

Jace snatched up my hand and guided me toward his room. "You're staying with me tonight." He pushed me into the room and shut the door behind him. "I'm not letting you out of my fucking sight."

"Jace," I whispered, looking back at the door, "I'm scared."

Nerves ran up and down my spine. I didn't know if it was a good idea to stay here tonight because I didn't trust Harlan. I fucking loathed that man after what he had done, but Mom was here. And by the sound of it, she wasn't leaving him anytime soon. I didn't want her to be here alone.

Chapter Sixty-Four

JACE

"Jace," Allie said, glancing at the shut door. She gnawed on the inside of her cheek. "Do you really think we should stay here?"

I clutched her waist and tugged her onto the bed with me, wrapping my arms around her stomach and grasping her belly. By the way she tensed, I could tell that she didn't feel confident in her body. She never had. But I loved to feel her flesh in my hands and loved every inch of her.

"Come here," I said, wanting to do more than just hold her.

She didn't want to leave her mother, and her mother wasn't going to leave my father. If he tried to do anything to her, we'd at least be here to try to stop him. That was the only fucking reason we were staying here. The only fucking reason, and it was a shitty one.

When she settled against me, her ass rubbing against my dick, I pulled her closer and murmured into her ear, "Wanna make my shitty day a little better?"

She smiled. "What do you have in mind?"

I pressed myself harder against her, and she turned over to roll her eyes at me.

"Jace, you're hurt."

"Come on, baby." I stroked her cheek with my thumb, my cock hardening against my gray sweats. "It'll help me heal *so* much faster."

She rolled her eyes again yet crawled down the bed and lay between my legs. "You are the most annoying person ever." She drew one finger up my bulge and curled her fingers around the waistband of my pants. "You nearly died last night, and all you can think about is a blowjob. Typical man."

I curled my lips into a smirk as I watched her slowly pull down my pants. My dick sprang out of it, hitting her smack across the lips. Squinting her eyes behind her thick lenses, she flinched away from me and puckered her lips.

"Damn it," she mumbled, wrapping her small hand around the base of my cock.

After sighing through my mouth, I relaxed against the mattress and gently stroked Allie's jaw with my thumb. She licked from the base of my cock up, swirling her tongue around the head and flicking the tip.

When she wrapped her lips around my shaft, I shuddered, then grunted. As she sucked more and more of me between her full lips, she stared up at me through teary eyes. Blinking a few times, she gagged on me yet continued to take every single inch until her pretty little throat was stuffed full with my cock.

"Fuck, Allie ..." I whispered, pulling hair from her face and holding it back in my fist.

She slowly pulled herself back up, my cock glistening from her spit and all the warmth from her mouth disappearing. She swirled her tongue around my head, then bobbed her head back down onto my cock.

Faster this time.

And over and over and over again.

I blew an unsteady breath out my nose, my cock becoming harder by the second. Allie lightly massaged my balls with her fingers as she continued to suck me off. Spit and slobber rolled down her chin.

When she came up for air, her cheeks were red. She stroked my cock up and down as fast as she could and gazed at me right in the eyes. "Are you going to come for me?" she asked, sticking my cock back into her mouth. "Come down my throat?"

She pushed me all the way down her throat again, stuck out her tongue, and licked my balls. Unable to hold myself back, I laced my hand in her hair, held her head down, and let my cum shoot into her throat. Pleasure washed over me, making my hips convulse and my toes curl.

My day might've been shitty, but she could make it so much better.

Chapter Sixty-Five

JACE

Since it had snowed on Friday night, the football game was postponed until Saturday night, which meant that I could go and actually coach alongside Coach. Allie had begged me not to go, had begged me to rest and relax. But I needed a pick-me-up after the past few days.

Carter walked arrogantly back to the sidelines, tearing off his helmet after his first touchdown of the game. He threw me a smirk and grabbed his water bottle. "You good, Harbor? Get into a fight on the wrong side of town?"

I ignored his comment and crossed my arms over my chest, watching the defense crumble under the other team. If I were out there, I would have picked up an interception or two by now. We would be winning, for Christ's sake.

Nonetheless, the team we were playing against was ranked number one in the state.

A running back from the opposite team ran forty yards to the five-yard line before Jamal tackled him. I sighed through my nose, watching the time tick down on the clock to three seconds before halftime. After glancing up at the bleachers, I caught Allie's eye. She signaled to her face, scolding me for not icing my swollen eye.

After giving her my best smile, I grabbed my ice packet, waved it in the air, and placed it on my face like she wanted me to. Then, I turned back to the game and slowly watched the time run down before our rival team was about to score.

A buzzer rang throughout the stadium, the bright white lights on the scoreboard reading 14–6. The teams retreated to their sides of the field, packing up to head to the locker room for halftime, when the lights in the stadium turned off.

Every single one of them. Even the scoreboard.

Phones started buzzing uncontrollably and lighting up across the stands. I pulled mine out of my jeans pocket and watched a prerecorded multimedia message pop up onto the screen of Principal Vaughn sitting, naked, in his office and masturbating to the videos he had recorded of the locker room.

Someone came over the intercom, using a voice enhancer to hide their true identity. But everyone knew who it was. The only people who would stir up any really bad trouble in Redwood were Poison.

"Redwood Academy, your principal is jerking off to the hundreds of recordings of Redwood students, naked in the locker rooms. Is this who you think is fit to lead your school? Is this who we're giving thousands of dollars to every year? Is this someone you think deserves to live?"

Gasps broke out through the crowd.

Knowing that this wasn't the worst Poison had planned for that fucking ugly excuse for a man, I continued watching the video of Vaughn jerking off. Suddenly, three masked guys—who were clothed in black and carrying different-sized weapons— stormed the room and caught Vaughn in a moment of weakness. With his cock hanging out, Vaughn scrambled to his feet.

One of the men forced him still.

Another one of the men handed the leader a knife.

The leader cut his cock right from his body and tossed it onto his neck like it was nothing.

"That's not the only punishment that Vaughn has received for his sins," João said over the speakers. I could tell it was him by the simple way he talked even though his voice was changed. I had been dealing with them for years now.

Suddenly, the lights turned on, and I caught sight of a ball hurling through the air from somewhere in the bleachers and toward the field. The ball bounced once, then twice, and then I realized that it wasn't a ball at all, but Principal Vaughn's head.

"Over the course of the next few months, all the lies, all the secrets, all the scandals that have run this town will be exposed. Nobody is safe from the truth."

Screams erupted through the crowd.

"Welcome to the end, Redwood."

Chapter Sixty-Six

JACE

The cheerleaders screamed around me, and the football players rushed off the field through a back entrance. Vaughn's head lay feet from me, blood splattered across the white field lines, and I didn't move.

Everything turned to pure chaos within mere moments, the crowd erupting into screams and shouts. Red and blue police lights turned on around the field. When Poison had told me to show up tonight, this was not what I'd fucking expected them to do.

People started rushing down the bleachers and knocking people out of the way. In a moment, I lost sight of Allie and Imani in the tall bodies of other students. My stomach twisted at how violent some of the students were being. I feared the worst.

"Jace!" someone shouted behind me, the voice lost in the crowd.

I turned around, expecting to see Allie, but Nicole rushed up to me in her tight cheerleading uniform with Redwood across the chest and goose bumps on her bare arms. After seeing her, I turned away and scanned the crowd for Allie, unable to find her in the large stampede of students rushing toward the exits.

Nicole wiped her cheeks with the back of her trembling hand. "We have to get out of here, Jace. My father is—"

When she grabbed my hand, I pulled it away. "Stop it, Nicole! We're not dating. We were *never* dating. Learn your fucking boundaries and don't fucking touch me again. I don't have the patience to deal with your fucking ass."

Yet Nicole didn't stop. She grabbed my wrist and tugged me toward the exit. "My dad texted me and told me to leave. I think he's going to blame you for this. He knows that you've hated Vaughn because of how much he hated you."

More and more people pushed and shoved down the bleacher steps. If Allie tripped over a single step, she could be fucking trampled because kids at Redwood were ruthless pieces of shit.

"Jace, listen to me! We have to go!"

"I need to find Allie first." I pushed through the crowd. "When I find her, we can talk."

"Jace," she shouted again, her voice getting lost in the murmurs.

But I didn't have time for her nonsense at the moment. Once I made sure Allie was safe, I could talk to her—maybe. I didn't want to. I really didn't fucking want to. But because everyone in Redwood seemed to hate me, I would get blamed for this. And Nicole's father definitely had it out for me, not only because I used to hang out with his daughter, but also because when I left Redwood in a few months, I would set out to do something he could never do—become one of the biggest things Redwood would ever see in the NFL.

Her father had played football all throughout college, and the last game of his senior year, he had gotten hit by a defenseman so fucking hard that he tore both of his ACLs and never recovered. Now, he wanted to destroy all my fucking chances at a life like that too.

People rushed past me as I hurried toward the bleachers, but I shoved them out of the way, pushing against the crowd. I raced up and down the student section, checking under the seats where Allie usually sat. Though I couldn't find her or Imani, I found Allie's phone, her screen recently broken in four places and kicked under the bleachers.

After shoving it into my pocket, I glanced up and scanned the area outside of the field. I caught sight of a red car with tinted windows sitting in the parking lot. The headlights flashed once, and my phone buzzed in my pocket.

João: Allie is fine. We have eyes on her. Meet at Landon's.

I let out a huge sigh, my shoulders slumping forward, and rubbed a hand across my face. Jesus Christ, tonight had not gone as I'd expected it to. I'd thought Poison would start small, not kill someone for the hell of it.

But I wasn't complaining. Vaughn deserved to be six feet under, just like my father.

Chapter Sixty-Seven

ALLIE

Everything happened so quickly. One moment, I cheered on Redwood's defense, and the next, I was pushing through a herd of terrified high school students with Imani in tow, trying desperately to find Jace.

Amid the craziness, I couldn't find him or any of the football players, which should've been easy because they were all so much taller than the typical Redwood student. Deep down, I knew Imani and I weren't in any big trouble. But ... still.

Imani suddenly stopped in the middle of the crowd as people pushed past us, shoving us out of the way to get to the exit of the field. Cops stood around, trying to calm people down and make sure they were safe, trying to be *nice*. Cops in Redwood were never nice; they were always corrupt. Now, they were scared that they'd be next.

"Come on, Imani. We need to go."

When I tugged on her hand, she didn't budge. I turned back around to see tears streaming down her cheeks. The bright red face paint in the shape of a *R* on her left cheek dripped down the side of her face from her tears. She went to wipe them away, but she couldn't even pull her arms up enough to reach her cheeks with her trembling hands. She mouthed my name, but no words came out.

Despite the adrenaline and nerves rushing through me, I wrapped my arms around her, like she had done to me countless times, and stroked her back. "Imani, we have to go. We don't know what else they have planned."

She shook her head, still unmoving. "They-they killed someone!"

I swallowed hard, not knowing how to react. My gut reaction was to tell her that I'd told her to stay away from Poison because they were no good and did shit that nobody else would do, but that would be rude—absolutely, terribly rude.

So, I pushed her forward with the crowd, so we wouldn't be trampled.

"That's what they do," I said, careful not to speak their name out loud and in public.

While everyone must have known that this was their doing, I didn't want to incriminate them. I needed to thank them.

She wrapped her arms around me as we kept up with the students. "I knew they were bad news, but ... I-I-I didn't think that they'd do anything like this. They took a life and put it on display like it was ... *nothing*." When we made it out onto the side-walks, where everyone was dispersing onto the streets and speeding out of the parking lots, she continued, "How many times do you think they've done that before? Once? Twice? Hundreds of times?"

After scanning the crowd again for any sign of Poison or Jace, I turned back to her. "I don't know, Imani," I answered honestly.

I wanted to tell her that they probably hadn't done it before, but that'd most likely be a lie. From the outside, they looked like they had done that *many* times before, to the point of perfection.

Past the point of shock, Imani shook her head and turned

back to the stadium. "I'm going to scream at them for this! How do you just kill someone and throw their fucking head onto the field during a football game?! You have to be fucking insane."

Never before having seen this side of her, I grabbed her by the wrist and dug my heels into the ground to try to stop her. "If you go back in there, the cops will question you and pressure you to give up any information you have on them. You don't want to get them sent to jail, do you?" I asked her. But honestly, the way she was reacting right now made it seem like she didn't care what happened to them, though I knew she did.

"They killed someone, Allie. Doesn't that scare you?!" she asked, continuing back to the cops at the gated entrance to the football field.

A couple looked over at her, giving us *that look* all cops gave when they thought that they had something stuffed in the bag, thought that they could coerce an innocent person into lying or spilling more than the truth just to prove their own beliefs.

She looked back at me with furrowed brows and a disgusted expression. Truth was, Jace and I were *living* with a murderer. We had been living with one for the past two years. And now, I would always be a bundle of nerves when I was with Harlan.

Murder shouldn't be positive by any means, but, sometimes and for some people—like Harlan and Principal Vaughn—it was needed.

"They won't even be inside," I argued. "They're probably watching from a distance."

After my last few words, she stopped abruptly. "Watching from a distance ..."

When she turned back around, a red car drove by, almost as if on cue. Though the windows were tinted, I didn't miss the small smirk I saw from the driver's window from João when they drove under a streetlight.

As the car drove down the street, Imani went to chase after it like a madwoman. I captured her wrist again and dragged her down the street toward the bad side of Redwood.

"There is no point in chasing them. They're already gone." And they were our damn ride.

I scanned the field for any sign of Jace and frowned when I still couldn't find him. After Poison's big reveal, the crowd had been pushing people down the bleachers so fast and so abruptly that I dropped my stupid phone and couldn't find it.

Imani hurried down the sidewalk and inched closer to me. It had to be below freezing out here at the moment. The frames on my nose felt like they were ice sitting on my face.

A car pulled up to the sidewalk a few feet ahead, and whoever was driving rolled down the passenger window. For a moment, I thought it was one of the Poison boys picking us up, but it was *Nicole.* Fucking Nicole, out of all the damn people it could be.

"Get in," she said to us. "You'll freeze out there."

My eyes widened slightly. What was she doing here, and why was she offering us help? I expected her to be the one to add to the drama, not help out with two students caught in the middle of it.

"We're not going anywhere with you," I said, hurrying down the sidewalk.

Nicole sped up to catch up with us. "Get in, Allie. Jace is looking for you."

Though I didn't want to believe that Jace Harbor had asked Nicole for help and though I knew it probably wasn't the best idea to get into the car with my sworn enemy, I knew that it would take us an hour to get to Poison's or even back to Harlan's house. And in this cold, we were bound to freeze one of our toes off.

Plus, if Nicole tried anything, I was sure Poison had something on her too.

I opened the car door and glared at her. "This doesn't make us friends."

"Fine by me," Nicole said, driving off once we were both in the car. "Poison's place it is."

Chapter Sixty-Eight

JACE

Impatiently pacing in Landon's basement, I rubbed my sweaty palms back and forth. *Where the fuck is Allie?* My fucking luck would be to save her from my father, only to hear that she had been fucking trampled in the crowd when I left the field.

I trusted Poison, but when they had told me that Allie got into the car with *Nicole* and that Nicole was bringing her and Imani here, I didn't fucking believe it. But Nicole had texted me ten minutes ago, telling me to get the fuck off the Redwood field and meet her at Poison's for a delivery of *special goods*.

That was what she had called Allie—*special goods*—probably because she was jealous.

Suddenly, the basement door swung open, and a furious Imani barreled down the stairs.

"What the hell was that?!" Imani screamed at João, who leaned against the wall with a cigarette between his lips. "Are you guys dumb?!" She shoved João. "You are the stupidest fucking people I've met."

Allie walked down the stairs, muttering something incoherent to Nicole. When she saw me, she walked away from her and wrapped her arms around my shoulders. "I lost my phone in the crowd. Everyone was going crazy. Sorry for making you worry."

After kissing her forehead, I handed her phone back and guided her toward the couch and away from Imani, who continued to scream at all three of the boys, who didn't look like they cared that they had killed someone.

"What's wrong with you guys?! You can be thrown in jail."

"Relax, Imani," João said.

"Nobody is going to jail," Landon continued, taking the pack of cigarettes from João and lighting one up. He drew on it once and blew out a puff of smoke, slumping down on the couch and sighing. "Nothing will happen."

"You don't know that!" Imani continued.

Kai placed a hand on her shoulder and glanced at Allie for the quickest damn second, probably to make sure she was okay. For some reason, he always fucking watched over her. And I didn't know if I liked that or not. Allie was mine, and I'd fought fucking hard to get her back. Nobody was going to take her away from me.

"We've done this before," Kai said. "We know how to clean shit up and hide the evidence. Don't make a big deal out of it."

Imani widened her eyes, shook her head, and backed away. "All three of you are insane." She looked at Allie and Nicole. "Why aren't you both freaking out more?! We just saw our principal's head in the middle of the football field."

Instead of freaking out like I'd thought she would, Allie blew out a long breath and shrugged her shoulders. She looked tired, and I didn't blame her. Neither one of us had gotten much sleep these past few days. This must've been another night in Redwood for her.

"You guys can't just—"

"Calm the fuck down!" João said, fury laced in his words. Though he led their little gang, he rarely lost control and usually kept himself calm—most of the time. He put out his cigarette. "You know what we did when you got involved with us. I gave you a chance to leave. You didn't. So, sit down and keep your mouth shut before someone hears you screaming at us for what happened."

Taken by surprise, Allie tensed next to me. Imani smacked João right across the face, leaving a big, fat red handprint on his cheek. João clenched his jaw and narrowed his eyes at her as she muttered something under her breath.

"You want to say that a little louder?" João asked her. "Because you're one more mistake away from me teaching you a fucking lesson on how to behave, Imani."

Though the words came out harsh, Imani seemed not to care. She turned on her heel, walked to the other side of the room, and sat against the wall. "Fuck you, João. I hate you."

When the room went quiet, Nicole turned to me. "Well ..." She cleared her throat and adjusted herself in the seat beside Allie.

Allie sat up taller and narrowed her eyes at Nicole, as if she was being protective of me ... which was cute, to say the least.

Nicole fixed her attention on me. "My dad is going to blame you. I know he will. He knows that you were the only person in my house the weekend all the files got stolen."

Allie looked up at me and frowned. "Is that true?"

I tensed at the memory of being with Nicole at her house. "Allie, you know that I went—"

Allie shook her head and looked back at Nicole. "He'll blame Jace?"

Nicole nodded, brows furrowed together. "I know he will. He hates him."

Landon waved his hand dismissively. "Don't worry about him. We're taking care of him next. He's the only person standing in the way of Redwood's fall. All the other police officers don't know shit about all the blackmail your father has been doing throughout the years."

Nicole teetered back and forth on the sofa, toying with the ends of her skirt. "And me?"

I rolled my eyes and sighed through my nose, rubbing a hand over my face.

"Piss us off, and you'll find out," João said.

Nicole pressed her lips together and looked down at her thighs. Yet again, we fell into another long silence, the tension in the air high—especially between Imani and Poison. Allie curled into me, resting her head on my shoulder.

"We need to talk about what we're going to do about your father," Kai said, tapping his fingers on a side table. "Once Nicole's father is gone, it will be easy to put him in jail. Is that what you want? Or do you want him tortured and dead?"

Allie tensed beside me and looked up at me, waiting for my answer. I swallowed hard and looked away from her, not wanting to say it out loud. She knew how much it'd hurt me to see Mom dead. She knew how much I'd hated killing the man who had burned Mom's body. I didn't want her to think less of me for this.

"Those are two different ball games," João said, sitting across from us. "Your father has increased his security, which I'm sure you saw. It's difficult to get him alone. If you want him dead—"

"We'll talk about this later," I said, ending the discussion. "When the girls are gone."

Chapter Sixty-Nine

ALLIE

Once we left Poison's house, Jace brought us home, guided me to his bedroom, and locked the door. We avoided Harlan and Mom in the living room at all costs. Part of me wanted to go see her, and the other part of me wanted to call it a night. I had been too exhausted lately to even think about pulling her away from Harlan and talking to her. They seemed to be joined at the hip or something.

Jace pushed me onto the bed, crawled up with me, and kissed me gently, moving his lips against mine in the same rhythm we used to have two years ago—the kind that was both slow and passionate and grew into something much hungrier.

"Aren't you ... still ... hurting?" I asked between kisses.

He moved his lips down the column of my neck and lightly sucked on the skin above my collarbone, the stubble on his cheeks tickling me. My head fell back slightly, and I let out a soft moan.

"Jace, I don't want it to hurt you."

"Oh, baby, this isn't going to hurt me." He slipped his hand underneath my leggings and rubbed my clit through my underwear. "Your little pussy is sopping wet." He sucked my bottom lip into his mouth and tugged on it gently, making me clench. "Does this feel good?"

Crawling further up the bed, Jace undid the button on his jeans and let his bulge push open the zipper on them. He pressed his hard-on against my entrance and thrust his hips back and forth against me. "Hmm?" he asked. "Does my good little slut like that?"

Heat pooled between my legs as I spread them even farther for him. I wanted to be stuffed full with his cock so badly that my pussy ached to feel him inside again. It had only been a few days, but after giving Jace a blow job last night, I had been dreaming of it.

Suddenly, he slapped my pussy. "Answer me."

"Yes," I whimpered. "I love it."

He sucked my bottom lip between his again and tugged on it harsher this time. "I bought something for you," he said, crawling off me and walking toward his dresser, tugging his shirt over his head.

I stared at the muscles in his back flexing hard under the moonlight. He pulled a box out of the drawer and looked over his shoulder at me.

"It came in the mail today."

"Something for me?" I asked with wide eyes.

When he turned around, he had a dildo in his hand.

And it wasn't any baby-dick dildo.

It was thick, fat, and long. Bigger than anything I'd ever had inside me.

Heat rushed to my core at the thought of pushing something that big inside of me as Jace fucked me from behind. He had told me so many times that he wanted to do it. I just hadn't thought he meant anytime soon.

"Jace ..." I whispered, sitting up.

He walked over to me, sat behind me with his legs by my sides, and stuck his thumb into my mouth. "Suck it, Allie." When he pulled his thumb out, he placed the head of the dildo against my lips and pushed an inch of it inside of me. "Get it wet for me, so I can slip it right inside of you."

I opened my mouth wide, letting him push another inch inside of me. I leaned back against his chest and pressed my legs together, feeling the pressure start to build inside of me. Jace pushed another few inches of the dildo inside of me and gently massaged my clit again, building me higher.

"You know how you're going to use this for me, right?" he asked low in my ear, trailing his nose against my neck. "You're going to use both hands and thrust this huge cock inside of your pussy as you watch yourself in the mirror."

Slobber dripped from my mouth and onto my chin. I whimpered and moved my hips back and forth against his fingers to feel more friction. Tension rose inside of me, more heat warming my core.

"You're going to be full with cock tonight." He captured my earlobe between his teeth and pushed another few inches of the dildo into my mouth until there was a bulge in my throat from the length. "Hold this for me and show me how you'll fuck yourself."

I grabbed the base of the dildo from him and closed my eyes as he snaked his hand around the bulge in my throat. Jace traced the edges of the dildo against my throat with his finger and stroked it up and down.

Thrusting the dildo in and out of my mouth, I curled my toes as my throat made gurgling sounds for him. The harder I throat-fucked myself, the faster Jace rubbed my clit.

He grasped my jaw in his hand and forced me to look in the mirror. "Look at the mess you're making of yourself, Allie." He sucked on my neck and stared at me through the reflection. "You love sucking cock so much that you're going to come from it, aren't you?"

I squeezed my eyes closed as wave after wave of ecstasy rushed through me. My pussy pulsed, aching to be filled. Jace pulled the dildo out of my mouth, pushed down my panties, and maneuvered his way out of his jeans. I lay in his arms, letting the pleasure overtake me for a few moments until I could finally move without twitching again.

After pulling me on top of him, he wrapped his arms under my legs from behind and spread them wide, his cock pressed against my ass. He spit on his hand, made his cock wet, then massaged my hole. He pushed a finger inside of me and groaned into my ear.

"Fuck, Allie, I've been waiting so fucking long for this." After a few moments, he pushed another finger into me, opening me up. "I've jerked off, thinking about fucking your ass so many times."

I clenched at the thought of Jace rubbing one out to the thought of me.

When he pushed in a third finger, I furrowed my brows at the feel of it and grunted softly. His hard cock pressed against my asscheek, inching closer to my hole and twitching against me.

"How does this feel?" he asked me, slowly thrusting his fingers in and out.

Unable to speak, for fear that I'd scream in pleasure, I nodded.

Jace pulled his fingers out of me and pressed the head of his cock against my hole. When he pushed himself inside and stared at me through the mirror's reflection, I gasped out loud and balled my hands into fists to displace the slight pain.

Inch after inch after inch, he continued until there wasn't any more left. He grabbed the backs of my knees, pulled my legs into the air, and spread them even farther, staring at my pulsing pussy hole as he started to fuck my ass. His balls slapped against it, hitting it hard.

"Put the dildo inside of you," Jace said into my ear, handing me the dildo. "Fill yourself."

I grabbed it from him and pressed it against my entrance, slowly sliding it inside of me. When I pushed it in all the way, I couldn't stop the moan from escaping my throat. I relaxed back against Jace and clenched hard.

Fuck, it felt so good. So much better than I'd thought it would.

As Jace started to fuck me harder, I used two hands to thrust the dildo in and out of my pussy. Pressure rose in my core, my pussy tightening every moment. The movement in and out of me made me nearly tip over the edge.

"Take this off," Jace said, grabbing at the ends of my shirt.

I tugged it over my head and let my breasts fall out of it.

"That's what I wanna see—your tits bouncing in the mirror as I fuck your fat fucking ass, Allie."

I grabbed the dildo tighter, not knowing how much longer I'd be able to keep this up. My legs were already trembling hard. I was about to tip over the damn edge in a second.

Jace grunted in my ear. "Fuck your pussy harder, Allie," he growled at me. "I want your cunt to be aching tomorrow."

At his demand, I fucked myself harder with the dildo, but it wasn't hard enough for him. He pushed my hands away from the dildo, and I let him, as all my trembling body could do was sink against his body.

"My little bratty bitch can't follow directions," he growled into my ear. Wrapping one arm around my waist to hold me still, he thrust his hips up into me as he pushed the dildo inside of me, all while staring at me intently in the mirror. "I'll have to do it for you."

Before he could even thrust into me again, I screamed out his name and let my body convulse in his arms as a toe-curling, hand-shaking, body-numbing orgasm ripped its way through me.

Jace continued to fuck me until I came down from my second orgasm. He pulled the dildo and himself out of me, stroked his dick, and sprayed his cum all over my pussy. Before I could stop him, he shoved the cum and the dildo back into me.

Though it was wrong—*so fucking wrong*—the thought of Jace

pushing his cum as deep into my pussy as it could go made me double over onto my side and come for him again. I slapped a hand over my mouth, not wanting him to know how much I secretly loved to be filled with his thick cum and that one day—not anytime soon—I hoped he'd fill me up with so much of it that he'd make me pregnant.

Chapter Seventy

ALLIE

Twenty minutes later, Jace shut the passenger door for me and slid into the driver's seat of his Maserati. When he started the car, I gazed out my window at Mom and Harlan's room and frowned at the light on and Mom's silhouette.

Every time I left her at the house alone, I felt guilty. I didn't want her to ever be with Harlan by herself because—though she was a bitch to me sometimes—I still loved her. When she had been with Dad, I could see how hard she could love. She had been my rock after he died.

I grabbed for Dad's dog tags and realized that they weren't there. Harlan still had them, probably had them stashed away in his office drawer or was hanging them over Mom's head, telling her that if I didn't straighten up, he'd destroy those too.

I needed to talk to her, but Harlan never gave her a spare moment. Whenever we were at the house, Mom was by his side at all times. She never left the room, always kept up a facade that everything was all right. Both she and I knew that she was lying.

And yet, even when Harlan had to work, Mom left the house with him.

It was constant.

Jace pulled out of the driveway and onto the road. Though it must've been nearly one in the morning, lights were on in nearly every house in the neighborhood, people pacing back and forth in their living rooms, cars started but nobody was in them. It hadn't even been ten hours since the football game, and the rich, snotty Redwood residents were already freaking out behind closed doors.

Imagine what would happen when more secrets came undone.

When Jace drove out of our neighborhood, I sighed and sank down in the seat. This was not how I'd expected my Saturday night to go—becoming acquaintances with Nicole, watching a penis get chopped off, seeing Principal Vaughn dead. It seemed so surreal that I thought it was a dream.

Jace pulled up to the side of the Overlook and glanced at me. "It's cold, but you wanna get out with me?" He cracked the faintest of smiles. "For old times' sake."

I arched a brow. "For old times' sake or to thank me for letting you fuck my ass?"

His smile turned into a sly smirk. "For a bit of both." He nodded to the rocks. "Come on."

After bundling up in the jacket Jace had bought me, I waddled out of the car and stayed close to him as we walked down the small pathway to sit on a couple of huge rocks. Still sore, I winced and scooted closer to Jace, resting my head against his shoulder and trying to shamelessly steal his body heat.

"Are you okay?" Jace asked after a few moments.

"As in ..."

"As in after everything that happened tonight."

Staring at the dark gray clouds sitting over the ocean, I shrugged. After everything that had happened with Harlan, learning that Jace had killed someone in his own self-defense, and worrying endlessly about what happened to him, I couldn't feel much worse. Jace and Imani wouldn't let Poison do anything to hurt me, so in that aspect, I was good.

It'd be nice to finally see some of Redwood's finest burn.

"Tonight didn't bother me as much as it should have," I admitted. "I thought it would, but ... I can't get myself to feel angry or upset that Poison killed Vaughn. I can't find myself to feel fear over what might happen to this town. Most people here deserve what's coming to them."

After a few moments, Jace hummed to himself and nodded. We sat in silence for a few more moments, questions starting to eat me alive, the longer we sat there.

Did Jace know that Poison would kill Vaughn? Or is he numb to the pain and terror and fear that most people from Redwood felt right now too?

"Jace," I whispered, letting the waves drown out my voice.

"Yeah?"

I gnawed on the inside of my cheek, threw one leg of mine over to straddle him, and grasped his face. There was one question I needed the answer to as soon as possible because the thought was killing me on the inside.

"What did you tell Poison about what you want to do to your father?" I asked, brushing my fingers against his cheek and pushing some strands of thick hair off his face. "You know, when you made Imani, Nicole, and me wait in the other room before we left, when they asked if you wanted them to kill him."

Jace stared out at the crashing waves for a few moments. "I told them no."

"No?" I asked in disbelief.

Ever since Poison had announced to Redwood that things were about to be different around here, I'd thought that Jace would jump on the chance to pay them to kill his father. I didn't think he'd ever have to think about it.

Jace swallowed hard. "I've thought about this for a long time. After he murdered my mom, I wanted him to rot in a jail cell for the rest of his life, wanted him to be tortured over and over and over for fucking eternity." Jace picked up a rock and threw it toward the water. "Now, I just want that son of a bitch dead, but I want to do it."

My eyes widened slightly. "You?" I whispered.

"He deserves all the fucking pain, Allie," he said to me. "And I'm ready to finally give it to him. No more wondering what life would be like if Mom had never cheated. No more dreaming of the past. No more living in fear. I'll give up everything I've worked for to protect you and your mom even if it ends up with me behind bars."

Chapter Seventy-One

ALLIE

Arm sprawled across my abdomen, Jace tugged me closer to him and mumbled something incoherent in my ear. Moonlight flooded into the room through the blinds, and I blinked my eyes open. After reaching for my glasses on the nightstand, I put them on my face and squinted at the clock on my phone.

Three-forty-five a.m.

"Jace," I whispered, pushing his arm off me. "I have to pee."

After pushing him onto his back, I scooted out of bed and glanced over at his bare abdomen, just barely covered by the thin sheets. I grabbed a plush teal robe that Jace had bought me and shrugged it over my shoulders.

Once I did my business in Jace's bathroom—yes, he had a bathroom in his damn bedroom—I opened his bedroom door and peeked my head out into the dark hallway. My mouth felt beyond dry. I needed something to drink. I hoped whoever was looking down on me that Harlan was asleep and hadn't gotten up for work yet.

Deciding that he was asleep, I tiptoed out of the room and down the hallway, careful not to make any noise. While the house was huge and had too many rooms to count, I had to be extra careful. If Harlan was still awake, he could be anywhere.

Something told me *not* to go down to the kitchen. It would be too far to run back to Jace's room without being trapped by Harlan, if he was down there, waiting for me like some psychopath. I didn't doubt it either. After last night at the game, he'd seemed on edge more than usual. *Everyone* was on edge, even the people I thought didn't have any dark secrets.

So, I decided to turn back around and get some water from the bathroom sink in Jace's room. I didn't care how nasty the water might've been. It would be better than dying at the hands of a known murderer. I walked quickly by the hallway bathroom and stopped when I saw a dim light flickering out from underneath the door.

The bathroom light wasn't on, but it looked like there was a flashlight or something.

Swallowing hard, I leaned closer to the door to hear someone gagging on the inside. I grasped the door handle and jingled it slightly.

"Mom?" I whispered through the door, brows furrowed together. "Mom, are you in here?"

Someone shuffled inside the room and opened the door. Creaking slightly, the door swung open a few inches. I walked into the room, turned the light on, unsure why she hadn't done it herself, and shut the door behind me.

"Mom? What are you doing here with the light off?"

"Shh, sweetheart, I don't want to wake Harlan," she said, glancing at the door. She puked in the toilet and looked back up at me. "He has a lot of work to do this week and needs his sleep."

I furrowed my brows. "He's your husband. He should be the one holding your hair back as you puke," I said, trying to get her to see what was wrong about this entire situation. A good husband wouldn't be angry that his wife was puking up her guts at three in the morning. "Dad would've woken up any night, no matter what he had to do in the morning."

After pulling her gaze away from me, she stuck her head back into the toilet and puked some more. "We don't talk about your father around here, especially not when *he's* in the house."

She went to push some graying-blonde hair behind her ear, but I held it back instead. She doubled over the toilet again and grasped her stomach, puking up some more.

"Why are you puking?" I asked, frowning. "Did you eat something bad?"

She tensed underneath me and nodded a bit too quickly. "It must've been the fish we ate last night ..." She grasped the toilet and squeezed her eyes shut. "Yes, that's what it has to be. It *can't* be anything else."

My brows furrowed, chest tightening. "Did Harlan—"

"No, he didn't." She stood on shaky legs and shuffled to the sink, washing her mouth. "This is my fault." Tears welled up in her eyes as she stared at herself in the mirror. "This is my fault, my fault ..." she whispered the last few words.

Though I didn't know what exactly she was talking about, I didn't need time to figure out that Harlan blamed her or *would* blame her for something.

She wiped the tears from her eyes and plastered a fake smile on her face. "Everything is fine, sweetie. You can go back to bed."

"Can we talk about Harlan?" I asked in a whisper before she opened the door.

Freezing in place, she glanced back at me. "About what? We don't have much time."

"Mom ..." I started.

Though she gave me an opportunity to ask questions and tell her everything, I didn't know what to say. I hadn't thought I'd get this far. She had been shut out for so many days, and I couldn't tell her about what Harlan had done. If she tried to leave, she might get killed.

"Mom, are you okay?" I asked, knowing that this was probably as far as I could take it. "Has he tried to hurt you? You don't seem the same, and I ... I never see your real smile anymore. So much has changed since Dad passed."

Mom swallowed hard, tears welling up in her eyes. Suddenly, she dropped her head and wept, placing a hand over her mouth so she wouldn't make much noise. Body trembling back and forth, she pulled me into a hug and rested her head against my shoulder.

"Sweetheart, I'm so sorry. I'm so sorry that I got you into this mess. I know ..." She swallowed hard against me, body still shaking uncontrollably. "I know what happened. I know what he does to Jace. I know that we can't get out. There's no getting out now. It's too late."

Lips trembling, I held myself together as best as I could and clutched her tightly to me, stroking her hair. I pressed my lips together, so I wouldn't make a sound and tensed to keep myself from bawling my eyes out.

"I miss Dad so much," I whispered.

It didn't have shit to do with the situation Harlan had trapped us in now, but I had wanted to say it out loud to her for so long. I wanted to scream at her for not letting herself take time to heal after his death. I wanted to fucking hate her for moving on with another man so quickly. But Dad wouldn't want that.

After a few more moments, Mom straightened out and wiped the remaining tears from her face. "I have to get back to our room before Harlan figures out that I'm gone." She shoved something into my hand and closed my fingers over top of it. "I love you with everything, baby. I will always love you."

And then she walked out of the bathroom and down the dark hallway until she disappeared into the maze Harlan called a house. When she was gone, I gently unraveled my fingers and stared down at Dad's chain that Harlan had stolen from me.

Chapter Seventy-Two

ALLIE

Monday mornings at Redwood were usually quiet, but not the day after Redwood's darkest weekend to date. There would be more dark times in the coming days. Poison definitely had more up their sleeves.

Though only half the student population actually showed up to school today, the halls were full with gossip and fear. Friends whispered to each other, glancing around at everyone, wondering who would be next to have their secrets exposed to the world.

Me? Well, I strolled down Redwood's hallways without a care in the world.

I had too much other shit to worry about than Poison exposing my secrets. All my secrets were already exposed to everyone at Redwood anyway. It didn't matter much to me, though I suppose that I didn't have any big secrets to begin with.

Opening my locker, I smiled at the bleakness of it. When the entire world was in chaos around me, nothing was stuffed in my locker today. It was my own space that I could keep and decorate however I wanted. I pulled out a couple of books for Biology, shut it, and leaned against the cold metal, yawning.

After my chat with Mom this morning, I couldn't fall back to sleep. I'd tossed and turned for two hours, then decided to study until Jace woke up for school. I tugged gently on Dad's chain, happy to have it around my neck again, and watched Imani storm down the hallways with flared nostrils.

Coiled black hair bouncing in a ponytail, she snatched my hand and tugged me past the three Poison boys without saying good morning. She actually snarled at them when Landon called for her down the hall.

"They're so annoying—so fucking annoying." She seethed.

"Well, good morning to you too," I said, pushing my glasses up my nose.

She stopped by her locker and fumbled with the lock. "Sorry, not sorry. They've been trying to contact me all weekend, and I'm done with it."

I leaned against the lockers and arched a brow. "Done with them? I'm surprised you haven't jumped back into bed with them already."

After giving me the deadliest glare I'd ever seen, she pulled some books from her locker. "Says the girl who's sleeping with her stepbrother after he broke her heart." She glanced back over at me and curled her lips into a smile, a giggle escaping her mouth. "I need to get more damn sleep." She wrapped her arms around my waist and rested her head on my shoulder. "Thanks for dealing with me when I'm cranky."

I patted her back. "Thanks for dealing with me when I make dumbass decisions."

"Anytime." She pulled the remaining books from her locker and shut it. We started down the hall toward our Biology class, her arm looped around mine. "Looks like Redwood is off to a *wonderful* start after what happened on Saturday night."

Students from AP Biology waited outside Mr. Barnes's classroom, gossiping with each other. I leaned against the wall and stared at the new young professor across the hallway, who chatted closely with another student inside the classroom. Brow arched, I nudged Imani. No doubt that man had some deep, dark secrets to expose too.

"Just be careful, Maddie," someone said to my right, breaking me out of my stare.

The shy girl in my class, Maddie, crossed her arms over her chest and nodded at her brother, Oliver. Oliver hiked a large duffel bag—probably filled with his hockey gear—over his shoulder.

Alec, another guy on the hockey team, slapped Oliver on the shoulder. "Come on, dude. Let her be. You think *she* has secrets worth knowing?" Alec threw Maddie a smirk behind Oliver's back and persuaded Oliver to leave.

When he was gone, Maddie inched closer to the wall and shuffled from foot to foot. She glanced over at us and her cheeks tinted red. "Did you see that?" she asked us, eyes wide in fear.

Imani and I burst out laughing at the same time.

"Girl, we don't care." Imani cocked her thumb at me. "She's sleeping with her stepbrother, and I'm about to forgive the three most fucked up guys in the entire school. Your secret is safe with us."

She moved closer and lowered her voice. "Are you talking about Poison?"

My lips curled into a smile, and I nodded. "Yep."

She widened her eyes even more. "Rumor has it that they are the ones who killed the principal last Saturday. Is that true?" she asked.

Imani and I looked at each other.

Maddie grinned. "Because I want to thank them. That man was nothing but a creep. Every time I was around him, I thought he was staring down my shirt. He ..." She shivered. "He always got way too close to me, and nobody would believe me."

Deciding that Maddie wasn't going to be a tattletale, I leaned closer to Imani. "Exhibit A for why you shouldn't hate them for what they did," I whispered. After turning back to Maddie, I grimaced. "He did more fucked up things than that. I'm glad he's gone too."

328

Chapter Seventy-Three

JACE

"Senior Night is this Friday," Coach said after practice on Monday.

Since Saturday night's game and Principal Vaughn's head being thrown onto the field like a football, Coach had been very hesitant to even continue the season. But we only had one home game left. Coach had reminded us multiple times today that security would be increased, so nothing would interrupt the game this time.

I'd have to talk to Poison about that one.

"Parents should arrive on the field thirty minutes before game time to walk you out during the ceremony, which will celebrate all the hard work each of you seniors have put into this season and all the seasons before this one."

Looking down at my feet, I kicked some dirt with my cleat. Dad wouldn't come to the game, and Mom was dead. I'd be one of the only seniors walking out onto the field alone. It kinda sucked, kinda didn't. Harlan didn't deserve any credit for raising me and making me into a football star. I had done that all by myself.

After practice, I nodded good-bye to Jamal and jogged over to the bleachers, where Allie sat with chattering teeth.

"Thank goodness you're done. I didn't want to go home alone, and it's freaking cold outside." She hopped down and wrapped her cold fingers around my palm, leading me toward my Maserati.

When we slid into the car, Allie slammed the door and looked over at me. "I was thinking ... I love watching you play football." Allie tucked some sweaty hair behind my ear and leaned in close. "I don't want you to sacrifice your career and *our* future to kill your father. He's already taken away your mother. Don't let him take away everything you've worked so hard for."

"Our future," I said, letting the words linger on my tongue. I had been so caught up in the now, so caught up in dealing with my dad and trying to get her to love me again, that I hadn't thought much about us.

If I killed my father and got caught, I'd be thrown in jail. I wouldn't get to see Allie. I wouldn't be able to build a family with her. I wouldn't be able to see her flourish and succeed as a biologist. Murdering my father would end my life and all hopes I had with her.

"Where have you been accepted to college?" I asked because we hadn't talked about our future—our immediate future—yet.

She grinned and looked out the windshield. "UPenn, Carnegie Mellon in Pittsburgh, Stanford ..." She squealed and jumped slightly in the car.

I smiled at her, but as she continued to list off the colleges she had gotten accepted into, I couldn't help but feel hurt. None of these colleges were close to where I was going. We would be so far away from each other, and I didn't know if I could deal with being so far from her for such a long time. We had been living together —*living together*—for the past two years. Being away from her would kill me on the inside.

"Stanford is so hard to get into." She looked back at me and dropped her grin, brows furrowing together. "What's wrong?"

Forcing myself to smile harder, I shook my head. "Nothing."

She frowned and moved closer. "Something's wrong, Jace. Tell me."

"Nothing is wrong, Allie."

Bullshit. Utter bullshit.

This was my fault. So caught up in what college would be most beneficial to *me*, I hadn't thought about Allie. I stupidly thought that she would follow me wherever I went, thought we could live together, wake up every morning and cook bacon and eggs together. Never had I thought she'd go off to her own college and we'd be away from each other.

"I'm happy for you," I said, grasping her jaw lightly.

After pushing back my seat, I grabbed her waist and pulled her into my lap. She giggled and sat on top of me, her ass against my thighs and her clenching pussy against my sweatpants.

"My girl has worked so hard for this. I'm so proud of you."

"Are you sure nothing is wrong?" she asked, resting her forearms on my shoulders.

"Never been surer in my life."

Fuck.

Setting my hands on her hips, I squeezed them gently. "Where, uh, where are you planning on committing to?" I asked her, staring at the way her father's dog tags glimmered around her neck. I couldn't look my own girlfriend, the love of my fucking life, in the eye because she'd see right through the lies.

She toyed with the ends of my hair and relaxed in my arms. "I'm not sure. They're all good colleges. If I like this internship that Imani's father found for me, I'll probably go to Carnegie Mellon. They have good interdisciplinary collaboration and are at the forefront of innovation, but th—" As she stopped, she tensed in my arms. "But ..."

"That's exactly what you want, right?" I asked, giving her my weakest smile.

The light in her eyes disappeared. "But you won't be with me," she whispered. Tears welled up in her eyes, and I watched them quiver, her tears seconds from falling. "Michigan is hours away ..."

My chest tightened. I wanted to be strong for her. She deserved that at least. She had been there for me through so fucking much.

Yet I couldn't stop myself from digging my fingertips into her hips because I wanted to savor every moment that I had with her. I didn't want to let the moments slip away.

"It's okay, Allie," I whispered, for fear that if I spoke any louder, I'd choke up.

Tears spilled down her cheeks, and I pushed them away with my thumbs.

"Don't cry, baby. It'll be okay. We'll get through it. We've gotten through everything that life has thrown at us already."

Lips trembling, she threw her arms around my shoulders and pulled me closer. "I don't want ... I don't want to leave you. We'll be hours apart, hundreds of miles away from each other for *four* years. I haven't been without you since freshman year."

Not knowing what to say—because I couldn't deny what she had said—I tugged her closer to me and kissed her softly on the lips, fingers trailing down her sides. Neither of us knew what the future held, but I wasn't going to let the present slip away from me.

Chapter Seventy-Four

JACE

I laid a trail of hot, needy kisses down the column of Allie's neck and sprawled my hands across her ass, fingers digging into her flesh. Allie tilted her head to the side, giving me better access, and laced her hand into my hair to hold me in place.

Windows foggy, she leaned against the steering wheel, reached between us, and pulled my twitching cock out of my sweatpants. After spitting on her hand, she wrapped it around my dick and stroked it slowly, each stroke becoming faster and faster.

Slipping my hand into her leggings, I pulled apart her wet folds with my fingers and massaged her clit. "Fuck, Allie, I wish you had one of those slutty little skirts on today," I murmured against her neck, sucking some skin between my lips. Determined to leave a love mark on her tonight.

She moaned softly, grinding her hips against my fingers. "Take them off me."

After placing her in the passenger seat, gripping the waistband of her pants, and pulling them all the way off her body, I set her down on my lap. The head of my cock pressed against her wetness, and she lowered herself. Her wet little hole tightened around me with every inch I put into her.

I leaned against my seat and undid the buttons on her shirt, grasping her tits through her bra. "Bounce on my cock, baby."

Placing her hands on my shoulders, she moved up and down on my cock and moaned. I pulled her breasts out of her bra, knowing that nobody could see in through the foggy windows, and ran my thumbs across her hardened nipples. Sucking one into my mouth, I tugged on it with my teeth and stared up into her eyes.

Allie moaned out, her pussy pulsing on my dick. She slowed to a stop and threw her head back, legs trembling around me. I grasped her hips and shoved myself up into her a few hard times until I came deep in her pussy.

I trailed my lips back up the column of her neck and kissed her. "I love you."

$$Chapter\ Seventy\text{-}Five$$

ALLIE

"Who's the chick?" Landon asked, staring at Maddie, who Imani had basically adopted since Biology this morning.

Imani ushered Maddie into Poison's filthy basement and toward the stained couch, near Jace and me. We had gotten here about five minutes ago and were waiting for Nicole because she apparently had *information*.

"We didn't invite her."

Imani crossed her arms. "Well, I did."

"It's okay. I can go," Maddie started, glancing nervously at all the boys. "I just wanted to thank you for what you did to Principal Vaughn. He—"

"What'd we do?" Kai asked from the other couch, drawing his finger against the muzzle of his gun he had on display for everyone to see.

I didn't doubt that he would use it within a moment's notice on anyone he might believe was a threat.

Maddie stopped short, cheeks flaming, and shrugged. "Um ..."

"Don't answer them," Imani said.

"I thought you hated us?" João said to Imani after inhaling smoke from his bong. He placed it down on the concrete floor and blew the smoke from his nose, eyes closing briefly. "Why are you here?"

After sitting next to me, Imani crossed one leg over the other and rested her head against my shoulder. "Because I'm not letting you guys make any more dumb decisions without my consent."

"What? You think you own us now?" João said to her, leaning forward with his forearms on his knees. He laughed lifelessly at her. "We make decisions around here. You take no part in it, not even if you fucking beg to."

After they quarreled back and forth for another five minutes, Nicole came clanking down the stairs in a pair of red heels and a small black dress. I rolled my eyes and curled my arm around Jace's. If she thought she could dress like this and get any man she wanted, she couldn't because Jace was mine.

Mine.

Nobody would take him away from me.

"Hey, guys," Nicole said when she stepped into the room.

Everyone, except Maddie, glared at her, not really wanting her here, but she was the only one who probably had solid information on her father.

She looked at Maddie and scrunched her nose. "Weird that you're here, but okay."

She kicked off her heels and sat on the sofa next to Jace.

I pulled him closer to me, so he wasn't even touching her, and clenched my jaw. "You said you had information. Tell us or get out."

Nicole widened her eyes at me, but I didn't have time for her bullshit. She was known to talk in circles and to talk forever, making up lies and gossip that the entire school would end up believing somehow. I just wanted to spend time with Jace and relax, not do this.

Jace placed a hand on my knee and squeezed gently. "We'll leave soon, baby. Settle down." He leaned closer to me and gently tugged on my earlobe with his teeth. "I'm yours."

Nicole straightened herself out and cleared her throat. "About my father ..." She looked from João to Landon to Kai. "This can't ... nobody can know that this information came from me. Please, if you can make it look like you got it some other way, do it. I don't want my father to be angry with me. I want him put away."

My eyes widened slightly. Put away? As in ... thrown in jail? As far as I knew, Nicole never seemed like she hated her father. She always gushed about how much money he would spend on her. She acted as if she hadn't moved from the bad part of Redwood to the rich when we were in middle school, acted as if she had grown up rich her entire life.

"He's using the cheer team to do his dirty work."

Landon rolled his eyes. "God, why is it always the cheer team in the drama?"

Nicole pressed her lips together, and I actually saw tears in her eyes. "I'm being serious. He found out that Principal Vaughn was taping people in the locker rooms. It started with the cheer squad. Vaughn let it slide as long as he was able to take some of the film of the girls. He's been using it against us and blackmailing us into getting information about people in Redwood for him, threatening to leak the tapes and ruin our lives if we don't." She turned to Jace. "That's why I slept with Carter. I never loved you. I just ... my father wanted me to get information out of you. I knew it was wrong. I fucking knew it."

"What?" Jace asked, staring over at her. "He's doing that?"

She wiped tears from her cheeks with a shaky hand. "That's not all. He roped some of the girls into a sex ring and was helping pimp them out at one point. He's doing it all for the money. He's so ... so greedy. He doesn't care."

My chest tightened. I wanted to hate her but didn't know that she had been through so much. I had prayed that one day, she would get hurt as badly as it'd hurt me to find her with Jace at the Overlook two years ago. But I hadn't meant like this. I would never wish this upon anyone.

"I-I-I'm one of those girls," she said, a complete and utter mess of tears and snot. "He used me, forced me to have sex with men sixty years older than me. Just to get a quick few bucks. I'm sorry for everything I've done. I'm so sorry."

Chapter Seventy-Six

ALLIE

Everyone stared at Nicole with wide eyes as she bawled into Jace's chest. Jace awkwardly patted her shoulder but inched closer to me, as if he was uncomfortable. I wanted to push her away, but I felt bad for her. She didn't have anyone.

"Prove it," Landon said, waving her off and lighting up a cigarette. "Why should we believe you? All you have done is lie for and protect your father for years. Why tell us now?"

Nicole sat back up and wiped her eyes. "Because ... because I know that you can do something about it now. I know that you can put him away for years, if you ... if you want to. And I'm begging you to do something. If you don't, I'll be stuck here for the rest of my life."

Staring back and forth between Nicole and Poison, I furrowed my brows. Did I want to believe this? No. Did I think that Nicole was lying? I sure hoped not. This was serious shit. If she was making this up to save her ass ... fuck, I didn't know what they'd do to her.

She stood up and shook her head. "You don't believe me, do you?"

João looked at Kai, who shrugged.

"I didn't find any of that footage when we went through the principal's computer, but he could've stashed it elsewhere. I don't know. She could be lying, or she could be telling us the truth about her father. We know he's a prick."

After a few moments, João nodded to the door. "Get out."

My eyes widened. "You're going to make her leave? After what she told you?"

"She can't prove this. We have nothing to go off of and nothing to hurt her father with," João said, glancing back at her. "You bring me all the shit you can find to prove to me that you're not lying, and we'll help you out. If you can't, then you're stuck."

Nicole shook her head, fear evident on her face. "But I-I— what am I supposed to get? How am I supposed to give it to you? What kind of evidence do you need? He doesn't let me into his office, and he somehow always knows if I try to sneak in there or not. I can't get you anything." She rubbed the back of her neck and stared at the ground with wide eyes. "Please, you have to believe me."

João sighed heavily through his mouth and stood, grabbing her by the arm and dragging her to the door. "I told you that I want you out," he said through clenched teeth. "Come back when you have something that we can use."

Nicole looked back at us, staring at Jace and then at me. "You have to believe me. Please, Allie, please. You're the only one who does—I can see it. Don't let them—"

João shoved her out and slammed the door in her face. I pressed my lips together to stop them from trembling. For some ungodly reason, I couldn't help but feel sad for Nicole. Don't get me wrong; I hated her with all my guts, but if she was telling the truth and João had kicked her out for nothing ...

"Jace," I whispered, curling closer to him. "Do you think she'll be okay?"

Jace grimaced at the door. "I don't know, Allie. I don't like her. She always lies about everything. And you can't believe a liar, not even when they're telling the truth."

Chapter Seventy-Seven

"Do you think Nicole is telling the truth?" Imani asked me at lunch on Friday, glancing over at the cheerleader table.

I looked over to see Nicole sitting at the end of the table, picking at some mashed potatoes on her tray. While I always thought that she was the head bitch of the cheer team, the others didn't seem to talk with her much. I'd almost go as far as to say that they *ignored* her.

Shrugging my shoulders, I turned back to my food and frowned. "I don't know." But I sure as hell wish that I did.

As much as I hated the woman, if she was being serious about this, then her own damn father had been pimping her out for money. I couldn't begin to imagine what that felt like—to be used by your own flesh and blood.

Imani munched on a carrot and opened her Biology textbook. "My dad wanted me to tell you that he got you an interview for next Monday after school. And when he says 'interview' "—she did air quotes around the word—"he means that you already have the internship. You just have to go talk to the guy."

For once, I had something good to look forward to. I hoped that life wouldn't get in the way and destroy this opportunity for me. The more I thought about my future, the more nervous I felt. If I ended up loving this internship, I'd probably end up choosing to go to a college that specialized in both biology and tech. But ... that would mean I'd be leaving Jace behind.

And I couldn't do that.

"Earth to Allie!" Imani said, waving a hand in front of my face. When I glanced at her, she nodded to the hallway, where we could see Maddie talking tensely with her brother's best friend, Alec. "Do you think that they're banging hard?"

I snorted and grinned. "I don't know. Are you banging Poison again?"

Upper lip curling into a scowl, she playfully rolled her eyes and looked behind me. "Speaking of the fucking annoying pricks, here they come." She bit down on her carrot, making it crunch, and looked away from the three guys as they approached.

"What's crawled up your ass lately, Imani?" João asked, sitting next to her.

Imani ignored them and smiled at Maddie. "Ugh, she's so lucky."

"Who?" Landon asked, following her gaze. "Maddie? Why is she lucky?"

Knowing that Imani wanted to make them angry, I played along. "Because she's with Alec." I leaned forward and winked at Imani. "He's like a walking hockey god."

"Who's a walking hockey god?" Jace said, arching a brow and plopping his ass next to me.

I cursed myself for actually saying that aloud, knowing that Jace would pester me about it if I didn't tell him more and admit that I had eyes for no one else but him.

"Alec, captain of Redwood's hockey team."

Jace placed a hand on my knee and squeezed, leaning close. "You think he's hot?"

Caught between telling the truth to my boyfriend and helping my best friend get back at the most ruthless gang at school, I gnawed on the inside of my cheek, furrowed my brows in a confused expression, and gave my best awkward laugh. "Um, yes?"

"The fuck you like him for?" João asked, scowling at Imani. "He can't even hold up a fight in any of his hockey games. He fuckin' sucks."

Imani flared her nostrils. "He doesn't suck."

João laughed lifelessly. "He sucks better than you do."

"If you want him to suck you off so bad, why don't you go ask him to?" Imani snapped, taunting him.

My eyes widened, and I nearly choked on my milk, my eyes darting back and forth between them.

Imani grabbed her food and stood. "Or maybe I could ask him to show me how a real man eats pussy. Either way is fine by me."

Imani stormed out of the cafeteria with all three Poison boys following behind her. I curled my lips into a smirk and turned back to Jace.

I patted his knee and winked. "Don't worry about Alec. I only date guys who are one thousand percent more asshole-y than he is."

Jace arched his brow and grasped my jaw. "Well, this asshole" —he pointed to himself—"expects you to be at Senior Night tonight. And you'd better not be late," Jace mumbled against my lips. "Or I'll excuse myself from the field to come find your ass."

<h1 style="text-align:center">Chapter Seventy-Eight</h1>

ALLIE

Jace hadn't been kidding when he said that there would be more security around Redwood tonight. I shut Imani's car door and hopped onto the sidewalk leading toward the bleachers. Cops were stationed at every corner, every block, and at least every twenty feet.

Maddie stood next to me, bouncing on her toes as we waited for Imani to text someone—probably João, as they had been fighting endlessly this past week. I crossed my arms and sank as far down into my winter jacket as humanly possible.

When she finally shut the damn phone off and walked to the entrance of the bleachers with us, two cops stopped us with hand-held metal detectors, waving them in the air.

"Arms up, girls," one said, lips curled into a smirk. "We need to check you."

I scrunched up my nose and held up my arms, letting him glide the detector across the front of my body. He instructed me to turn around and then swiped it across my back, stopping when he reached my ass.

While no damn beep came, he cleared his throat. "Do you have anything in your back pockets?"

Reaching into my back pocket, I pulled out my wallet and handed it to Imani, who waited beside me with Maddie. Imani glared at the police officer with a scowl, knowing exactly what he was really doing.

"She's fine," Imani snapped. "She doesn't have anything."

The officer swiped his detector against my backside again and paused. "Anything else back there?" he asked, crouched down behind me with his head parallel to my ass.

Wanting to just sit down, I reached into my pockets again to feel around, knowing that there wasn't anything. I pulled my hand back out and shook my head.

"There's nothing," I said, glancing back down at him and catching the *fucking bulge* in his pants.

"We're going to have to search you," he said.

My heart dropped, and I shook my head. "No, you're not searching me."

"If you want to make this difficult, ma'am, you can leave."

But I couldn't leave. I needed to be here for Jace. Nobody else was.

"Just let me pass. I don't have anything."

"Says everyone who's guilty."

"Please," I whispered.

"I'm so, so, so late!" Nicole said, hurrying in behind us in a scandalous cheerleading uniform that barely covered her ass. She pushed me to the side, whispering for me to hurry past the officers, and held her hands up. "Please, let me through."

The officer whisked his metal detector over the back of her body, then the front, stopping when he reached her breasts.

"What do you have under your shirt?" he asked her, shamelessly staring at her breasts.

She gave him a sweet smile, but it didn't reach her dull eyes. "Do you want to check?"

"I'll have to take you somewhere private to be certain. We aren't taking any chances tonight, especially after what happened at the last game," the officer said, but I knew that was a lie. He wanted to touch her, to feel her up, to break the fucking law and fuck a minor tonight. He didn't care about the death of the most hated man in Redwood.

"All right," she said, glancing at me, then at the field, as if to tell me to get out of here.

I pressed my lips together, my heart aching at the thought of Nicole doing this for me. I wanted to go after her and tell her not to do it. I wanted to fucking hate her for everything she had done to me. I didn't want to believe her, just like Poison didn't. But I did. This proved to me that she had been dealing with this sort of thing for God knew how long. And I fucking hated this town and everything about it.

Imani grasped my hand and pulled me up to the bleachers. "Come on."

When Nicole and the police officer disappeared into a small building, I clenched my jaw and continued up to the bleachers. Poison walked in a few moments later, not being harassed by the police at all. Hell, they didn't even get fucking scanned for guns and weapons—a test that I knew they'd all fail.

They sauntered up the bleachers and toward us. I balled my hands into fists, watching as the police stopped girl after girl to *check* them for weapons of any kind.

Fuck the fucking police for thinking that they owned this entire town and could do as they pleased. One day, they'd get what was coming to them.

Chapter Seventy-Nine

ALLIE

"Let's welcome our seniors!" Coach said through the microphone, introducing the seniors as they walked out onto the field with their parents or guardians.

Carter walked out first with his millionaire mother and father, giving the crowd that ugly smile of his. A couple more guys on the offense walked out with their families. Jamal came next with his mother and Marquis, who blew kisses to every cheerleader he walked by.

I cheered for him, though I couldn't quite get into the spirit because Nicole hadn't come back out from the building yet and joined the others on the field. My stomach tightened at the mere thought of what that officer was doing to her.

When the coach called Jace's name, I turned my attention back to the field and cheered for him as he walked out onto the field alone. Harlan had always hated football, so it wasn't a surprise that he hadn't shown up for the night he should've been proudest to be called a father.

Cheering in the stands in one of Jace's many jerseys, I grinned at him and felt nothing but pride. This man had been through so much these past couple of years. I was glad that his father hadn't taken football away from him. Football had been the only thing motivating him to push forward after the loss of his mother.

Jamal clapped Jace on the back and pulled him closer, both wearing huge grins. My heart warmed at the sight of them with Jamal's mom in between, her hair done up and her nose scrunched as she smiled. I was so grateful for her, and I knew Jace was too.

"Let me take a moment to congratulate all these fine men," Coach said. "I've watched them play since they were peewees, running down the field and scoring points at six years old. I'm both proud and sad to watch their last game as Redwood athletes. Thank you for twelve years, boys."

The crowd roared in excitement, and I tried to get into it, too, but still, Nicole hadn't come out yet. Determined to find her, I told Imani that I'd be back and started through the crowd. But just as I made it to the stairs, Nicole walked out of the building, wiping some mascara from her cheeks, grabbing her pom-poms, and running onto the field with a fake smile plastered across her face.

"Go Redwood!" she cheered, though the excitement didn't make it to her eyes. "We love you, Redwood. We love you."

Chapter Eighty

ALLIE

Thrusting a hand into my jeans, the officer fondles my pussy and sticks a finger inside of me, like he owns me and everything in this town. I scream and yell as tears stream down my face. He pushes me to the bathroom mirror, grabs a fistful of my hair, and forces me to stare at our reflection.

Nicole stares back at me, cheeks stained with ugly streaks of mascara and her red lipstick smudged all over her chin and cheeks. She weeps as she takes it from behind, biting her lip to hold back her sobs.

"Fucking slut," the officer growls in her ear. "This is all you're fucking good for."

I shot up in Jace's bed, my chest rising and falling in a ragged and unsteady rhythm as tears streamed down my face. Realizing that it had only been a dream, I pushed my tears away and scrambled out of bed, needing to pace and think, to get my mind off of that horrible nightmare.

After slipping out of the room, I walked back and forth in the hallway, a small night-light brightening the floor around my feet. Though it was still dark, at least I could see where I was going out here. I didn't want to turn on the light in our room, knowing that I'd wake Jace after his strenuous game.

Rubbing my face and trying to stop thinking about my dream, I walked into the bathroom and turned on the sink to listen to the soothing sound of rushing water. I sat on the toilet with my head in my hands and forced myself to take deep breaths.

If that was what happened to Nicole every fucking day, I ... I wanted to apologize *for* those men. Nobody deserved to be treated so poorly, and tonight, I'd let it happen to her without a second thought. I let that man touch her because I didn't want to be touched. She had disappeared into that back building for me.

Tomorrow, I had to make it better. I had to do something. As much as I hated her, I couldn't let her continue to be abused like that. The longer I stayed here, the more I learned that this whole fucking town was shit. People weren't who I thought they were.

Once I splashed some cold water on my face, I shut the light off and opened the bathroom door to go back to Jace's room. All I wanted to do was curl up in his arms and fall into a better night's sleep, forget about my problems for a long damn time.

Someone bumped into me and cursed.

"Harlan?" Mom whispered, nervous.

"Mom?" I said, turning the bathroom light back on to see her.

She stood in the center of the hallway with a metal hanger in her hands, which looked to be uncoiled and bent in directions that it shouldn't be. She stared at me with wide eyes and swallowed hard. "Honey," she said, placing the hanger down by her side. "Go to bed. Now."

I furrowed my brows and eyed the hanger. "What are you doing up and with that?"

She placed a hand to her chest, pressed her lips together, and rushed into the room, puking into the toilet.

I shut the door behind her and poured her a cup of water, crouching by her side. "Mom, what's wrong with you?" I asked, handing her the water and holding back her hair. "You keep getting sick in the middle of the—" I stopped short and glanced between her and the hanger. "Mom ..."

She grasped my hand and gave me a pitiful frown. "I'm sorry, sweetie. I'm so sorry. I-I'm pregnant."

Chapter Eighty-One

ALLIE

"Oh my God," I whispered, grasping the sink counter to steady myself.

Out of all the damn freaking ways that this could've played out with Harlan Harbor, this was the worst-case scenario. Mom was pregnant by him. *Pregnant!* He would never let her go now, no matter how damn hard Jace and I tried to peel her away from him. Jace or Poison would need to kill him, like they had talked about.

"Honey, I'm so sorry," she said, gripping the hanger.

When I glanced at it, I doubled over and clutched my stomach, unable to hold myself up anymore. Pain shot through my body, my heart aching. "Mom ... Mom, how could you even think about us-using that?" I asked, knowing that she had only brought it to the bathroom with her for one reason and one reason only.

To try to stop this pregnancy.

"Baby," Mom said, crouching down beside me, tears spilling down her cheeks. "Don't cry."

I placed a hand over my mouth to muffle my sobs. If she

needed to get an abortion, then she needed to get an abortion, but ... not like this. This could kill her. If I hadn't found her before she did something to herself, she could've ... she could've died. Just like Dad.

"Mom," I sobbed.

She sat on the ground next to me and cradled me in her arms, gently stroking my hair and rocking us back and forth. And while she tried to be strong behind me, her chest heaved back and forth too. "I'm sorry," she said through the tears. "I'm so sorry."

"Why?" I asked, grasping her arm and lying in her lap. "You could've died."

While she didn't respond right away, she held me tighter in her arms and continued to rock us, like she used to do on the couch when I was five, when we used to talk to Dad over video chat while he was deployed, her cheek against mine and a big smile on her face.

But I hadn't seen her smile her real smile for years now. I didn't think I ever would.

"Do you want to leave me too?" I asked, unable to stop myself before the words decided to tumble out of my mouth.

We hadn't been on particularly great terms since she'd married Harlan, but I didn't want to live without her too. It had been hell, trying to get over that I would never see Dad again, but Mom too? I didn't know how I'd be able to survive with both parents gone at such an early age. It'd be so damn difficult.

"Don't you dare say anything like that again," Mom said, voice tense. "I love you more than you think I do. I was doing this for us. There isn't any other way about it. I don't want to be stuck with him forever. If I have his baby ..."

I turned in her hold and pushed the tears from her cheeks. "There has to be another way. You can't do this to yourself." I ripped the hanger from her hand and placed it on the counter. "Promise me that you won't ever attempt to do that yourself. You can shove it up into you, hit an artery, and bleed out within minutes, Mom."

Her lips quivered. "Honey, there's no other way."

"Go to the doctor. Please, Mom, go to the doctor."

She shook her head. "I ... Harlan won't let me out of his sight. And if I tell him that I'm pregnant, he won't let me get an abortion. He's fucking psychotic, Allie," Mom whispered. "He'll kill me before he ever lets me abort it. I ... I can't have a baby with him. I'm afraid he'll hurt it or ... or kill it."

I sat back on my heels, trying to come up with any sort of plan. We were stuck in a corner that we couldn't get ourselves out of, and Mom was right. Harlan liked to control. I had witnessed that firsthand when he brought me into his office and forced me to watch as he burned that fake file.

The stupidest idea popped into my head, but it could work. *Could.*

"What if ... what if you make an appointment for me to go to the gynecologist?" I asked, brows furrowed together and an uneasy feeling in the pit of my stomach. "What if you tell Harlan that I need to get on birth control?" Because I still hadn't yet. Jace and I had been relying solely on the pull-out method and the day-after pill. "I'll tell him that I want you with me because I'm scared of having them shove an IUD up my uterus."

Mom swallowed hard and shook her head. "I don't know if that'll work. Putting an IUD in only takes a few moments. Abortions can take hours. Harlan isn't stupid. He'll put two and two together."

I swallowed hard, my heart racing. "Tell him that I'm pregnant then. You can't use a hanger to do this, Mom. Please, tell him that I'm pregnant and that I want to get an abortion, so I can focus on my studies. He knows that I have goals and work hard. He'll believe it."

After taking a deep breath, Mom rubbed her forehead. "You can't tell anyone the truth. This can't leave this room," she said to me, pressing her lips together. "Please, this is beyond dangerous to even consider doing this. You know how insane Harlan is."

"I promise that I won't say anything to anyone," I whispered.

But I knew that I'd break that promise at some point. If Mom told Harlan that I was pregnant, Jace would find out, and he would freak. Being pregnant at Redwood Academy was like digging your own grave and slipping down into it. High schoolers were ruthless pieces of shit sometimes.

Mom gnawed on her lip. "Okay," she finally said. "I'll tell Harlan that you're pregnant and make an appointment for you at my gynecologist."

Chapter Eighty-Two

JACE

Allie tiptoed back into our room and shut the door behind her, sniffling. Sunlight flooded into the room through the curtains, hitting her blotchy red face. I shuffled up in the bed and leaned against the headboard, frowning as she walked to her side in my T-shirt and sank under the blankets without even saying good morning.

"What's wrong?" I asked her, pulling her into a hug on the bed with my chest against her back and my legs curled up behind hers. I kissed her on the side of the neck and stuffed my nose into her hair as she placed a hand over her mouth and cried harder. "Baby, tell me what happened. Why are you crying?"

She sniffled and turned toward me. "My life is a mess," she sobbed.

"Talk to me, Allie. What's wrong?"

"We might go to different colleges. Nobody believes Nicole. And Mom ..." she started. She slapped a hand over her mouth and squeezed her eyes closed. Cheeks red and eyes puffy, she shook her head. "Mom is screwed. We're screwed. And I hate how I can't stop crying!"

Knowing that my father's psycho side had taken a toll on me, too, when I first learned about it, I wrapped her into a hug and kissed her on the forehead. "It's going to be okay, Allie. I told you that I'm going to take care of it. We need to get information on Nicole's father first. And once we do—"

Allie wiped her cheeks with the back of her hand and sat up, crisscrossing her legs, my shirt riding up her bare legs and giving me the best damn view of her bare pussy.

Since when has she slipped those lacy little panties off her?

"Nicole isn't lying about being pimped out," Allie said.

"We don't know that. She could be doing it for attention. She does everything for—"

"No," Allie said firmly. "Last night at the game, cops were checking students for weapons because of what Poison had done. They checked me and told me that they needed to search me in one of the back rooms."

I stiffened and growled, possessiveness taking over every part of my body. "They what?"

She placed a hand on my chest. "Jace, listen, please ... I told them no, but they refused to let me into the bleachers without a search. I knew that they wanted to feel me up. I fucking knew it. Nicole ... Nicole ... she ... she was taken by one into the building for me, and they let me go." She shook her head, disgust washing over her features. "I hate that I just let her go. I need to visit her today. I need to apologize."

Balling my hands into fists, I clenched my jaw. I couldn't fucking believe that those asshole officers had done that to her and to, I was assuming, a bunch of other girls too. This town was too corrupt for its own good.

"I need to go alone," she whispered. "I need to talk to her by myself."

After inhaling sharply, I nodded. "Okay, but was that it? Is there any other reason you keep getting up in the middle of the night to cry?"

She paused and looked down between us. "No," she whispered. "There's not."

Chapter Eighty-Three

ALLIE

After sliding out of Jace's Maserati, I walked up to Nicole's front door and gulped. For years, I'd hated this woman with my entire being, and now, I needed to apologize to her for not believing her sooner and not stepping up at the game. She should've never had to go into that building with that officer, but she had done it for me.

I glanced back at Jace, who offered me a supportive smile. Taking a deep breath, I turned back to the door and knocked twice, hoping that Nicole was the only person home. I didn't know what I would do if her father answered the door and saw Jace out in the driveway.

When she didn't answer the first time, I knocked again.

"One sec!" someone called.

A few moments later, Nicole opened the door in some fluffy cheetah-print pajama pants and a Redwood sweatshirt. "Allie, what are you doing here?" She glanced over my shoulder to see Jace and scrunched her nose at the car, as if Jace Harbor, who she had once claimed to love, was nothing to her. "Why is he waiting there? Do you guys wanna come in?"

My eyes widened slightly. "Oh, um, I ... can I?" I asked. I hated barging in on people, but I needed some time away from the Harbor drama to think, and I really needed to apologize to her for everything.

She opened the door wider to let me in. "Is Jace coming?"

"No, he's going to Jamal's."

After waving Jace off and texting him to reassure him that I'd be fine, I walked farther into her house and stared around at all the stuff. Nicole wasn't *rich*, rich like Jace was. She had gone to elementary and middle school with me and Poison, but she had suddenly come into money when the high school that poor kids on this side of town were supposed to attend suspiciously burned down. The town claimed that some of the rich kids had done it— and that was why us "trashy" kids could attend the great and pres- tigious Redwood Academy—but I thought Poison had secretly been behind it. I just didn't know how Nicole fit into any of that.

"Do you want something to drink?" she asked me, heading toward the kitchen.

I followed her and nervously rubbed my sweaty palms together. "Sure," I said awkwardly, not knowing what to say to her.

I needed to apologize, but how? How could I casually bring up something like that? Did she even want to talk about it? Did she just want to forget it?

She pulled some orange juice out of the refrigerator and grabbed a glass, her hand trembling as she poured me some. She spilled some over the edge and cursed when it rolled down the side of the cup and onto the granite countertop. "Sorry, I have, uh ... tremors," she said, whispering the last word. She grabbed a rag from the sink and wiped up the spilled orange juice, then handed me the glass.

"You do?" I asked, raising my brows.

Cheeks flushing, she nodded and sat on a stool at the kitchen island. "Um, yeah." She tucked some hair behind her ear. "The only people who really know about it are Jace and some of the girls on the cheer team."

"Oh," I said, sipping my orange juice. "There's nothing wrong with that."

She stared at the countertop, frowned, and shrugged. "There's nothing wrong with it until your friends stop inviting you to their sleepovers and want nothing to do with you because all they want to do is do each other up in makeup and eyeliner, but you ... you can't even hold your damn hand straight." She blew out a breath and looked back over at me. "Sorry, you probably don't care. I'm just salty."

"If it means anything, I really like the way you do your makeup."

She gave me half a smile. "Thanks. I wake up a couple hours before school to get it done. I really love doing it, but it's hard, especially when you don't have anyone to practice on besides yourself."

After taking another sip of my orange juice, I slid onto the stool next to her. "I, um, I wanted to apologize for last night. I shouldn't have let you leave with that officer. I ... I don't want you to feel like you're alone. Poison might need proof, but I don't. It's terrible, what you're going through. And I'm so sorry that nobody believes you."

Instead of crying like she had the other night, Nicole just looked empty. "It's okay."

"No," I said, shaking my head. "It's not okay. We're going to stop it."

"Poison won't ... not unless I give them proof," she said, drawing her finger against the countertop in patterns. "I don't have proof. I can't get proof, not alone. The girls on the cheer team don't even speak to me because of what my father has made them do in the past. They won't admit to it either."

Unsure about what to do, I gently patted her shoulder and turned toward her. "For what it's worth, I believe you. I'll try to convince Poison to believe you too. You ... you took the fall for me yesterday with that man. I don't need any more proof than that. You're so strong, and I'm sorry for thinking that you were a bitch all these years." A tear rolled down my cheek, but I quickly pushed it away. "I could only think about myself. I wasn't thinking about what could be happening to you to make you act that way. I'm sorry."

"I'd do it again for you," she whispered. "I'm numb to most of the pain. Nobody should have to live through something like that ..."

A deafening silence fell upon us, and I swished the rest of the orange juice around in the cup. "Why don't you come hang out with Imani and me today?" I asked her, hoping that Imani wouldn't mind.

She knew how much I'd hated Nicole these past few years. If I asked her, she'd think I was on drugs or something, so I just wasn't going to ask Imani. I'd bring Nicole and deal with Imani later.

"As you can see," I said, gesturing to my face, "I have not worn makeup for two years. I think having a makeover done by a friend would be fun."

Nicole's eyes widened. "Really?" she asked, hope in her eyes. "You would really let me?"

I smiled at her. "Yes, I would."

Chapter Eighty-Four

ALLIE

"What the hell is she doing here?" Imani asked, pulling me aside after Nicole and I showed up at her front door for a girls' day. Imani grabbed my hand and looked over her shoulder at Nicole, who walked up the grand staircase and gawked at the paintings on the walls that must've been worth millions of dollars each. "I thought we hated her?!"

I shrugged my shoulders. "She doesn't have any friends."

"She has the entire cheer squad."

My lips curled into a frown, and I grasped Imani's hands. "Just for today. If it doesn't go well and she doesn't fit in with us, then we don't have to hang out with her like this anymore. I promise. I just ... please. I need to do this one thing for her."

After rolling her brown eyes, Imani cracked a smile and gently shoved me. "Only because you're my best friend. If you weren't, I would've thrown her out the second that she stepped onto my driveway." She pointed a finger at me. "But don't make me regret this."

I wrapped my arm around her and rested my head against her shoulder. "Thank you."

Maddie peeked in through the side-door window and waved at us, then opened the door and sprang into the room with a huge smile. "I brought my friend Vera to our girls' day! I hope you don't mind. She really needs to get out of the house and stop writing those smutty stories of hers."

With long, silky hair and bright brown eyes, Vera stepped into the room and shut the door behind her, cheeks flushed red—and not because of the searing wind outside. "Can you not?" she said to Maddie, narrowing her eyes and pushing up her glasses. "I don't need the entire world knowing."

Imani rocked back on her heels as she stared at Vera. "Where have I seen you before?" she asked, tapping her finger against her lips. "Wait, don't you hang out with that guy who's always buying weed from Poison? What's his name again? Blake? Blaise? Is that his name?"

"I do not hang out with Blaise," she said, her thick Latina accent coming through.

Imani ushered them up the stairs and to her room, shutting the door behind us. "Sure you don't. I bet you don't even like him either, like Maddie doesn't like her brother's best friend." Imani wiggled her brows at me. "And Allie over there *hates* her step-brother."

I rolled my eyes playfully at Imani. Though that girl hated big groups of friends, she damn well liked to troll them.

She grinned at me wickedly, then peered over at Nicole, her smile dropping a bit. "Do you *hate* anyone, Nicole?"

Nicole placed down her bags of makeup and sat on the bed, looking between Imani and me. Her lips curled into a half-smile, the expression on her face seeming like nobody had asked her something like that before.

"Maybe ..." She glanced down at her freshly manicured nails and smiled wider. "I have my sights set on one boy, but he'll never date me. He's way too smart, and he makes me feel like such a fool sometimes." After a moment of silence, she unzipped her makeup bag. "So, makeovers?"

I plopped myself down in front of her, pulled my hair into a ponytail, and placed my glasses on the side table. "So," I said once Imani, Maddie, and Vera started bickering about how they all *hated* their boys, "you going to tell me about this boy?"

She rummaged through her supplies and pulled out some mascara. "Maybe one day."

$$Chapter\ Eighty\text{-}Five$$

JACE

"You want a smoke?" Landon asked me, pulling a cigarette from the box and handing it to João. He pulled out another one and pushed it between his lips, lighting it up when I refused. "So, we really going to believe Nicole?"

After hanging out with Jamal earlier, I'd decided to come over here and try to talk some sense into Poison. Allie had looked really shaken up today about what had happened at the game with those officers groping Nicole. If Nicole hadn't been there, they could've tried to do something like that with Allie. And I couldn't let either of those things happen.

Someone knocked on the basement door, and we all looked over at it.

"You invite someone?" João asked, cigarette hanging out of his mouth. After I shook my head, he set the cigarette down in the ashtray and walked over to the door, reaching into his back waistband for his gun. He opened the door a few inches and grumbled something to himself. "What are you doing here?"

"Imani?" I asked, glancing over at Landon with furrowed brows.

"Jace, your girl's here," João called.

I shot up from the couch, grabbed my coat and keys, and hurried over to the door. "I'll see you guys later. Text me when you come up with a plan. I'm down to meet whenever now that football is over for the season."

Standing at the door, Allie had her hair and makeup done and a sleek dress that must've been Imani's because it was two sizes too tight. I didn't mind that though—easier for me to see up her short little skirt.

"Thought I'd find you here," she said. "Nicole just dropped me off."

"Baby," I cooed at her, burying my face against the crook of her neck and breathing in a sweet vanilla perfume. "You look so good. You haven't done your makeup, put perfume on, or straightened your hair like this for what, two years now?"

She giggled and playfully pushed my chest. "Jace, stop it."

I gently bit down on her neck, rubbing my stubble against it as she liked and running my hands all over her body to feel her up. I hadn't gotten to taste her today, and I had been craving to have my way with her since I'd found her in my oversized T-shirt this morning and nothing else. Not even panties.

After turning around in my hold, she raised her brows at me. "So, I thought you were hanging out with Jamal today. How'd you land here?"

"I came here to convince Poison that Nicole was telling the truth," I said to her, gently stroking her face. Snow drifted down around us, some landing on her glasses and melting. "After what you told me this morning, I thought it was necessary."

A smile stretched across her face. "You really did?"

I nodded and grabbed her hand. "Now, come on. I want to take you out. Once they have a plan, they'll text me. We're going to bring him down, one way or another." I tugged her to the car, and my phone buzzed in my pocket.

As I opened the passenger car door for her, I pulled out my phone to see messages from Dad.

Dad: You got your stepsister pregnant?!

I stared down at the messages with wide eyes. Pregnant? Allie was pregnant? Surely, it couldn't be true. Allie would've told me about it as soon as she found out. But she had been getting up in the middle of the night to pee lately, more than she usually did.

Dad: Her mother just told me that she's pregnant!

Dad: What the fuck, Jace?

My hand slipped from Allie's, a warmth spreading throughout my body. Allie was pregnant with my child. We weren't even finished with high school yet, but she had our baby inside of her. My breathing hitched at the thought of seeing my Allie sitting on our bed, holding a tub of ice cream on her swollen stomach, smiling at me with her eyes through those thick frames of hers.

"Jace, what's wrong?" she asked, brows furrowed.

"You're pregnant?" I whispered.

Her eyes widened, and she placed her hands on my chest. "No."

My heart dropped. "No?"

She scrunched her nose. "No, I'm not. Don't be weird about it either. We can't have a kid now. We need to finish high school and college before we even think about something like that, Jace."

"But—"

"No."

I sighed in defeat, knowing that she was right. "Then, why does my dad think you're pregnant?"

Allie gulped and looked around, as if to make sure nobody was listening. "You have to swear not to tell anyone," Allie said. She gnawed on the inside of her cheek and curled her fingers. "My mom is pregnant."

Everything around me stopped, my chest tightening at her

words. She had to be lying. She couldn't be telling the fucking truth. She couldn't. I ... I couldn't accept it if she was.

This was ... bad.

Real fucking bad.

Worse than I had originally thought. Allie nor her mother knew that ... that Dad ...

"Jace," she whispered, "you're scaring me. Say something."

"Allie"—I took a deep breath—"my dad had a vasectomy years ago."

Chapter Eighty-Six

ALLIE

"No, Jace," I whispered, shaking my head and backing up until my back hit his Maserati, unable to believe what he had said. "Don't lie to me like that. You're lying. You ... you have to be lying. This can't be true."

Jace frowned and grasped for my hand. "After he started to suspect Mom was cheating, he got the surgery and didn't tell her. That was how he knew that her child wasn't his before he killed her. He's a fucking psychopath, Allie. If he finds out that your mother cheated—"

"My mom didn't cheat," I said, fingers trembling.

"Allie, she—"

"No. There's no fucking way that she cheated on Harlan, especially after ... after she found out about what he did to your mom." I lowered my voice and pulled Jace close, so nobody in this shitty part of town could hear our drama. "She knows that Harlan killed her. She knows why he did it too. She has to. I can see the fear in her eyes. She wouldn't do that to me."

It didn't make any sense. Harlan barely let Mom out of his

sight anyway. It had been that way for two years now, so ... so this baby had to be Harlan's. It couldn't be anyone else's. And even if Jace thought that she had cheated, my mom was loyal. She had waited years for my dad to come home from the military, years spent without the love of her life, and she hadn't cheated on him.

But then again, she loved Dad.

From the look in her eyes last night, I could tell that her love for Harlan was all a lie.

"What are we going to do, Jace?" I asked him, a searing wind chilling my face.

Jace looked around the neighborhood and grimaced. "Get in the car. We'll figure it out."

After locking ourselves in the car, Jace started down the street and toward home. My heart raced inside my tightening chest, my hands sweating.

What the fuck are we going to do? How are we going to do it? Has Mom ... really cheated?

"How do you explain it, Allie?" Jace asked, hand tight on the steering wheel. "How else could she have gotten pregnant? My dad can't have children. He made damn sure of that when my mom was still alive."

I gnawed off the lip stain that Nicole had decorated my lips with. So much for getting dressed up for Jace and having an easy night. My anxiety was through the roof now. Now, Harlan really couldn't find out that she was pregnant.

"I don't know, but she couldn't have cheated. Your dad never lets her out of his sight." I stared out the windshield at a good ole car fire that some kids had started on the bad side of town and sighed through my nose. "She basically spent the last month with Harlan on vacation, and then when they came home, he ... he's been way too protective of her."

"There was one night that he let her leave," Jace said, swallowing hard. "You remember the night he kicked my ass and nearly killed me? He forced your mom to leave for almost an entire day. He didn't take her anywhere, just told her to leave and be back later."

"But ..." I whispered, unable to believe that Mom would do something like that. "She couldn't have cheated. She ... fucking couldn't have. She knows Harlan and how violent he is. As annoying as she is sometimes, she wouldn't do that to me."

Jace pulled up our driveway and parked the car, hitting off the lights and staring into the living room, where Harlan paced in front of Mom, who sat on the couch nervously. I rubbed my hands over my face, tears pricking the corners of my eyes.

What the fuck are we going to do? What if Mom really has cheated on Harlan? I don't believe that she would, but ... but what if I am wrong?

"Fuck," Jace muttered. "I've been trying so fucking hard for the past two years to keep you and her safe. If my father finds out that your mother is pregnant, he'll go so fucking insane that he'll kill all of us."

My chest tightened, and I grabbed on to Jace's hand. "We can't let him find out. We have to ... have to go in there and pretend that I'm pregnant. This has to work. I can't ... I can't lose you or her."

Jace grabbed my hand and walked with me to the front door. "What are we going to say—"

The door swung open, and Harlan stood before us with his arms crossed over his chest.

"Get the fuck inside now," he said to Jace, grabbing him by the collar and yanking him inside the house.

Eyes widening slightly, I hurried in behind Jace and shut the front door behind us. Harlan pushed Jace into the living room and sent him stumbling over onto the couch next to Mom.

Mom stood up and placed her hand on Harlan's chest. "Sweetheart, it was just a mistake that we're going to fix. You don't have to worry about it."

Harlan ignored Mom altogether and directed his attention to

Jace, his jaw twitching. "You fucking got your stepsister pregnant?! Your fucking stepsister? I expected that you'd knock up that whore Nicole, who you always fucking hang around with, not her."

"I'm sorry," Jace said, placing one hand on the couch near Mom, almost in a protective manner. "I can't do anything about it now. Allie is pregnant."

"That's your fucking stepsister!" Harlan shouted, getting in Jace's face.

My heart raced as I looked between the two of them, and I was afraid that Harlan would go berserk again and beat Jace to a pulp. Jace was still recovering from last time. I didn't want him to get hurt again. I needed to do something, but what could I do?

"You know what people in this town are going to fucking say to me about that? How shitty of a father I'll look like to them?"

"You are a shitty father," Jace said.

Harlan slapped him hard across the jaw. "We're going to clean this fucking mess up."

Mom cleared her throat and tried desperately to pull Harlan away from Jace. "It's okay, sweetheart. I already made an appointment for Friday at noon. We'll have to get Allie and Jace out of school for the day. Nobody will find out about it."

"You'd better hope nobody finds out about it," Harlan threatened, glaring at Jace.

I stared at Mom, pleading with my eyes to her to talk to me alone in the other room, but she gave me a sharp shake of her head and ushered Harlan out of the room and to their bedroom. When they disappeared down the hall, I collapsed next to Jace and took his face in my hands, rubbing his reddening cheek, where Harlan had struck him.

"It's going to be okay, Jace," I whispered, fearing for my life. "We'll get him."

Chapter Eighty-Seven

JACE

Sitting in Chemistry with the most boring fucking teacher ever, I blew out a breath and checked my phone, placing it strategically behind my textbook. I hadn't been able to sleep all last night, and I was damn glad I didn't have football practice every single afternoon anymore. If Dad found out about Allie's mom being pregnant, we were all fucked.

My phone buzzed on the table, the teacher arching a sharp brow at me. Ignoring her, I tapped open the message from Allie. It was a picture of her taken from below, so I could see up that tiny little plaid skirt she wore today.

Allie: Hope this will get you through Chem. xx

I placed a hand on the bulge in my jeans, hoping that nobody would see how fucking hard my stepsister had made me. I tilted the screen away from everyone else, about to tap on the picture to expand it, when another one came through of Allie in a tiny white tank top and no bra, her nipples poking straight out.

Allie: See you at lunch. <3

Pressing my hand harder against my crotch, I nearly groaned

in front of the entire class. Allie knew how to fucking tease me to the point where I wanted to rip off all her clothes and take her mercilessly in class. And she surely knew how to get my mind off my father.

Me: Meet me in the library in five.
Allie: But I'm in class.
Me: Don't be late, or I'll punish you.

I gathered my books and shoved them into my backpack. The teacher looked over at me, hands on her hips and that annoying glare she always gave João when he came into class thirty minutes late.

"And where do you think you're going?" she asked me. "Class doesn't end for another twenty minutes."

After swinging my backpack over my shoulder, I walked out of the room. "Just to the restroom. See you later, Miss Mifstien," I shouted over my shoulder, walking down the hall toward the library.

I guessed one of the benefits of killing off the principal was that there weren't any consequences now, not until Redwood found a new principal.

"Jace Harbor!" Mifstien called.

"Love you too, Mifstien. Have a great day!" I shouted back, smirking to myself. I knew I would after my library retreat with Allie.

I sauntered to the back of the library, tossing my backpack onto the ground and settling onto one of the many empty couches, waiting for Allie's cute ass to walk through the door.

Five minutes passed. Then six. Then, Allie finally walked through the door with flushed cheeks and a nervous expression stretched across her face. When she saw me, she inhaled sharply, eyes darting around, and made a beeline for me.

Before she could say anything, I grasped her wrist, bent her over my lap, and watched as her skirt rode up her ass.

"Jace!" she squealed quietly, glancing up at me through her glasses.

I pressed my hardness up against her stomach and tucked some hair behind her ear. "I told you that I'd punish you for being late." I drew my finger up her stocking that ended right above her knee. "Now, be a good girl and cross your legs for me."

"There are people," she whispered, struggling to move away.

But I shoved two fingers past her panties and into her wet hole and immediately made her still. I grasped some of her hair and pulled it up gently. "Cross your legs and stick your ass up, so I can spank it. Do it before I make you scream so loudly that everyone in the library knows that your stepbrother is touching you."

Allie crossed her legs and stuck her ass up a few inches, her pussy tightening around my fingers and her juices already starting to run down her thighs. I couldn't fucking wait to be inside of her. When I pulled my fingers out of her, I placed my hand over her mouth and smacked her hard on the ass, right in the corner of the quiet library.

She furrowed her brows the way she did when I fucked her and whimpered into my hand. I smacked her again, this time harder, and groped her ass, loving the way she felt. It made these jeans too uncomfortable.

"You wanna help me get through my day, Allie?" I asked, brushing my thumb across her bottom lip and spanking her again. When she nodded, I gestured to the bookcase behind us. "You're going to crawl behind that bookcase for me and pull your shirt down so I can see those nice tits, and then you're going to swallow my cock."

"But, Jace—"

I wrapped my hand around her throat and gave her a stern look. "But what?"

She glanced around to make sure nobody was watching and slunk to the ground on her hands and knees, crawling behind the bookcase, as I'd asked. I stood, my cock hard inside my jeans, and walked over to her. She pulled down the top of her shirt, her tits spilling out of it, and stared up at me hungrily.

Resting one hand on the bookcase, I pulled my cock out. "Are you going to be late next time?" I asked, placing the head of my cock right on her lips.

When she shook her head, I shoved myself between her lips and all the way down her tight, wet throat, grunting. She placed her hands on my thighs, relaxing back on her heels, and bobbed her head back and forth on me, spit and drool and slobber running down her chin and dripping onto her tits.

I reached down and pinched both her nipples so hard that she moaned on me, louder than she should've. Someone shushed us from somewhere in the library, and I tugged on her nipples even more, so Allie would moan for me like that again.

She pushed a hand between her legs and teased her pussy, her fingers wet. She moved closer to me until her lips pressed against my hips and stared up at me with teary eyes. She swallowed, sucking harder and harder and harder until I couldn't handle it any longer. I pulled out of her and tugged her to her feet, twirling her around and lifting up her short skirt.

"Fuck, baby," I grunted, ramming my cock into her sopping cunt.

Wrapping my arm around her neck, I pulled her closer to me and made her arch her back. "Moan for me, Allie," I murmured into her ear, loving the way her pussy clenched and tugged on my cock every time I pulled it out, her walls wrapping around me tightly. I thrust back into her and sucked on her neck, wanting to leave a bright red hickey on her so everyone knew that she was mine.

Allie pressed her lips together in defiance and squeezed her eyes closed. Thrusting into her and already about to tip over the edge, I rubbed her cheek soothingly.

"You're so pretty, Allie … so fucking pretty."

She opened her eyes and bit down on her lip, her pussy tightening around me.

"So pretty," I cooed, rubbing her face softly. When she leaned into it, I smacked my hand against her cheek, making her moan out loud.

She cursed under her breath and gripped the bookshelf, fingers turning white, and almost instantly came all over my cock.

"Come in my panties," she whispered, sticking her ass out even more.

After grunting in her ear, I pulled out and came inside her underwear until I ruined them. Instead of stripping them off of her, I pulled them up and pressed my fingers onto them to rub my cum into her pussy. "You're going to walk around for the rest of the day with your underwear drenched in my cum, and if it starts leaking out and running down these fucking sexy thighs of yours —where everyone can see it—you're going to let it happen. When we get home tonight, I want your stockings to be fucking stained with me."

She beamed up at me, her eyes wide with excitement.

I grasped her jaw. "Do you understand me, Allie?"

"Yes," she whispered.

<h1 style="text-align:center">Chapter Eighty-Eight</h1>

ALLIE

"Where were you guys?" Imani asked, arching a brow and picking at her turkey sandwich that her father usually made her. She rolled her eyes and briefly glanced over at her three lovers. "I had to spend the majority of lunch with these assholes."

"That must've been *terrible*," I said sarcastically to her, cracking a smile. "Especially when Landon can't stop touching you under the table."

She sneered and pushed Landon's hand away from her, scolding him to stop it because people could definitely see. Redwood was full of lurkers who nobody expected. Nothing was really private here, especially not with Poison.

"He's not touching me."

"I'm claiming her," Landon clarified.

Rolling my eyes at him, I glanced over at Imani. "And you think we"—I gestured to Jace and me—"are messed up. You can't even decide if you want them or not." I leaned closer to Jace. "At least I know what I want."

Jace unwrapped a sandwich. "To be fucked in the library."

Imani laughed, and I cut my eyes to Jace and slapped his chest. "Thanks for the help."

"Anyway," Jace said, looking at João, "we need to move things along. My father is about to snap." Jace placed a hand on my thigh and squeezed. "And when I say move them along, I mean, by the end of this week. We can't wait much longer."

Nicole walked into the cafeteria, glancing from the cheerleader table to ours and gnawing on her cheek. I gave her a smile and waved her over, patting the seat beside me.

Though she looked nervously between Poison, Jace, and me, she sat on the bench. "Hey."

"What are you doing here?" Jamal asked, taking a seat across from her.

She pressed her red lips together. "I'm sitting with my ... my friends." After whispering the word, as if she didn't know if we considered her a friend yet, she pulled her backpack onto her lap and rummaged inside of it. "I have something that might help prove myself to you."

"You don't have to," I said, leaning closer to her. "They believe you."

Nicole looked between the Poison boys and shook her head, giving them a flash drive anyway. "I spent all night trying to find it on my father's computer. I'm not going to let all my hard work go to waste. I just ... I need a place to crash for a couple nights. As soon as my dad gets home from work tonight, he's going to know that I went in there."

When nobody offered Nicole to stay at their place—I would've, but with Harlan, it wasn't a good idea—I kicked Jamal under the table and narrowed my eyes at him. Jamal would probably be the only person who Nicole's father wouldn't check. For the most part, Jamal stayed out of trouble with the police.

"You can stay at my place, but what's on the flash drive? Why do you need it?" Jamal asked.

Jamal knew nothing about what was happening behind the scenes. I didn't even think that Jace had told him about Harlan killing his mother yet. He was behind, and I kind of wanted to keep it that way. I didn't want to drag his family into this. His mother worked so hard for him to have a good life.

"It's ... a video of my father and me," Nicole whispered, thrusting the flash drive into Kai's hand. "If you can't find anything incriminating on my father, use this. I want this to be over as quickly as possible. I don't want any of you guys getting hurt anymore."

Kai pulled out his computer and stuffed the flash drive into the USB port, eyes widening. Almost immediately, he snapped the computer closed and looked around the cafeteria to make sure that nobody had seen. "You're not fucking with us."

Nicole pressed her lips together and looked down at the table. "Please, use that. I don't want any of the other girls to have a video of them leaked or ... or something worse. If you can incriminate him with this, then do what you need to."

Kai leaned closer. "Nicole, this is a video of your father mol—"

"I know it is," she snapped. "It fucking happened to me. I don't need to relive it. Do what you have to do with it and fucking destroy that fucking bastard, so he doesn't hurt anyone else like he has me."

Everyone at the table went silent, and I gently rubbed Nicole's shoulder. I didn't want to even see what was on that flash drive. By the mere way Kai—*Kai!*—had paled when he saw it, I knew that it'd sicken me right down to the very core.

I rested my head on her shoulder. "Thank you, Nicole. You don't know how much we needed this right now," I whispered because it was true.

Without this video and without evidence, we wouldn't be able to get anywhere. Jace and I would be stuck in this situation for even longer, always worrying if Mom would be alive once we made it back home for the night.

"Jace and I are in your debt," I said to Nicole.

She gave me her best smile. "No, you're not. I did this so nobody else will get hurt or used by the Redwood Police or disgusting old teachers who have nothing else to do than jerk off to underage students."

"Sorry that we're late to the party!" Maddie said, approaching our table with Vera in tow. "Did we miss anything good?"

"Nope," Imani said, cutting her eyes to the rest of the table.

We hadn't had many friends before, and neither she nor I wanted to get them involved in our messy drama. We had other things to deal with and to worry about.

Imani pushed over to make room for them. "We were just waiting for you."

Chapter Eighty-Nine

ALLIE

"**W**hat time do I have to pick you up?" Jace asked me from the driver's side of his Maserati, glancing down at his phone when a text message from Kai appeared.

I pushed the door open and frowned at his phone. It wasn't that I didn't trust Poison; it was that I knew they were bad news. I wanted this to all be over with, and they were the only people we could trust. Everyone else in this town was shit.

"Seven, I think."

"Do you want me to walk you in?"

I leaned over from the passenger seat and kissed him on the lips. "I'm capable of walking twenty feet by myself, but thank you."

"Don't want anything to happen to that baby of yours." Jace winked.

After playfully rolling my eyes, I watched another text come through and gave Jace a pointed look. "Don't do anything stupid while I'm at this internship, please," I pleaded with him. "I know you want to protect us, but I don't want to learn that you confronted your dad and he killed you while I was trying to figure this all out."

"I'm not going to confront him yet," Jace said.

"You'd better not, Jace, because I love you," I said, kissing him one last time. I shut the door and waved at him through the window. "Seven o'clock. Don't be late!"

Once he drove off, I walked into the building and gave the man at the front desk with thick blue-framed glasses my name. "I'm here to see Mr. Abara. He works in the biochem department."

A young man peeked his head out of an office down the hall and smiled at me. "You're looking for Jahari Abara?" he asked, gathering some papers and walking toward me. "You must be Allie Hall. Jahari has spoken much about you."

Shifting awkwardly from foot to foot, I nodded and glanced around in hopes that Mr. Abara would come save me because I hated small talk and got so nervous while chatting with someone I didn't know. It was why I'd really only had Imani as a friend for the past seven years.

"I'm Colton," he said, sticking his hand out for me to shake. "I've been interning under Jahari Abara for the past three years."

Taking it hesitantly, I shook his hand and smiled at him, wondering if I had met him before. He looked oddly familiar, yet I couldn't quite wrap my head around where I had seen him. "Do you go to college around here?"

"About forty-five minutes away, but I live right in the heart of Redwood."

"Oh, uh, cool. I go to Redwood Academy now, finishing up my senior year."

"My brother goes to Redwood," Colton said to me, walking into a large room with people finishing up work. He slouched down at his desk and smiled at me, those brown eyes seemingly familiar, yet I didn't know who they belonged to. "Maybe you know him."

"What's his name?" I asked.

"Carter. He's the quarterback of the football team."

My eyes widened, and I held back a gag. "Carter is your brother? You guys don't seem alike in the slightest. He's so ... so" —*dickish*—"um ... different from you."

"You mean that he's kind of an asshole?" Colton asked me, playfully shoving my arm and cracking a smile so sinister that I definitely saw the similarities between them. "So am I, once you get to know me."

Mr. Abara walked into the room, just his presence commanding attention. "Allie! You made it!" He walked over to us and placed a hand on Colton's shoulder. "I see that you've met Colton already. You two are going to be working closely together for the next few months. I was hoping you'd get along."

Colton leaned back in his seat, a smirk plastered across his face. "Oh, I think we're going to get along quite nicely."

I gave Mr. Abara a tense smile, my stomach tensing. "Yeah," I lied. "Me too."

Chapter Ninety

JACE

After dropping Allie off at her internship, I opened my glove box to make sure I still had the gun that I'd picked off the man who had killed my mother, then drove to Poison's place. I needed to protect Allie and her mother, and if this was the way that I needed to do it, then I would. I needed Poison to hurry the fuck up and get along with incriminating or just fucking killing Nicole's father already.

The chaos from Principal Vaughn's death was slowly dying down, but everyone was still worried about who would be next. Poison had leaked secrets here and there throughout the week, but nothing as huge as the police chief—the one person who people should trust the most—molesting his own daughter and pimping out the cheer girls.

My phone buzzed.

João: 8th St. Five minutes. Alone.

Making a U-turn, I merged onto the highway toward 8th Street and parked at the curb until I saw Kai stuff his hands into his pockets and walk out of a run-down house with broken windows and beer bottles littered in the front yard. When he spotted me, he nodded to the house and walked back inside.

I shut the car off and stuffed the gun into my waistband, pulling my hood over my head and starting toward the house. Checking around to make sure nobody was watching, I slipped in through the side door and locked it behind me.

After following the dim light, I made my way down the stairs and into a basement of a house that I had never been in before. While the house looked run-down, the basement was fucking stacked with computers, hardware, money, and guns.

"This is your place, Kai?" I asked, studying all the up-to-date tech they had down here.

"How'd you know?" Kai asked, leaning against one of the many desks.

"Couldn't picture João or Landon being a tech geek."

Kai laughed and deadbolted the basement door behind us, leading me to another room, where Landon and João were looking through ammo and loaded guns.

João looked over his shoulder. "Which one you want?"

I pulled my gun out of my waistband. "I have this."

Kai whistled and grabbed the gun from me, looking it up and down. "This is pretty nice, but"—he pointed to some part of it and tossed it down—"it's broken. Won't shoot cleanly or accurately. Pick something else out. There are tons of them here."

Staring around the room, I studied each one, not knowing what the fuck I was looking at. I didn't know shit about guns, but I needed to if I wanted to protect my family. Allie might not really be pregnant with my baby, but someday, she would be. If we didn't get through these next few months, that someday would never come.

After glancing around a couple, I walked over to one and brushed my fingers against it. "How about this one?"

Kai looked over his shoulder and tensed. "Anything, except that one. That one was my—" He paused and looked down for a moment. "That one was Allie's father's from when he was in the military. You're going to want something lighter and newer."

"Why do you have his gun?" I asked.

"His business is his business," João said, nodding to the other guns. "Pick a gun and get out of here. We have shit that we need to figure out and to plan for Nicole's father. We can't spend all day holding your fucking hand as you pick your poison."

After sighing through my nose, I picked up a handgun that seemed light enough. "How about this one?" I asked, still not knowing what the fuck I was doing. I hated the fucking thought of killing someone, and I really hated actually picking out a gun to do it with.

Landon tossed me some ammo and nodded to another room. "Practice in there and don't come back out until you hit the center of the target. You'll get one, maybe two shots in real life before your father reacts. You can't miss."

My fingers curled around the ammo, and I headed to the other room. One to two shots at the most, and I needed to make them count. Because if I thought Redwood had been in chaos before, Redwood was about to drown in it soon. This was how I'd ensure a better life for Allie.

Chapter Ninety-One

"Great work today, Allie," Mr. Abara said, gently squeezing my shoulder as we walked out of my first, apparently official, day at his company's internship for me.

After I had *pleasantly* met Carter's brother, Abara had taken me through every aspect of the company from the bioengineering section to the mechanical engineering sector they'd just started.

With the newest tech and some of the most innovative engineers in the entire country, it was a place that I wanted to be before college. It'd give me a huge upper hand when starting a bio career and some real-life experience to add to my résumé. Jobs *loved* this kind of stuff, especially if I had someone to vouch for me and if recruiters knew that this place was the highest of the high.

"Thanks, Mr. Abara." I zippered up the coat Jace had gotten me and lingered by the doors.

"Do you need a ride?" he asked me, brown brows furrowed.

I checked my phone, the bright *7:03* p.m. lighting up the screen. Jace would be here any minute to pick me up, and I didn't want him to get nervous about me riding home with someone else. Plus, I didn't want to be in the same house with Harlan alone.

"No, thanks," I said, sending a quick text to Jace.

He was never late, picking me up.

"Well, have a—oh, wait. There's one thing that Mrs. Abara wanted me to ask you about." He sighed and stuffed his hands into his pockets. "I know you probably don't want to hear about it, but she keeps nagging me to ask you about those Poison boys that Imani has been hanging around with. Do you know anything about them?"

Sinking deeper into my coat jacket, I shrugged my shoulders. I did not want to tell them that they had killed the principal or that they did shit that nobody wanted to even know about. So, I smiled sweetly at him. "Not much."

"She's been out with them a bit too much, and we're both worried about her safety. Next time she goes with them, could you maybe go with her and let us know if you think she's in danger?"

"Sure," I said, my glasses fogging up. "But I don't think she's in danger."

"Thanks, Allie. It will really help alleviate some of Mrs. Abara's stress." He leaned in and smiled. "You know how she can get about her only baby."

"I know; I know."

"Well, I'll see you tomorrow evening. Call me if you change your mind about that ride. I don't mind coming back here to get you, if yours doesn't show up." He hiked his bag higher up his shoulder and ran out into the blizzard happening and to his car.

Tugging my glasses off because they were too foggy and I couldn't see anything anyway, I bounced on my toes and tried to stay warm as the snow piled up by my feet. I glanced down at my buzzing phone, Jace's number popping up.

Jace: Sorry. Be there in two minutes. Lost track of time.

I pulled my hood over my head and held it tight around my face, so the wind wouldn't sear the skin on my ears off. A car pulled up, the headlights illuminating the thick and heavy snow-fall. Glasses in hand, I hurried over to it, careful not to fall, and was about to rip the door open when I realized it wasn't Jace at all.

From the driver's side, Colton pushed the door open for me to sit. "Get in. It's freezing out there."

I stepped away from the car and forced a smile. "I have a ride."

"I'm not that nice to take you home," Colton said, lips curled into a smirk. "I can let you sit in my car for a bit though until she gets here."

"I don't think Jace would like that," I said to him, pushing my glasses back onto my face.

"Jace Harbor?" Colton asked, gripping the steering wheel a bit tighter. "He's picking you up? What are you doing with a guy like him? When I went to Redwood a few years back, he was nothing but a player."

After moving back another inch or so, I said, "He's my boyfriend."

"Guys like him don't stay in relationships," Colton said.

"You would know that, wouldn't you?" I snapped, then smacked a hand over my mouth.

It was my first fucking day at this internship, and I had already insulted someone. But he had been a dick first, right? I pulled my hand away from my mouth and pressed my numb lips together, squinting at Colton through the snow.

Colton leaned back and chuckled. "You have a mouth on you, Allie."

And I also had a knee that could do terrible, terrible things to his groin.

Jace pulled into the lot and right behind Colton, flashing his lights at me, as if I hadn't seen him. After giving Colton my best *I'm smiling, but I hate you* smile, I hurried against the snow to Jace's car, yanked open the door, and slipped into the warm interior.

"Sorry I'm late," Jace said, pulling around Colton's car and glancing over at him with furrowed brows. "Who's that?"

"Carter's brother," I said, unzipping my jacket and stomping out my shoes. "He works under Imani's father."

Jace tightened his grip on the steering wheel until his knuckles turned white. "Colton?" he asked through gritted teeth. "Stay away from him, Allie. He's bad news."

"You know him?" I asked, placing my hands in front of the heater.

"When I was a freshman on the football team, he was one of the seniors. He's a fucking dick. Nearly flunked out of school. His daddy must've gotten him this internship with his money because I don't know how the hell else he would have scored anything here."

"He's kinda rude."

"He and Carter are basically the same person. Don't trust him and don't talk to him if you don't have to."

"Noted." I glanced over at him, a look of bewilderment on his face. "Where were you?"

"With Poison, buying this ..." When he pulled up to a red light, he opened the glove box and pulled out a fucking huge gun that I knew he probably didn't even know how to use. "They have a shit-ton of stuff at Kai's place."

I arched a brow. "You know how to use that?"

"I told you that I need to protect you and your mother."

After exhaling sharply, I frowned at him. "And I told you that I would rather Poison deal with him. If you get caught, you'll go straight to prison for life, Jace. You won't be able to play college football or be with me or—"

"I know," Jace said, cutting me off. "I know what I can lose if I kill him, but I also know what I can lose if I don't or if Harlan finds out about your mother before Poison can expose Nicole's father. It's my life or yours, Allie."

Letting it really sink in, I blew out another breath and rested against the seat until we pulled up to the house.

Before Jace shut the car off, he looked over at me. "You know, I didn't know if Kai wanted me to tell you this or not, but he has one of your father's guns from the military. I thought you should know. I don't know what's going on with him though."

"One of Dad's guns?" I whispered, brows furrowed.

I had looked endlessly for them after he died and couldn't find them anywhere. Why did Kai have them? Sooner or later, I would have to find out what this favor Dad had done for him was or at least get his gun back. I had too many other things to worry about now.

Chapter Ninety-Two

ALLIE

K nowing that Mom was bound to get sick this morning, like she had every morning lately, I set my alarm for three a.m. and snuck out into the hallway before I could wake Jace. I didn't want Mom to be in the bathroom alone, especially if Harlan woke up and decided to look for her.

Then, he'd find out that she was lying about me being pregnant.

If I had to lose sleep over this, then I would in order to keep Mom alive.

So, I slipped into the hallway bathroom to see Mom sitting in front of the toilet with her plush robe covered in puke. Tears streamed down her face, eyes puffy and red. I locked the door behind me, gave her some dirty clothes from the hamper to wear, and pulled off her puke-stained robe.

"Mom," I whispered, chest tightening.

She looked so tired and not from the lack of sleep, but this constant charade we had to play because Harlan would murder us if we didn't. And nobody would care if he did, especially because the chief of police cared only about money. He must have hidden Jace's mother's murder.

"I'm fine, Allie," she said, clutching her stomach. "I'm fine."

After glancing at the door, I crouched by her side. "I have something to ask you," I whispered into her ear, pulling some hair behind her shoulders and tying it with a hair elastic so nothing would get in her hair too.

"What is it, sweetheart?"

"Did you ... cheat on Harlan?" I asked, voice barely above a whisper.

Mom froze and looked back at me. "Do you think I'd do something like that?"

My lips curled down into a frown. "No, but ... Jace told me that Harlan had a vasectomy."

All the blood drained from Mom's face, tears welling up in her eyes. "No, he didn't. He couldn't have. I ... I don't believe it. He never told me about it. If he finds out that I'm ... I'm pregnant, he'll really kill me, kill us." She rubbed a hand over her face. "I need to figure something out."

"How are you pregnant? What happened? Is he ... doing something to you?" I asked, thinking back to how Nicole's father had been pimping out the entire cheerleading squad. If he and Harlan were friends, maybe Nicole's father had done something to Mom too.

But how would that explain him killing his first wife for cheating?

"Honey, you have to believe me when I tell you that I would never cheat. I can't ... I can't tell you what happened right now," she said, placing a hand over her mouth to stop a whimper. "I'm too ashamed."

"Mom, there's nothing to be ashamed of," I said to him. "Please, tell me."

"Not now," she snapped. "Please, not now."

After stepping back, I nodded and heard something creak in

the hallway. I peeked my head out the door to see nothing and shut the bathroom again.

"I have another question, completely unrelated too actually. Before Dad died, did he ever talk about anyone named Kai Koh?" I asked, running the sink water so nobody would hear Mom throwing her guts up at three in the morning on a school night.

Mom tensed for a brief moment, then turned back to the toilet and puked more. "Lord, I want this to be over. I had too much morning sickness with you. I can't do this again for two more months." She looked back up at me. "I don't—"

Someone knocked on the bathroom door, and we froze.

"*Sweetheart*," Harlan called from the hallway, acting freaking nice, like we all didn't know what kind of psychopath that man really was. "Sweetheart, are you in there?"

Almost instantly, she widened her eyes in fear, tears filling them to the brim.

I coughed over the running water and whimpered. "Mom, I-I'm going to puke," I said, acting the best I could to get Harlan *not* to come in.

"Harlan, I'll be out in a few minutes. Allie is getting sick," Mom called, putting her head in the toilet and puking up some liquid that seemed like the last of her sickness for tonight. She cursed to herself, quickly swished some mouthwash around in her mouth, and spit it out, taking my hand.

I flushed the toilet and clutched my stomach, acting as if I were sick, and walked out into the hallway, where Harlan stood in a pair of sweatpants and a nightshirt, lips pressed together and a scowl written all over his face.

Mom squeezed my shoulders and ushered me down the hall. "I'm going to get you a glass of warm milk, sweetie. I used to drink some every morning in my first trimester with you. It'll be all right."

"*Sweetheart*," Harlan said tensely behind us.

We stopped in the middle of the hallway, and Mom glanced back. "Yes?"

Harlan smiled at her, evil intent under it, and stepped between us. "I'll get it for Allie. Why don't you go lie back down? We have to get up early tomorrow, and you've been getting up every night this week."

At that moment, I feared that Harlan was onto something. He wasn't stupid.

"I want my mom," I said, brows furrowed together and clutching my stomach. I did my damn best to have tears well up in my eyes, too, because I fucking needed answers from Mom as soon as humanly possible. "Please, I need her. Just a glass of milk, Harlan. Just one."

Halfway to the kitchen, Harlan tightly grabbed Mom's arm and mine. "Then, why don't we *all* get some milk and relax? It's been a long night for all of us, hasn't it?" He looked over at Mom with a tight smile, as if he knew something that we didn't know. "Hasn't it, sweetheart?"

"Yes, Harlan," she said. "It has."

Chapter Ninety-Three

JACE

"**P**lease, Harlan!" Mom cries, kicking and screaming as Dad drags her by the hair down the hallway and past my bedroom.

I slam my door closed, hating the sound of them fighting over and over and over. It never ends—ever.

And as much as I love Mom, she cheated on our family with my peewee football coach.

She traded her life with us for a night with him.

I hate her for it. I fucking hate her.

She knows how abusive Dad gets and decides to leave me at home with him to go off and fuck a loser from the bad side of town. It is selfish and disgusting of her to do, and I am ashamed to even call her mother. I loathe that she has done that to our family and to me.

"Think about Jace, about the baby, please! Don't do this."

Balling my hands into fists, I let a tear fall down my face. While I might hate Mom, I hate Dad more for making her beg and *scream for him like this. I want to both stop this myself and drown out their screams. It is constant arguing, constant torture for a kid just trying to get through school and make it big one day.*

I collapse onto my bed and grab the football, tossing it into the air and listening to Dad scream at Mom and Mom scream at Dad and them both scream so loud that I can tell neither one of them is listening to what the other is saying. They are yelling to argue, not to understand.

Unable to take it any longer, I rip open my bedroom door. "Can you guys please stop screaming?" I shout over the noise and glance out the hallway to see Mom storming toward me with a fresh black eye and Dad with a bruised lip.

"Fucking bitch," Dad snarls at her. "You deserve to be put six feet in the ground."

I woke up, covered in a layer of sweat and my heart pounding inside my chest at the thought of losing Allie's mother like that. I might've hated Mom at some point because of what she had done to our family, but she hadn't deserved that.

And Allie's mother ... she had been nothing but sweet to me, a motherly figure even.

If Allie only knew half the stuff Dad had done to Mom, she'd flip.

Needing to get a fucking drink to clear my mind, I walked down the hallway and into the kitchen, where Allie, her mother, and my fucking father sat tensely around the kitchen island at three-thirty in the morning, nobody speaking a word and each drinking a glass of fresh milk.

Allie gave me a *help me* look and glanced back at Harlan, lips pressed together tightly.

Dad turned to me with a huge fake smile and pulled out the chair next to him. "Jace, why don't you join us? Since you got your stepsister pregnant, might as well learn how to be a father, getting up at all hours of the night to deal with your son, who'll grow up to be a loser."

I swallowed hard and pulled out the chair next to Allie, knowing that something was up. By the looks of it, milk wasn't the only thing Dad had been drinking tonight.

"Allie and her mother have been waking up by themselves for the past week. It's only right to help out, don't you think?" he said to me.

"I was sick," Allie said. "I don't need Jace to help me puke."

Harlan looked over at her. "You're right. *You don't need Jace at all.*"

Nostrils flared, I grabbed Dad's elbow and pulled him to the side of the room.

What the fuck is he up to? What does he know already?

It hadn't even been a couple days yet, and he was acting too fucking suspicious about everything. Maybe this whole *Redwood will burn* thing was getting to his head too.

Before I could even get a couple words in, Dad leaned in close to me. "I don't know what you're up to, but I'm going to find out," Dad said, squeezing my shoulder harshly. "I can play the same fucking games you are. I've been doing it for years, Jace. So, quit talking to those Poison boys, who don't know how to do shit, or else someone you love is going to get hurt."

I flared my nostrils, rage pumping through me. "I'm not doing anything with them."

"Don't give me that shit." Dad seethed. "I know they killed your principal, like I know you've been hanging out with them too much lately to just be buying bags of weed that you don't even smoke."

Balling my hands into fists behind my back, I had to hold myself back from swinging at him right then and there. The gun was back in my bedroom, and I didn't know where the fuck Dad had guns anywhere in this house. I wouldn't be surprised if he had one stuffed in his waistband at all times.

And, plus, I didn't feel confident enough with shooting that I could kill him in one shot and not miss. I needed training, and I needed it fucking bad because nobody threatened Allie ever, especially not my father.

Chapter Ninety-Four

ALLIE

"What did your dad say?" I asked, lying in bed with Jace twenty minutes later and staring up at the ceiling.

My mind raced with a hundred thousand different thoughts about what Mom could have gone through with Harlan. She had refused to tell me, told me that she was too ashamed to even think about it, and it kind of hurt because we were risking everything for her.

Jace slid his hand across my chest and to my heart. "Your heart is racing, Allie." He kissed my neck softly. "Why don't we calm you down before going back to bed? Hmm? Would you enjoy that?"

I pushed his hand away. "Not now, Jace. It's four in the morning, and we have school tomorrow."

Instead of listening, Jace rolled between my legs. The moonlight flooded in through the windows, hitting his chiseled face and illuminating his dark brown eyes. "You and I both know that you won't be able to fall asleep after that." He kissed down my neck, slipped his hands underneath his oversize nightshirt that I wore, and tugged on my nipples.

"Jace," I whispered. "I don't think—"

"You don't think what, Allie?" Jace asked, kissing down my body, placing his mouth on my panties, drawing his tongue against the lace to make them wet. He looped a finger around them and tugged them to the side, giving himself better access, then drew his nose down my inner thigh.

A shiver ran through my body. I whimpered slightly and arched my back, pussy pulsing with anticipation. And Jace knew it, too, because he hovered his mouth right above my clit and breathed against it.

I lifted my lips, wanting him to kiss me there, but he moved his lips away, always keeping them centimeters from my flesh.

"I'm only going to eat your wet cunt if you ask nicely for it, Allie."

"Jace," I whimpered, annoyed.

I could almost feel him sucking and licking it.

He pushed a finger inside of me, and I tightened around him as he moved it in and out, curling it in the right spots for my body to jerk into the air.

"Don't you want to come for me? Relax a little?"

"Please," I whispered. I wanted to relax after this week; a couple minutes wouldn't hurt.

"Please what?"

Digging my heels into the mattress, I lifted my hips and pulled down on his head, desperate for him to eat me out. He smirked against me and pulled his fingers out, crawling off the bed.

"I have a better idea." He grabbed the dildo he'd bought me, and then he lay on the bed beside me and sat me right on his face. He eased the dildo inside of me until the hilt met my pussy lips and lifted his mouth to lick at my cunt.

Arching my back, I rested one hand on his abdomen and the other on the bulge in his basketball shorts, stroking it quickly and gently massaging his balls. Waves of pleasure washed through me as he fucked me with the dildo and flicked his tongue against my folds.

I pulled his cock out of his pants and dipped my head to take it in my mouth. Jace groaned and lifted his hips off the mattress, thrusting himself into me. He wrapped his strong arms around my thighs and spread them apart farther, forcing me closer and closer to his face.

He pulled the dildo out of my pussy, pulled apart my ass cheeks, and gently placed the head against my hole. I sank my head down on his dick, taking it all inside of me as he shoved the dildo into my ass and groaned against my clit, vibrating it.

"Fuuuck, Allie," he grunted, thrusting his hips up and his cock deeper down my throat. "Your ass just fucking swallows it. Ride my face, baby. Make yourself feel good."

As I ground my pussy against his lips, Jace thrust the dildo in and out of me and reached down to tug on one of my nipples. My bare pussy clenched over and over and over, and I moaned hard on Jace as I came, finally relaxing for a few moments tonight.

Chapter Ninety-Five

ALLIE

Yawning from lack of sleep, I walked with Jace into Redwood and to my locker, resting my head on his shoulder. People looked over at us, pointing at me and whispering behind our backs like we didn't notice. It felt too much like when the entire school had found out that Jace and I were fucking and Principal Vaughn had posted flyers all over the corridor about it.

I ignored their stares and opened my locker, pulling out my books for Biology class, a sticky note that I was *damn sure* I hadn't left sticking out of one of the sections. I flipped open to it, wondering if this would give me a clue as to whatever everyone was whispering about, and found myself staring down at the reproductive health section.

After rolling my eyes and thinking nothing of it, I handed the book to Jace and continued rummaging through my locker for my tablet that I used to take notes. And as I found it, the notorious quarterback *god*—not—sauntered up to the lockers and smirked at Jace.

"Heard you're pregnant with someone else's baby," Carter said to me.

My eyes widened slightly as I shut my locker and narrowed my eyes. "Who told you that?" I asked him, completely taken aback. I grabbed my books from Jace and inched closer to him to keep my distance from Carter.

Who knew what he had up his sleeve today? It was always something.

"The good ole *Redwood Journal*," Carter said, tapping on his phone.

The school newspaper, run by a bunch of nerds, had an entire article titled "Redwood Will Burn" and their predictions about which great Redwood star would fall next.

And today's headline was "Unexpected Pregnancy and Even More Unexpected Baby Daddy."

I ran my hand over my face and snatched his phone, scrolling down as Jace looked over my shoulder at the article that had nothing but lies written all in it. Lies that said, *Allie Hall is pregnant, the father is Carter, and that is why Jace and Carter have been fighting these past few weeks.*

"Looks like we're having a baby together, princess," Carter said, throwing me a wink.

"Why don't you fuck off, Carter?" Jace said, shoving the phone against his chest. "What'd you do to have the newspaper run some shit like this? Fuck one of the writers or something?"

Carter smirked. "Actually, I didn't do anything. I'm as shocked as you are. Who knew I'd find out that Allie was pregnant with my child? I thought it'd be just another day at Redwood Academy, and I guess it is." Carter shoved his phone back into his pocket and walked down the hall, holding up one hand, as if in victory. "I'm going to be a teen dad!"

Before Jace could go after him, I caught Jace by the wrist. "Don't bother. He's not worth the time or the punishment," I said, gnawing on the inside of my cheek. But I was worried about the fact that someone had found out that I'd had to lie to Harlan about being pregnant.

"How do you think everyone found out?" I whispered to Jace, ignoring the stares as he walked me to Biology.

"My dad," Jace said through gritted teeth.

"I thought he didn't want anyone to know."

"He doesn't want anyone to know that *I* got you *pregnant*. He wants the attention off him, so he can still be that perfect fucking father that everyone in Redwood thinks he is. He fucking pisses me off."

"We can't ... back out of this lie though. We have to keep up the pregnancy act at least until we handle him, which means that" —I glanced down the hall to see all our friends waiting outside of Biology class—"we have to lie to everyone, even our friends."

"You have to lie to them," Jace said, letting go of my hand. "I gotta head over to gym class."

"Jace, you're just gonna—"

He kissed me on the lips and winked. "Good luck."

I glared at his departing figure, wanting nothing more than to give him the middle finger for leaving me to answer all the questions. But this *was* my idea, and I'd rather endure the terrible high school drama and bullying than have Mom dead.

Chapter Ninety-Six

ALLIE

"Tomorrow," João said, scooting into an empty seat across from us at lunch and referring to when Poison was going to leak information about the police force. "We talked to Nicole about what's going on. If everything goes smoothly, I'd suggest not returning to school tomorrow. This town will go fucking insane when they learn about it."

I blew out a deep breath and slouched in my seat, ignoring the stares from half the student body. This entire day, I had been faced with never-ending questions from Imani, Nicole, and the rest of the girls about being *pregnant,* and as much as I loved my friends … I hated the attention *and* that everyone thought my fake baby was Carter's.

It was getting on my nerves.

João leaned closer, spotting Imani walking through the cafeteria doors, and pulled a box of cigarettes out of his back pocket. "And your pregnancy rumors are a perfect distraction for the student body right now, so bravo to you on that. You and Carter

..." He lit up right in the middle of the cafeteria and blew a cloud of smoke out of his nose. "Never would've guessed."

Not having the mental capacity for any more rumors, I kicked him hard in the shin and hoped that it left a nasty bruise. All I wanted was for people to shut the fuck up about it because it was a lie fabricated by Harlan, Redwood's most fucked up devil.

Imani sat at the table beside João, tugged the cigarette out of his mouth, and stomped on it. "I told you to stop that. It's bad for your health. You're going to get lung cancer and die." She frowned. "On second thought ... why don't you smoke all of them at once to speed it up a little bit?"

Stifling a laugh, I smiled at their interaction and rested my head on Jace's shoulder, stuffing some more of my sandwich into my mouth. At least by pretending that I was pregnant, people couldn't judge me for eating and feeling tired all the time. I could have cravings for coconut shrimp in the middle of History, and nobody would say a word.

I guessed it worked out that way.

A few moments later, King Carter sauntered into the cafeteria, pulling the stares away from me. And while I thought he was going to walk to his normal table with the rest of the football team, he stalked right up to our table, sat in the empty seat next to me, and said, "What's up, babe?"

Jace curled his fingers into my thigh harshly. I gently rubbed his leg and ignored Carter, hoping he'd get the hint and walk away before Jace did something stupid. Jace was already on edge from his father and my mother. I couldn't imagine how much anger he'd take out on Carter if he—

Carter had the damn audacity to wrap his arm around my shoulders. And before I could stop anything, Jace stood up and grabbed Carter by the collar.

"Get your fucking hands off my girl," Jace said through clenched teeth.

"I can do what I want with her. She's carrying my baby," Carter said.

Leaning my elbows on the table, I placed my face in my hands and blew out a deep breath. Whatever Jace gave Carter, he fucking deserved it. I didn't know what the hell his problem was or who even believed the rumor that Carter was *supposedly* my baby daddy. But Carter didn't have to keep rubbing it in.

"Allie," Imani said, staring worriedly at the scene behind me. "You should stop Jace."

I looked over my shoulder at Jace, who straddled Carter's waist in the middle of the cafeteria and rained down a series of punches on that pretty boy's face. I smiled. I actually smiled at it and wanted to pat Jace on the back. But instead, I turned back around and continued to eat my lunch.

These rumors and keeping up with Mom every morning really wore us out.

A crowd gathered around us, whispering and recording the fight—well, more like the smackdown on Carter. I sank deeper in my seat, hoping nobody would ask me any questions. I could only imagine how the school newspaper would spin this story ...

Jace Harbor fights his stepsister's baby daddy.

Is Jace Harbor jealous of Carter?

Who is Allie Hall's real baby daddy? Find out today!

"Break it up!" someone shouted over the crowd.

The crowd of students parted ways for Jace's football coach—who I guessed was now subbing as the principal until we found someone suitable.

He grabbed Jace and yanked him off Carter, shoving him toward the office. "Get in my office. You know better, Harbor."

After Jace stormed out, I handed Jace's coach Jace's backpack and smirked at the puddle of blood under Carter. That man had been nothing but a prick to everyone since freshman year.

I just hoped that Jace wouldn't be suspended for this.

Chapter Ninety-Seven

JACE

With fury raging through me, I sat in the principal's office with my arms crossed over my chest and Carter's blood on my hands. He fucking deserved everything that I gave him, even Allie agreed. She hadn't stopped me. He had been damn set on getting on my every last nerve since he couldn't do it in football anymore.

"What the fuck was that, Harbor?" Coach Carol scolded, shutting the door behind him. He dropped my backpack by my chair and walked around what once had been Principal Vaughn's desk, giving me a look of disapproval. "Shit like this will get you kicked out of Redwood, and everything you've worked for will go down the drain."

I balled my hands into fists and pressed my lips together, glaring at the mahogany desk. I didn't have an answer for him because I wasn't going to let Allie get disrespected and touched by scum like Carter. She hadn't asked for him to touch her, so I hadn't asked if I could hurl my fist into his face.

Simple as that.

"What's gotten into you?" Coach Carol asked. "You've been hanging out with the Poison boys too much. Something isn't right with you. I can tell. I know when you're holding something in, Jace. I've coached you for years."

Growling under my breath, I looked up at him. "What do you want me to say? That I'm fucking tired of all these stupid fucking rumors? That I can barely sleep lately because of my father? That I worry endlessly if Allie and her mother will survive another day in that house?" I snapped, unable to keep it all in anymore.

Coach Carol was the only adult that I had ever really opened up to; the words seemed to flow from my mouth when I was with him. I didn't know how to shut the fuck up, and he didn't know when to stop pushing me for information.

Don't get me wrong. I loved the guy, but some things were better left unsaid.

Almost as if he didn't know what to say, Coach frowned, leaned back in the seat, and adjusted the Redwood cap on his head. He twirled a pen between his fingers and stared out the window. "You get into another fight, and I won't be able to protect you next time. Get help, Jace. Don't do this alone."

After relaxing my fists, I looked him in the eye. "I'm not doing it alone. Don't worry."

Coach looked over. "I didn't mean ask Poison to help you with ... whatever the fuck you're up to. If you get in trouble, you ..." He shook his head and grimaced. "I don't want to see you dead, Jace. You're like a son to me, and I know how corrupt Redwood is. People go missing, and nobody says a word about it. You need to be careful with who you trust and what you do."

Unsure if I should tell Coach about my plans, I clenched my jaw. "I will be, but I can't endure this anymore. I'm prepared to do what it takes to protect my family from assholes like my father. And you should prepare too," I warned him, knowing that Redwood was really about to turn on its head tomorrow once that video was released.

"I don't know if I should ask you what that means, son," Coach Carol said.

I licked my bottom lip, nerves zipping through me. Allie and I had to get through the next couple of days in peace and without Dad finding out about her mother, so she could get an abortion, and I could finally give Dad everything that man deserved.

Tossing my backpack over my shoulder, I stood up. "Thanks for always being there for me, Coach. But you don't want to know. Redwood is about to turn into chaos. Protect yourself and your wife. I thought I should tell you that at least because ... you've been more of a father to me than anyone else."

Chapter Ninety-Eight

JACE

Later that night, while waiting for Allie to finish her internship, I sat in Mustang Ranch to have dinner by myself because I really just wanted to be alone. If I hung out with Jamal, like he wanted me to, he'd want to talk about Allie, and I would want to tell him about what was really going on. So, I couldn't do that. And Poison was out, preparing for tomorrow.

"Burger with fries," the waitress said, placing a plate in front of me. "Anything else?"

After shaking my head, I grabbed the burger and watched the ketchup ooze out of the sides and onto my fingers, as Carter's blood had done this morning. I had taken the rest of the day off, sitting in the locker room and tossing a football around, my mind not really with it today.

"I looked all fucking around Redwood for you," João said, sliding in on the other side of the booth. "Check your fucking phone next time. Allie could've been calling you."

"Allie's at her internship," I said, biting into the burger and staring emptily at him. "What do you want?"

"Who made up the rumor about Carter getting Allie pregnant?"

"It's not a rumor," I said, lying through my teeth.

"It was your father, huh?" João took one of my fries. "Fucking bastard."

"What's it to you?" I asked, wanting to continue my dinner in peace.

"Nothing."

"Then, why're you here?"

João shrugged one shoulder and looked around. "We have to release the video tonight. Kai is picking Allie up from her internship, so nothing will happen to her when it releases. We don't know how people are going to react."

Placing my burger down, I sat up straight and leaned forward. "Why? I thought the plan was to release it tomorrow during school? What happened to it? Who found out about it?" I asked, worried that Coach Carol had said something to someone.

"Nicole's father found the missing footage. He knows that Nicole took it. She's with Jamal now, so she should be fine until the video releases at least. She called me earlier, a snotting mess, and told me to do it as soon as possible."

I swallowed hard and cursed under my breath. As much as she annoyed the fucking shit out of me, I didn't want her father to hurt or even kill her. She was a bitch, but Allie was becoming fond of her.

João leaned closer. "We're going to fucking destroy all the billionaires in Redwood, all of the fucking assholes here. Don't fucking worry about it."

"That's not a nice word," a young girl with brown hair said, walking past our table with a big glass of root beer that she was spilling everywhere. She couldn't have been older than three years old, maybe younger. "Not all rich people are bad."

"Who the fuck is this?" João asked me, brows furrowed.

I shrugged a shoulder and looked back at her, her eyes, big and brown. She smiled and tilted her head, sipping the drink that she could barely hold straight. "Me and my mommy got saved by a rich person. She said that they were so nice."

"Olivia," a woman a few booths down called, her back turned toward us.

"That's me," the girl said, grinning even wider at us. She held out her hand, as if she wanted me to shake it, her soda beginning to spill off the side of her glass. "What's your name?"

I grabbed the glass to hold it upright so she wouldn't spill it anymore and took her hand hesitantly. "Jace," I said to her and actually smiled back. My entire world felt like it was falling apart, and a stranger could bring a smile to my face. It fucked me up, but it felt good to see such innocence.

She turned to João and held out her hand, waving it as if she was waiting for him to shake it too. But João just stared at her and curled his lip into an ugly grimace.

She placed one hand on her hip, giving him an attitude. "I'm waiting."

"Shouldn't she be afraid of me?" João said.

Olivia pulled her hand back and wrapped it around her soda, taking another sip. "I'm not afraid of you because you have tattoos and look like a monster. My mommy has tattoos, too, and hers are soooo much cooler than yours. They're white."

"White tattoos?" João asked.

"Yeah!" Olivia said. "All over her body, even her head!" She pointed to a scar on João's forearm. "They look like that."

"Olivia!" her mother scolded, still turned. "Come back here."

Olivia departed back to her booth. And almost immediately, her mother picked her up and placed her on her hip, placing her soda on the table and walking with her out of the restaurant.

Olivia waved. "Bye, Jace!"

My lips curled into a small smile, and I waved back to her.

João arched a brow at me and nodded over his shoulder. "Who was the kid? She seemed to like you."

"She would've liked you too, if you'd told her your name."

"I don't fucking give my name out to strangers."

"She was a kid."

"A fucking smart kid."

I rolled my eyes and called for the waitress, wanting a box and the check. If Redwood was going down in flames soon, I wanted to see it burn with Allie. Maybe it'd give us both some peace.

The waitress brought over a box without the check and smiled at us. "That woman with the cute little girl paid for your food," she said to me. "I guess there's always some good in Redwood after all."

$$Chapter\ Ninety\text{-}Nine$$

ALLIE

"So, after your introduction yesterday to what we do ..." Mr. Abara said, walking down the hall with me and Colton at my internship. He held a couple files by his side and beamed at everyone who greeted him. Apparently, he was the big cheese around here. "What would you like to learn more about? Any specific department?"

Eyes widening slightly, I turned to him. "I get to choose?"

"Of course you do, Allie! I'm not going to force you to do something you hate," he said, clapping Colton on the back. "All the interns, like you and Colton, get to choose as long as there aren't too many interns in the same department."

Colton gave me a half-smile, and I couldn't tell if it was genuine or not. Knowing who his brother was and what had happened last night, I wanted to say that it was fake, but honestly, he looked serious and happy here, working under Mr. Abara.

"Um ..." I said, stopping in the hallway and glancing at all the different departments. Between biomedical, bioengineering, biotech, artificial intelligence, and even cyber engineering, there were so many to choose from that I didn't know where to even begin. But I was damn glad that I had taken him up on this internship.

Colton leaned toward me. "I had a hard time choosing too."

Mr. Abara glanced toward the cyber engineering offices and smiled. "You don't have to choose now. I'll give you one more day. But we could really use some help in the cyber engineering offices. It's the newest sector we have and a subsection of bioengineering. Engineers are working on tech to implement into the body that can be integrated and controlled by the mind—think being able to control prosthetics or contact lenses that not only let you see better, but ones that you can also zoom in or zoom out with. Things like that."

"That's a ... a real thing?" I asked, completely amazed.

"It will be," he said, chuckling.

"Allie," the woman at the front desk said, hurrying up to me while I chatted with Colton and Mr. Abara. She swept some blonde hair from her face, cheeks flushed. "Someone is here to see you. They say that it's urgent."

I glanced over at Mr. Abara to ask if it was okay. He gave me a smile. "It's almost time to leave anyway. Why don't you head out? It seems like whatever it is, it's important." He glanced at the woman. "Isn't it?"

After she nodded, I grabbed my coat and purse, gave a slight nod to Colton because I didn't want him to say anything about me being rude to him the other night to Mr. Abara, and hurried to the front office, where Kai paced around and rubbed his hands together.

When he saw me, he grabbed my wrist, thanked the woman, and pulled me out the doors and into the frigid December air. "We have to go. I already texted João, who's with Jace. He knows that I'm picking you up."

My eyes widened as I stumbled after him, my flats being drenched in snow and slush and sliding over the ice. Kai tossed me a helmet for his motorcycle, and I stared at him like he was absolutely insane.

"What's going on, and why are you driving a motorcycle in the middle of winter?"

"It's the only thing I have." He kicked one leg over the bike and sat. "And I'll explain later."

"If you want me to leave with you, you'll tell me now," I said, scrambling through my purse to find my phone.

What was going on? What was wrong? Something had to be because Jace had told me not to go with anyone, especially after what had happened yesterday with Colton.

Kai placed his helmet on my head and strapped it on. "We have to release the information about Nicole now instead of when we planned to tomorrow. Her dad found out. And when it's released, you need to be safe. This town will fucking blow up over the police force pimping out underage girls."

Chapter One Hundred

ALLIE

After we pulled up to Kai's run-down house in the center of the Redwood slums, I texted Jace so he knew where I was and handed Kai his helmet. We walked into his house through a nearly broken, unlocked door, then down a set of creaky stairs to a basement. Filled with cobwebs, spiders, and cockroaches, his house didn't even look livable.

He typed a code into what seemed to be a high-tech lock, clicking the metal door open and gesturing for me to walk in. Hesitantly, I stepped into the room and stared in awe at all the computers, monitors, and screens. Well, I'd spoken too soon.

This place looked like a damn underground shelter for the richest of the rich.

Kai typed another code into his security system, then placed his jacket and the helmet down on a table, flicking on the lights and making the room come alive. Monitors turned on, lights flashed, computers pulled up programs that I couldn't quite understand.

"Make yourself at home," Kai said, sliding onto a seat in front of the main computer. "We need to release the video as soon as possible, before Nicole's father finds her at Jamal's place."

I sat beside him and looked over his shoulder, watching him type a string of letters, numbers, and words I didn't quite understand into a program, the screens around us changing colors and pulling up websites like Facebook, Twitter, and Instagram and even the Redwood news stations.

"Nicole is safe though?" I asked, brows drawn together in worry.

"For now," Kai said, grimacing. "Landon is with Imani and João with Jace. Don't worry."

"Why'd you come to get me?" I asked because Kai seemed somewhat protective of me. He always had been. I wanted to know why. I never quite understood it. I never did anything to him or really helped him in any way.

Kai froze for a second, then continued typing, as if his body hadn't reacted that way. "Jace would kill me if we left you at your internship when this all went down."

"Jace wouldn't kill you," I said, crossing my arms and staring at the side of his face. "You know how to use a gun. You've been in way more street fights than he has. There's something else. Why can't you tell me?"

He paused for a moment and looked over. "Why can't I be nice?"

"Being nice would've been texting me and telling me to leave my internship, not picking me up from it in the frigid snow when all you have is a motorcycle," I said to him, arching a brow.

Things weren't adding up in the slightest. First, Kai had told me that he owed my father a favor, then he put a gun to Carter's back when he was harassing me in Redwood's halls, then Jace told me that he had one of my father's guns, and now, this?

The Poison boys weren't nice for no reason at all.

They always had something up their sleeves.

Swiping a hand across his face, Kai sucked in a sharp breath and focused on his computer screen. "Wait," he said, fingers moving even faster. He paused for a moment and looked up at the screens with worry on his face. Then, he pressed the Enter key and sent the video out to the world from anonymous accounts that I'd bet couldn't be traced back to him.

My phone buzzed almost immediately, social media lighting up with videos, retweets, and chaos about the police force, the video being shared almost a thousand times within the first few minutes. Kai knew how to make stuff go viral, and I assumed he knew how to make stuff disappear too.

After a few moments, Kai sat back in his chair and spun, so he was facing me. "How's your internship?" he asked me.

"That didn't answer my question," I said.

"It will." He stood and nodded to another locked room. "Come with me."

Hopping up, I followed him into a room filled with all types of guns from ceiling to floor, wall to wall. He locked the door behind us and leaned over a table in the center of the room. "How's your internship?" he asked me again.

"It's good," I said, staring wide-eyed at all the guns and walking around the room in amazement.

For someone who lived in the shitty part of town, he sure had a lot of money to buy all these and stash them here.

"What department are you in?" he asked me.

"None yet. I have to choose by tomorrow. Why?"

Kai paused, as if he was debating on whether or not he wanted to tell me the real reason why he was asking and truthfully answer all my questions that I had for him. Eventually, he sighed. "Because this is just the start of the chaos in Redwood. The rich will try to silence the poor, like they've done for fucking decades. They'll kill them with no repercussions, and I want to give us a fighting fucking chance."

"And you're suggesting ..."

"Work with me," Kai said, fingers paling on the table. "You're the smartest person to come out of Redwood in years, and Mr. Abara's company is making tech that is only seen in cyberpunk fiction, tech that will change the world of war and of life forever."

My eyes widened. "You want me to ... to steal their ideas and make it for you?"

"It's fucking crazy, I know. I didn't even want to get you involved in it in the first place, but we're not prepared for what's to come. You know that the rich will slaughter the poor, will walk all over us and put the blame on *us*. They'll split the town up, so kids in the slums won't get a proper education anymore. They'll leave us homeless. You saw it when you lived here. I know you did."

"Kai ..." I whispered, completely taken aback. "You're asking me to make you weapons."

"Not for me," Kai said. "To level the playing field."

I paced around the room and shook my head, unable to believe that this was even happening. I couldn't do that at all. As much as I wanted the poor to succeed, I couldn't steal ideas and hardware from my internship. He was asking too much.

Seemingly knowing that I wouldn't agree, Kai grabbed my hands. "Dad wanted this."

"Dad?" I asked, brows furrowed. "My dad or yours?"

"*Our* dad."

My lips curled into a smile, and I found myself laughing. "What the fuck, Kai? What are you even saying? My dad ... isn't ..."

"Yes, he was. He didn't want you to know that he had another family, that he had gotten another woman pregnant before he met your mother. He didn't want you to see him in a bad light."

I shook my head, unable to believe this. "You're not serious, are you?"

"I'm not lying. I have a DNA test to prove it." Kai walked around me to grab Dad's handgun and placed it in my hands. "That's why I have this. That's *why I'm telling you this* and pleading with you to help me. A rich motherfucker killed our father and got away with it. They do this shit all the time and never get punished for it. It's time that stops. It's time we fight back."

"Kai," I whispered, the gun trembling in my hand. "That's why you ... you've been so protective of me?"

"You're the only family I have left," he said. "My mother over-dosed three months after Dad died. The rich rip families apart and leave us with nothing. *Nothing*, Allie. And your mother ... is in the same boat as Jace's mother, isn't she? She might die, too, and if she does, you know that nobody will give a fuck."

Tears welled up in my eyes.

As much as I hated to think about it or believe it, Kai was speaking nothing but the truth. We needed to fight back, more than just releasing tapes of sexual assault or masturbating to illegal porn. We needed to make a damn impact before anyone else died.

JACE

"It's fucking insane out there," João said as I parked my car behind Kai's motorcycle. He looked behind him at the smoke coming from two streets down and cursed under his breath, glancing around the street. "Where the fuck is Landon?"

Needing to see Allie, I walked into the house without him and down the creaky steps to Kai's underground hideout, gun parlor, whatever the fuck he wanted to call it.

I banged on the heavy metal door three times. "Open up. It's Jace."

When nobody answered, I banged again.

João grumbled under his breath and typed in a code into the lock. "If they're in the back room, they won't hear you." When the door clicked, he shoved it open with his boot.

All the computers and monitors were on, some with the local news, others tracking social media, like Facebook, Instagram, and even Redwood Academy news activity, which was blowing up with articles about the police force already, the hashtag *#SaveNicole* trending across the entire state, not only the town anymore.

"Allie!" I shouted, hurrying into the back room to see her arms around Kai.

Overcome with so much fucking annoyance over tonight, I ripped Kai off her and took her in my arms. She widened her eyes and hurried back over to make sure that he was okay.

"What the fuck, Allie?" I asked her through gritted teeth.

"He's my brother, Jace," she snapped, then turned back to me, regret written across her face. "Sorry, I didn't mean to snap at you. I just ... he's my brother." She looked over her shoulder at Kai and gently grabbed my hands. "My dad had another kid, I guess ... I still can't wrap my head around it."

I glanced over at Kai. "You're Allie's brother?"

Kai gave a half-smile and looked at Allie. "You know, I always hated that Dad lived with you and not my mom and me, but after he died ... I, uh ... I realized that we were both the same—both lost a parent, both grew up on the bad side of town, both had mothers who kinda spaced out after he died."

Allie smiled at him. "I'm still mad that nobody told me sooner, but I'm glad you did."

"Yo, enough with this lovey-dovey shit. Where the *fuck* is Landon?" João asked Kai, lighting up a cigarette.

Kai shrugged and placed Allie's father's gun back on the shelf. "Probably fucking Imani somewhere. I don't fucking know. I've been here, making sure the video is out and going viral. He hasn't called."

"It's fucking crazy out there already, dude." João paced around the room and shook his head. "If they don't get back here in the next five minutes, I'm going out there to find them."

Kai walked back into the monitor room, and we followed to sit somewhere that wasn't surrounded by ammo. Kai sat down on a swivel chair and kicked one leg up onto a table.

"Does the one guy who hated Imani the most now care about her?" Kai asked, lips curling into a smirk. "Cute."

João growled and cut his eyes to Kai. "Don't push it."

Pacing around the room, João ran a hand across his face.

I leaned closer to Allie, resting my head on her shoulder. "I'm glad you're okay. I don't know what I'd do without you, Allie." I kissed her temple, watching as she looked over at me with big eyes. "What's wrong?"

"I'm worried about Nicole," she said, gnawing on the inside of her cheek. "What if her father finds her at Jamal's and … and does something worse than rape her? What if he kills her, Jace, and we never find her body? She disappears out of nowhere?"

"If anything, her father will come here before he checks Jamal's house," Kai said, typing something on his keyboard. One of the screens that showed the local news channel changed into a live feed of a camera outside of Jamal's house, the screen split to see both the front and back doors. "And I got it covered."

I blew out a deep breath and relaxed back against the couch. This was all going to be over soon. I wouldn't have to worry about Allie, Allie's mom, or Dad killing us all. After all this chaos, there would be nothing but peace, and we could finish our senior year without the constant threat of murder.

"All right, I'm fuckin—" João started.

The door opened, and Landon walked in with Imani, who looked up and smiled at him.

"I hate you, you know that?" she said to him, then stopped and turned to us. "Why is everyone staring at us? What's wrong?"

After Landon shut the door behind them, João clenched his jaw and glared at him. "Answer your fucking phone next time and get back here sooner. It's fucking crazy outside. She shouldn't be out there."

Allie moved closer to me and giggled—actually giggled—in my ear, the sound giving me butterflies, even now. "They're so in love with her. I never thought that I would say this, but it's actually cute." She reached for Imani's hand and pulled Imani down next to us. "I'm so glad that you got back safely."

"You too, girl. I already texted Maddie and Vera. They're safe with Maddie's brother and some of the guys on the hockey team." Imani glanced between Allie and me, brows furrowed together. "Have you spoken to Nicole? How is she? I saw that video ... and ..." Imani choked up. "And I feel so bad about this entire thing."

"You saw the video?" Kai asked, then turned to Landon. "I told you not to show her."

Imani hopped up. "It's not his fault. I snuck a peek at it while using the bathroom."

Feeling the tension, Allie tugged on my hand and pulled me up to my feet. "We should go back home. I don't want Harlan alone with Mom."

"You should wait a little bit," Kai said. "If Nicole's father finds any of us out there, he'll do God knows what to find Nicole. Wait a couple hours until he has other shit around Redwood that he has to deal with—angry rioters, murders, fires. You can't go now."

Chapter One Hundred Two

Dozing off on one of Kai's couches, I desperately tried to keep my eyes open as the clock read two thirty-five a.m. Jace rubbed my thigh, telling me every five minutes that we'd go home soon but knowing that it wasn't safe at all to leave, especially not now.

Imani had fallen asleep on Landon's chest, both of them snoring away. João sat in a dirty white lawn chair by the locked metal door with a gun in his hand and a jealous expression on his face as he stared at Landon. Kai sat at his computer, looking more awake than anyone here, eyes jumping from monitor to monitor.

"I know what we can do to keep us awake," Jace whispered into my ear.

"Why are you always horny?" I whispered back, not complaining but wondering *how the hell* he could be horny at a time like this, especially while we were with other people. When he moved his hand down the front of my body, I pushed him away. "Quit it. We can't have sex here in front of everyone."

Jace took my earlobe between his teeth and tugged gently.

"We're not going to have sex. I'm just going to play with you. Relax, baby. You need this." Jace pulled me into his lap and ground himself against my ass, making me shiver in pleasure. "See? You need it."

Closing my eyes so I wouldn't get embarrassed if Kai or João looked over, I relaxed in Jace's arms—only slightly. He slipped his hand into my leggings and played with my pussy, drawing his long and rough fingers against my folds.

"Grind your pussy against my knee," he said, lifting his leg a couple inches higher.

With a leg on either side of one of his, I bucked my hips back and forth very subtly so nobody would see me do it, the warmth gathering in my core. Jace placed his free hand over my mouth, letting me whimper into it, and continued to push apart my folds until he came to my clit.

Moving his fingers in small circular motions, Jace rubbed me faster and faster. I squirmed in his grasp, but he held me in place and grunted into my ear.

"Fuck, I wish you were wearing a short little skirt, so I could slip myself inside you and fill this tight little cunt, make you beg, cry, scream for me in front of our friends."

I curled my toes and bit my lower lip, squeezing my eyes shut as the pressure rose in my core. Jace continued, the motions so unceasing and steady. I dug my fingers into his thigh, pleasure rushing through me, and a—thankfully—calm orgasm rolled through my body. Though I still couldn't help but moan quite loudly into his hand.

"We should go," I whispered, body finally relaxing against his.

"Just a little longer," Jace murmured against me. "I'm not finished yet."

Chapter One Hundred Three

JACE

"**W**e have to go back to the house," Allie said, trying to convince both of us that driving through the Redwood chaos in the middle of the fucking night was the right thing to do.

We needed to make sure her mother was okay, and I didn't want to leave her alone with that bastard.

But it had only gotten worse out here since João and I had been out.

The police department had been set on fire, flames lighting up the dark sky and smoke settling over the town. The poor looted the rich areas, throwing rocks into their glass windows and stealing shit from inside. And the rich stayed in a state of panic, pacing back and forth in front of their house windows and packing their cars for an easy escape, if needed.

Ahead and on the only route back home, two police cars were parked right in the street, blocking all traffic. I rolled up to a stop and saw the police chief himself storm out of his car and to mine, gun drawn and pointed at me.

"Jace," Allie whispered, clutching my hand with her trembling one, tears welling up in her eyes that reflected the shining police lights. "What are we going to do? This is our only way home ... and he ... he looks like he wants to kill you. I'm scared, Jace."

Watching him approach the car, I squeezed her hand. "It's okay. He won't do anything to hurt me," I said even though I was sure that he would. I grabbed her chin and forced her to look at me. "If anything happens, take the gun in the glove compartment and protect yourself, baby. Do you understand me? Don't let him or any of the other officers touch you or force you into anything. You fucking kill them."

Tears raced down her cheeks. "But, Jace ..."

The driver's door was ripped open, and Nicole's father yanked me out by the collar and onto the concrete. All I could hear was Allie screaming at him not to hurt me, that she loved me more than anything, that she wouldn't be able to live without me.

Nicole's father laid me flat on the ground and shoved his knee across the side of my neck, making it hard for me to breathe. He pressed his gun to my temple.

"Where the fuck is my daughter?" He spat down at me. "Where the fuck did you take her?"

"I don't know what you're fucking talking about," I said through gritted teeth. "I don't know where she is."

"Is she with Poison?" he asked me, nostrils flaring, that gun pressing harder against me. He put more of his weight on my neck, and I gasped for air, my vision blurring slightly. He knocked me in the head with the side of the gun. "Huh? Is that where that fucking bitch is?"

When I refused to say anything, he slammed the muzzle into my fucking temple. "Jared, get his fucking whore out of the car. If he won't talk, we'll make him."

"Don't fucking touch her!" I shouted, scrambling to get out of his hold and ready to put up a fight now because Allie was fucking mine. I wouldn't let any one of those fucking corrupt cops touch her like they had Nicole.

"Don't fucking like it, do you?" Nicole's father asked. "I've been waiting to kill you, Jace. I just didn't think I'd get to toy with your stepsister and make you watch before I put a bullet right through your skull. She's so fucking pretty though. No wonder Vaughn wouldn't give me your and Allie's video. He wanted to keep her all to himself."

All I could feel was rage rushing through every one of my veins. I wanted to fucking kill this man more than anything. He wouldn't even get a chance to touch Allie before I did it too.

"Get the fuck off me," I shouted at him, shoving my elbow back. "Touch her, and I'll fucking kill you."

"You won—"

A gunshot rang out to my left, and I twisted my head to see the body of a police officer hit the ground from under the car, blood seeping out from a bullet wound in the middle of his head. Allie stood up and aimed the gun at Nicole's father with shaky hands and blood splattered across her face.

"Let him go!" she screamed. "Let him go now!"

Nicole's father gently released me, his gun still aimed at my head but his grip looser. He chuckled at her. "What are you going to do? Shoot me? You'll fucking kill your boyfriend if you do," he said to her, grinning like a fucking madman. "Do it. I'd like to see you try."

And when I saw an opening, I grabbed that gun from his hand and aimed it anywhere that wasn't right at me. We struggled with it for a few moments, bullets flying everywhere, and another bullet shot through the air, hitting Nicole's father right in the ribs. When he doubled over to grasp his ribs, I grabbed his gun and sprinted over to Allie, needing to get out of here as soon as humanly possible.

Hand trembling in mine, Allie gave me the gun and looked

back at the police chief, suddenly ducking behind someone's car parked in a driveway.

"He has another one," she said to me, grasping my hand harder. "We have to get out of here."

Not willing to stop now, I pulled Allie behind the house and through yards of the Redwood rich until I knew that he wasn't following behind us. Yet we continued to run toward my father's house.

"How did you do that?" I said. "You know how to shoot a gun?"

She gave me a half-smile under the moonlight and shrugged. "My dad taught me some things before he died, and I'm glad that he did." She spotted our house in the distance and pulled me faster. "Do you think he's going to follow us back home?"

"He's looking for Nicole. He won't follow us. He'll go to Poison's next."

"I'm scared, Jace," she whispered. "I'm so scared."

Stopping at our back door, I wrapped her up into my arms. "We're so close to finishing this," I whispered, stroking her hair. "We're so fucking close, baby. After your mother gets an abortion, we'll be fucking free, and I can kill that son of a bitch."

"Why can't we do it now?" she asked, brows drawn together.

"Because he won't let her out of his sight. And he'd make sure to kill her before I could even get close enough to kill him."

Chapter One Hundred Four

ALLIE

I hadn't shot a gun in years, not since Dad used to bring me to the shooting range. It probably hadn't been the best idea to bring his barely teenage daughter out to shoot guns, and Mom had especially hated it, but I was now grateful toward him. He'd taught me how to protect myself.

Jace grabbed my trembling hand and kissed my knuckles. "Calm down, Allie. It's okay."

Though Dad had taught me how to protect myself, I hadn't thought that I would ever have to kill someone with a gun. I hadn't known I would shoot a police officer dead and run through a chaotic Redwood like I was running away from the police.

"I'm just ... Jace ... I've never done that before."

Wrapping his arm around my shoulders, he pulled me into his chest and gently stroked my hair. "I know what it feels like, Allie. You're scared, and you're hurting. That's how I felt after I killed that son of a bitch keeping me hostage. I'm here for you, and I'll always be here for you. No matter what."

My lips fell into a small smile, and I curled my fingers into his back. "I love you, Jace."

And I fucking meant it more than anything. Not only had I killed that officer because he was going to take me and do God knew what with me ... but I couldn't stand to see the chief of police—the one man who was supposed to protect this town— throw Jace onto the ground, hold a gun to his temple, and threaten to put a bullet through his head.

Killing that officer had been more than just for me.

"We're too deep into this now, Jace," I said, tears welling up again. Between the nerves, finding out that Kai was my brother, and shooting a man dead tonight, I couldn't hold it together anymore. I rested my hands on his taut abdomen. "We're in this together."

Jace rested his forehead on mine. "Always."

After a few moments, I grabbed his hand. "Come on. Let's go see my mom."

Stepping into the house, I tiptoed through the darkness, careful not to slam into anything so I didn't wake Harlan, and walked up the stairs, seeing a sliver of the bathroom light glow against the hallway wall. My stomach tightened, and I hurried up the stairs, taking two at a time.

The sound of puking echoed through the hall, and I hoped to God that Mom wouldn't wake Harlan up because the door wasn't closed, like it usually was, and the light was so damn bright. When I made it to the top of the stairs, I let go of Jace's hand and rushed to the bathroom, my heart stopping when Harlan stood over a puking Mom.

"Where have you been?" Harlan asked, not even pulling Mom's hair back.

"Out," Jace said, wrapping his arm around my waist and holding me to him.

"It's three in the morning."

"It's actually four."

"What's on your face, Allie?" Harlan asked.

I dragged my palm across my chin, hoping the only blood from the officer was on my chin, and sucked in a breath, remembering that I had to keep up this facade even though Mom was the one puking up her guts because of morning sickness. "Puke."

"Mother and daughter, puking up a lung tonight." Harlan rested a hand on Mom's shoulder and squeezed tensely. "Isn't that right, sweetheart?" He looked back over at us with dangerous, dark eyes. "We had steak for dinner last night. She must've gotten sick from it. Nothing to worry about though. Why don't you kids head off to sleep? I can take care of this."

My stomach tightened. I didn't want to leave Mom alone with Harlan, but it was too late. He had already found her puking, could already be suspicious that she was the one pregnant, not me.

Chapter One Hundred Five

ALLIE

I hadn't slept at all last night, or the night before, or even the night before that one. I was in a constant state of worry that Harlan had seen right through Mom's lie about *me* being pregnant and needing an abortion when, really, it was her. He had caught Mom puking the other night, in the midst of morning sickness.

Originally, I had thought he'd put two and two together, but for the past few days, he hadn't said or done anything that made me think he was suspicious of us. And I was thanking whoever the hell was watching over us that we had made it to Friday without a scratch on her from Harlan.

Sitting in the doctor's waiting room, I grabbed Mom's hand and squeezed hard, my knee bouncing nervously. This was it. We were so damn close to getting her an abortion and setting her as free as she could be from Harlan. At least then, he wouldn't get that urge to kill her over *cheating* on him, which she certainly hadn't done.

But ... she hadn't told me what she had done to get pregnant.

And I was afraid that I didn't *want* to know.

Though chaos unfolded outside, the doctor's office was deathly quiet, and it made me so freaking nervous. Jace placed a hand on my thigh to stop it from bouncing and squeezed gently.

"It's okay, Allie," he whispered into my ear. "Deep breaths. We're almost through it."

After blowing out a couple deep breaths, I squeezed my eyes closed. "What is happening?" I asked, stomach in knots. "The appointment was scheduled for a half hour ago. Why aren't they calling us in?"

The clerk sitting at the front desk smiled at us. "It'll be a few more moments. With everything that has been going on these past few days, we're having trouble finding nurses and doctors to come into the office. Most live on the bad side of town, so it's difficult for them."

Nodding my head politely at her, I swallowed.

Mom squeezed my hand tighter. "It's going to be okay, sweetie," she said, pulling me closer to her and talking as if she was really trying hard to remind herself that this was the end, that she'd soon be free. "You're going to do great. Nothing to worry about."

"I want this to be over with," I whispered.

"Me too, sweetie. Me too."

"Allie Hall," the nurse called from the back door, adjusting a clipboard in her hand.

I shot up and pulled Mom up with me, my stomach in knots. This was it. We were about to finally finish this after living through the past week as bundles of damn nerves. It was about to be over for good.

Before I could get two feet, Harlan grabbed Mom's wrist. "You don't need to go in with her, honey. This town is in too much chaos already. I'm sure they don't need a woman who's going to do nothing but cry hysterically back there with them."

Mom tensed, and I pulled her back anyway.

"It's okay if my mom comes in with me, right?" I asked the

nurse, pleading with her with my eyes. If this didn't fucking work, I would be devastated—absolutely devastated.

The nurse smiled. "Of course. It's no problem."

When I continued to tug Mom, Harlan tightened his grip on her.

"*Honey*," he said in the strongest, strictest tone I had ever heard from him. "You're not going in there with her. You're going to stay out here with me. Do you understand?"

Mom smiled nervously with her brows furrowed together, grabbing my shoulder. "Harlan, she's my daughter. I don't want her to go in alone. She's terrified of what they're going to do to her and the baby. It's this one time, and it'll only be for a few minutes."

"If she was terrified, she shouldn't be fucking my son."

"Harlan, she—"

"You'll stay out here with me, honey." Harlan stuffed his hand in his right pocket jacket, and Mom's face paled, her whole body going rigid. "Do you *understand* now?"

My entire body tensed because ... I didn't have to see what was in his pocket to know he had brought a fucking gun to the doctor's office and was threatening to shoot Mom dead here if she didn't cooperate.

I just ... didn't know how to tell Jace that his father was armed without something happening to Mom first.

I glanced over at Jace, who stared at me with both worry and a quizzical expression, as if he didn't understand why my expression had turned from anger to terror in a matter of milliseconds. Wanting to show him somehow, I very slightly nodded to his father, but he still didn't get it.

"Allie, it's okay if your mother doesn't want to come in," the nurse said.

Fuck, this was not what I ... had wanted to happen. Not now. Not fucking now.

As if she realized that Harlan wouldn't let her go anyway,

Mom ushered me along with tears in her trembling eyes. "It's okay, sweetheart. You'll be fine. I'm sure it's a quick procedure. A few minutes, and you'll be back out. Go on."

"Jace can go with you," Harlan suggested. "He was the one who got you pregnant."

Swallowing hard, I bit back my tears and held myself together. "No, I don't want him to come in with me," I said because I needed him to stay out here and make sure that Harlan didn't take Mom away and kill her then.

All I wanted to do was run into Mom's arms to tell her that I loved her more than anything, but I couldn't do that. I sucked it all up, turned around, and walked to the nurse who held the back door open for me. We were fucked—absolutely fucked.

Chapter One Hundred Six

ALLIE

"He didn't say anything?" I whispered to Jace later after we got home from the doctor's office with an IUD stuck up my vagina and a severe cramp pinching my insides.

While I had been way too nervous to tell the nurse that the abortion wasn't for me, she had made me take a pregnancy test beforehand to confirm. When it came back negative—thank God because I couldn't have Jace's baby at the moment—she offered to give me some birth control.

The nurse told me that I'd have some side effects tonight and tomorrow, like cramps and nausea, and that I had to wait an entire week to have sex again—not sure how that was going to happen, but we'd see. I wasn't too upset about me at the moment; I had Mom to worry about.

Jace shook his head. "No."

"Not even when I walked into the back? He didn't take Mom anywhere, right?"

Jace turned in his bed and rubbed my stomach. "No."

I gnawed on the inside of my cheek and stared up at the ceiling, watching the moonlight flicker against the walls. It didn't make sense in the slightest. Harlan had been dead fucking set on keeping Mom out of the doctor's office with me. He had to have known that something was up; I couldn't believe that he hadn't said anything.

But maybe he was waiting until we got home, until he couldn't be stopped.

"Jace, I have a bad feeling," I said, grabbing my stomach and curling into a ball. And it wasn't the side effects of the IUD either. It was a feeling that something really fucking bad was going to happen, a feeling that Mom was in danger.

And as I was about to jump out of bed, I heard Mom scream so fucking loudly.

"I'm sorry, Harlan! Stop it, please!"

My eyes widened, and we both got out of bed.

Jace caught my wrist. "Wait, I need to get that fucking gun." As I waited by the door, bouncing on my toes, he hurried around the room and pulled open a bunch of drawers, tossing things out of them. "Where the fuck is it?"

"Harlan!" Mom shouted.

"Fuck it. I can't wait." I rushed out into the hallway.

Jace hurried after me, grabbing my hand and pulling me behind him. "It's not where I left it. He must've fucking taken it. He's a fucking psychopath, Allie. Stay here in the hall. I can't let anything happen to you."

Tears welled up in my eyes, but I refused to let them fall now. Nothing good would come from me crying my eyes out. We had to deal with Harlan one way or another.

So, I shook my head and continued forward. "No. My mom is out there. I won't stay calm, and I won't let him kill her. She's the only family that I have left, Jace. I fucking love her."

"And if he kills you too?"

Knowing that we were losing precious time, I kissed Jace on

the lips and pulled him toward the living room. "We don't have any time. What happens tonight happens. I love you. I hope you know that."

Mom lay in the middle of the living room, grasping her stomach, blood smeared across her teeth, as if Harlan had punched her in the mouth.

Drunk off his ass and waving a gun in the air, Harlan swayed and stared at Jace with wide, devilish, horrifying eyes. "Look who thought he could come save the day."

I lurched forward to help Mom, but Jace held me back.

"Don't be stupid."

My stomach tightened, throat closing up. *Don't be stupid? Don't be fucking stupid? Let Harlan wave a gun at Mom, punch, kick, beat her while she is pregnant?* I couldn't fucking do that. I couldn't.

"Let her go!" I yelled at Harlan, tears in my eyes. "Please, she didn't do anything wrong."

"Didn't do anything wrong?" Harlan let out a lifeless laugh. "She fucked another man behind my back, like your stepbrother's whore mother did. She did plenty fucking wrong, Allie. Don't fucking tell me she didn't."

"She's not preg—"

"I made her take a pregnancy test two minutes ago. She's pregnant." He leaned down and trailed the gun up Mom's throat, making her whimper out. "You are, sweetie, aren't you?"

Mom looked over at me through teary eyes. "Go back to your room. You don't want to see this."

"They're staying." Harlan swept the gun down her chest, between her breasts, and to her stomach. "They're going to see what happens to whore women like you who cheat on their husbands."

And then, Harlan pulled the trigger.

Everything stopped.

Every.

Fucking.

Thing.

Blood pooled out of Mom's abdomen. Her body went limp.

I collapsed onto the ground and used the rest of my strength to crawl over to her, clutching her body in my hands and putting pressure on her wound. "Mom, no, please, no. Stay with me."

"Where's your gun, Jace?" Harlan asked, cracking a smirk. "Did you lose it? Did you decide that you couldn't kill your old man? You fucking should've done it sooner because I'm not fucking stupid. I figured it all fucking out. And after I put another bullet through her head, you're next."

"No," a woman said, stepping out from behind Harlan, the muzzle of her gun against the back of his head. "You're not going to lay another hand on my son."

Chapter One Hundred Seven

JACE

"No," I whispered to myself and shook my head, staring at the figure behind Dad.

She couldn't be real.

I was hallucinating.

Mom was dead.

"Put the gun down now, Harlan," Mom said to Dad, unflinching.

Dad froze and stared at me with wide eyes, loosening his grip on the gun but refusing to drop it. Allie doubled over her mother, in perfect fucking range for Dad to shoot her dead, too, and pressed on her mother's stomach, where Dad had shot her. Blood seeped between her fingers, and Allie started to hyperventilate.

"You're alive?" Dad asked without turning around.

"Put the fucking gun down now," Mom said through gritted teeth.

When Dad refused to drop the gun, Mom shot him in the hand. The gun *and* some of his fingers fell from his hand and onto the ground. In a rush, I picked up the gun and pointed it at him, not sure what the fuck I was doing or how this would all play out.

"Mom!" Allie screamed, hovering over her mom and staring down into her dulling eyes. With both hands pressed against her stomach to hold the wound closed, Allie shook her head. "Don't go, please. Stay with me, Mom. Please, stay with me."

I knew that I had to leave and get Allie's mother to the hospital now, but I felt like I was fucking hallucinating. I had seen Mom dead. She couldn't be here now. She couldn't. If I turned away and ran out of the room, would Harlan still be here when I got back? Was this all in my head? Was Mom real?

"Jace!" Allie cried. "Please, help me. Please, I'm begging. Save my mom."

"Mom," I whispered, eyes widening. "Mom, you're ... you're ..."

Mom pressed the muzzle of the gun against Dad's head. "Take Allie's mother to the hospital. Take care of your girlfriend. And protect those you care about. I'm going to be the one to finish this and end your father's life." Before I could say another word, Mom cut her gaze to me. "Now, Jace."

After cursing to myself, I threw the gun onto the glass living room table and picked Allie's mother up in my arms. "Grab my keys, Allie. Quickly."

When Allie grabbed my keys from the counter, I rushed out of the room and to the front door.

And as we stepped out of the house, I heard the gun go off three times. Then, there was silence and a sort of peace that I couldn't even begin to explain. But it only lasted for a couple moments because I found myself hurrying with Allie to the car.

I had so many questions to ask Mom, but I didn't have time for that either.

Maybe one day, I'd see her again.

Squealing into the hospital front door, I parked the car and grabbed Allie's mom from the backseat. We hurried through the automatic sliding doors and into the lobby, Allie screaming and crying next to me that there was way too much blood everywhere.

"Mrs. Abara!" I shouted, spotting Imani's mother down the hall.

She looked over her shoulder at us, widened her eyes, and sprinted over. "We need to bring her to the ER now. What happened, Jace?" she asked, ordering someone to take Allie's mother from me and bring her to the other room.

Allie grabbed on to her mom's hand and shook her head. "No, I don't want her to go. I lo-love you. Don't leave me, Mom, please."

As a nurse tried to pull Allie off her mother, I grabbed Allie by the waist and tugged her toward me, hugging her to my chest.

"My father beat her and shot her," I said for the first time aloud. I hadn't told many people about what Dad was capable of, but now that he was gone ... I didn't have to keep it a secret anymore.

Mrs. Abara cursed under her breath and hurried down the hallway toward the ER. "Call Imani!" she shouted over her shoulder. "Make sure that she gets here to calm down Allie. I'll do my best to help the main surgeon out."

"Wait!" I said, pulling Allie closer. "Did you ... did you save my mom?"

Mrs. Abara was the best neurosurgeon in the area. Mom had been shot straight through the head. She had to have known and helped her recover somehow. She had to have. Nobody else would've, especially in this town. People couldn't keep secrets as big as this one.

Instead of answering me aloud, she gave me half a smile, then disappeared into a back room. My chest tightened, and I scooped Allie into my arms. I would figure it out sooner or later. After settling down on a chair in the ER waiting room, I pulled Allie to my chest, stroked her hair, and called Imani.

"It's going to be okay, baby," I whispered to Allie, rubbing her hips. Mom had told me to protect the ones I loved the most, and that was exactly what I was going to do for forever. "We're going to get through this. I'll make sure that we do."

Chapter One Hundred Eight

ALLIE

It had been hours, days maybe. I didn't know.

Imani and Poison sat in the corner, quietly chatting with each other. Doctors rushed up and down the hallways toward Mom's room and some other rooms. I still sat wrapped in Jace's arms, refusing to move in case Imani's mother came back with some news. *Any news.*

A back door opened, and two doctors, along with Mrs. Abara, walked through them, scanning the emergency room for me and Jace. As soon as I saw them, I hopped up and rushed over, wiping the tears from my cheeks.

"When can I see her? Is she okay? How bad is it?" I asked, unable to hold myself back.

Mrs. Abara placed a hand on my shoulder and showed no emotion on her face. None. No smile. No frown. No sense of relief or despair. Instead, she looked at me and swallowed. "Allie, your mother lost a lot of blood—*a lot.*"

Before she could even continue, I took a step back and shook my head. "Please, don't continue," I said, knowing this conversation was going nowhere good. My knees gave out, and her voice became distant.

From behind, Imani caught me and held me steady. "Be strong, Allie. It's what your mom would've wanted."

So, I stood up a little straighter on trembling legs and grabbed Jace's hand as hard as I could. "If you're going to tell me that Mom died, I can't … I can't hear it." My lips trembled. "Please, spare me the pain and heartbreak, Mrs. Abara, please."

Mrs. Abara swallowed hard and took me into her arms, rocking us back and forth. She and Jamal's mom had always been like second mothers to me, especially after Dad died.

Resting her cheek on my head, she said, "Your mother has fallen into a coma and is in the ICU. We don't know when or *if* she'll awaken."

My entire body fell weak, limp almost.

Mom might not be dead, but she was unresponsive, in a coma, near death maybe.

"You can see her now," Mrs. Abara said, looking up at Jace. "Please, go with her."

Scooping my hand in his, Jace followed Imani's mother and pulled me down the hallway toward the ICU. We waited in an elevator, went up three floors, and paused when we reached a frighteningly quiet one. My stomach turned and twisted, nerves getting the best of me.

I squeezed Jace's hand and walked into Mom's room, smacking a hand over my mouth and letting out a sob.

"Mom," I whispered, though I knew she couldn't hear me. I walked over to her and doubled over her bedside, taking her fragile hand in mine. "Mom, I love you so much—so freaking much. You can't leave me. Please, don't ever leave me."

And while I didn't expect a response, I still felt like shit when all I heard back were my sobs echoing through the halls. Jace crouched behind me, sliding one hand around my waist and pulling me close. All I could do was turn toward him and wrap him into a hug.

Jace Harbor was the only family I had left.

471

Chapter One Hundred Nine

JACE

"I'm nervous," I said to Allie, rubbing my sweaty palms against my jeans and staring at the door, waiting for Mom and my sister to walk into the diner.

It had only been a few days since what had happened with Dad, and I so desperately wanted to stay with Allie at the hospital, but Allie had urged me to go out to breakfast with Mom. And I'd told her that I would only go if she went with me.

Not only did she need some fresh air—that hospital brought out the worst in people—but I needed her with me. Meeting my mom again and my sister for the first time in years wasn't something I could face alone. I so desperately needed her to be with me because Allie was my only constant in this life.

Allie grabbed my hand in her weak one and gave me her best, "It'll be fine."

Though I could see she was still struggling on the inside. Her mom hadn't woken up yet.

Mom walked into the diner, holding Olivia's small hand. Olivia wore her hair in pigtails that bounced up and down every time she took a step and a Redwood football shirt that made me grin even though I wanted answers more than I wanted Mom back.

It felt wrong to think that, but it was true. She had left me for years without a call, without a trace, without letting me know that she wasn't dead like I thought. Instead, I'd had to endure the pain of Dad's wrath every single fucking day.

I wanted to hate Mom, but she was all I had left.

"I remember you!" Olivia said, smiling at me.

Mom let go of her hand and crouched next to her. "Sweetie, remember how I told you that I had a secret and that Mommy would one day let you in on it? Well, Jace is your big brother."

Olivia stared at me with big eyes. "What does that mean?"

Though I tried to suppress my grin, I couldn't. Instead, I found myself grabbing Olivia and setting her on the table, her light-up princess sneakers on my thighs. "It means that we get to hang out all the time, that I get to bring you to Redwood sports games like hockey and baseball, and we get to watch whatever kinds of shows kids your age are into nowadays. You like *Paw Patrol*?"

Olivia wrinkled her nose. "I like *Cops*."

Allie giggled into my shoulder, her body trembling in a fit of laughter next to mine—the first real smile I had seen from her in days now.

Mom smiled at her, then looked back at Olivia and me with a glimmer in her eyes. "Tell him what else you like, *Olive*."

Throwing her hands up into the air the way refs did when signaling a touchdown, Olivia showed me all her little teeth and shouted, "Football! I'm gonna be the best football player who's ever lived. Mommy even got me one to play around with." She leaned closer to me. "Do you like football?"

"I love it."

"Mommy, you hear that?" Olivia asked, turning around and

jumping off the table. She grabbed Mom's hand. "Maybe Jacey can come over, and I can teach him how to play."

Mom ushered her into the seat in front of Allie and me. "I'm sure he'd love that."

Allie placed a hand on my thigh and leaned in closer as Mom got Olivia settled into the seat and stopped her from squirming around.

"About those babies you want ..." Allie whispered, her voice a bit stronger than it had been this morning.

Getting her out of that hospital seemed to be a good thing even if it was just for an hour.

"Don't tease me because we can definitely go against doctor's orders and do it before your IUD starts working," I whispered back to her and relished in the way she blushed hard. If she thought *that* was cute, I couldn't fucking wait to have kids with her and make a family.

When the waitress came over, I ordered Allie four pancakes and some eggs. She hadn't been eating much lately, and I hoped to God that she'd start now. It had only been a few days, but this had taken such a toll on her body already.

As Olivia and Allie started eating breakfast, I turned to Mom. "Why?" I asked. "Why'd you leave me alone all those years? Why didn't you get me out of that situation? He fr-freaking abused me, took another wife, and threatened to kill her."

Mom glanced down at her untouched food and pressed her trembling lips together. "I needed to protect Olivia and get stronger. After what had happened, Mr. and Mrs. Abara—Imani's parents—found me. Mrs. Abara saved our lives, and her husband helped me through physical therapy with the latest technology that his company had been producing. It took me years to be able to walk again, Jace. We've been staying outside of Redwood in a secure location. I'm sorry."

Allie squeezed my knee and inched closer to me, not saying a word, though I knew that she had something to say. Or maybe I wanted her to say something because ... I felt so bad for being pissed at Mom, but I couldn't help it.

"Your father was a monster. If I'd contacted you, he'd have found out, and he might have ... done something to you or to Olivia to get back at me for ... for cheating on him." She stared up at me with wavering eyes. "I came to all your games with Olivia. I so desperately wanted to see you again, but I couldn't."

"Why now?" I asked, balling my hands. "Why not sooner?"

"Because I knew he was days away from killing Allie's mother. I watched him for weeks, waiting for the opportunity to step in. I should've barged in sooner before he had the chance to hurt Allie's mom, but I... I didn't. I'm sorry. I'm not a hundred percent healed yet, but ... I couldn't bear to see anything happen to the both of you."

We fell into an awkward silence, and Allie inched closer to me to whisper into my ear. "You should forgive her, Jace. Don't let her slip away again. Life is too short and too precious. If you don't want to do it for yourself, please, do it for me."

I gazed down at Allie and kissed her on her forehead. I would do anything for her.

Chapter One Hundred Ten

ALLIE

Kai: You in?

I stared down at the text message from Kai and gnawed on the inside of my cheek. It had only been a week since everything had gone down, and I hadn't found the energy to get back to my internship. Mom being in a coma weighed so heavily upon my shoulders, but this morning, I'd woken up and reminded myself that she was there because a rich Redwood man had gotten away with murder.

This town was so damn corrupt. I couldn't sit around and do nothing.

Me: We'll meet you at your place. Twenty minutes.

Jace sat up on the hospital waiting room chair and rested his head on my shoulder. "I've been thinking," Jace started. "As nice as our lives could be, I don't want any of that dirtbag's money. I'll save enough to put us both through college and for your mother's hospital bills, but I'm going to use the rest for charity."

I glanced over at him, butterflies in my stomach. "Really?"

Jace paused, brows furrowing. "Do you think that's a bad

idea? I can—"

"Not at all!" I reassured. "Who are you going to donate it to?"

"I wanted to start my own foundation to help women who are being abused, give them a secure place to stay, food, and necessities while they get back on their feet and until they feel safe again to live on their own."

My heart swelled, pride rushing through me. "Jace, that's wonderful."

Blushing, Jace looked over at me. "You think?"

"Yes!"

"Will you help me? I can't do it alone."

"Of course I'll help you." I turned around to face him and swallowed. "There's actually something I wanted to talk to you about too. I'm going to stay in Redwood until Mom wakes up," I said, nails digging into my palms.

It broke my heart. It really fucking did, but I couldn't leave Mom. Not only was she the only family that I had left, but also, if she didn't wake up and the doctors decided to take her off life support ... then these would be the last few months that I had with her.

"I'm going to stay even if she hasn't woken up by the time college rolls around. I got accepted to a college an hour north. I'll commute every day."

"I'll stay with you," Jace said, slowly unclenching my fists and drawing me closer.

I gave him the best smile I could muster and shook my head. "No. I won't let you. You have dreams of going into the NFL, and going to Michigan is the only way that you're going to get there. It's one of the best and biggest football schools. I won't let you throw away your dreams."

Jace curled his fingers into my hips. "I'm not giving up my dreams. You're the only fucking thing that matters, Allie. I want to finally be with you without all this shit going on. I want to be able to love you without worry anymore."

"We can still love each other. We'll just be a couple hundred miles apart."

"A couple hundred miles would be fine; I could come back to see you every day. But Michigan is nearly a thousand. I'll barely see you for who knows how long, Allie. I need you. I fucking need you."

I grasped his face, drawing my fingers down his cheeks and holding back a sob. I needed this man, too, but I also needed him to enjoy the freedom he finally had. He had already sacrificed so much for me, and football was his life. I wouldn't let him choose.

"Go to Michigan. Play football. Get into the NFL. Set up a good life for us and for … the babies that I know you so desperately want to have. Okay, Jace? Make a life for us there, and I'll come once my mom heals from her wounds. I promise that I'll transfer there when I can, so we can finally be together. No more holding each other back. We're going to thrive, Jace."

Cursing under his breath, Jace looked at me through teary brown eyes. "I fucking love you, Allie. I don't want to go."

"Don't cry, Jace," I whispered, knowing that once he did, I would start. "I love you too." I rested my forehead against his and kissed his lips. "We'll make us and this work. We always do."

This is end of Stepbrother (for now)! Preorder the next book in the series today, which follows Imani and Poison > https://books2read.com/Poison-Redwood-Academy

I'll be writing a sequel about Allie and Jace *together* in college <3 The next books will answer all your questions about other characters like Nicole and her father, Imani and the Poison boys, Vera, Maddie, and more! Make sure to subscribe to my newsletter to stay up to date on this series: https://www.emiliarosewriting.com/

Also by Emilia Rose

ALSO BY EMILIA ROSE

Paranormal Romance

Submitting to the Alpha

Come Here, Kitten

Alpha Maddox

My Werewolf Professor

The Twins

Contemporary Romance

Poison

The Bad Boy

Excite Me

Erotica

Climax

About the Author

Emilia Rose is an international best-selling author of steamy romance. Highly inspired by her study abroad trip to Greece in 2019, Emilia loves to include Greek and Roman mythology in her writing.

She graduated from the University of Pittsburgh with a degree in psychology and a minor in creative writing in 2020 and now writes novels as her day job.

With over 18 million combined story views online and a growing presence on reading apps, she hopes to inspire other young novelists with her story of growth and imagination, so they go on to write the stories that need to be told.